THE FALLEN HERALD

A Tale of Heaven's War

SIMON P. EDWARDS

authorHOUSE®

AuthorHouse™ UK Ltd.
500 Avebury Boulevard
Central Milton Keynes, MK9 2BE
www.authorhouse.co.uk
Phone: 08001974150

This book is a work of fiction. People, places, events, and situations are
the product of the author's imagination. Any resemblance to actual
persons, living or dead, or historical events, is purely coincidental.

First published by AuthorHouse 9/24/2010

ISBN: 978-1-4490-2494-9 (sc)

Printed in the United States of America
Bloomington, Indiana

This book is printed on acid-free paper.

Cover art by Roger Garland.
View Roger's other work at www.lakeside-gallery.com.

THE FALLEN HERALD

Simon read his first fantasy novel when he was 'just knee high', courtesy of his beloved father, Michael. Since those youthful years he's devoured endless quantities of Feist, Eddings, Tolkien and more recently Erikson, to name but a few. His bookcase burgeons.

To pay the bills Simon works in marketing, and holds the Chartered Institute of Marketing's highest professional qualification. Though enjoyable, he admits that marketing is a dull place, compared to the world of Rune.

When not spending time with his family or writing, he's either jogging or playing games with the 'Wednesday night crowd.'

He lives in Watford, England with his wife Kim and daughter Chloe. He thanks them both for the time allowed to him in 'darkest' Cornwall (cider not withstanding!), where most of The Fallen Herald was written.

The Fallen Herald is his first novel.

Visit Simon online at: www.simonpedwards.co.uk

DEDICATION:

For my father, Michael Edwards. Since I penned the first words to *The Fallen Herald*, this novel has always been for you. Thank you for placing my feet upon this road. Though the years have now passed, I miss you as much as I ever did, and know that you still walk the road beside me.

ACKNOWLEDGMENTS

It's been a long road to this place, and the journey is far from over. These fantastical lands it seems know no bounds.

Kim, thanks for being the light in my life, I'd be completely lost without you. And thanks for delivering my little candle; Chloe - welcome!

Grandma Edwards, I always remember when you said you'd 'buy the first copy.' I hope that they have book shops in heaven! Thanks for the games, the sweets and the puppet shows. I'll always remember.

Paul 'Dream-Chaser' Shedden; this book would never have made it to the shelf without you. Thanks for believing and always listening brother. And Amanda, thanks for the perpetual multiple copies!

Bobbe, put simply this is a better book for your input, though at first I never believed you.

Thanks also to the 'Wednesday night guys' aka my guinea pigs- Neil (for the copious notes!), Martin for the tremendous enthusiasm, and Luke (and Ali), Mark and even the elusive Tony for your patience as I waffled on during our gaming sessions. Thanks for being my guinea pigs and then also believing. Your lively discussions after reading the drafts brought Rune truly alive beyond my mind, for the very first time. Your joy truly became my joy.

And last but certainly not least, thanks to my hosts! Martin and Wendy at Penquite; thanks for always making my 'lair' available. The views are unforgettable.

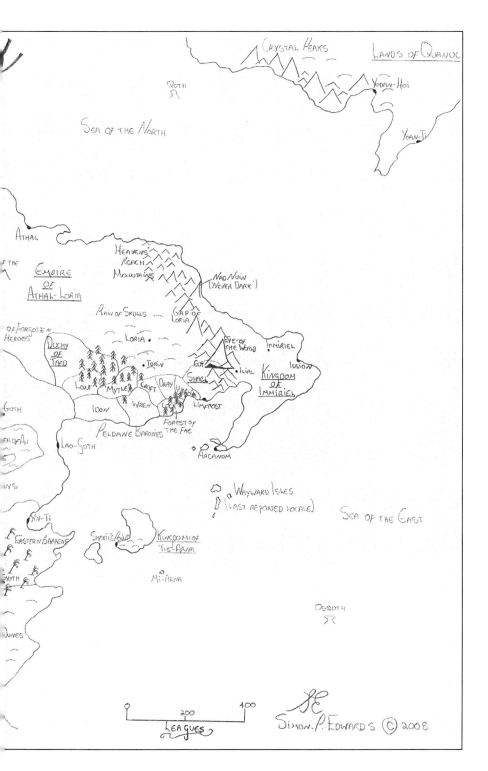

CONTENTS

PROLOGUE

Prior to the settlement of Rune

'D'you reckun there's more to life than this?'

'More than wot?'

'Y'know, waitin to be eaten.'

Yalk looked up from where he sawed at the thick green Tolp stalk with a serrated stone, and scratched his weathered face. 'Wouldn't think so meself. We's always been meat. Wonder what we taste like though – bit like this Tolp maybe?'

Rek frowned and gazed at the vast fields of thick, thigh-high Tolp, in which the endless lines of hunched humanity laboured, under a blazing, emerald sun. 'It's just, well, y'know, I might wanna do somfin else.'

Yalk hawked and spat. He wanted to laugh, but daren't. No one ever laughed. Sure way to draw attention that. 'Sumfin else?! Wot, you been chewin that damn grubby root again, Rek? Does mighty strange things t'you dat!'

They shuffled aside for a six legged Ilapod that scuttled by with panniers loaded with Tolp stalks. Its scores of facetted eyes were constantly scanning the endless fields, of toiling people. It was both beast of burden, and watchdog.

1

Rek shook his head insistently, when the Ilapod had passed. Under the blistering sun his hair had long ago bleached to the same sand colour as the earth, in which they perpetually scrubbed. 'I fink there's more we could be doing dats all. Go some place way from the draguns, someplace we can laugh n stuff.'

'Ain't nowhere way from draguns Rek' said Yalk, his gaze drawn to where a vast shiny black resinous mound rose out of the earth, its shadow stretching across the fields. Several holes suggested entrances and hundreds of Ilapod scuttled across its surface, where their woven saliva kept the structure strong and raised it ever higher for the draconic resident.

Yalk and Rek had lived under the shadow of that vast mound for their whole lives. Scores of similar ones dotted the horizon for as far as the eye could see. They'd seen the serpentine dragon come slithering down that mound many times, where it grazed casually on the humans. Some people still tried to run, but most just accepted their fate. It was the crunching of the bones that Rek hated.

'Dragons've got gods y'know' said Rek, tying off a bundle of Tolp with some gut string.

'Course I knows' replied Yalk. 'Not allowed to worship em, is we? Too good fer us!'

Rek nodded, and started to hack at another stalk with his serrated stone. Stone tools were all they were allowed and each of them guarded theirs jealously. 'So, do yer recon we's got gods then. Y'know if dey have, musn't we?'

Yalk spat again. 'Nope. If we ad gods n stuff, where is em? Nope. We's just food. Just meat.'

Rek could see that he'd probably exhausted Yalks' ability to comment on the matter, but he tried anyway. 'Might not'n be no harm saying a prayer though? Y'know, like we sees Ilapods doing to dem dragon gods; that Ione´ and gorGoroth.'

Yalk shrugged, his thoughts perhaps set on their usual evening meal of pulped Tolk stalks, Rek considered. Tolk was all they got to eat, except on prayer days, when they also got a small piece bitter sap taken from the bark of the Yan tree. It wasn't much to look forward to, since prayer days were also the days when the dragons came down to feed. The male dragons were the worst, being much larger than the females, their hunger was ferocious and hundreds of families could be eaten by just one of them.

When the burning emerald sun finally dropped behind the horizon darkness fell across the fields like a cloak, and the relentless heat swiftly dissipated to be replaced by a bitter cold.

Yalk and Rek tucked their precious stone tools into their belts and began to shuffle with the endless tired lines of humanity back to the caves that helped to shelter them from the bitter cold. There was no conversation, and the outlines of countless Ilapod could be discerned guarding the edges of the herd.

The caves were deep in the mountains and were naturally warmed by pools of scalding water that boiled from the depths of the earth.

Rek and Yalk reached their blankets and Yalk began to grind the meagre supply of Tolk they were given into the paste that would barely sustain them.

When Yalk spooned some for Rek onto a large leaf and handed it to him Rek just stared at it.

'You's got to eat Rek' said Yalk, his deeply lined face creased with concern. 'You get weak and don't do your quota dats it, dey'll take you off, chop you up and make things outa ya!'

Rek shook his head. 'Dunno what it is Yalk, just can't get this god thing outa my head. S'not right, dem havin gods an us jus bein meat an all.'

Yalk looked about nervously, noting that where the nearest Ilapod clung to the gloomy cave walls was some fair distance. Ilapod hearing was very sensitive and they were both strong and fast; they'd probably not even see them coming.

'You's gotta stop this Rek. It wos interesting an all, but there ain't nothing else. I don't wanna be chopped up.'

'Prayer day tomorrow Yalk. Draguns gonna come down again. He's a biggun that male. Recon we'll make it? We's twenty summers old now. Not many round here got to that old Yalk. Gonna be us soon. Can't keep being lucky.'

Rek could see the fear bright in Yalks eyes and continued. 'I'm gonna say a prayer.... just dunna wot to do though.'

Uncertainly Rek shut his eyes, and Yalk looked about nervously, his eyes darting around the walls. Rek had seen the Ilapod and dragons at prayer, but that involved feeding on the humans, screaming and bellowing and raging fires that reached for the skies. He couldn't do any of those things, so with his eyes squeezed tightly shut he settled for a few words. 'If we've got human gods out there, you's need to listen now. We's not happy. We's bein eaten and when we's not being eaten we's bein chopped up and made into fings. You gotta help us.' He paused then as if uncertain whether there was anything else that he could say and then added 'please, help us. We's miserable.....I wanna be happy.'

Rek opened his eyes and smiled slightly at Yalk, it felt good.

'Stop dat smiling' hissed Yalk, 'you'll get us noticed!'

Rek continued grinning.

'Well?' asked Yalk.

'Well what?' said Rek.

Yalk scrubbed at his long matted hair in frustration. 'You know. Any message or anyfin?'

'Nope. Jus felt good is all.'

Yalk sighed, lay down on the cold rock floor, and rolled himself into his threadbare blanket; they were rare and tended to be passed from one person to another, usually when someone had been eaten.

A boom shook the cave. Stalactites swayed alarmingly, and water blasted in small geysers from the scolding pools.

Rek grinned.

Yalk mumbled and rolled himself further into his blanket. 'S'nother mountain rumble is all. Get yerself some kip.'

Somehow Rek knew that it wasn't another rumble. It had felt different, like the mountain was being hit by something and he felt strange inside, warm almost.

The detonation, as the large rock sealing the cave entrance was blown away, was tremendous. The cave trembled and rubble showered down across the thousands of slaves.

All of the slaves were now on their feet, including Yalk and Rek, and they could see a figure standing in the cave mouth. Towering to the height of several men it filled the cave mouth and the sense of its presence was immense, as if the cave could not contain it; the very walls seemed to shake. Coiled silvers scales were wrapped like cloth about a muscular scarlet body that was somehow intensely female. Fiery hair boiled about a beautiful face filled with outrage and love.

For a frozen moment nobody moved and then the Ilapod surged down the walls with appalling speed. Their razor sharp chitinous forearms were raised before them, as they descended in a whistling swarming pack onto the scarlet creature, in a blur of whistling blades.

In one fluid motion the creature in the cave mouth drew an enormous silver sword that was sheathed between the two ivory wings folded across its back, and then it was engulfed by the Ilapod.

The silver sword met the chitinous blades of the Ilapod, in a blur. Black and silver rose and fell and then the high pitched whistles of the Ilapod turned into hoots of terror and they were mown down.

Fast though they were they were no match for the creature and in a moment it was over. The creature was surrounded by the steaming, twitching, body parts, of the dying Ilapods.

The creature's voice was soft, but carried through the entire cave across all the silent ranks of stunned humanity. And then her smouldering eyes met those of Rek and she smiled. 'Your gods are coming.'

Rek smiled in return, and for some reason, he felt completely calm. He pushed his way through the stunned and silent throng until he stood before the creature who utterly dwarfed him. 'Thanks' he said simply 'you gonna to take us away?'

'Yes, Most Beloved Son Rek I'm going to take you to safety. I am Riva-Tri and I serve one of your gods; Balor, god of destruction.' Rek had no idea what she meant referring to him like that or who the god of destruction was, but thought that this was probably not the time to ask.

'My brothers and sisters, the other avatar who are heralds to your gods are here, and we are at war!'

'Where's you takin us?' asked Rek. No one seemed interested in challenging that he was asking the questions.

'To safety' said Riva-Tri. 'To a world of your own!'

Rek began to ask another question, but the avatar held up a scarlet hand to forestall him. 'I know that you have many questions Most Beloved Son Rek, I also know that you *all* have questions' and she looked about the sea of pitiful upturned faces. 'But, your gods are coming and this entire world is now at war. We must leave and immediately.'

As if to make her point, the mountain trembled as if struck.

Numb and hardly daring to hold to hope, thousands of slaves followed Riva-Tri out onto the mountainside. There, spilling from countless other cave mouths came the desperate lines of ragged humanity, where they milled looking down on the scene unfolding before them, and felt what little hope they had dared to believe in crushed.

The endless fields of Tolp were gone, replaced by rampaging armies of Ilapods. They seethed like a living sea, of glittering black carapaces, apparently without end. The giant resinous mounds that abounded the plains frothed with them, and they spilled from the sides as if being vomited from an enraged earth.

Amongst the sea of Ilapods slithered the dragons, the illapods seething like tiny insects about them. The scales of the mighty serpentine giants rippled as they slithered along the plains, propelled by their small taloned legs. They raised elongated maws to the sky, filled with razored fangs bigger than a man and billowed vast gouts of sooty flame that filled the air with dark clouds, and the acrid stench of sulphur. Poisoned saliva dripped from maws, where it collected in deadly pools on the earth. Hard metals and diamonds glittered from the scales of many dragons, sealed by their own fiery breath.

Rek looked to Riva-Tri. The face of the Avatar was impassive, as she shifted her gaze from the seething plains to the skies above where a moon rode, that burned low and fat in the sky, lending at best, a surreal metallic grey cast to the unfolding scene of terror.

'What's we doin?' hissed Rek, trying hard not to soil himself. The throngs behind him had started to scream. Ilapods had begun to spot them and were racing up the mountain slopes. Many people started to run back into the caves.

'Waiting, Most Beloved Son.'

'Stop callin me that, don't knows what it means anyway. But, wot I means is waitin for wot?'

Yalk was tugging on his sleeve. Rek turned to him in irritation. 'That's what, I fink' said Yalk pointing at the sky.

Ranks of winged creatures had come into sight, though they were still far up in the pallid grey sky, they were getting rapidly closer every moment.

Rek knew they must be huge, but he could feel, as much as see them coming. The thrum of their wings made the air tremble and their presence rode before them like a storm. And it seemed that the dragons could feel them too, as they roared and bellowed their challenges to the skies.

Riva-Tris' gaze never left those ranks as the Avatar came into full view. Skins of every colour hove into sight, from the deepest azure blue, to white, emerald and gold, and they blazed with an inner power. Snowy wings graced their backs, and each carried a glittering blade, that rippled in deadly menace and challenge.

'Shoot, must be more'n a hundred of em' said Rek.

Riva-Tri flashed him a silvered smile. 'Ninety nine to be exact Most...Rek, that is. I am the one hundredth.'

Tearing his eyes for a moment from the descending avatar Rek asked, 'so where'r we tryin to get ta?'

'There' pointed Riva-Tri with the blade of her massive sword.

Across the plains, past the dragons, the vast resinous mounds and seething Ilapods, was a small standing stone, speared by a shaft of white light that descended from the heavens to illuminate it, like a candle against the dark. Rek found it odd that he could see it with such clarity.

'Sure is a long way' said Rek.

'Yup' agreed Yalk.

'So what it is?' asked Rek. 'Someplace safe?'

Riva-Tris' smile was soft and though the racing Ilapods were just moments away, she stroked Reks' hair with a giant hand. 'Very,very safe.'

The avatars dropped from the heavens then. They extended their dreadful blades pointing earthwards before them and literally fell from the skies. As their wings folded about them protectively, they appeared to super-heat as they dropped from the skies, becoming wreathed in white-hot flame and then they struck the earth. Where they hit, the earth boomed and trembled, cones of fire blasted skywards, rocks rained down for miles around, and Ilapod bodies were cast into the air like childrens' toys.

As Rek watched, one of the avatar comets slammed into a dragon mound. Where the fiery avatar struck, the mound erupted like a volcano, spewing resin and dust for miles into the air. Moments later, with a bloom of sooty flame, a massive ebony dragon burst out of the mound with an avatar caught in its titanic jaws. The dragons' slitted eyes, that gleamed hard as diamonds, were focused solely on the silver Avatar that, despite the fangs that pierced, it hacked at the dragon with staggering strength, sending chunks of flesh and scales raining onto the mound below.

The dragon screeched in appalling pain, and with a wrench of its head threw the silver Avatar away from it. The Avatar struck the ground, tumbled and in one fluid motion sprang back to his feet, his ivory wings snapping out behind him for balance and the two titanic opponents launched themselves at each other with a crash. The mound, unable to cope with the forces at play, collapsed burying the raging battle from sight.

Where the avatar had struck the Ilapod army that filled the plains below, they had cleared massive areas. A broken path to the light, and hopeful salvation in the distance, was beginning to emerge, though it still seemed like a very long way indeed to Rek.

Other dragon mounds across the plains burst open, disgorging their draconic occupants. Brightly coloured dragons with gossamer wings leapt into the sky, those wings beating frantically to give them height.

'Oh no, they's gonna drop on them avatar' groaned Rek in horror.

Riva-Tris' eyes were fathomless as she replied. 'No Rek. They are leaving this world. The female dragons and their goddess, Ione', will take no part in this war.…..this is just between us, gorGoroth and His servants.'

'Hope' said Yalk faintly 'means there's hope.'

'Time to move' said Riva-Tri and suddenly descended like scarlet death into the Ilapod hoard streaming up the mountainside. Their razored forearms never touched her, and her wings seemed to shield her from many blows, as she spun through them, her sword dealing dreadful death and dismemberment. Their high-pitched dying hoots joined the roars of the dragons, and the screamed challenges of the Avatar, to create a cacophony never before heard on this world, or any other.

Rek, not really understanding why it was him that was doing it shouted 'move, you's lot, move' and started shoving and bullying the terrified human herd after Riva-Tri, as she carved a path through the Ilapod army.

Riva-Tri was skilled beyond anything that Rek could have conceived in his wildest imaginings. She was a living blade that winnowed the black ranks in front of them, carving a swathe wide enough for her gods' children to pass through. And though they linked up with other avatar, whose skills in battle created 'pools' of calm on the plain, even the avatar could not be everywhere at once. And so, the terrified ranks of humanity were hunted down from the edges. Men, women and children, all were pulled from the edge of their pack, by pincers and black carapaced limbs. Dark figures would dart in and drag them away screaming, before a beleaguered Avatar could get there.

They huddled tight together, herd like, their Avatar protectors racings around them, silvered swords a blur and yet still humanity continued to bleed and die. They were like a giant beast being harried, run down, getting slower and slower, until finally the relentless black mass would descend.

A massive red scaled dragon almost reached them then, and for the first time, Rek saw Riva-Tri hesitate, unsure of whether to launch herself at it. It loomed over their ragged line, steaming saliva dripping from its enormous maw, the eyes burning with a hunger that they all knew too well, when suddenly an avatar suddenly streaked in from the side, as if propelled by a gale, and struck the dragon in the side of its serpentine head, with a dreadful crack. Draconic scales shattered to rain down in chunks on those below, and the two went down in a flash of silvered blade, fire, and talon, into the Ilapod hoard, where they tumbled over and over crushing scores of Ilapod beneath them.

They didn't wait to see what happened.

And then the earth suddenly bucked and groaned, fissures ripped through the plain. People tumbled down the rents with screams, and the agile Ilapods took advantage of the chaos to dart in a drag more people screaming to a death of hacking blades.

It seemed as if something heavy had entered the world. The earth dropped slightly like an immense force was pushing down on it.

From the head of the throng Rek strained to see what was happening. If anything, the three avatar that were now with them seemed even more alert.

Rek screamed 'Wuts happenin?'

Despite the din of battle Riva-Tri turned to him. Strangely, in that moment, she seemed very vulnerable. Her smile was sad. 'He's here Rek.'

'Who' Rek asked dully, hoping to hear something else.

'The dragon god – gorGoroth. He has come.'

Reks mouth flapped uselessly for a moment. 'Whut we gonna do?

'We will answer!' said Riva-Tri.

As gorGoroth stepped onto the world it groaned beneath his weight. The sky darkened and a dreadful silhouette lit the moonlit sky. It towered taller than a mountain, and the outline of weaving heads seemed to snap at the moon.

As if in answer, a rumble shook the plains, but this time it seemed to come from deep within the earth. Gradually the rumbling became stronger and stronger, until they could barely stand. More fissures split the earth, rocks tumbled from the mountain side and then figures burst up from the earth. A grey marbled hand rose from the bowels of the earth, higher than the tallest man, followed by the figure of a man, it rushed ever upwards until it obscured the sky. All across the plain dozens of giant male and female figures rose and then they became scores. Their gods had come. At last the entire plain was full of the towering marble figures. Ancient and weathered faces, bearing looks of anger, sorrow and humility, looked in impassive stony regard to where the silhouette of gorGoroth stained the night sky. Though it could not be seen, a sense of outrage blazed from those figures, hotter than the sun. And then with a grinding of rock, they began to move.

'Run!' boomed Riva-Tri. And they did, all that was left of humanity surged then like a battered and beleaguered river of broken flesh and rags, towards the heavenly light that marked the standing stone.

Rek was aware of the boom of huge feet running that rocked the earth. He chanced one glance over his shoulder then, and that moment stayed with him for the rest of his life. The vast grey gods moved with a life of their own and sped with dreadful purpose toward the titanic draconic figure on the horizon. Spears the size of trees were already howling towards the draconic figure. A single grey stone god launched hundreds of huge stone arrows without even slowing, and another surrounded by a web of pulsing light sent a blast across the plain, so bright that it would have eclipsed the sun.

The crash as those forces met was titanic, and the fragile world beneath their feet began to break apart.

When the ragged remnants of humanity finally stepped through the stone and onto a slim ivory bridge that led to another world, Rek was the last to leave.

- CHAPTER 1 -

Star Fall

The army of cheerful imps hammered at the inside of Thorn's head. They hammered, they marched and they sang bawdy songs.

Putting his head in his hands did not seem to help, so he opened his eyes instead. That proved to be a mistake. The imps started banging and crashing even harder, and appeared to have found bin lids and drums as well.

'I'll kill Alazla,' he mumbled. 'That green ale hits harder than Mum's skillet.'

'Still, no reason to kick us out though.' He cautiously rubbed his temples as he continued his mumbled monologue.

Recalling the previous night cracked a smile on his parched mouth, which also felt as if a small family of birds had nested in it. He chuckled as he remembered the nobles' outrage when they had discovered the seriously uninvited Thorn, and best buddy Alazla, at their posh dance.

'Plenty of ale and roast to spare – could have watered and fed twice that number' he mumbled.

Thorn neglected to remind himself of the fact that they'd only really been discovered because they'd sneaked off with the host's twin sisters. Naturally the young count had come looking for them. The tussle with his guards had been somewhat less than legendary, half-cut as they were, and they'd been forced to flee – in separate directions. Thorn had lost his own pursuers by diving into the woodland that had hosted his night's sleep.

'Decent of you, certainly,' Thorn said, patting the tree limb that had unexpectedly hosted him for the night, 'but seriously lacking in the comfy bed department.'

'Wonder if Alazla got away too?' he mused, rubbing more firmly at his temples. The imps appeared to have found something more interesting to do, he noted with interest; their cheerful thumping was becoming much subdued.

Feeling slightly encouraged, Thorn reached to his belt for his last skin of wine. The imps hooted in glee, but his hand grasped only his leather belt.

'Oldoth's shiny balls!' he cursed as he recalled how the wineskin had been torn from him by one of the guards last night. 'Nice vintage too.'

As the reluctant half-light of dawn crept across the sky, Thorn ruefully considered that he should perhaps make his way down from his nocturnal woodland perch. With the family inn full to bursting with patrons staying for the Festival of Seventy-Seven Blessings, there would be a fine breakfast to be had from the inn's kitchens. His stomach growled in anticipation and the imps fled.

Resolved on consuming the mother of all fry-ups, Thorn steeled himself for the drop, swung his legs over the blue bough of the tree and dropped to the damp woodland grass.

Thorn stopped. Lank dark hair fell about his face and his brow furrowed in sluggish thought. 'Odd. Something… odd.'

Pushing back his overhanging and bedraggled locks, he looked up to stare at his impromptu bed. The tree was blue – and not only blue, but also crystal.

Thorn took a deep breath and looked down, focusing on his feet.

'This is not usual,' he muttered, 'not right at all – bloody imps!'

Perhaps they'd mixed their drinks too much or smoked some bad Jack's Folly. Likely the latter, he realised. Alazla was ever one to buy the cheap stuff.

Sighing, Thorn scrubbed a hand through his hair and tried again.

'Bugger. Blue tree… and still there,' he cursed.

Not only was the tree still there but it seemed very healthy to boot. Its crystal trunk exhibited the intricate swirls and whorls of bark, and the branches and crystal leaves sighed and whispered gently in the chill breeze. And if he was not mistaken, there was even a family of crows nested in it. Thorn swore at them. They took no notice.

Thorn reluctantly looked farther about him and saw that the crystal tree also had many crystal tree friends, in fact a whole wood of them, and they surrounded a small glade.

The blue-grey light of dawn was mixed with starlight from the retreating stars and it set the crystal trees to a gentle shimmer. If he weren't hung over, Thorn would have been enchanted.

Soft, luminescent green light pulsed gently upward from crystal roots, through trunks into the reaching branches and into the shimmering tips of every crystal leaf. As a strong wind stirred the leaves, they rang, shimmering like a thousand tiny silver bells.

The tranquillity of the chimes soothed the ache in Thorn's head, and he stood for a moment, allowing it to wash over him. Oddly, he felt his languidness lift from him like a cloak, as if it had never been. He no longer felt either hungry or thirsty. Astonished, he opened his eyes.

'Now that's a strange thing, and no mistake,' he started, and trailed off.

There were figures in the glade. They seemed translucent, ebbing, almost ethereal. He was so startled that the music slipped from his head and the figures vanished.

Perplexed, Thorn stared at the glade.

'Okay. I'm getting that I'm not drunk any more.' He stood on one leg. 'Yup, balance okay.' He felt around his head, pushing and poking. 'No bumps on the noggin either. So that means…'

As he so often did when thinking, he began to chew his lower lip. With his hunger and thirst apparently slaked, his most urgent cravings had vanished. Thorn knew with the certainty he always felt before he landed in deep trouble that he should probably leave. He also knew that he wasn't going to. He'd always had a talent for finding trouble, although this time his partner in crime Alazla wasn't there to rescue him.

'No helping it then. Let it never be said that good common sense ever ruled what I did!'

Resolved, Thorn took a deep breath, closed his eyes and concentrated again, seeking to find the crystal music. As soon as his eyes closed it was there, in the darkness of his mind, and his awareness was whisked away like a leaf riding a stream.

The pace of the chimes rose quickly, becoming faster, until they raged within his mind, no longer a stream but now rapids across which he fell and tumbled.

Thorn snapped his eyes open.

Dozens of figures danced and spun in the glade. Without exception they were tall and supple, flitting with willowy grace to the chiming beat from the trees. Gossamer-thin dresses and gowns covered skins of copper, gold and bronze, that burned with an inner radiance. As they danced, sparkling motes of light span into the air about them.

The festivities of the night before were all but forgotten and Thorn's mind wallowed in stupor, churning, trying to make sense of what he saw. He'd never seen, or even imagined, creatures like these, and he scrambled frantically, trying to make sense of it. Briefly he looked away, not entirely trusting his tired eyes, but when he returned his gaze, the ethereal figures still danced and swirled like dozens of golden fireflies.

Even though he knew he was bright, there were few things that Thorn actually liked about himself. One of the qualities that he actually fostered, though, but which also so often led to his ridicule, was his passion for the study of ancient lore, and it was this knowledge that finally delivered his answer, but he could scarcely find it in himself to believe it. These creatures could only be Randaerren, he realised. To say that they were fiction or myth was understatement. In religious myth, Randaerren were highest servants and caretakers to the Great Wyrms, dragons, who in themselves were but legend. The same dragons who, legend told, had fought with the dragongod against the younger gods of human-kind.

Chilled, Thorn slipped back behind the bole of his tree. All thoughts of flight had now wholly left his mind. Astonishment and fear warred with his thirst for knowledge.

The spinning Randaerren slowed and parted, forming a row between them towards a large crystal rock that sparkled green in the half-light. Wide oval eyes settled expectantly upon the rock.

Slowly, a single Randaerren maiden stepped forth from the throng, walking between her parting brethren towards the rock. Thorn was awestruck by her alien beauty. Proud cheekbones cast shadows across a skin of sullen gold, as her oval violet eyes fixed upon the rock. She swayed with an almost impossible sensuality, her golden feet not even seeming to touch the lush grass.

Such alien beauty left Thorn feeling cold, even though he was drawn to her in an almost painful way. He felt somehow unworthy even to rest his heated gaze upon her.

The maiden climbed gracefully atop the rock, its green hue lending an odd, sinister cast to her beautiful features. She raised willowy arms and turned her face towards the sparkling stars and skies, crying out alien words in a rich musical voice.

Silence dropped across the glade like a shroud. The Randaerren did not move, and gazed in beatific expectation upon the fading stars.

Thorn too searched the heavens until his gaze fell at last upon a star that he'd never seen before; it smouldered a sullen red. His mind raced across maps of the heavenly constellations and he still failed to place it. A light dropped out from the red star and, hurtled across the dawning sky like a fiery comet, its tail a streaking banner. The humble hue of the other stars fled before it, until it became the sole light in the sky.

Thorn's attention, like that of the Randaerren, was fixed in unerring attention as the comet thundered deadly straight from the heavens towards the glade. The glade became immolated in its fiery red light.

The Randaerren's gaze never wavered as the molten mass raced ever closer. Determined not to look away, Thorn was finally forced to shield his eyes as tears streamed down his face.

The comet streaked down with impossible speed towards the glade, the maiden apparently its target, though she did not move. Thorn wanted to cry out to her, but knew that he'd never be heard over the deafening roar. With certainty he knew too that the impact would immolate not only her delicate form but himself too, and most of the surrounding forest. There'd be nothing left of him even to send to the sky god. Thorn knew this and still he didn't move. The certainty that he was witnessing something momentous drew him, like a moth drawn to the enchanting lure and yet deadly embrace of the candle flame.

The comet was vast now and blotted out the entire dawn sky. Lava boiled across its surface. Tears evaporated in tiny moist wisps from his face as it loomed over the maiden like a mountain, her face upturned and calm beneath its cosmic fiery rage.

Thorn clutched the bole of the tree, bracing himself for its terrible impact. Then just as it seemed that the comet must strike and bury the maiden's body deep in the bowels of the earth, scattering the Randaerren like so many autumnal leaves, the comet simply shattered, raining downing in shimmering bursts of gold, russet and bronze.

The raining sparks lit the wide, saucer-like eyes of the Randaerren, where they were captured as glowing embers. Any resemblance to humanity fled with the feral and alien cast it lent them.

As the raining sparks faded, accompanied by the light within the Randaerren eyes, darkness fall upon the glade. Whether it was owing to the bright glory of the comet Thorn was not sure, but the dark seemed unnaturally deep. He was aware of the rasp of his own breath.

Thorn sought for something on which to focus within the darkness. The raging glow of the comet hung across his vision as his eyes struggled to adjust, but as the moments passed he became able to make out the forms of the Randaerren at the edges of the glade, where they were frozen like statues. Of the maiden, he could see nothing.

Thorn could see nothing in the very centre of the glade; it was as if it had been swallowed into a dark hole in the night. Concentrating harder, he suddenly understood that he could see nothing, because something obstructed his view. The light in the glade actually seemed to warp in towards that centre, where it was swallowed.

Thorn's stomach lurched into his throat as he began to drink in the scale of the creature that blocked and drew in the light from the heavens.

Feathered wing-tips swept beyond the treetops, fanning out from vast shoulders, human in appearance but unlike those of any mortal creature. Naked save for a breach cloth, his skin was of the deepest blue. The creature's physique was stupendous, muscles rippling across his torso. His presence and beauty were unearthly.

And then the creature stirred, looking down on the maiden, and as it did so the gargantuan wings momentarily eclipsed the moons.

The earth groaned under his weight and crystal leaves chimed out as branches swayed.

Thorn suddenly understood that he was in the presence of an avatar; herald to one of the younger gods, of men. And here, that the avatar now faced the Randaerren, caretakers of the Great Wyrms and the most ancient enemies of the avatar.

Oddly, Thorn felt no terror as he waited for the blow that would destroy the Randaerren and scatter their flesh as ash on the wind. He knew that the blow must come; this creature summoned here to face these audacious but nonetheless ancient foes. Nothing but a Great Wyrm could face an avatar. As deep as their craft might be, the fate of the Randaerren maiden and her kin was nevertheless certain.

The form of the avatar wavered, and his presence washed about the glade like a soft, summer night's breeze. The avatar slowly diminished in size, allowing light to flood into the glade, until the winged herald stood at no more than the size of a mortal man.

With the return of starlight to the glade, Thorn drank in the sight of the avatar. He swam in the beauty and divinity of the creature, in the skin of deepest blue, the feathered wings of purest white and the eyes: eyes that pierced the soul, eyes that now gazed at Thorn.

Thorn froze, his breath fixing in his throat as he hung in that unearthly gaze. He felt his soul laid bare, and it trembled. Beads of quivering sweat traced down his nose and his heart beat so hard he thought it would burst. Unbidden thoughts raced through his mind, his essence laid bare: thoughts from his past, dreams of his future, his failings and the selfishness of his own petty ambition. Why these thoughts? Why should they assail him as he hung there frozen, a rabbit caught in the hypnotic gaze of a stalking wolf, wanting to move, to flee and yet able only to watch death approach.

The Randaerren began to stir, seemingly sensing that something was wrong.

Thorn recognised the selfish regard of his own ambition. The unexpressed mockery of his parents' achievements. Their desire for him to take over the inn they ran and owned had been spurned by him; such menial work was beneath him. He'd always set his sights higher, and so very high, upon the heady ranks of Arcanum and the League of Mages. Even his attachment to Alazla was perhaps no more than self-preservation: Thorn's mind was strong but his body was weaker. Didn't he cast scorn on his friends for their lack of intellect?

And then those black eyes that spoke of a power so ancient and vast slid past him and back to the Randaerren.

Thorn clawed a rasping breath and wept at the sense of shame that lingered within him.

As the avatar's returned gaze swept over the Randaerren, they bowed low, as wheat before the storm. The avatar smiled, and with it starlight bloomed throughout the glade. As if taking that as their cue, the Randaerren began to sway and dance; the crystal music burst joyously forth from the trees once more.

The Randaerren maiden leaped from the rock and the avatar took her outstretched hand. The dance that began then was of a faster tempo and it centred about the heavenly creature.

The Randaerren spun about the avatar, like myriad rainbow planets orbiting a sun.

The avatar drew the porcelain-like maiden to him and, with a feline grace that belied his massive strength stepped into the swirling dance. The avatar led the dance and the Randaerren swirled in his wake.

The dance seemed to go on forever, and yet to Thorn, who drank in its every detail, it also seemed so short.

The dawn starlight eventually began to fade before the eager sun, and with it the crystal music also started to slow. The swirling Randaerren slowed to a halt about the avatar, who, with the maiden at his side, fixed his gaze upon the fading light of the stars, now finally surrendering their silvered dominion to the morning sunrise.

Hush descended on the glade and something deep within Thorn whispered in concern. Thorn pushed the feeling to one side, determined to remember the details of this immortal event for ever.

And yet Thorn could not seem to allay the gnawing concern in him. He noticed then that the glade had become slightly shadowed, in fact unnaturally so. And yet the avatar and the Randaerren, with their gaze fixed upon the fading stars, appeared not to notice. No, that was not quite right, he corrected: the maiden had noticed.

From where it came Thorn had no idea, but suddenly a blade was present in the hand of the Randaerren maiden and a twisted smile broke across her golden face. From Thorn's vantage point he recoiled at the dreadful malice in that smile, even as he physically felt a rotten taint washing from the blade. The twin points of the dagger writhed and twisted in her hand like venomous serpents and her figure.

The maiden began to raise her hand and her awful intent struck Thorn like a blow.

The gaze of the avatar remained fixed upon the fading stars.

The dagger was framed for a terrible moment between the avatar's white wings and then the maiden plunged it downward with an awful strength. The black blade struck the avatar in the spine, plunging in to the hilt. The divine creature staggered forward with a cry of agony and surprise that pierced Thorn to the heart. His cry blasted across the glade like a gale and the crystal trees sang with the power of it, shattering and cracking, boughs crashing to the earth.

Randaerren began to scream as they saw what had happened, and many were physically blown to the ground with the force of the avatar's cry, their gossamer gowns torn from their bodies and cast rag-like into the gale.

The avatar staggered forward, clutching vainly at the writhing and rotten blade protruding from between its ivory wings. Dark blood ran down the muscles of its back, staining its wing feathers a dreadful scarlet and pooling on the grass of the glade. Turning, the avatar looked down on the maiden. Its twisted face was terrifying and the sinews in its mighty arms bulged.

Closing his eyes, Thorn waited for the certain blow and scream that would signal the end of the maiden's life. But it did not come.

When Thorn opened his eyes he seemed to look straight into those of the avatar and his immortal soul cried out in sorrow. He saw in those eyes a depthless compassion and an intense love for all life.

And the maiden remained alive, though she cowered prostrate before the dying avatar.

Slowly the light in those depthless eyes began to fade as the avatar staggered forward and fell to his knees, now making no attempt to remove the pulsing black dagger from his back. With an arm that could fell trees he reached out and stroked the hair of the cowering Randaerren maiden, sparkling tears running down his now calm face.

And then his wings seemed to fold in upon themselves and his entire form began to crumple slowly inward, hand still resting on the maiden's head, until he was gone. The form of the avatar was but sparkling motes of light on the dawn breeze, which softly began to settle upon the dew-damp grass.

There was no sound. The wind whispered no more. The animals of the forest were still. The trees had ceased their crystalline wail. Mortal and immortal worlds were caught between time, stunned with horror and disbelief.

Randaerren stood still as statues, frozen in the early morning mist, ebbing slowly from sight.

The maiden stood alone for a moment as the avatar's dust settled on the grass at her feet and then she too vanished, folded into the embracing shadows.

Seconds passed, each like an hour, as Thorn struggled to draw breath through his terror.

'By all the nine gods. What have I just witnessed?' Thorn croaked. 'Must leave. Need to get out of here.' 'No telling who's going to come by next. Some other immortal or legendary type, knowing my luck. I'll need Faed's own skill with shadows to get out of here with my skin intact.'

If the god of deepest shadows heard Thorn's muttered reference to him, he certainly didn't cloak him in darkness or whisk him out of there unseen.

He made to turn and leave this place far behind him, but a dull, nagging voice, within his sub-conscious told him that he must tell someone what he'd seen, but it warred with his ever present instinct for self-preservation.

'No way to be sure whether any of the Randaerren saw me,' he muttered, chewing his lip again. 'With crystal trees and all, it's not your everyday forest, and likely to be sacred. So if I'm not tracked down by the magic types and turned into something unnatural, the guards will still find me and likely lock me up for trespassing. Bugger. But what if I tell the truth? No one will believe me for sure.'

He blew into his hands to test his breath and could not help but recoil. 'Great, I smell like a dwarven brewery. They'll think it was drunken imaginings for sure!'

One of Thorn's talents had always been to think quickly under pressure. It was one of the reasons why he'd always excelled at college exams. This proved no exception. 'Evidence, that's what I need. Keep your trap shut, Thorn, and hopefully hear nothing. But, if someone comes knocking on your door' (he winced visibly at what his mother would say) 'I'll show them the evidence. Yup, that's the way!'

That decided, Thorn turned back to face the silent glade. Fragments of crystal trees lay scattered on the ground, their trunks shattered as if struck by blasts of lightning. Dust glittered sadly upon the grass in the soft dawn light. Heart in his throat, Thorn stepped cautiously into the clearing.

'Easy now, Thorn. Nothing about right now; quiet as a grave, in fact.' He winced at his choice of words and muttered a curse.

He let the breath out slowly when he realised that no terrible force had yet rent him limb from limb.

The grass was bedecked with tears of dew as he crept slowly towards the avatar's dust. Reaching it, he knelt down and looked upon the remnants of the fallen herald. Grief wrenched him then as the true enormity of the tragedy struck him. His throat clenched and tears fell from his eyes. Thorn suddenly wept in wrenching, unashamed gasps, mortal grieving for immortal.

Minutes passed as Thorn struggled to control his grief. He wiped at his tears, which continued to fall regardless.

'Like it or not, Thorn, you need evidence if anyone's ever to believe you,' he whispered softly. 'Be strong now. There's no help for it.'

Reaching to his belt, he tugged loose a small pouch and emptied its contents onto the ground. Grimly Thorn scooped a little dust into the pouch; it was cold to the touch. Somehow he felt dirty having to do this. Thorn talked quietly to himself all the time, keeping up his courage.

Tying the pouch drawstrings, Thorn noticed his tears had been falling into the avatar's dust. Where the tears had fallen tiny diamonds now lay in small wet craters.

'Now that's a strange thing and no mistake. There's magic still at work here, not to mention the fact that that's the first time for sure that my tears have been worth anything but the salt that's in them!'

Amazed, Thorn reached down and gently picked up one of the diamonds. It seemed flawless, with a slight bluish cast that winked at him in the sluggish light of dawn. Several score more glimmered within their dusty bed.

'You're worth more than that inn my parents have worked their whole life to pay for,' he said, shaking his head in amazement.

He paused only for a moment, though, before placing the diamond back amongst its fellows, where it continued to wink at him.

'Would just seem wrong to take you, somehow. I think you just need to stay right there. Something needs to mark where that avatar met his end, after all'

Gathering himself, Thorn stood and attached the pouch to his belt. He rubbed his hands together to free them of the dust, idly noticing how the wetted dust clung tenaciously to them.

He left the glade in silence and didn't look back.

- CHAPTER 2 -

Thorn

Winged messengers fled from the Citadel of Storms. Aolandar, most blessed son of Oldoth, god of sun and storms, stood on battlements on restless smoke. His ancient eyes making out their airy forms, he watched the messengers rush away with impossible speed towards the greater cities across the face of Rune.

He then turned his attention back to the ebbing and coalescing shape before him, of Balthazar his second in command, and head of the divine house of Oldoth in Korth. Balthazars' spirit hung like a dark, brooding cloud over the battlements, where occasionally it took on the shape of a shifting face.

'I saw the blade fall, my beloved son' said Aolandar, his ancient voice heavy with sorrow. 'Oldoth delivered the vision to me. I see it every where I turn, I cannot escape it – that fell twisted blade and the scream of the dying Avatar. All of the gods now gaze upon this place, upon Rune.'

'You mean our gods, the younger gods, sire?' questioned Balthazar, the voice from the ebbing cloud was vast.

Aolandars golden shoulders slumped wearily. 'I think not, my son. Can there be any other answer to this, dark though that answer may be? We had thought the war in heaven over. We believed that six thousand millennia past, when at last, gorGoroth the dragon god fell, we had won, if such a dreadful cost as the death of ninety one of our own gods, could even be called a victory.'

The dark cloud of Balthazars' spirit seemed to hang its head. 'You believe that gorGoroth has escaped from his bonds most beloved son? That he now seeks to wage a new war on humanity – a last war?'

'Perhaps' replied Aolandar, and there was steel in his voice again. 'That, or his mate, the female dragon goddess, Ione', has at last decided to enter this war.'

'But why would she do that sire? Why now? The female dragons tooks no part in the last war. Had they done so, we would certainly have lost.'

'I know not, Balthazar…..but we *must* have answers. Yet, for now, you must put those concerns aside.'

'But which god did the fallen avatar serve?' continued Balthazar regardless.

Aolandar crossed golden skinned arms on his muscled bare chest and fixed a grim stare upon the ebbing son. 'Harken to me Balthazar. We do not know…. as yet, but you must focus, something else is of far greater concern!'

'I do not understand sire.' Balthazars' face shifted in the winds that stirred the battlements of smoke on which Aolandar stood.

'There was a witness!' Lightning flickered around the citadel of storms, where it rode banks of dark clouds across a night sky.

'What!?' hissed Balthazar. 'Who?'

Aolandar smiled, and for a moment, the shifting battlements flooded with sunlight. 'The air spirits have given us a name and it is a most portentous one – Thorn, his name is Thorn. Find him and we may also find the answers that we seek. That task, Balthazar, I give to you.'

****

The old trollish teacher was so venerable and diminutive that to Thorn's eyes it seemed that he'd shrunk from the inside out, leaving bones too small for his skin. Barely able to peer out from watery eyes beneath folds of thick brown skin, he shuffled about the classroom, expanding on points with rangy arms that varied between wagging at pupils and helping him to knuckle across the floor.

Thorn knew that given the previous day's events it was a major achievement for him to have made it to college at all. On returning home to his parents' inn he had attempted to catch some sleep, but nightmares of twisted blades and screaming avatars had finally forced him from his bed. His parents had certainly been shocked to find him helping the head cook Janine with early morning chores in the kitchen. Recognising the enquiring look on his mother's face, he had headed the questions off by then making his excuses and rushing off to college.

With the Festival of Seventy-Seven Blessings starting only the day before, college did not begin until midday, and Thorn had arrived so early that he'd had to spend four hours in the library before lessons began. The words of the textbook on the pantheon of the younger gods had not registered at all, and after trying to read the same page eight times he had given up and eventually sat alone with his harrowing thoughts.

Thorn found himself grateful for the comforting presence of his fellow pupils in the class. Oddly, it meant that he could go through his memories of yesterday without the same mind-churning terror that they evoked when he was alone. However, paying attention to the old trolls' ramblings concerning the events leading to the creation of the Southern Alliance, of which his native city of Korth was a part, was taking it several steps too far.

Thorn was unaware of the glances from his friend Alazla, who had noted his friend's withdrawn appearance and had several times during that class endeavoured to catch Thorn's attention. Unknown to Thorn, Alazla was also somewhat miffed that Thorn had all but ignored him that morning and not even enquired as to how Alazla had managed to extricate himself from the hospitality of the city guards after they'd gate-crashed the noble's party.

Thorn replayed the events of the previous day in his mind again, absently scratching at the palm of his right hand. In his mind's eye he saw the twisted dagger fall again and again and again, the dreadful malice in the eyes of the maiden and the avatar crumpling inwards. Though he was sure in himself, Thorn's mind recoiled from the terrible belief that the creature slain was an avatar, a herald to one of the nine younger gods. How could this be true, he wondered? Such beings were both divine and immortal and so surely immune to death. And so, when logic concluded that it simply could not be true, he remembered how the beautiful winged creature, though impaled by that twisted and befouled blade, could still strike down the maiden with a single blow, instantly sundering the life from her frail form – and yet it had stayed its hand. With tragic and utter certainty Thorn knew that such dignity and forgiveness could only be divine.

What did such a dreadful thing portend, he wondered? It was believed that each god had only one herald. And to which god did this herald belong? Surely their reprisal would be absolute. Struggle though he might, he could conceive of no power capable of striking down an avatar, and certainly not one with a reason to do so.

And what did it mean for him, for Thorn? Such a thing could not go unnoticed, he knew. The divine orders must know, or would do so soon, he was sure. Did they know that he had seen it? Was the gaze of an angered god now resting on him? Sweat broke out, cold on his brow. He recalled the avatar's dark and depthless eyes boring into his. His innermost thoughts had been laid bare in that brief glance. The avatar had *known* Thorn was there.

Thorn's throat constricted in fear and he glanced down at where he now scratched at his hand. The palm was blue, as if it had been washed with a stain. He knew from his furious scrubbing with the dish brush earlier that the stain would not come off. His vision swam at the horror of it all. The blade, the dust, eyes boring, screams, blades and screams, screams. An angered god.

From a distance Thorn could hear his name. Echoes were all about him and he struggled to bring the class into focus. He fought to slow his gasping breath and became aware that the old troll was standing by his desk, or rather his watery eyes were just looking over the top of it.

'My, my, Thorn,' clucked Master Fafner, sucking at his huge yellowed canines. 'Seems to me that someone had far too much cider last night! You look decidedly unwell, young lad.' Fafner ignored the jeers from the class at this revelation, as he wagged old curled claws in Thorn's face. 'I think you'd better go and get some fresh air, Thorn.'

Thorn could barely manage a nod as he got up from his desk, and the world tilted under his feet. Unable even to thank the old troll for his kindness, he lurched out of the class, barely aware of the laughter that followed him.

Strong hands eventually lifted Thorn to his feet from where he knelt retching in the college courtyard. Alazla's rich voice swam through the haze. 'You're as cold as ice, Thorn.'

Thorn nodded, grateful for the calming presence of his best friend. His vision cleared gradually to reveal Alazla's handsome face, his grin framed by a shock of blond hair.

'You never could take your drink, you know.'

Thorn could only nod weekly, with a half-smile, as Alazla's presence was taken away from him by a group of college girls who flitted around him like so many butterflies. Never one to be shy and turn down such attentions, Alazla began to entertain them with a ribald story of how he and Thorn had gatecrashed the noble's party the previous night. Thorn had never been so lucky in his attentions from the fairer sex, nor had he been able to exude the sheer charm of his friend.

Growing more bored by the minute and becoming irritated despite himself at the endless laughter, Thorn eventually moved away, deciding to wait for Alazla at the college gates. The old iron gates were thrown wide and pupils frothed gleefully out, looking forward to another night of celebrations for the Festival of Seventy-Seven, when all things harvested were abundant.

Thorn lounged against the gatepost where it opened out onto the cobbled Square of Mahomet, named after the immortal scion of Lorethian, god of justice.

'Guess I'll just wait here, then,' he muttered to himself. 'Of course I could go and join in the conversation and enjoy being ignored by Alazla's various girlfriends again. But, somehow I think I'll forgo that and stand here pretending that I've got no friends.'

It was in fact not unusual for Thorn to recriminate himself for his shortcomings, but most especially for his lack of charm in conversing sensibly with the opposite sex.

Waiting for his friend, Thorn knew better than to expect greetings from many students. Brighter than most, although sociable, he was prone to darker introspective moments that drove many would-be friends away. Alazla, though, had proved immune, or just pig-headed regarding such moments, and usually dragged Thorn out whether he wanted to go or not. Quite why Alazla had decided to befriend Thorn so many cycles ago he wasn't sure, but Thorn knew that he was immensely grateful for the gift of his friendship.

Thorn couldn't help but enjoy himself occasionally by greeting some students anyway, calling the odd hello as they passed, knowing they'd ignore him.

'Afternoon. How you doing? Good evening last night?' All such jovialities were consistently ignored.

'Must be something I said. Maybe I should change my underwear?' he wondered half aloud. 'Yes, that must be it. I'll change my pants immediately when I get home.'

All such amusing anecdotes were knocked soundly out of Thorn's head as he was slammed face first onto the cobblestones.

'Shit, what the blazes?' Thorn cursed.

Blood dripped from his lips onto the cobbles as he pushed himself onto his knees.

Suddenly a weight landed on his back, knocking the wind from his lungs with a terrible whoosh and driving him back down. Nose driven into the stone, Thorn gasped for breath and tried to move his head round, yet as he did so something slammed into the side of his face. The world began to tilt and spin, and again something struck the side of his face. Blood ran down Thorn's face, the salty tang bitter upon his tongue. With a yank his head was wrenched back by the hair and he heard cruel laughter, then with a crunch someone drove his face down again into the unyielding stone.

Thorn's world was a haze of blood, impotent anger and distant, echoing voices. He was vaguely aware of laughter and the dark smear of his blood on the cobbles, but it seemed oddly disconnected, as if it belonged to someone else.

As if at a great distance someone said, 'Let him be.' Other voices just cajoled. It was all so far away as to be almost meaningless. His hands clutched feebly at the cobbles in an attempt to push himself up, but the weight; the mocking weight was just too much; he simply didn't have the strength.

Then suddenly the weight was gone; there were shouts followed by the sound of blows being struck. Moments later gentle hands lifted him firmly to his feet. Gradually his eyes focused and Thorn peered into the concerned and undeniably handsome face of Alazla. Surprising even himself, Thorn managed a rather weak but bloody grin.

'You'd better let me set that,' Alazla said softly, looking askance at Thorn's face.

Thorn just nodded glumly as Alazla took hold of his nose and gave it a sharp twist. There was a soft crunch, and more warm blood ran down Thorn's face. He teetered to keep his balance amidst the spinning.

'Can't have your good looks ruined during Seventy-Seven, can we?' quipped Alazla. Unfortunately his humour had always been contagious: Thorn couldn't help but smile. Almost at once he wished he hadn't, as pain shot from his nose.

'Don't you get tired of being a ruddy hero?' Thorn asked as he spat blood onto the cobbles.

Alazla showed no surprise at the caustic remark. 'Where would heroes be without some poor ordinary person to save, Thorn? We'd just be the same as everyone else!'

Thorn grinned, which was not a pretty sight. 'I guess I deserved that. Sorry. Oh, and thanks.'

Alazla clapped him on the back with a meaty paw. 'Always a pleasure!' He beamed as he said it.

Thorn was caught between wanting to throttle his stalwart companion and hugging him. Drawing a deep breath instead, he looked around and noticed that they'd drawn quite a crowd.

'We're fine,' Thorn said to the onlookers. 'Don't worry. No need to rush and help. Crisis over. Thanks for your help.'

Alazla pulled Thorn away at that point. 'Please try not to make any more enemies, Thorn. You've got quite enough to handle with Lorm and his gang taking out their woes on you. What is it they've got against you anyway?'

Thorn did not reply, preferring instead to dab at his nose.

Alazla, it seemed, had not finished, though. 'If you become half as good an innkeeper as you are at winding up Lorm and his mates then you can look forward to a very prosperous life, my friend!'

Thorn had decided at that point to feel sorry for himself, so he just nodded.

'Say now, I think we'd better get you home,' Alazla said kindly. Thorn nodded glumly, anticipating his mother's matronly reaction and his father's anger at his taking another beating. Inevitably they'd both be down the college again berating his tutors, which was actually significantly more mortifying than getting another thumping.

They walked home in awkward silence. The bustling streets of radiant Korth slipped by almost without notice, though citizens laughed and joked in anticipation of more festivities.

Thorn knew, of course, what Alazla was thinking; he was feeling sorry for his friend, wishing he could do more to help. Certainly at times it was all Thorn could do not to ask for that help or even indulge himself in a reservoir of self-pity and sorrow, a black pit of anger and self-recrimination that would sometimes threaten to overwhelm him. It was not even that he was ugly or for that matter stupid; in fact he was far from stupid, which in its own right would often draw recrimination. It was just that he seemed to draw unwanted attention and even hostility from life's disreputables. He simply couldn't seem to get away from it. He didn't look for it; it came to him and struck him in the small of the back when he least expected it. And what did he do about it? Nothing, absolutely nothing, and more to the point he actually could do nothing! He simply didn't have the physical strength or athleticism of many other students. So good old Thorn just had to get up and carry on as always, with a ready grin but tense for another kick in the face. One of these moons Alazla wouldn't be there to pick him up: Thorn had no idea what he'd do then. Now there was a sobering thought, he realised.

Looking up, a slight lump in his throat at the notion, Thorn realised that they had reached his parents' inn. The half-open shutters on the long wooden façade were thrown open to reveal the cheery welcoming glow of oil lamps. He really didn't feel like going in.

Suddenly he recalled that Alazla was still with him, and snapping momentarily out of his melancholy he regarded his stalwart friend.

Judging by Alazla's darting but longing glances towards home, with those deep blue eyes into which many of the fairer sex had stared, he was obviously eager to be off and prepare for the evening, yet he made no attempt to leave. Again, Thorn wondered why Alazla hung around with him.

Thorn looked gratefully at his friend and even managed a weary but slightly battered grin. 'I owe you, yet again, Alazla!'

Alazla nodded, his normally cheerful face stern. 'You know, if things don't sort themselves out with Lorm and his buddies, I may just have to take a little more direct involvement.'

Thorn did not miss the way Alazla's meaty fists clenched when he said this, or the feral glitter in his eyes, rarely there, and only so when he was truly and deeply angered.

Certainly Alazla was right, but Thorn was too bone-weary to consider Lorm again right now. That knucklehead was frankly way down his list of important things to do. Thorn needed to clear his head and decide what to do. For this he needed to be away from Alazla too, even though he desperately yearned for his friend's cheerful companionship at that moment. Alazla's more simple perspective on things could be just what he needed.

He'd decided to ask Alazla to stay when he noticed his friend glancing back towards his home yet again.

Thorn sighed in resignation. 'Look, you'd better be getting on. You don't want to miss out on that hot date at the Badgers' Den now, do you? Besides, the more time you waste here the less time you've got to tidy yourself up, and by Sha's Blade you look a state!'

'Besides,' Thorn added belatedly, 'if I came with you you'd stand no chance! Look at the state of me!'

'Now with that,' said Alazla, 'I can't argue. You'll meet me at the Den later, though. I won't take no for an answer! Dina's got a friend I think you'll like! If you come really late, she'll be so drunk she may not notice that you look like you've been dredged up from the harbour.'

'Go on, bugger off, you know there's no hope for me, so stop trying. I might as well become a monk!'

Alazla laughed openly, blue eyes sparkling. Giving Thorn a cheerful jab on the shoulder, he ran off down the cobbled alley away from the inn.

Thorn watched his sturdy friend receding into the press of people, his blond head standing out for a while above the crowd.

Going into the inn was the last thing Thorn wanted to do, and given his wounds he knew that his mother's matronly reaction was going to be more extreme than ever.

'Oh well,' he sighed 'the night, or evening that is, is still young! Can't be going in, so what I need is some company – and company that won't talk back!'

Decision made, he walked round to the rear entrance of the inn. Opening the wooden gate cautiously, he peeped into the courtyard. 'Great; coast is clear and all is well!'

Stepping in, he froze momentarily as he noticed Obelisk, the family bear hound, sprawled nonchalantly by the inside wall. However, the great old beast, now seriously grey around the chops, just thumped his tail happily and put his head back down.

'Good Obelisk,' Thorn muttered. The old hound thumped his tail but didn't bother to get up. 'I always forget you're almost as old as I am.'

Reaching the outhouse, where his father kept many of the inn's non-perishable stores, it didn't take a moment to remove a rather venerable and decidedly dusty bottle of Apple Spirits from the shelving. He paused and put the Apple Spirits back, instead taking a slim, spiralled, smoky glass bottle.

'Black Spite: the very best, all the way from the jungles of Ylith. If there was ever a time to drink it, I think this is probably it,' said Thorn. Slipping it into his pack belt, he took a quick look across the yard and went for the gate. As he ran he could hear his mother shouting at one of the serving wenches in the kitchen.

'Poor old Lisa, burnt the roast again!' he chortled.

The thought of a little normality brought a grin to Thorn's face, which in turn made him wince in pain. He wasn't sure whether to laugh or cry at his predicament.

Still wincing, he shut the gate behind him (don't want thieves getting in, he noted) and sauntered innocently off down the street.

'So where to, then, I wonder. Korth's a big place, after all. Grandest city in the whole of Rune… or so they tell us,' he amended.

'What I need is a place to sit down and think. Just me and the Black Spite. I've heard it's hallucinogenic.' That last gave him pause. Given the shocks he'd had over the last day or two, drinking an alleged hallucinogen might not be the best thing to do.

He shrugged mentally. 'What's the worst that could happen? Not much compared to what I've seen. It may even dull this bloody pounding in my nose. By the nine, it hurts!.'

Thorn did not, or affected not to, notice the strange glances he got from passers-by, who noted his rambling conversation with himself.

He continued. 'Of course, if I keep drinking, I'll never have to deal with the matter at all!' He scratched his two-day stubble at that, although also did not actually notice that he needed to shave. 'Some would say that's burying your head in the sand, Thorn. To me, who's seen an avatar slain, it just sounds like good common sense!'

Pausing briefly, Thorn wondered where to take his night of self-imposed bachelor revelry and decided that the Broken Square could well be the place. Adjusting his pack, he loped off cheerfully in a westerly direction, trying hard to ignore the insistent pain from his nose.

His route took him along the south wall of the inner city, and he decided to take the parapet route, which strictly speaking you weren't meant to do, it being off-limits to non-military personnel. Shrugging his shoulders nonchalantly to himself, he carried on anyway, slipping cautiously past the guardhouse and up the imposing stone steps to the inner wall.

'Crikey, Thorn, you really are being risqué today,' he quipped to himself. 'Is this a new you, I wonder? You're making a habit of going into forbidden areas after all. All you need now is an extra span in height and shoulder width and you'll have new and wonderfully shallow friends flocking to be your best buddy.'

Some few minutes later Thorn reached the top, his breath clouding in the cooling evening air.

Thorn realised that he was wheezing slightly. 'You know, I really do hate physical exercise. I wonder if there's some way that I can have shoulders like Alazla's but do nothing but push a quill all day? I should write to Arcanum and ask the mages. If anyone would know, they would.'

Thoughts of exercise brought to mind Master Lackweed, and Thorn shuddered involuntarily. The college's master of exercise was a small but physically robust type, who had an odd penchant for wearing tight vests. In Thorn's opinion the diminutive chap was always trying to make up for his lack of height by flaunting his physical prowess. He also seemed to think that Thorn (who tragically shared a similar physique) should be able to keep up. Needless to say, Thorn did not share his enthusiastic opinion and often skipped exercise, preferring a good book and a roll or two of Jack's Folly.

'You know, in fact, I'm only slightly winded. Lackweed would almost be proud!'

'Actually, I'm not sure I'd go that far. Although you do bear a striking resemblance to Lackweed.'

Thorn whipped round to see Alazla walking up the last few steps. Alazla, Thorn noticed, was not out of breath.

'It's uncanny, I'd say,' continued Alazla. 'Are you absolutely sure you're not related in some way?'

Thorn was not sure whether to be mad or happy. He'd been looking forward to trying to sort things out in his head, but knew that he'd likely fail. There was probably no making sense of it after all. He'd also dreaded the deep melancholy that he knew would settle on him as a result.

Thorn settled for smiling. 'By the trickster, Alazla, how did you know I'd be here!?'

His friend chuckled and propped himself on the parapet next to him. 'For a bright lad, Thorn, you can be remarkably stupid. You've been coming to this spot "to work things out" ever since you were knee-high. You were too serious….even then.'

There was no denying the truth of it and Thorn felt his spirits lift in his friend's reassuring presence. He felt obliged to try once more, though. 'What about your hot date at the Den though?'

Alazla had pulled out a brown clay pipe and was tamping it full of Jack's Folly. The 'therapeutic' dried yellow herb was commonly available in Korth, though frowned upon. It was also not terribly cheap, and Thorn briefly wondered how Alazla had paid for it. His family were not well-off.

'You're a fool, Thorn. On a night like this even you could have got laid. Yes, and even looking like that. Ola is just about as desperate as you are. She's no wood nymph, that's for sure….but beggars can't be choosers.'

Thorn had no answer, knowing that his friend was probably right.

'Anyway, you've had a face like a troll all day. I know you've got your problems, my friend, but laughing at life has always been one of your talents. Something happened after we legged it from that party last night, or I'm Sea Monkey.'

Thorn could have wept then at Alazla's insight and the compassion he'd shown in following his friend. For a moment he didn't trust himself to answer, as his emotions grew thick in his throat. Instead he gazed out over Korth's lower city, a view that he loved very much. As always, it took his breath away and a little calm settled on him in return. The evening was particularly beautiful and the lower city was illuminated a burnt orange as it rambled erratically downhill towards the ocean.

'Qizoth's still down there, you know,' said Alazla, pointing with his pipe.

Thorn laughed at that, recalling the small skiff with which they'd often menaced the larger ships in the harbour. Qizoth was grandly named after the silver-crested sea beast of legend. Their antics in the tiny skiff had become well known to some of the regular ship captains, and as their reputation for menace grew, the ships' crews had often pelted them with fruit, wood and even other less savoury items. They'd even tried to steal aboard a ship one night. Swift discovery had found them dumped straight into Korth's chilly harbour.

'Took me hours to get those eels off,' Thorn said.

Alazla laughed, a rich and vibrant sound, and drew deeply on the pipe.

'How come they didn't get you?' Thorn muttered, only slightly sour.

'Sweet flesh, my friend, I guess you're unspoiled! Bless. Maybe you should give your life over to Eli-shar – I hear they're always seeking the untainted!'

Thorn laughed again, feeling a little more cheered, and uncorked the Black Spite. He took a swig of the viscous Ylithian liquid and gagged as it scorched the back of this throat, travelling slowly to his gullet, where it lingered like smouldering coals. Coughing briefly, he took another deep swig.

'Careful there, lad,' Alazla said, raising an eyebrow. 'Looks like someone's getting used to drinking that stuff!' He leaned closer and peered at the bottle. 'And the black, too. Someone also has expensive taste.'

Thorn shrugged and watched the ships bob gently in the harbour, enjoying for the moment the short but companionable silence.

'So what was with the disappearing act last night, then?' Alazla said at last.

Thorn had known the question was coming, of course, but in truth still had no answer. He stared unseeing for the moment at the ships, and in their place a twisted dagger rose and fell. Crystal trees shattered and the sky bled tears of flame.

'Thorn,' Alazla's hand shook his shoulder. 'What by the nine gods is it? You've gone as pale as the solstice moon.'

Still he had no words. What could he say? Thorn had no doubt in his heart that Alazla would believe him, but where to start? And would telling Alazla place him in terrible danger too? So far no threat or accusation had found Thorn, but that was not to say that he was not being hunted? By what right could he share that burden with his friend? As Thorn's closest friend he knew that he deserved to know, but in telling him would he also betray his trust and place Alazla's life at risk?

Thorn took a swig of Spite, now barely tasting the strong liquor. His thoughts spun far away, perhaps seeking momentary sanctuary in the temporary haven of the familiar, tracing the lower city from the harbour in a series of what appeared to be randomly determined streets and allowing their tranquil solidity to soothe him. Perhaps in those twisting labyrinthine streets he could somehow find the courage he needed.

He knew too, with certainty, that Alazla would not push him until he was ready to answer. Often they'd sat just there after one escapade or another, laughing and joking. At other times they'd simply enjoyed the vista and the warm familiarity of each other's company.

Thorn allowed his mind to wander for a moment, enjoying the solace of lighter thoughts, recalling the tales of how Korth had grown, in harmony with the land about it. Most dwellings and structures in radiant Korth were grown from living crystal where they flourished to the exclusion of all other places in the world of Rune. To Thorn it seemed at odds that such a wonderful city could have played host to the death of an avatar.

Lulled by the Black Spite and the reassuring presence of radiant Korth, Thorn's thoughts begrudgingly twisted back to the avatar like a lodestone, and what to tell his friend. Why would a Randaerren maiden slay an avatar? It made no sense. Was it not written that they were servants of another race, the Great Wyrms, those who swam through the darkness between worlds? There was no accounting in all the histories for such a meeting.

That this terrible act had occurred on the first night of the Seventy-Seven Festival had not escaped Thorn. The Festival came only once every seventy-seven cycles and it was celebrated across the whole world of Rune. It was a time of abundance, when harvests overflowed and all disease simply ceased. Even warring nations would halt hostilities for the seven-day duration. The Seventy-Seven was held sacred to the full pantheon of nine younger gods.

'Damn, this just makes no sense!' said Thorn.

He muttered and mumbled to himself as the sun sank at last, unnoticed, into the sea with a final flash of red fire. Alazla waited patiently, puffing on his pipe..

The avatar's eyes held Thorn again. Their dark, fathomless depth pinned him like a shrew beneath the talons of an eagle. The strength within them was vast and unstoppable, yet bound by equal compassion.

Thorn lurched upright, sending the bottle of Spite bouncing across the battlements. He knew! The avatar's eyes had told him. It had been there, in those depthless eyes. He had known that he was going to die. Tears traced Thorn's face, the salt stinging his wounds unnoticed. Why did he not flee? Why stay?!

Alazla scrambled to snatch up the bottle, endeavouring to save its expensive contents. 'What is it!? Come on, Thorn! For pity's sake!'

Again the dagger plunged and again Thorn was torn by the avatar's death cry, its sound like a shattering glass. Crystal trees exploded and tumbled, the Randaerren fleeing. He was faced again by the terrible malice contorting the maiden's face into something obscene.

'In the name of the nine gods, Thorn, what's eating you? Just tell me. Please trust me now, as you always have.'

And so Thorn did. It spilled from him as if from a lanced wound, and he wept when it was over. Alazla cradled his head against his shoulder when it was done, and Thorn cried in shuddering gouts of both relief and sorrow.

'You're not alone,' Alazla said, placing his head against Thorn's. 'I'll always be here for you, you know.'

Thorn looked up and nodded, trying without success to wipe the stinging tears from his numerous cuts and burns.

The solstice moon was high and bright as a candle now, and its glowering sister, the violet moon, also known as Veylistra's Face, named after the capricious immortal scion of Nim, god of magic, hung low and menacing in the night sky.

'You're not alone,' he repeated.

Thorn knew that, but had needed to hear it again. There had been no laughter, no mockery, and no suggestion that the whole thing was the result of his imagination or wishful thinking – just simple and straightforward acceptance. That was so Alazla. It was everything that Thorn had expected and hoped for from his friend.

Alazla gently lifted Thorn's hand from his shoulder and raised it to the sky. Thorn did not resist. The silvered light of the solstice moon bloomed across his palm, revealing the dark blue stain remaining from where the avatar's dust had touched his skin. Within that darkness a universe revolved now. Stars chased across the night sky, and the sparkling hue and flitting shadows of infinity hung like a ghostly cloak across the dark.

Unable to look any longer, Thorn let his gaze fall, by coincidence or not, upon the Heart of Korth, where nine mighty edifice faced the Heart of Korth itself. There the crystal singers had created their most beautiful works; towering statues of the nine younger gods in crystals of purest emerald, sunstone, sapphire and ruby. Under the solstice moon they blazed like fallen stars. Did the gaze of those angered gods now rest on him, he wondered?

Alazla noted Thorn's gaze and there was no smile upon his face. That absence seemed odd, and that too momentarily added to his melancholy.

'You can't face this alone, Thorn.' There it was again.

And which of you this night is without his herald, Thorn wondered of those gods. Which of you this day rages at the sky? Whom do you blame? To whom do you look? Does anyone know the truth but me?

'You must tell someone, Thorn. You need help.'

Thorn's smile was simple as he turned from the faces of the gods. 'I *have* told someone. I've told you.'

'My dearest friend, had we been born brothers we couldn't be closer. But you *must* listen to me. You need to tell someone. People need to know. We should go to one of the temples. Perhaps to Oldoth: his revered brothers and sisters tend to be quite… approachable.' Alazla referred to the god of sun and storms, and Thorn knew that his divine order was much loved in Korth. Most households had at least a bronze disc with the beaten face of the sun god above a door lintel.

'And what would they do, do you think, Alazla? Punish me? Almost certainly for trespass, in what was obviously some form of sanctuary. Or perhaps just lock me up while they try to understand this mess?!' Thorn thrust his sparkling palm at Alazla's face. The whirling stars within for a moment cast a puppet master's orbiting shadows across his face.

Alazla pushed the hand away, his expression never changing. Thorn's harrowing palm, it seemed, had no fear for him, or he hid it well indeed. 'No, they'll help you. You know yourself how benevolent most of the divine orders are. I can't recall that they've ever punished anyone for anything: that's the job of the Fist, Thorn.'

Thorn's face remained set. He wasn't actually sure what he even wanted, other than to be rid of the damn stars in his hand and to no longer feel afraid. Though it had been only yesterday, the whole thing felt like a lifetime ago. He'd just not thought beyond simply sharing the burden with Alazla.

Alazla drew deep upon his pipe, apparently watching the ships at peace below, nodding gently on the turning of the waves. 'We can't face this alone. What's happened is bigger than you, Thorn, and it's probably more important too. People need to be told.'

Alazla was not one prone to wise and startling insights, but the truth of his words struck Thorn, though he despised them too for their clarity. Fear curled in his belly, a deep-seated knowledge that life would never be the same again. As miserable as much of it had been, he still did not want to let it go.

'No one need know, Alazla. No one even knows I was there! And what difference does it make? What's happened has happened and there's nothing that either you or I can do about it!'

Disappointment was painted thick on his friend's face as he turned from the battlements. Veylistra's Face hung glowering behind him, for a moment framing him in a violet shroud.

Alazla's words were pitched low, anger taut and coiled in his voice. 'You're better than that, Thorn. You always have been. And I see it, even if you don't! I always have. I know you're not that selfish, even though you might like to think that you are.'

Thorn wished then that his friend wasn't right, and it must have shown on his face as Alazla smiled. Thorn still resisted, however, though his arguments, even to himself, felt weak and at best spurious. 'I'll not place either you or me in any more danger. We can just ignore it and carry on as normal.'

'And what's *normal*, Thorn? The death of yet *another* avatar because you didn't warn them? If that happens, everyone will despise you, Thorn, including yourself. There'll be no "living normally" after that!

'Do you think that blue mark on your hand's going to scrub off with brushes and soaps in your mum's kitchen? No you don't, and neither do I.'

Thorn found suddenly that he had no arguments left. He was beyond anger, fear and even recrimination. The burden had been shared, and that in itself began to lift him. Alazla and Thorn had never failed at anything they'd tackled together – and they both knew that. 'Fine. You're right. Just let me sleep tonight; I need some rest. We'll go in the morning.'

'The morning, then,' Alazla reiterated, and clapped Thorn on the shoulder, making him wince. 'They may even heal you too if you ask them nicely. You need to keep what good looks you've got, after all.'

Thorn laughed and it felt good. 'You'll only have more competition if I do that.'

'I think I can handle it.'

- Chapter 3 -

Possession

The wispy, ebbing messenger from the Citadel of Storms had instructed Balthazar to trace the witness. Though the messenger had been clear that the witness had not been observed, in a 'traditional' sense, Balthazar did not need anything as crude as a description to help him, he had certain skills, which was of course why he'd been chosen.

Indeed Balthazar already knew this person to be a man – he could taste him in the air, the tiniest particles like a residue left lingering; they were there to be tasted, if you but wished to do so. The man scent was overlaid with an unusual mix of profound sorrow and overwhelming fear, but also and most unexpectedly a sense of anger and utter outrage, the sense of which was sharp and bright. Balthazar found this latter particularly strange.

Balthazar moved through a world of particles and the tiniest matter. His form was insubstantial, unseen to the natural eye. He ebbed and flowed with the slight breeze through the streets of radiant Korth. Although his form was in a sense cohesive, a strong wind could easily scatter his essence, making it difficult for him to piece himself together again. Never know what body part you might end up without, he thought to himself with a shudder. Concentrating hard on following the scent from the crystal glade, at one point he was drawn into a horse's lungs, a truly unpleasant experience, and upon exiting was left feeling damp and in need of a good bath. Naturally, the horse hadn't even noticed.

Floating through woven baskets and market stalls, over roofs, through windows and around the citizens of crystal Korth, Balthazar occasionally picked up a particle or two of divine power. This was not surprising, of course, if this mortal had touched the remains of an avatar, but nonetheless, he prudently scooped them up into his own being. No sense leaving spare power around, after all. Even a single particle of such power could leave a citizen impossibly strong or long of life.

Balthazar, beloved son of Oldoth, god of sun and storms, beloved son Oquanar and beloved daughter Reon, had moved from the glade within the crystal wood, following the man's scent as one combined essence. Their love for each other, united by their common belief in the guidance of Oldoth, made their joining both intimate and without reservation. They had joined forms largely out of prudence, since anything capable of slaying an avatar was likely to be more than a match for a single beloved, despite cycles of hard study and training. The feeling of their combined power at that time had been immense, their very beings mingling.

It was with a deep reluctance that Balthazar had gently asked Oquanar and Reon to withdraw. At times it had seemed that their combined essence had become something much greater than themselves, hinting at a greater awareness, and at parting it was lost.

The scent had become somewhat scattered within the busy streets of Korth, pieces sometimes clinging to beasts of burden or to the clothes of the citizens, taking divergent paths. Separating, they had followed differing trails across the city.

Then Balthazar picked another scent up: bitter and damp, overlaid with a vague scent of power. Confused, he hovered for a moment, thinking. Although both trails were fresh, this was slightly younger. Intrigued and slightly concerned, he followed the particle scent, tasting the bitter tang, and he decided that there was a slight canine essence to this new being.

Following the new scent, he realised that it moved parallel with that of the man into a bustling market place, known as Rounders Place, primarily for its circular shape. The market was awash with numerous wares and hawkers. At a fish stall manned by a plump but hearty good-wife the scent changed somewhat, although Balthazar couldn't quite put his finger on how it had changed. Concerned, Balthazar was able to do little but continue to pursue his quarry.

It was late morning by the time Balthazar traced the scent to the Three Barrels Inn. He flowed in through one of the open windows. The Three Barrels was a cheery place, obviously run with pride by its owner, judging by the colourful curtains at the windows and the table tops which gleamed deeply from cycles of loving polish.

The Three Barrels was already coming alive with revellers eager to enjoy the third day of the Seventy-Seven. A slim but athletic-looking man in his late forties was in charge behind the bar, but he took orders from his numerous customers with an easy smile and directed the goings-on with the grace and ease of someone born to his craft. Occasionally he would spare a smile for a slightly plump lady with brown hair functionally coiled atop her head who bustling in and out of the kitchen, bearing steaming platters and wearing a constantly harried look.

Balthazar floated easily through the smoke and revelry. The scents were more difficult to follow in such a crowded area, particularly one filled with so many strong odours. He cast about, carefully tasting the air by drawing it into himself, moving slowly throughout the common room. After a few minutes of cautious tasting, he realised that the scent must lead up the stairs, which he glided over to, following one of the inn's patrons. The patron, a well-built male in the simple clothing of a labourer, took the stairs with ease and on reaching the landing walked past a number of doors, halting at the end door. The man paused and looked back down the hallway behind him and right through Balthazar. Seemingly satisfied, he turned back to the door, where he placed his ear against it, listening.

A moment later the man stepped back from the door, and as he did so a shadowy form separated from his body, which dropped to the floor like an empty sack of grain. The hovering form was misty and only the size of a plump child, with a sinister green cast. Its features were human, but the hair was spiked, its mouth twisted into a vicious grin from which rows of razor sharp teeth protruded. Wicked sharp talons flexed as it looked at the door. It was completely naked and covered in a fine haze of hair.

'May the sun god look over us,' hissed Balthazar in shock. The hissed words seemed but the murmur of a breeze.

He was unable to make out whether the creature had any gender, not that he had expected to be able to identify one, for he knew that he looked at a deviant – creatures created aeons past by the magi in their games of power. With the power of possession, the magi had primarily used them to enslave high-profile figures, and further the shadowy reach of their domain.

The grinning deviant, its greenish hue casting a nimbus upon the hallway floor, flowed under the door.

'Move, Balthazar, move, damn it!' the beloved brother berated himself, and slipped under the door after it.

Beyond the door, Thorn slept.

The Black Spite and Alazla's companionship had at last dampened the memories of the avatar's sorrowful eyes and its dying screams, allowing an exhausted Thorn to drop into a sleep so deep that it was devoid of dreams.

With blankets tucked up under his chin, had it not been for the rather battered condition of his face he would have looked for all the world like just another young man, sleeping in after a good night's carousing. Not even the sound of the banging skillets from downstairs disturbed him.

The deviant cared for none of this as it coalesced spectre-like above Thorn's peaceful face, its ebbing childlike form very slightly disturbed by the gentle rise and fall of his breath. It hovered above him like a dread spirit risen from the grave, casting a sickly green shadow across his face.

As Balthazar's airy form emerged from under the door he was in time to see the misty deviant hovering over the face of a young man in bed, obviously asleep and utterly oblivious of the dreadful peril that now threatened him. Drawing the scent of the room into his being, Balthazar knew immediately that he had found the young man he sought. He had found Thorn.

The young man, who could not have been more than twenty cycles, mumbled something and rolled over onto his side. As he inhaled, the deviant was drawn completely into his lungs.

Balthazar was shocked at the speed of the deviant's attack, and realised that if he didn't act immediately the mage-born creature would assume utter control of the young man, putting him beyond help. The damage that a deviant did to the mind of its host in suppressing its natural will was irrevocable. The deviant also usually took great delight in inflicting as much pain on the host as possible. The pain manifested greater mental energies which the deviant then fed off, becoming even stronger.

As Thorn cried out in his sleep, Balthazar raced forward with the force of a thunderstorm and grasped the deviant with talons of air. He captured it just as it disappeared with the inhalation into Thorn's mouth. And there the deviant hung, struggling. Balthazar slowly and with utter resolution began to carefully draw the creature back out. The deviant hissed and spat as claws and a face manifested themselves within its greenish form, the lower portion of its torso trailing down into Thorn's mouth. It lashed out at the airy Balthazar, but its talons passed harmlessly through him. It shrieked and spat in anger and frustration.

Balthazar cautiously drew the deviant farther out until it almost seemed to be standing on Thorn's face. Quickly then Balthazar threw coils of air round the deviant, binding it in bands stronger than the toughest iron. It shrieked and gibbered at him in some foul arcane tongue and its slitted eyes cast frantically about for a means of escape; the door, the window, as its coiling bonds became ever tighter. Then just as Balthazar sought to place the final bindings it broke an arm free. With a hiss of spiteful glee it plunged its misty claw straight into Thorn's forehead. Thorn's skin didn't crack or bleed as the insubstantial claw penetrated his skull, but his eyes flew open and he screamed a wretched cry of primal agony.

Cursing, Balthazar wrenched the deviant away from Thorn. It came free, but giggled even as it was bound immobile, hanging in the air in the middle of Thorn's bedroom.

As the deviant hung there, the door to the room flew open and the plump woman with brown hair and the slim middle-aged man that Balthazar had seen in the bar burst into the room. They stopped, horrified at the sight before them, the childlike deviant hanging in the air and Thorn writhing on the bed, thrashing from side to side, screaming in pain, but with his eyes remaining closed.

Balthazar muttered a string of curses and cast about him for his essence. He dared not do this too quickly less he miss a part of himself or even add something to himself which did not belong, which could be disastrous, potentially leading to a corruption of his very being. Thus, it was some moments later that Thorn's mother and father became aware of another presence in the room with them. Slowly Balthazar's form came into view, first becoming just a misty outline and then building moment by moment, becoming more substantial.

By the time Balthazar had fully drawn his essence together, his face a mask of determination, the man had braved the hissing deviant and was bearing the unconscious Thorn from the room.

He halted in the doorway as Balthazar spoke through a partially misty mouth. 'Please wait, I can help you! I am Balthazar, beloved son of Oldoth. Your son has been placed in grave peril and he is hurt. He is beyond your means to heal. Allow me to help you.'

Jouran held a limp Thorn cradled in his arms; tears trembled unshed in his eyes. His watery gaze took in Balthazar and noted the intense strength that seemed to radiate from him – but not a human strength, he thought, more like the feral strength of nature; a storm, vast and ominous, yet presently leashed, silent and controlled. His toned bare upper torso had a slight golden hue, accentuated with arm-bands of gold and jewellery. But it was his eyes that unnerved Jouran though, for they were almost without pupils and within them a cloudy sky seemed to roil.

Jouran's eyes slipped back to the spitting deviant briefly, but his stance was proud and angry rather than afraid. Catherine, his wife, wrung her hands at his side.

Though his face showed profound shock, Jouran's voice was strong. 'I recognise you, brother. I've been to Oldoth's House and sought blessing from time to time. Can you really help my son?'

'Yes, I can. But it needs to happen now. The wound is likely deep and he is in great peril.'

Thorn whimpered and trembled in his father's arms. Looking only at his son, Jouran replied, 'Very well, brother, and may Oldoth bless you for helping. But please do it quickly: he's our only son.'

Nodding, Balthazar could not keep the relief from his voice. 'Thank you. Now I must ask your forbearance… just for a moment.'

With that he turned to the deviant and the clouds within his eyes seemed to boil darker. 'Your kind are rare, creature. Who is it that sent you?'

The deviant did not answer: it merely grinned and gesticulated obscenely.

'Think not to take me lightly, demon. You will pay for such folly and so, if I am not mistaken, will your master.'

With that the bands of air about the deviant began to draw apart. Briefly the deviant hissed in delight and, thinking it was free, lunged towards Jouran, who stepped back involuntarily. And then the deviant realised its dilemma: it was actually being drawn apart. It began to struggle and shriek. Its face then became almost fully childlike and innocent; tears began streaming down it.

Gibbering, it cried out now in the common Runic language, its forked tongue lisping the words, 'Please don't; have mercy. I am just a child. My mistress made me. I could not disobey.'

'Then tell me whom you serve,' Balthazar cracked.

'I cannot!' it shrieked. 'I cannot. I beseech you, spare me!'

The airy bands had now drawn the deviant so far apart that it was almost transparent.

Catherine stepped forward, shouting at Balthazar, 'You heard it; it's just a child. Don't hurt it. Let it go. Please.'

Jouran, cradling Thorn, just watched, transfixed.

Balthazar continued, relentless. Moving his arms outward, the deviant stretched. 'Speak now or die!' he thundered.

The deviant shook its head and with a wail fell apart, its form becoming wisps of ebbing green cloud.

The room was quiet.

Catherine and Jouran stared transfixed at where the deviant had just dissipated.

Balthazar sighed and his shoulders dropped as he turned towards Thorn's parents, his face creased with worry. 'I understand that a hundred questions now chase unanswered through your minds, but I must ask you to wait. Soon you will have your answers, as best I can tell you, but at this present time we must consider first your son, Thorn.'

Jouran spoke softly, as Catherine smoothed the hair back from Thorn's face. 'Please hurry, brother, he's all we have.'

'Place him upon the bed…. and I will do what I can.'

Jouran ever so gently lay his comatose son back upon the bed. 'He is so pale,' he said, stroking dark hair back from his son's face. 'His breathing is so shallow, but I can't see a wound. What was that… that…thing?'

'Please, these questions must wait,' replied Balthazar, firmly but not unkindly. 'The creature you just saw has wounded him grievously and I must fully understand his ailment if I am to help him.'

Sitting down on the bed beside Thorn, he placed a golden skinned hand upon his head. Thorn felt cold to the touch. Gradually Balthazar allowed his consciousness to be drawn into Thorn. In moments his mind was flowing through him, one moment as a particle of water, another as a particle of air. Moments became minutes and it seemed as if Balthazar did not breathe.

Balthazar roamed through Thorn in a way that only a son of Oldoth could. He came to know Thorn in ways that he would perhaps never know himself and thus came to understand that, as he had suspected, that Thorn's wound was not physical. The deviant had damaged his mind. Even now, Thorn's mind bled; it struggled and fought to remain alive, but the wound was open and deep. Balthazar knew that as the minutes passed, Thorn's mind would begin to lose control over his vital functions, his breathing, his heart, his organs; essentially his body would begin to close down.

Withdrawing from Thorn's body, Balthazar whispered into the air. Within moments a slight form appeared before him, invisible yet tangible. He knew that Thorn's parents could not see it. The sprite landed on his hand and waited patiently while Balthazar gave it urgent instructions.

Perfect in its diminutive form, human yet not, tiny gossamer wings protruded from its back, a blur even while it was still. Finally it nodded, bowed briefly and flew from his hand and out of the window faster than the human eye could follow.

To Jouran's eyes it had seemed that Balthazar held something that moved faster than his eye could see within the palm of his hand. He struggled to overhear what was whispered, but heard only 'A sacrifice may be required.' This last chilled him even further and he didn't dare ask what it meant.

Turning his attention back to Thorn, Balthazar placed his hands upon his chest, leaning so close that he could feel Thorn's shallow breath on his face. Thorn's body strained beneath his hands, organs faltered and convulsed as they received halting instructions from his mind. Then, as Thorn breathed out, Balthazar breathed in, taking all of Thorn's breath into his lungs. He then pulled back and sighed gently, being careful not to expel the air within him that was Thorn's.

Catherine, concerned, moved to the bed. She gasped. 'What've you done? He's not breathing! You bastard, he's not breathing!' She moved to strike him.

'Peace,' said Balthazar, more calmly than he felt, and stepped away from the bed and Catherine. 'I have taken his breath. If you will, I now carry Thorn's next breath within me and until such time as I expel it, he cannot die.'

Catherine and Jouran both looked in horror and amazement at their son, who lay so utterly still as to be dead.

'Is he truly so badly wounded, then?' asked Jouran, as if seeking to deny the truth. 'There's not even a mark on him.'

'I'm sorry… but he is,' Balthazar replied solemnly. 'He is also beyond my simple arts to heal. We require help from the divine order of Eli-shar, the goddess of life herself, if we are to save him.'

At this Catherine dropped onto the bed beside her son and lowered her head onto his chest, weeping.

'I have sent a messenger. I *believe* that they will come.' Balthazar added the last belatedly and did not relate how poor relations had been between some of the divine orders in recent decades. He just had to trust that someone would come. If not, when Balthazar next fully expelled his breath, Thorn was dead.

It was some hours later when a serving lad brought the beloved sister of Eli-shar upstairs. The sister was young and slim, perhaps only Thorn's age. Her long tawny hair was tied back at the neck, cast over her blood-red sleeveless dress. At the nape of her neck a simple gold chain carried the symbol of an intricate knot; the symbol of her order.

The sister looked briefly at Balthazar and did not greet him. Balthazar bowed slightly and said only, 'Welcome, beloved sister. You have my most profound thanks for coming. We are in your debt.'

Her countenance was stern as it moved to Thorn and she walked to his side, placing a hand on his cool brow.

When she spoke, her voice was crisp and assertive. 'You hold his last breath within you, son of Oldoth. The god of death may have fallen, beloved son, but his dominion is still not without power. You imperil yourself with each moment.'

Jouran and Catherine exchanged alarmed glances.

Apparently not noticing the exchange, the sister continued, her smooth and slightly childlike face showing for a moment great compassion. 'His wound is to the mind and it is terribly deep. It would be better to let him go.'

Catherine shrieked and threw herself at the feet of the young daughter of Eli-shar, clutching the hem of her red dress and sobbing. 'No. Please, no. He's all we have. I beg you, beloved daughter, please, in the name of all the younger gods, please!'

The daughter stood up, her face sorrowful. 'I'm sorry, there is nothing that can be done.'

Jouran gathered Catherine into his arms.

Balthazar stepped forward. 'Beloved daughter, this young man is important. I believe that you may have known that before you were sent.'

The eyes of the two locked then and something seemed to pass between them.

'What was it that did this?' she asked after a moment.

'A deviant,' Balthazar replied without a flicker of emotion.

A silence stretched then in the room; even Catherine's sobs stilled. Minutes passed as she apparently just stared into Thorn's face.

The young daughter hung her head for a moment. When she looked up again, her eyes appeared to stare beyond Balthazar and into another place. 'Do you know what you ask?'

Balthazar paused and then with great deliberation replied, 'Yes, I'm afraid that I do.'

'Very well,' the beloved daughter said softly.

Turning to Catherine and Jouran, her face composed and devoid of any apparent emotion, she said, 'Your son must be very special.'

Catherine nodded, unable to speak, reaching for her husband's hand.

Sitting beside Thorn and stroking the hair in an almost familiar manner from his face, she whispered, 'The fallen we lift. The injured we bleed for. The mortally wounded we die for. We do this in joy and in love. I beg you, beloved Eli-shar, cradle me and lift up your son.'

The sister raised the twisted symbol of her goddess to her lips and kissed it. Then, leaning forward, almost with reverence she placed a firm kiss upon Thorn's lips. At that her back suddenly arched impossibly and a shudder shook her slender frame. With a soft cry she dropped lifeless to the floor.

At the same moment Balthazar breathed out and Thorn took a deep breath of air, his eyes flying open.

Catherine flew to Thorn, enfolding her son in her arms.

Jouran ran to the fallen form of the daughter of Eli-shar and knelt beside her. Blood trickled from the young sister's mouth; her eyes were wide and stared sightlessly. Jouran felt for a pulse and found nothing. He looked to Balthazar, horror contorting his face.

Balthazar nodded. 'She made a great sacrifice for your son,' he said sorrowfully.

Two men entered Thorn's room then, wearing plain and unadorned red robes. They gently lifted the sister's lifeless body from the floor and bore her from the room without a word.

Balthazar turned to follow them and paused for a moment by the door. 'You must come to me at the House of Oldoth; there we will talk. Come at dawn tomorrow. Your son will sleep well tonight. And fear not, for he has received the blessing of a goddess this day.'

Thorn slept deeply that night and the only thing he dreamt of was a young girl in red, who took away his pain and carried him back to the light. He would never even know her name.

- CHAPTER 4 -

The House of Oldoth

Thorn insisted on going to the House of Oldoth alone. His parents had protested, beside themselves with worry for his health and desperately concerned about what the future now held for their only son, but he had insisted. Thorn was a young man now and it was his right to face up to his own responsibilities; amazingly he felt absolutely fine in doing so.

His father had sat Thorn down and gently explained much of what had happened. Thorn had a hazy recollection of the deviant and a searing pain within his mind, but it now seemed dull and very far away. He didn't care to try too hard to remember.

His father, of course, had been at first kindly and then increasingly stern. He was no fool, and he'd pushed Thorn hard as to what could have led to such an extraordinary set of incidents. Thorn pleaded ignorance at first, and when that didn't work he just asked his father to give him time. With that Jouran agreed to relent, though only until Thorn returned.

The part that Thorn struggled with the most, though, was the undeniable and inescapable fact that a daughter of Eli-shar had sacrificed herself for him. She had taken his mortal wound into herself and died so that he could live. Thorn found this impossible to reconcile, not only for the terrible sacrifice but also as to why he should be singled out. Such treatment was beyond rare, reserved for the mighty. To the common masses it was simply the stuff of folklore.

His father had already practically beggared the family by sending offerings of thanks in both gold and goods to the order of Eli-shar, indeed far beyond what the family could genuinely afford. Jouran had simply said that his son was worth more than anything they possessed. Should the divine order of Eli-shar require even more from him (not that they had actually asked for a single gold coin) for the sacrifice of their daughter, well then, he would happily sell the inn and they'd go back to live with his brother in the Bay of Gulls.

Respecting Thorn's wishes to go to the meeting with Balthazar at the House of Oldoth alone, but fearing for his son's health, his father had insisted that Thorn ride, not walk, even though the House was within the city of Korth itself. And so Thorn found himself riding Ranticus, one of the family's draught horses, whose usual task was drawing the ale cart. Certainly there was no danger of the old beast injuring Thorn in a headlong rush after some young filly.

Ranticus's plodding journey to the House of Oldoth allowed Thorn some much needed time to think. The rhythm of the old horse was comfortable and soothing.

Thorn recalled almost nothing of the attack by the creature his parents had called a deviant, and for that, given their description of events, he was profoundly grateful. He was mystified, though, as to why a daughter of Eli-shar should sacrifice herself for him, although some connection with the fallen avatar seemed at the very least highly likely.

As Thorn reflected on the fallen avatar once more he realised that the horror accompanying the memories had gone. Another gift from the daughter of Eli-shar, it seemed.

Ranticus bore an unseeing Thorn past people he knew and places with which he'd been familiar since childhood. A few of these folk hailed him in greeting, but he did not see or hear them.

Certainly his palm remained blue, though, as he gave the stain another futile rub. He was grateful that it wasn't sparkling as it had been the previous night, and even more so that his parents had not spotted it amidst the turmoil. That would have made explanations or deflections of topic simply impossible. His father's mind was at least as quick as Thorn's own.

Ranticus had stopped.

Coming out of his reverie, Thorn looked upon the House of Oldoth. It was not so much a house as simply an outer wall that ran in a single perfect circle about the enclosed area. Rising to perhaps thirty spans (a span being the width of an open hand), it bore an unusual golden hue that shimmered gently in the early morning sunshine. A single circular opening served as the entrance, although no gateway to bar it was in sight. A stylised sun had been painted around the entrance itself so that those coming and going would have to pass through the mouth of the sun.

Taking a deep breath, Thorn urged Ranticus forward and into the circular entrance. It was only then that the unseen airy denizens set by Balthazar to guard Thorn during his sleep and journey departed.

'Well, here goes. I suppose that things can't get much worse. At least here I should be safe from the likes of deviants….or anything else for that matter.'

Ranticus, of course, made no response.

'If Alazla was amazed before, he's going to be dumbstruck this time. I think last night's events are likely to test even his incredulity.'

They emerged onto a single unbroken expanse of green grass, essentially a vast field of lush green grass within the confines of the outer circular wall. Gasping in surprise, Thorn saw a glittering dome above, spanning the entire house. Rising directly from the outer wall, it shimmered in golden waves one moment and then blue the next. Beneath the outer dome and in the shadow of the spire were scores of small azure and grey domes dotted across the lush meadow, like oversized mushrooms. Thorn watched in avid fascination as a sister of Oldoth walked right through the wall of one such dome but did not emerge on the other side.

'Now, this is an eye-opener, eh, Ranticus? Strange that it didn't look like this last time we were here, though.' This set him chewing his lip thoughtfully.

Beloved brothers and sisters of Oldoth strolled casually about the meadow and in and out of the domes, apparently deep in conversation. All of them Thorn regarded as being in various states of undress.

'Crikey, mother would have a thing or two to say about this, I reckon! Not that I'm complaining, mind.'

The brothers frequently sported bare upper torsos, and the sisters; brassiers of gold, red or blue with open wispy skirts. Clearly they all also adored gold ornamentation, which was exhibited everywhere, including armbands, necklaces, hair clasps, rings and other things more exotic. He wanted to say that the sisters were the closest thing he'd ever seen to a naked woman, but thought better of it given where he was.

Thorn was vaguely aware of laughter. Looking down, his eyes met those of Balthazar, the sun highlighting his toned form, golden hair waving behind him as if upon a summer's breeze. The previously roiling grey eyes of the beloved son sparkled now, in mirth, bright as a morning sky.

'You are welcome, Thorn. Few are permitted to see the truth of Oldoth's house, and I notice that you see it as true as the sun upon the grass. How is that, I wonder?'

Balthazar paused and smiled at the perplexed expression upon Thorn's face and said, 'Forgive me, let us make you welcome. I trust that you are feeling better?'

Thorn nodded and accepted Balthazar's hand as he dismounted.

Balthazar settled a hand familiarly onto Thorn's shoulder. 'First we must see you settled and then I will send for you; clearly there is much that we need to talk about.' The last was said with a penetrating although not unkind stare.

Thorn felt his throat constrict under the scrutiny and he did not reply. Concern clutched at him. He was uncertain what the brother of Oldoth actually knew, but he was fairly sure that it was more than Thorn wanted him to.

Balthazar gestured and a young daughter of Oldoth stepped forward. 'Alicia, see that Thorn is settled in and made comfortable.' With that, Balthazar strode away across the grass, towards the distant spire.

Thorn watched the receding back of Balthazar with unease, suddenly feeling unexpectedly alone. Switching his gaze back to the young daughter, he realised that he was being frankly appraised. He took in his would-be guide's freckled complexion, quirky smile and slightly wild red hair and immediately thought that he could like her.

'The name's Alicia,' she said, jovially thrusting out a hand. Thorn solemnly shook it, inwardly remarking the firmness of her grip.

'Don't know what all the fuss is about myself. You sure don't look like much to me. You can leave your horse there. Come on, what are you waiting for?' she said, already starting off across the meadow.

'Wait, where are we going?' asked Thorn.

She did not reply and Thorn was forced to run to catch up, desperate to ask more questions but forced through circumstance to concentrate on jogging, though that did not stop him mumbling, 'Typical: you seem to know about me but I don't know about you. That's usually the way things go, it seems. No change there.'

He did not catch Alicia's amused glance as she marched briskly across the meadow, weaving easily between strange blue and grey domes. Thorn noted that the domes stood about fourteen hands or so high and as much wide, with sons and daughters appearing to come and go from them at a whim. Alicia seemed quite nonplussed by it all and began what was, Thorn realised, a stream of largely rhetorical questions.

'You'd think that you were the son of the Guardians themselves for all the fuss they've been making here. For Balthazar to come and find you, you must sure be important. I suppose that stuff about being an innkeeper's son is all just a front?'

Thorn was not even sure what to say to that.

Alicia looked over her shoulder, appraising Thorn as they walked, but he steadfastly refused to look her in the eye. She carried on as if Thorn's silence were affirmation enough. 'Some sort of holy messenger, I expect? Word is that your summons came direct from the Citadel of Storms! Maybe it was Aolandar himself who sent for you! Gracious, that's something, isn't it? Say, are you related to him, maybe?'

Dignified silence was the way now, Thorn decided. Aolandar? The Citadel of Storms? A few days ago he'd have laughed at such mythical nonsense. Now he just became more chilled by the moment. It was now utterly apparent that someone certainly knew all about what he had witnessed, or at least knew some of it. The question was, what the heck did he do about it?

By the time they reached their destination Alicia had apparently practically convinced herself that Thorn was a divine emissary of Oldoth, alighted directly from the heavens. Awe-inspired from her own suppositions, she gaped at Thorn. Thorn didn't know what to do. Realising that denial would probably just mean digging himself an even deeper hole with this youthful fanatic, he kept silent.

Taking the chance to look about, he wasn't surprised to find that they'd stopped outside a grey dome. Thorn waited.

Alicia continued to gape at him.

'Okay… thanks, Alicia.'

That elicited nothing.

'So, what now?' he tried lamely.

Apparently snapping out of her runaway thoughts, Alicia broke into a smile. 'This is yours... er... sir.'

Thorn looked dubiously at the winking dome.

'No doubt you know all about these, so I'll just leave you to it. Balthazar will send for you later, I expect. Bye for now, sir.' And with that Alicia turned briskly on her heel and marched off.

Spinning towards her with a dozen questions suddenly on his lips, Thorn was too late and glumly watched her rapidly receding back.

'Great. This just gets better and better,' Thorn thought. Then the rain started.

'Oldoth's bright golden balls, where on Rune did that come?!' Thorn cursed. He froze when he realised what he had said and where he'd said it. Still, no lightning appeared from the god of sun and storms to smite him.

It was a light drizzle, the sort that would usually interfere very little as you went about your day, provided you kept to some modest cover, like most sensible people. Truly better and better, he thought. Thorn realised that outside the dome above it was actually black with cloud and a heavy rain fell in droves, yet only a light drizzle fell within. It even seemed that the light drizzle sparkled merrily.

'Cheerful drizzle, now that's got to be a first. What on Rune is there to be happy about?' Just for good measure, he shook his fist briefly at the sky dome. 'I really do think that given my fairly dire personal circumstances you could be a little less chirpy.'

This did not elicit any obvious response, so Thorn turned his glum thoughts back to the small dome beside him. He couldn't help but think that it somehow seemed pleased to see him.

'Go on then, do something – whatever it is you're supposed to do.' The dome said nothing.

'Well, I'm not going to touch you, if that's what you're thinking! I've got into enough trouble touching things I shouldn't.' He didn't bother to look at his palm, dreading to see the blue stain and what it could portend.

'I'll study you instead. Leap before you look and all that. Yes, that's it.' And so Thorn studied the dome. Some time later he was still studying it and was also soaked to the skin. He was definitely not going to touch it. He'd got himself into enough trouble already, it seemed, intentionally or not, and he certainly was not going to make matters any worse by dabbling with more foreign things.

Defeated, he finally sat down on the grass, which he noted sourly was now very damp.

Several hours later and just as the day was beginning to turn into evening, a youthful and rather bemused son of Oldoth presented himself before Thorn. Thoroughly wet, miserable and really very put out, Thorn glared at him angrily.

'What?' Thorn said curtly. 'Please don't do anything to interrupt me, your hospitality is overwhelming! No, don't tell me; you treat all your guests this way.' He knew it was likely unfair when he said it, but he was really feeling a bit sorry for himself.

Seeming surprised, the young man composed himself and with an almost concealed smile replied, 'If you would follow me, sir, beloved son Balthazar would like to see you now.'

'Of course,' replied Thorn, 'I'll jump right to it.' Grumbling to himself, Thorn clambered to his feet.

Thorn set off after the son, taking the opportunity to glance daggers at those who dared to be moving freely in and out of their little domes.

Ultimately, Thorn and his guide moved out of the dome village and walking past the towering golden spire proceeded into a wide and open meadow, free of domes or other strange artifice of divine magic. What must have been about fifty sons and daughters seemed to be holding some form of service beneath the open sky, just as the timid stars were appearing from behind the clouds, to greet the rusty setting sun. Their soft chant was reassuring in the light evening air and Thorn felt his temper begin to melt away.

Skirting the service, they came to a halt some distance beyond and the son looked at Thorn expectantly. When Thorn's face registered only blank incomprehension, the son said, 'You may enter.'

Thorn looked blankly about him. There was only grass and the dome far above, and beyond that the evening sky. An awkward silence prevailed. Giving up, Thorn turned to the son. 'Help me out here: enter what?' The question died on his lips as he addressed only thin air.

Bemused and angered at his treatment for the second time that day, Thorn felt his temper begin to fray once again.

'Tyche trip them up! Enough is enough; I'll have a look around anyway.'

As Thorn stepped forward, he felt the atmosphere about him change. The air went from calm to utterly still. There was not a sound. Looking up, Thorn realised that the sky dome was no longer present. A breathtaking evening sky soared above, as the setting sun bade goodnight to the cheerful stars. There was an intense peace about this place: a spiritual peace, he realised.

'You are perceptive.'

Thorn jumped.

Balthazar stood before him where only a moment ago there had been just empty air. 'The air is never empty, my child,' said Balthazar, as if reading his thoughts. 'It is as alive as you and I. It is a world of wonder, a place of creatures fair and fierce, all of whom serve our god.'

Balthazar regarded Thorn gently, his eyes unreadable, golden earrings and armbands winking softly in the starlight. About him was an aura of intense calm or as of a soft mountain breeze. No, Thorn thought, stepping back slightly, this is the tempered strength of a storm.

Balthazar moved forward and placed a strong but gentle hand upon Thorn's shoulder as if to stop him from fleeing. 'Fear not, Thorn, you will come to no harm here. You are under the protection of Oldoth now. Tell me, Thorn; do you know why you are here?'

Those words struck Thorn like a blow. A whirlwind of responses and options crashed through his mind. Lie, he thought: he'll never know. You've done nothing wrong, perhaps you trespassed at worst. Make something up. Tell him just some of what you saw. Protect yourself. If you tell him, he'll be sure to tell others, and where will it stop? At best he may think you're mad. Dozens of replies and options lay open to him. Yet warring with these was the overriding belief in honesty that his parents had worked hard to instil in him.

Thorn caught himself as he realised that judging from the scrutiny he was receiving from Balthazar, many of his emotions must certainly be playing across his face. Balthazar in turn revealed nothing, his face impassive in its chiselled perfection. He waited patiently for Thorn to speak.

Opting for a true but tempered course, Thorn finally replied, deciding to omit the avatar from his reply. 'I, I guess that you probably want to know about the glade?'

He paused to see what response that elicited.

Balthazar simply nodded.

Another pause. Best not to mention the Jack's Folly, Thorn thought.

'Well, as you're aware, it's the Seventy-Seven Festival at the moment and my friend Alazla and I had a few drinks at the Badgers' Den.' He decided not to mention the fact that they had actually gatecrashed the party of a well-respected nobleman (who had particularly beautiful twin sisters). He carried on: 'We had a few drinks and lost each other after that.' Again he left out the ensuing fight leading to their ejection and Alazla's night in the care of the city guard. He shrugged, 'I was looking for somewhere to crash out' (hide, more likely, his conscience reminded him). Ignoring the nagging in his subconscious that blandly suggested his own cowardice, he continued. 'I entered a private wood, admittedly passing a few guards and all. I spent a night in a tree.' He finished the last rather lamely, even to his own mind.

Balthazar said nothing. Face impassive, his restless eyes seemed to bore into Thorn.

Thorn shifted under the scrutiny and continued half-heartedly. 'Maybe there was a storm that night or something. When I woke up, there were trees and branches everywhere.'

Thorn barely believed what he was saying himself, but his need for self-preservation seemed to be overwhelming his intellect. Somehow he also knew that he just could not yet talk to Balthazar of the tragedy that he had witnessed. He nevertheless felt somehow ungrateful for not telling everything to a person who had certainly saved his life.

Balthazar waited patiently.

Belatedly Thorn endeavoured to add a little more embellishment. 'I know that I trespassed on private grounds. I'm sorry.'

Still Balthazar said nothing and Thorn shifted awkwardly from foot to foot.

When it was clear that the beloved son would say nothing else he continued again, skirting closer to the issue, but again not quite touching on it. 'That sister of Eli-shar gave her life for me and I honestly don't know why. Her life was certainly far more precious than mine. She'd been chosen by a god and would have given more to people in her few cycles than I probably will in my entire life. I don't know why she saved me. I certainly didn't deserve it. I'm really very sorry that she died.'

With the last Thorn felt weak to his stomach. He grieved for the sister of Eli-shar and deep down believed that she should never have given her life to save him. He also knew that he'd actually rather have died than have to live with the fact that she was gone and he was here. Thorn could feel his heart hammering in his chest as he waited for Balthazar to reply, his gaze boring into Thorn's soul.

Eventually Balthazar replied. 'You are wise for one who is so young, Thorn.'

Certainly this was not what Thorn had expected to hear.

'Are you aware, Thorn, that the sunlight and the wind reach all corners of this world? It is everywhere and gives life to everything. There is nothing that our father Oldoth does not see.'

Relieved that Balthazar did not appear to be berating him, Thorn nevertheless felt small and vulnerable with that statement. He was just a student, caught up in something of which he had almost no real understanding, and beloved son Balthazar commanded the entire House of Oldoth in Korth! The son could probably see through Thorn's attempts at evasion like air on a sunlit morning!

'I could not help but notice the mark on your hand yesterday, Thorn. Would you mind if I took a quick look?'

Thorn paused, his heart skipping a beat. Game up, he thought. Nowhere to run. He gingerly held out his right hand. The palm was stained deep blue; motes of light were scattered across it like glitter.

Balthazar took the proffered hand and Thorn felt a warmth in the beloved son's grip. Under Balthazar's touch the motes of lights began to swim gently under the skin, like miniature stars. Thorn could not help but squirm, his stomach wrapped in knots of fear.

The son peered into his palm for several minutes and then released his hand, with only a cryptic 'Hmmm.'

'Is there anything else that you would like to share with me, Thorn?' Balthazar asked calmly. Trying to wrestle with the fact that Balthazar had said nothing directly about his hand, Thorn thought furiously. No matter which way he came at it, he found that he was simply not able to talk to him about the avatar's death. He shamefully admitted to himself that he was also afraid. Afraid for himself.

Eventually, though, Thorn just replied, 'No, sir, I don't believe that there is.'

The look on Balthazar's face, although not unkind, said it all.

Sighing and raking back his long golden hair, Balthazar responded, 'Very well, Thorn, if nothing else your compassion and perhaps caution is commendable and bespeaks a wisdom that could one day serve you well. But, remember this: you must also learn to recognise friend from foe. Allow those who deserve your trust to aid you. Listen to your heart, Thorn. Think on this and we will talk again tomorrow.'

There was a gentle whisper of wind and Thorn had a feeling of being lifted. Blinking to reorientate himself, Thorn realised that he was now outside his (as he immediately thought of it) dome. Alicia was already waiting for him there and didn't look in the slightest surprised at his sudden appearance.

The shame of Balthazar's gentle rebuke settled on Thorn's shoulders like a blanket and he looked morosely at Alicia.

'Hungry?' she asked, breaking the silence.

Thorn realised that he was famished and nodded a somewhat sullen affirmation.

'Come on then,' Alicia said, and marched off, weaving her way between various domes, illuminated in the silvered half-light of a brightening night sky.

Later that evening, Alicia returned a sated and moderately cheered Thorn to his 'bubble'. Smiling slightly, she appeared to relent at his perplexed expression. 'If you've forgotten how to use Oldoth's shelter, just remember that it's like many things with our god: just breathe and take him into you. And all shall be as you wish.'

Thorn then noticed two figures waiting in the half-light, beside his shelter. From her surprised expression it seemed that Alicia had not expected people to be there either.

His mother, Catherine, was clad in a simple grey woollen dress with a brown cloak thrown across her back. Even in the subdued starlight his mother appeared haggard, the lines at her eyes deeply emphasised, lips pursed in worry. Beside her, clearly wrestling between excitement and apprehension, was his closest friend Alazla. A shock of blond hair framed a slight smile on his mischievous face. He shifted slightly from foot to foot, obviously waiting for Catherine to take the lead.

'Mum, Alazla,' Thorn greeted them both. If anything, this slightly perfunctory greeting caused his mother's concerned frown to deepen even further.

'If you will excuse us, young lady, I'd like to talk to my son,' Catherine said, addressing Alicia.

Alicia nodded politely and sauntered away with a poorly concealed smile, glancing back only once.

'Well, I don't see anything as civilised as tables and chairs here, so I guess we'll just have to sit on the grass,' Catherine said matter-of-factly.

Glum, Thorn sat down beside her.

Catherine reached out and took her dejected son's hand in her own. 'I'm sorry to come here so quickly after last night,' she apologised, 'but your father and I are desperately worried about you. Do you have any news, son? Has Balthazar seen you yet?'

Thorn sighed. 'I've seen him, Mum, but I'm none the wiser yet than I was yesterday. We're going to talk again tomorrow.' He omitted to explain that he and the beloved son were meeting again to give Thorn another chance to tell the truth.

Stroking the side of her son's face, Catherine said, 'We must be honest with each other, Thorn. Your father and I know you well enough to be sure that you're holding something back. We need to know what it is. We only want to help you, to protect you.'

Thorn remained silent, thinking. He was shattered from an emotionally exhausting day and realised that he was also probably still recovering from the injury inflicted by the deviant. He also knew, though he understood that it would test him gravely, that even should he never tell Balthazar, of all people his parents deserved to know the truth. He wondered where he would find the strength.

At that point and true to form, Alazla stepped in to save him. Although there was a smile on his face, it never reached Alazla's eyes as he said, 'Rumour has it that you stole and ate moonberries from the Guardians' forests and that now you can speak with the spirits. Oh, and some people are saying that you entered the crystal woods and had a night of passion with the wood nymphs.' He couldn't help but laugh at that point. 'Of course there are other stories too, but I'm plumping for the last one at least!'

Thorn exchanged a lingering look with Alazla, unable to offer his thanks for the reprieve.

'Alazla, that's enough,' Catherine snapped. 'And don't think I don't believe you're in on this somehow! You two have been conspiring together for the last fifteen cycles.'

Had the light been better, Thorn knew that he'd have seen a ruddy blush staining his friend's cheeks at that point. Alazla had never been great at hiding the truth, even from strangers, let alone from those who knew him well.

In a more moderate tone Catherine continued, 'Let Thorn answer, please, Alazla. We're not trying to judge you, son, we just want to help.'

That cut Thorn to the heart. He loved his parents dearly, but he just didn't know what to say. What could he really tell them? That he'd trespassed within the sacred crystal woods and witnessed not only the immortal Randaerren, but a holy ritual resulting in the descent of an avatar and its destruction by some apparently innocent but dreadful force?! Oh yes, and then there was the avatar dust caught in the skin of his hand. Even if he did tell them, his tale was so far-fetched that he didn't know whether she would even believe him.

In a flash of insight Thorn suddenly understood that no matter how concerned they were, there was nothing that his parents could do to protect him from what he'd inadvertently stumbled into. More to the point, he might also place them in danger by telling them, and that was something he could never live with. He needed time to think, to make sense of everything that he'd seen, time to piece it all together. Telling the truth would have to wait – again.

Squeezing Catherine's hand gently, he replied, 'I know, Mum, and I will tell you; it's just that I'm not sure what it is that I actually know. I'm trying to make sense of it myself. Just let me sleep on it tonight and we'll talk tomorrow, I promise… please.'

Catherine frowned slightly and made as if to say something, but then apparently thought better of it. 'Very well, Thorn. But we *will* talk tomorrow. The order has been kind enough to allow us to sleep here tonight, although I'm not quite sure where, mind you,' she said, looking in concern at Thorn's dome. 'We'll see you in the morning.'

With that she kissed him tenderly on the forehead and began to walk towards the dome village.

Standing too, Alazla hung back for a moment. He pitched his voice very low as he spoke. 'By all that's holy, Thorn! Your mum told me a bit of what happened last night. Are you okay?'

Thorn nodded, grateful for his friend's presence and for the fact that at least to him he didn't need to lie. 'I think so. But it's like I can feel a scar in my mind, where the deviant hurt me.' He struggled for a moment to find the right words. 'You know when you get wounded and it heals all fresh and pink, you know it's going to be okay, but for a while you need to be gentle with it while it heals. Well, it's like that in here,' he said, and tapped his head.

Alazla nodded, his normally bright eyes clouded in thought. 'I take it the dust is still in your hand too.'

'It is, but it's not really dust on my skin any more, but it's more like it's part of me. Somehow, I know it's never going to go away,' said Thorn.

Alazla placed a hand on Thorn's shoulder.

'Come on, Alazla,' called Catherine from where she waited.

'We're going to have to tell them something, you know,' said Alazla. 'If you want my advice, it would be to confide in Balthazar. He can help you and protect you if you need it. He can probably also help you cook something up that will satisfy your parents, without placing them in danger.'

Thorn did not miss the reference to 'we' and was profoundly grateful that he had confided in his friend. He also saw the sense of his advice. 'Right… I think that's what we're going to have to do then.'

With a reassuring smile, Alazla turned and walked to where Catherine waited. They moved off together into the darkening night.

Tired and almost sick with worry, Thorn looked forlornly at his dome. Too tired to care anymore, he then simply did what he had seen others doing and stepped into it. A sensation like warm silk brushed across his skin as he stepped inside.

The simple interior was illuminated by a sourceless silver glow. Deep, soft, woollen blankets had been laid out to form a bed upon the lush grass. There were no other furnishings. Too tired think any more, Thorn dropped down onto the blankets and fell into a deep sleep.

- Chapter 5 -

Shadow's Touch

When Thorn's dreams came, they were troubled. His mortal mind sought to make sense of that which made no sense. He wrestled with concepts of which he had little or no understanding. Images of boiling skies with racing thunderheads filled his dreams. Stricken winged creatures fell from the sky and he didn't know what they were, but felt as if he should.

In the dreamscape he found himself on his back, and boiling clouds filled his vision. A wound of some form pulsed in his mind, the taste like that of an infected rancid cut, disease lurking just beneath the surface.

A shadow fell across him and he felt the heat of its gaze, unable to tell whether it pitied or mocked him. The figure raised a shadowed foot and brought it down hard on his skull, which crunched with the impact. Thorn cried out with pain and shock in his sleep, but seemed somehow unable to awake.

The wound in Thorn's mind was almost healed, but still fresh, pink and tender. Against this scar the voices now pressed. Pulled taught, it stretched and then finally split, giving in to the insistence of their power. The voices slipped quietly into his dreams.

The clouds were gone now, replaced by shadows racing through the dreamscape. Yet the shadows moved with a ghastly life of their own, pulsing with malevolent intelligence. Whispers, whispers. Thorn strained to hear.

'Closer, yes, come closer and we will tell you all.'

Horrified yet fascinated, Thorn stepped within his dream towards the ebbing shapes. Soft tendrils surrounded him, embraced him, and Thorn felt comforted.

Whispers, whispers. 'Answers you can have. Protection too. Love you we will. Come with us… come with us.'

Protection, that's what I need, Thorn realised within his dreams; protection. He almost sobbed with relief. Persecuted most of his life by people with greater physical strength than he, Thorn had been forced to hide behind those stronger than himself. Though he recognised this weakness, he had also never come to fully understand his own gifts.

Witnessing the death of the avatar, Thorn had become afraid again, and fear was his greatest enemy. There had been an attempt on his life and he knew that he didn't deserve it. He was now being persecuted by both Balthazar and his parents, seeking information from him and likely the opportunity to blame him for all that'd happened. It was like he was some form of criminal. Thorn's deepest consciousness rejected this last, a reasoning voice within telling him that this simply wasn't true. His father and mother supported him and had not judged him. The divine order too had not condemned him, but so far had merely sought to listen and understand. But the cycles of persecution rose to the fore, fuelled by his irrational fear, smothering these thoughts.

As if in answer, the voices whispered from the shadows, 'Yes, yes, we understand. Blameless you are. Ashamed they should be for treating you so. But more is to come, Thorn, much more. Now they will judge you. Blame *shall* be yours to carry. It is inevitable. And the punishment – it will destroy your life!'

Fleeting images flashed through the dreamscape: condemnation, Balthazar's face contorted in rage at Thorn's sin, countless faces shouting at him in righteous anger and then the mines, cycles of back-breaking labour in the slave mines! His youth would be lost, his back becoming cramped and hunched in a permanent rictus of pain and his skin hanging in grey folds. He died there in the darkness of the mines and no one knew, or cared.

The whispered voices now rose to a crescendo, rolling around him in waves. 'Come with us. Let us protect you. We can defend you from those who are wicked and self-righteous. We can give you the *strength* to overcome them! No answers will you have to give us. A normal life you can lead. We can come for you now. All you have to do is ask. All you have to do is ask. *Ask*!'

Within his dream Thorn wrestled. This was just a dream. Such questions were foolish and meaningless even, shouted his deepest consciousness. Yet how did he have this tangible awareness of thought within his dream? This too made no sense. But, they'd offered him protection and strength! He would have strength at last – the strength to cast down those who mocked him. How that lured him! Again his subconscious shouted that this simply could not be, he could never ignore what he had seen that evening in the glade and he could never ignore the sacrifice that the daughter of Eli-shar had made for him. He knew that this was true.

The tendrils about his mind drew tighter. Thorn fought, but the voices were so strong. After all, he was sure that they only wanted to help, as they'd said. And if he was wrong about that, well, it was only a dream.

Thorn felt his resistance fading as fast as a setting sun. And then he accepted.

Soft, comforting shadows enwrapped Thorn like a blanket. He fell into a deep and comforting sleep.

Deep within his dreams Thorn did not notice as the bloated red spider crawled out of his mouth. Scores of yellow eyes gleamed with a terrible intelligence and it peered at Thorn, its mandibles clacking under his nose. Then still covered in Thorn's saliva, it dropped to the ground, and scuttled out of the shelter.

Time passed, and the soft blankets of darkness wrapped and comforted Thorn. He luxuriated in the eiderdown of safety, snuggling ever deeper. Yet at the edges, the darkness occasionally flickered, almost as if an annoying light were pressing inward, sparkling at the edges of the shadow. It made no difference. The sleep was so comforting and tender. It was protecting him. But again that light would flicker at the shadow's edge. It was a nuisance and disturbed the tender comfort of his slumber. Irritated, Thorn focused upon the flickering.

The shadows whispered, gently, 'No, do not look. Sleep you need and rest you must have.'

Thorn wavered on the brink of restful darkness. There it was again. He focused. Shouting: he was sure that he could hear shouting now.

'Ignore it you must. Fear not, all will be well. We come for you now.'

The shouts became screams. Thorn began to battle upward from the depths of darkness.

Soft tendrils enwrapped him.

'No, you must not leave,' they whispered, the anguish apparent in their tones. 'Hurt you they will. Stay with us. We come for you.'

Thorn's will wavered. It was then that he heard his mother's voice screaming his name. Thorn struck at the shadows and they scattered.

Thorn opened heavy eyes. The soft grey light of his shelter had gone, replaced by a pulsing, ebbing, inky blackness. He could see nothing. From within or beyond the darkness he could hear shouts and screams, voices calling. Casting the blankets aside, Thorn lurched upward and lunged towards what he assumed was the shelter wall and the outside.

He burst into silvery moonlight and beheld a scene of chaos.

A battle raged within the House of Oldoth. The meadow was carpeted in a stinking black fog that coiled thick about his ankles. Sons and daughters of Oldoth screamed the name of their god and battled armoured warriors on horseback. The warriors were everywhere and in great numbers. They galloped across the meadow, wicked axes and flails dismembering the ranks of sons and daughters fleeing before them. Blood ran freely across the grass and the warriors delivered utter carnage.

Where the circular entrance to the House of Oldoth had been in the outer wall, now was just a pool of inky darkness, from which issued the stinking fog. Above this darkness sat a small spider, its mandibles weaving back and forth, seeming to spin shadow amidst the dark. From this darkness thundered horsemen at full gallop, their chargers carrying them crashing into the mêlée.

All of the horsemen wore bear skins and chain mail. Upon their heads were full helms, obscuring their faces, carved into the likeness of various beasts, from lions and wolves to griffin and dragons. As each charged from the pool of darkness, he bore a short javelin which he would hurl into the fray and then draw a smaller, wicked, hand-to-hand weapon, usually an axe or flail.

As Thorn watched in horror, sons and daughters slowly began to rally, desperately forming pockets of resistance against the wholesale slaughter. Crying out in pain and love to Oldoth, they beseeched their god for aid, and aid he granted them. Thorn watched as a group of warriors charged three daughters and a son of Oldoth. As the chargers struck, the wicked axes and flails whistled downward to cries of triumph, but the son and daughters simply faded away onto the wind, their essence now the slightest mist on the breeze.

Others, though, were not so lucky. Two sons not forty hand-spans from Thorn did not finish their calls for aid to Oldoth and were simply trampled beneath the churning hooves of the chargers, their white skins and golden hair smashed into the green grass, now no more than tattered red flesh.

Terror struck Thorn like a lance into the heart and he staggered. Somewhere out there were his mother and his best friend, almost everything that had any meaning in his life. Sweat sprung from his pores and he cast frantically about. Nothing, nothing but swirling black mist and figures rising and falling within.

'Mother!' Thorn screamed, 'Alazla!' He could barely hear himself above the din of battle and immediately knew that it was hopeless.

Suddenly there was a warrior before him, his black charger rearing, pawing the air. Steaming breath blasted from its nostrils. The visage of the warrior stared down at him, helm shaped like a tusked boar, making him seem like some vast, grotesque creature. Blood, flesh and clumps of hair clung to his axe-blade. The warrior shouted in some harsh language and pointed his dripping axe at Thorn. Thorn felt weak and cold and knew that he could not escape, facing his executioner with a grim inevitability. Somewhere deep inside he thought, Alazla wouldn't feel like this.

Unexpectedly the warrior then dropped off his horse and ran towards Thorn, his chain mail rattling. Thorn remained transfixed in horror, vaguely aware of the mist beginning to whip and churn, as the warrior grabbed for him. Aware of the thumping of his own heart, he could smell the warrior now, the very stench of his armour. Beads of sweat glistened upon his neck. The size of him was overwhelming.

And then the warrior was lifted clear off his feet. A massive swirling fist crashed into the side of him. There was a crunch of bone and a splintering of mail and the warrior was hurled into the mist like a child's doll. Blood splattered Thorn's face.

Stunned, Thorn looked up at a towering, swirling image of something vaguely human in shape. Hair streamed out behind it on the wind like a banner. Seemingly composed only of air and mist, the creature towered to fifty spans. As it watched Thorn, its shape ebbed and flowed with the breeze. Oddly, Thorn became aware that the creature was female, and that it now smiled at him. Briefly it placed a huge cloudy hand softly upon his head and, turning, thundered back into the ebony mist with the force of a gale.

Making a decision, Thorn swallowed hard and followed the creature. The mist swirled about him with the din of battle. He pursued the outline of the creature ahead of him, but it swiftly became impossible to distinguish it from the mist.

A young daughter staggered into him, blood pumping from the stump where her arm had been, her chest and shirt soaked in her blood. Reacting instinctively, Thorn grabbed her as she slumped to the earth. It did not even occur to him now to be terrified. Ripping off his shirt, he tore a strip off and quickly tied a firm tourniquet to the arm stump. He knew that he did not have the strength to carry her, and her flesh was so cold that he knew she'd lost a lot of blood. Although she could well die, right now there was little else that he could do for her, so he laid her gently upon the grass and then continued into the mist that reverberated with the sounds of concealed battle and death.

Terror for his mother and Alazla tightened like a band around his heart. Plunging past knots of raging combat, he grabbed fleeting glances at faces but could not see them, and the mist seemed relentless. He felt so helpless and inadequate, but didn't know what else to do. Guilt gripped him that as sons and daughters about him were fighting and dying, all he was able to do was run and hide. Thorn despised his own weakness.

Skirting knots of mêlée, he became aware that the mist was receding, or rather it was flowing away, back across the battlefield. Thorn halted. As the mist drew back, moonlight fully illuminated the meadow once more. The knots of combatants seemed to pause. Thorn saw bodies crushed, fallen and butchered. Beloved sons and daughters lay in unnatural repose. Eyes stared sightless into the realm of their god. The dark warriors too were not without casualty and many dark forms could be seen lying beside or crushed beneath their chargers.

As the mist reluctantly withdrew, Thorn realised that it was actually being forced back. Some twenty sons and daughters stood arrayed behind Thorn, their skin golden even in the moonlight. Several of them had their arms outstretched and a powerful wind thundered past them, forcing the black mist before it. The mist coiled and snapped as if alive, retreating into the black gate. The small spider above the gate chittered to itself in anger.

Before the gate sat a warrior of fearsome proportion, revealed by the retreating mist. An obvious giant of a man even in a saddle, he was clad in blood-red chain mail, with a black fur cape draping his huge shoulders. His helm was carved into the image of an eerily handsome man, although a scar ran across the left eye and cheek. Clutched easily in one hand was the biggest double-bladed axe that Thorn had ever seen in his life. If it were not Thorn's eyes playing tricks, the axe seemed to writhe in his mailed fist.

Thorn could sense the power and rage of this man, even at such a distance. His horse, a red charger, seemed to sense his master's anger and pawed the earth in frustration.

A mounted standard-bearer behind the dread warrior bore the device of a circle of chains, set upon a steel pole.

Arrayed behind the standard-bearer were more armoured warriors, possibly as many as a hundred. Most bore javelins and axes, but a unit at the back also bore wicked bows of an enormous size. Thorn's heart sank in despair.

Silence dropped like a shroud across the meadow. Thorn cast frantically about and realised that he was directly between the two opposing lines. He saw that this realisation too was striking many of the presently engaged combatants.

As one, the remaining horse warriors in the midst of the meadow disengaged from the mêlée and wheeled their horses, racing back to their lines. The sons and daughters left behind turned to their wounded, picking up fallen companions and hastily binding mortal wounds that could not wait.

It was then that Thorn spied his mother and Alazla. Their faces were ashen and covered in blood, but from what Thorn could see they did not appear to be injured. Between them they carried a daughter of Oldoth.

Not daring to shout and draw unwanted attention to them, he began to run across the meadow. Thorn didn't notice that the chieftain's helmeted gaze swung with him as he ran. Alazla, staggering slightly under his burden, noticed Thorn. A look of intense relief spread across his face and he leaned towards Catherine, saying something.

Raising a red-mailed mist, the chieftain signalled the charge. Warhorses leapt forward, hooves churning the lush grass. The thunder of their assault shook the earth.

The chieftain led, his massive bulk and the size of his mount making him look like a giant amidst dwarves. Thorn watched in horror, understanding that they were directly before the murderous onslaught. Not knowing why, he turned and sprinted towards his mother, Alazla and their charge. Whether it was for self-preservation or to protect them, he was never quite sure.

He reached them when the screaming wall of horseflesh and armour was about fifty spans away. Launching himself, he landed square on his mother, driving her to the ground beneath him.

At that very moment, unknown to Thorn, the divine order of Oldoth struck back. Winds such as they had never encountered in the world slammed into the horse warriors. So great was the force that it snapped necks on impact. Warriors were torn from their horses and thrown forty, even sixty spans to land with bone-rending crunches on the ground.

The first wave of the warriors' charge faltered, and then the second struck. It raged directly over Thorn and Alazla, miraculously without harming them. Arrows sang over the heads of the charging horse warriors, raining down upon the ranks of the divine order. Yet just as the arrows approached, screaming winds tore them away, rendering them as harmless as leaves on the wind.

Thorn picked himself up off his mother, helped her up and crushed her to him in a brief and desperate hug. As he held her to him, Thorn realised that his mother's tunic was damp with blood. His stomach lurched as he pushed Catherine from him and lifted the tunic away from her shoulder. A deep and ugly gash ran from her shoulder across her breast. She was pale from loss of blood.

'Hold still, Mum,' he said, more calmly than he felt. 'You'll be okay, but I need to stop the blood loss.' Catherine smiled at him wanly and nodded. Thorn began to tear strips from her tunic, stuffing and binding the wound quickly to staunch the flow of blood as best he could.

While Thorn did this, Alazla comforted the injured daughter of Oldoth. Her head wound did not appear grievous and she was beginning to regain consciousness.

Satisfied, Alazla then moved to the body of a fallen horse warrior and relieved him of an axe. The weight of it was immense, but Alazla thought he could probably get a few good swings in if need be. Noting that the warrior stirred slightly when he removed the axe, Alazla levelled a good kick at the warrior's ribs and smiled in satisfaction as the recipient groaned in pain. He noticed then that this warrior seemed somewhat different from the others; there were the markings of rank on his armour. With his attention focused upon the fallen officer, Alazla did not hear the axe whisper in malicious delight as he lifted it.

'I don't mean to be the bearer of more bad news,' said Alazla casually as he returned, inspecting the axe-blade, 'but we appear to be completely caught between two enemy lines.'

Looking up, Thorn realised that it was true. The cavalry had thundered over them and now, racing across the meadow, it was about to hit the lines of the divine order of Oldoth. At the other side of the battlefield, by the gate, some twenty mounted archers were reloading wicked longbows.

Oddly, the giant chieftain had not followed his troops into the mêlée and leaned on his saddle horn just fifty spans away, watching them. His standard-bearer sat behind him impassively, holding aloft the metal insignia of the circle of chains. With the clang of armour the chieftain dismounted and, hefting his twin-bladed battle-axe, strode towards Thorn's group.

'This is not good,' murmured Alazla. Despite their straits, Thorn could not help but quirk a dark smile at his friend's gross understatement.

The wounded daughter of Oldoth, a lady in her later cycles with a careworn face and silvered hair, rose shakily to her feet. Wobbling slightly, she stepped forward and pushed the others firmly behind her.

In a remarkably firm voice the daughter said, 'You will halt there. Proceed no farther, lest you would face the wrath of Oldoth.'

The chieftain halted for a moment and regarded the daughter. The handsome but scarred face carved into the helm twisted and sneered, speaking in a grinding, metallic voice. 'Stand aside, witch. The powers of your petty god are no match for me.'

Raising her chin slightly, the daughter replied, 'I will not.'

Thorn was vaguely aware of the air about them beginning to darken, snapping the heavy furred cloak of the chieftain in the wind.

The chieftain stepped forward, his huge size making the aged daughter seem quite tiny. He hefted his twin-bladed axe.

The daughter, wobbling slightly, whispered gentle prayers to Oldoth, and as she did so the air about her darkened further. As she held her hands cupped together a ball of light and warmth began to grow in her palms, until within seconds it burned furiously, seeming to suck all light in the vicinity into it. The chieftain continued to stride unerringly towards her as without hesitation she drew the pulsing ball of sunlight into one hand and cast it directly at him. It flew like a miniature star and struck him in the chest. Sunlight washed over them with a roar that shook the earth, and reflexively the group threw their hands over their eyes.

Stunned, moments later they withdrew their hands. As they re-focused their eyes they beheld the massive red armoured figure apparently unhurt and now directly in front of the daughter.

In his gravely voice he spoke. 'Weak indeed. How little I truly knew.' With that he swung the double-bladed axe in a terrible, horizontal sweep. As Thorn watched, it seemed to him as if some creature was imprisoned within the axe-blade, for it seemed that he could see a twisted and eager face drooling in anticipation. Then the axe struck and the image was gone. The daughter screamed briefly as the blade sliced straight through her waist, neatly dividing her. Her two halves fell twitching to the earth, spraying blood. Thorn fell to his knees and vomited.

Moments later, his shadow fell across Thorn. Looking up weakly, Thorn stared into the impassive and twisted face of the chieftain's helm. His whole body shook with fear.

He heard his mother's shrill voice. 'No, I beg of you, spare him, please. He's just a boy. You can gain nothing by killing him. I beg you.'

The visored head swung to where his mother stood.

Catherine's face was drawn and gaunt, and her usually immaculate hair had fallen from its coil atop her head, hanging in disarray about her shoulders. Fresh blood was seeping through the wound that Thorn had just bound.

She held out her hands imploringly. 'Tell me, you must be a father. You will understand a parent's love for a child. Please, do not take the life of my son.'

Surprisingly the armoured figure replied, 'Very well, mother of a son, I shall not.'

Hope blossomed through Thorn.

Then his arm lashed out with inhuman speed and swept the head clean off Catherine's shoulders. Her body teetered for a moment headless and then collapsed. The head landed next to Thorn with a wet smack. His mother's eyes were opened in surprise, but oddly not in pain.

Somewhere in the distance Alazla screamed.

Thorn was not aware of his own screaming. Tears traced tracks unnoticed down his face and his world collapsed in ash and ruin with the head that wept blood onto the muddy earth beside him.

On his knees, he stared in numb horror at the head – the mouth was wide, caught in a silent scream, where it lay beside her corpse. He wanted to rush to her and cradle her, and shout and rage in denial, but he seemed paralysed and unable to touch the horror of what lay beside him. Instead he vomited, gagging and retching, drawing air into his lungs in ragged, rasping breaths.

Though the battle still raged, Thorn's world had shrunk. He heard nothing. He saw nothing other than his mother's lifeless remains. Reaching out trembling hands, he tried to touch them but could not. Tears streamed unheeded down his cheeks. 'No. No. No,' he sobbed, rocking back and forth.

This was not real.

The chieftain loomed over him like some form of dread executioner. Thorn watched his mother's lifeblood run slowly down the axe in utter incomprehension.

This was not real.

Where were the sons and daughters? The thought knifed through the haze of incomprehension like fire. Thorn lurched to his feet, tottering as if drunk. Minuscule before the looming chieftain, he screamed, 'Balthazar, Balthazar, Balthazaaaaaaar!' Nothing. Where was he? They *must* help him. Please gods, let them help him.

'Stop your whimpering, child.' The moving mouth of the visor twisted the metallic words, making them echo with distance. 'She had her wish and I have not taken your life. Not that I had intended to anyway,' and he laughed a deep and inhuman sound.

An armoured hand lashed out and grabbed Thorn about the neck, even as his mind warred between incomprehension at the chieftain's words and the rage that began to consume him. He hung like a netted fish from the armoured fist as the giant turned him this way and that, inspecting him like some interesting specimen.

Alazla had stood transfixed in horror, the axe hanging numb in his fingers. Clearly the armoured giant had all but forgotten he existed.

Lifting the axe in numb fingers, Alazla walked towards the back of the figure. He would never let his friend down.

Thorn's eyes bulged with the giant's hand wrapped around his neck, and he tried to shake his head. But because of his predicament it went unnoticed, not that it would have made any difference to Alazla.

Alazla hefted the axe, and didn't notice how the blade adjusted its balance for him. He took the greatest swing that his strength would allow. Always agile and strong, Alazla had become the envy of most of his friends, good at most sports and anything physical, though he had usually relied on Thorn to do most of the deep thinking. But he didn't need to think now. The axe struck the giant in the middle of the back with every ounce of strength that Alazla could muster. It was like striking stone. The axe rang like a bell and jarred out of Alazla's numb hands. The red chain mail had not even moved.

With a sobbing, gasping Thorn still clutched in his armoured fist, the giant turned towards Alazla. He chuckled, a sound that seemed as if it came from within a cavern. 'Brave, young one, very brave indeed. You have great strength for one so young. I could use you, but

I dare say that you would not be pliable, unlike this one here,' he said, shaking the dangling Thorn for emphasis. And he laughed again.

The figure seemed to dismiss Alazla then, and turned to look up the battlefield. Alazla followed his gaze. It was immediately clear that the horse warriors were defeated. Giant figures composed of air strode amongst the remnants of the warriors, smashing them with massive fists or sending them swirling up into the air within maelstroms of impossible strength.

Striding towards their group from the remaining combat came a mighty figure. Composed of mist and cloud, the creature was vast, and its rage was awesome to behold. Storm clouds boiled within it and thunder shook the ground as it strode. Where its feet struck the ground, lightning flickered and raged about its head like a halo.

Somewhere within Thorn knew that the striding figure was Balthazar, but come too late. He would have spat a desperate curse had he the air to breathe.

The giant appraised this for a moment and calmly noted, 'It seems that I may have outstayed my welcome.' And to Alazla he said, 'Farewell, young one… perhaps we shall meet again.'

With that he slung the struggling Thorn over his shoulder like a sack of meal and strode towards the gate. The standard-bearer trotted obediently after him.

Alazla watched the retreating figure helplessly. His eyes locked with Thorn's for a brief heart-wrenching moment of impotent agony and then the giant disappeared into the gate, his remaining troops following.

'No!' Alazla screamed. 'Noooooooo!'

The black gate vanished.

- Chapter 6 -

The Assembly

The wispy figure before him was almost translucent, and just half the size of a human. You could barely discern the outlines of flowing hair, a gentle face and perhaps even wings, although they could just as easily have been tendrils of the mist.

Balthazar stood in the absolute tranquillity of the House of Oldoth's inner sanctum, although there were no walls to define it as such. The battle had not reached this part of the house. A horse warrior had attempted to penetrate the inner sanctum, but he was vastly inadequate to the task and had been struck by a howling gale that shredded his armoured body like paper.

Outside the inner sanctum, blood stained the grass and, despite the rains that the sons and daughters had called, would continue to do so for many days. After examination, the warriors' bodies had been burned on a pyre. No rites had been said for them.

A detailed inspection of the warriors had revealed little, little that is that did not suggest they could have hailed from one of several northern realms, including the empire of Athel-Loria. What was more concerning to Balthazar was the nature of the enchantments that had borne them here, and the obvious magic that had been imbued in a select few, especially the giant leader.

Over one hundred sons and daughters of Oldoth had lost their lives that night, more than half the complement of the house. The order had been set back two generations in Korth. Yet tragic as this was, the potential reasons for it were even more terrifying.

Balthazar focused his attention on the ebbing and coalescing figure before him. As the figure spoke in a gentle breeze as soft as a summer wind, the face occasionally took on the form of the most holy Aolandar, Guardian of the Citadel of Storms and Head of the Order of Oldoth.

'The enemy has struck, though we do not yet know his face. Grievous has our loss been. Yet, even now, that foe has not revealed his hand my son. The boy Thorn is gone. We found him and lost him. For that we may be truly punished.' At this last, Aolandar's ancient voice broke and the shifting figure fleetingly lost its substance.

A moment passed and Aolandar's whispering voice came again, stronger this time. 'From what we have seen, Balthazar, we must assume that our foe could strike anywhere and at any time, although I do wonder whether they have already found what they need. Nevertheless, we shall not allow them to pick and choose their battleground again my son. Our sanctuaries must now be properly guarded. Aerial hosts fly as we speak to guard our most sacred places. They and our brethren must be protected at all costs.'

Grim-faced and nodding, Balthazar crossed gold-banded arms upon his chest. 'But what of the boy Thorn, Holy One? I am certain that he carried some seed of power within him, although of the extent of its potency I could not say. But I do believe that he was alive when they took him, which suggests to me that someone wants him, or failing that….what he carries.'

The airy outline of Aolandar nodded its head in agreement and Balthazar continued. 'Aolandar, most high, I also believe that Thorn, though unknowing, may have embraced a darkness. Only in this way, through one that we had welcomed into our midst, could the dark powers have found their way into our sanctum. Should that power take complete control of him, it could undo us.'

Balthazar hesitated then, his face set and expressionless as he said, 'Master, I tremble to say this, but I believe that we must find Thorn and slay him.'

'No!' cracked Aolandar. The smoky figure for a moment churned like a roiling black cloud. 'If indeed Thorn still lives, I will *not* sanction his demise. If he can tread our holy places without feeling the wrath of Oldoth, then that mistake is *ours* and not his. I will not see him punished for our own folly.'

Balthazar hung his head at the remonstration. 'Very well, Holy One, but how can we even determine whether the lad lives? Our foe will almost certainly seek to conceal him, he is almost without doubt beyond our sight, and our messengers will likely not locate him, no matter what realm he is now in.'

Responding, Aolandar simply said, 'Then we must call an assembly, Balthazar, and a most special one at that. *All* of the divine orders must now be made to know of what peril we face. Now, let us pray together that Oldoth will guide us.'

****

Even with his substance composed of the very wind, the journey to the small island of Mi-Arna took Balthazar several days, covering as it did thousands of leagues.

Balthazar had never set foot on Mi-Arna before, but knew of its significant history. Mi-Arna was where a ravaged humanity in flight, had first set foot on the world of Rune, and in doing so, had at last found freedom from slavery and death at the hands of their draconic masters.

A simple circle of stones marked the place where the gate to the Bridge of Mourn had then been. There were one hundred stones within that circle; a sorrowful testament to the majority of younger gods who had fallen in the battle against the dragon-god gorGoroth, in their desperate attempt to free their children.

Divine powers could not carry you into the island itself, but only to its borders. So, on a shingle beach surrounded by rearing grey cliffs that were brightening slightly in the dawn light, Balthazar found that his mortal body was forced on him and he dropped easily from the air.

Grey sea beat against the base of the cliffs with a roar that shook spray into the air and dampened Balthazar's golden hair. He decided it was fortunate that he never felt the cold, as he looked momentarily at his bare chest. He smiled and started forward.

The beach carried him up into hills and onto a white gravel road which appeared to lead a gentle but slightly circuitous path towards the centre of the island. From where he stood, Balthazar could immediately see that the island was not large, certainly no more than a league across.

The white gravel road eventually led Balthazar to a lush bowl shaped valley. Sparkling rivers plunged in waterfalls from the hillside to rush foaming over rocks, downward in azure torrents. Scattered around the valley walls shaded by slight trees bearing heavy blue and yellow fruits, were scores of small, pristine, white buildings. They appeared to be miniature temples; with domes and peaks but also open to the sun, without walls.

At the valley's centre sat a lake. A single-arched slender bridge ran from the shore to a small island in the centre, upon which sat small stone seats arrayed in concentric circles, within a circle of lopsided and ancient grey stones. Balthazar knew without having to look that there were one hundred seats and one hundred stones.

Noticing figures on the valley floor, Balthazar started downwards.

He was passing a small white pavilion when he heard a lush, female voice call out, 'You certainly took your time.'

Turning, Balthazar saw a woman leaning against a pillar, gazing at him with wide, luminous eyes. Easily described as beautiful, she wore a tight emerald-green dress that had been artfully woven about her, showing off her richly curvaceous figure. About her, there was a sense of animal magnetism that tugged at Balthazar, at some deep, primal level.

'Most Beloved Daughter Dynnari, it is a pleasure to see you again,' Balthazar replied, bowing deeply.

The most beloved daughter pouted for a moment and said, 'Oh, Balthazar, don't be such a bore. Come here and give me a kiss.'

Balthazar scowled slightly and said, 'Dynnari, that would be most improper; we have not seen each other for many moons now and this is a most sacred place.'

Dynnari scowled ferociously, stamped her foot and retorted, 'Unless you give me a kiss right now, you foolish son of Oldoth, I'll make sure that no woman ever looks at you again, *and* that parts you probably consider quite important to you become quite inoperative!'

Balthazar felt a distinct tug pulling him forward. As he waved his hand nonchalantly, the feeling vanished.

'Oh, I don't know, you're a lot older than you used to be. Younger women and all that.'

Dynnari's face could have curdled custard.

'Ha!' cried Balthazar. Leaping forward, he landed on the pavilion within two bounds and swept Dynnari into his arms.

She struggled briefly and then relented, kissing him soundly on the lips. As always happened when she did that, Balthazar felt his stomach flutter and warm, as delightful desire coursed through him. He pulled her deeper into the embrace, lingering. Her lips were full and delicious.

Some time later they separated and settled beneath a small fruit tree beside the arbor. Dynnari's head was on his chest as he regarded a small statue within the arbour depicting Aevarnia, goddess of love and healing. A small bowl at the goddess's bare feet held an offering, obviously placed there by her highest devotee, whose lustrous hair he now stroked.

'I've missed you very much, you know,' Balthazar said.

'Have you really, truly?' Dynnari asked, looking up, her brown eyes liquid.

'Very much,' Balthazar responded. 'I'm sorry that I have not replied to your messengers,' he paused. 'It's just that there has been some trouble lately.'

Dynnari lifted her head. 'I've received visions too; an avatar slain. It's almost unthinkable. Do you know which avatar it was?'

Balthazar could easily list the names of all nine avatars, as could any son or daughter of the orders: they were as familiar to him as his own face in the morning mirror. That one of them was simply gone seemed, somehow, incomprehensible.

He shook his head. 'That's one of the things we're here to find out.'

'By the way,' said Dynnari, 'you do know that only *most* beloved sons and daughters are traditionally meant to attend an Assembly. You're too junior to be here Balthazar. That old fusspot Sorbek has already been complaining to Aolandar, you know,' she teased, laughing.

Balthazar laughed too. 'Well, Aolandar was quite clear that he needed someone to carry his bags. So I'm afraid I got the job.' Blowing out his cheeks, he huffed, 'I expect they have realised that I'm here already.'

'Almost certainly,' Dynnari replied, caressing his stomach with her fingernails. 'They'll be sending someone to get us if we don't go down soon.'

'Well, we'd better be quick then,' murmured Balthazar, kissing her deeply again. As he did so, the sun set across the valley, seeming to slowly drop in the liquid heart of the lake.

The shadows beneath the standing stones began to steadily lengthen, as the most beloved sons and daughters argued about who should proceed first onto the island and in what order. Balthazar sat to one side in bemusement, since he was apparently too junior to get involved. Sorbek, the fussy old son of Lorethian, god of courage and justice, was a stickler for tradition and he had with him a dusty old tome that he claimed set out the processional order exactly. Accordingly, he was busy telling everyone how to organise themselves, which most were ignoring, having their own views on the subject. Dynnari was busy chastising Tiaa, most beloved daughter of Faed, god of shadow and stealth, who had originally ignored all propriety and simply gone onto the island and sat down. All in all, it looked like it could be a long night.

Balthazar took the opportunity to watch Anemon, servant of Nim, god of magic. Anemon was an unusually tall man, Balthazar noted. His hair was silver and bound into plaits, and his slight beard was so neatly trimmed as to suggest a degree of vanity. He wore purple robes that bore a single golden rune repeated over and amongst a simple twisted golden thread. Balthazar did not know what the sigil represented. Anemon leaned upon a light wooden staff wound about with golden wire.

Balthazar realised that his scrutiny had been noted and that Anemon now stared at him with violet eyes. Calmly returning the arch-mage's regard, he considered that Anemon was the only divine representative present who was not actually a most beloved son or daughter. Nim, the god of magic, had apparently never subscribed to the principle of supporting a divine order. Instead his servants were known as magi and they served primarily to further the pursuit of knowledge. Unlike the divine orders that drew their power directly from their deities, the magi drew theirs from life-energy.

The cessation of argument brought Balthazar out of his contemplation. Apparently a processional order had been agreed. Dynnari, using her significant persuasive power, with the odd wink and carefully placed smile, was getting everyone into position. Even old Sorbek, with his trimmed forked beard and silvered robe and train, appeared happy.

Beneath the fading red light of a setting sun, the most beloved sons and daughters of the nine younger gods proceeded at a slow pace in pairs over the graceful white bridge to the island beyond. Old Sorbek, son of Lorethian, god of justice, was first to proceed arm in arm with Dynnari, daughter of Aevarnia, goddess of love. They were followed by Aegon, beloved son of Ondalla, goddess of the harvest, hand in hand with Valeya, daughter of Sha, god of war, her golden armour and headdress a fantastic spectacle. Both had to be careful not to tread on Sorbek's enormous train and upset the entire processional.

Next came Aolandar, his golden skin bright, and though the air was still, his hair floated about him like a cloud. He was accompanied by the slight Tiaa, daughter of Faed, goddess of thieves; her shadowy form almost impossible to make out.

The final couple in the processional were Jord, son of Tyche, god of luck, who sauntered beside the stately Imdalla, daughter of Elishar, goddess of healing, resplendent in her blood-red satin dress and train. Following them, alone, came Anemon, Arch-Mage Primus of Nim, a lonely purple spectre.

Balthazar remained seated beyond the island at a respectful distance.

As each couple reached the end of the bridge and stepped onto the island, they knelt and kissed the earth. They then entered the concentric circles of white stone seats and, moving to different parts, seated themselves.

Yet the formality of the occasion could not change the fact that ninety one seats then remained utterly empty. The overall effect was of a meeting that most people had already left, and where just the stragglers remained.

There was an awkward silence as all seemed acutely aware of the emptiness.

The silence grew for several minutes, each divine head seemingly too self-conscious to break it.

Unexpectedly it was Dynnari who finally broke the silence. She rose gracefully from her seat, amidst a gentle rustle of emerald silk. As she stood, the rest of the theatre seemed to dim and she became illuminated by a column of soft light. To Balthazar's eyes, she looked magnificent.

When Dynnari spoke her voice barely carried. 'The thanks of the order of Aevarnia are extended to Most Beloved Son Aolandar for calling this assembly. We're aware of the ill tidings that we must sadly speak of.' She glanced about then at the empty seats. 'Such tragic news not reached us… for many cycles.'

From his perch Balthazar realised that by opening, Dynnari had removed any issues of rank and politics. The order of the love goddess was the furthest removed from such things. A flash of insight made him wonder whether she was in collusion with the crafty old Aolandar.

As Dynnari sat, Aolandar immediately stood and was illuminated by the same light, which Balthazar was personally thankful for, as at least it served to hide the haunting empty seats.

Aolandar's face was grim and the deeps of his eyes unreadable. Holding up his arms, with golden armbands and rings winking softly, he said, 'Most beloved sons and daughters of Rune, I give you my thanks for heeding my call. Not for four centuries has a Divine Assembly been called. Sadly, though, as Dynnari has said, you all know why you are here.'

His last words seemed to echo and multiply off the encircling standing stones and he took a moment before he continued. 'Your gods and goddesses have sent you visions – one of the nine avatars has fallen, lured from the heavens and slain.'

Aolandar waited for his words to sink in. There was utter silence. Even the creatures of the hillside and woodland were still. 'It is beholden upon us all to understand how this could happen, and not least of all why.' This statement was accompanied by a soft murmuring and nodding of heads from all nine.

'One of our beloved gods has lost his or her herald. Each and any god would be dreadfully wounded by such a loss. We need to know whose avatar it was. Be not afraid to speak, for all here share the profound depths of your sorrow and pain.'

Aolandar turned to look at each most beloved son and daughter in turn, seeking an unspoken answer. Slowly he turned around the circle, each son and daughter shaking their head, until he came to the last son: Aegon, most beloved son of Ondalla, goddess of the harvest. Aegon's skin and form were so closely aligned with his goddess's power that he appeared to be composed mostly of earth and stone. His eyes glittered hard as agates. Aolandar's heart welled up with sorrow. Other sons and daughters began to rise in sympathy, and then Aegon too slowly shook his head.

The silence then was profound. The wind did not stir, and even the trees seemed to have ceased their endless whisper.

Deep in his heart Aolandar shared the sorrow that the most beloved son or daughter must be feeling for the loss of their avatar. He was profoundly grateful, however, that it was not that of Oldoth. He had personally received a visitation from the winged herald of Oldoth, instructing Aolandar to call this assembly.

Aolandar was also not altogether surprised that the order concerned chose not to reveal their appalling loss. To him it seemed a sad indictment of the state of relations between certain orders of late. This could appear a great admission of weakness and perhaps even vulnerability.

Compassion etched on his lined face, Aolandar continued, looking from son to daughter as he did so. 'All here understand that the loss one of us bears is grievous. But we are all sons and daughters of the younger gods, we are a family! We would help you, share your loss. And be assured that our wrath will be terrible upon those who have committed this heinous crime!'

The light about Aolandar darkened as he said the last. Certainly no one present doubted the ability of the assembly to seek utter retribution upon any foe. In most minds there was little doubt that this collective might was soon to have focus.

Again no one answered, the silence broken only by the rustle of clothing or the chink of armour.

Though he had half-expected this, Balthazar was bitterly disappointed that there was obviously such a total lack of trust. He sighed, and the golden shoulders that harboured such immense power seemed to slump wearily. Meeting Dynnari's shadowed eyes, he knew that the most beloved daughter felt the same sorrow.

It was no surprise to Aolandar when the contentious Sorbek, most beloved son of the god of justice, stood. The light dimmed about Aolandar, illuminating Sorbek in his glittering metallic robe, a mesh of fine steel links. He unconsciously stroked his forked black beard as he swelled his chest, readying himself for an impressive oratory.

'Though most beloved son Aolandar is correct in seeking to identify the god or goddess whom the fallen herald serves, in my view this in only part of why we are here,' said Sorbek.

Balthazar shifted uncomfortably at this contentious statement. Already divisions were beginning to show, and the Assembly had only just begun.

'I for one respect the privacy of the order concerned if they are not yet ready to reveal their dread loss,' said Sorbek, and his glance towards Aolandar was pointed.

Aolandar returned Sorbek's stare with icy regard. It always turned to politics, he knew, but the taste of it was bitter in his mouth. The order of Lorethian was foremost amongst the conservative faction and they rarely missed an opportunity to meddle, it seemed, or to express contrary opinion.

Sorbek continued, his voice rising. 'We must respect that privacy and focus instead on the force that committed this atrocity, and then' he continued, clenching a scarlet-gauntleted fist for emphasis, 'introduce them to the wrath of the collective assembly.'

Although Balthazar was reluctantly in agreement with Sorbek on this, he also personally doubted the ability of the assembly to agree on anything collectively. Our enemy will be laughing, he thought to himself bitterly.

Aolandar rose back to his feet, suddenly looking very much his age. Sorbek did not sit back down immediately, though, and began to draw breath for what would likely be a long-winded speech. Aolandar ensorcelled his words slightly; and the boom of his voice cracked around the theatre and valley.

Birds burst from their trees, squawking in outrage.

He did not notice Dynnari's smile as a scowling Sorbek dropped back onto his seat.

'Given that the order that has lost its herald is reluctant to speak of its tragedy, we must respect this and, it seems, turn instead to seeking the enemy that committed this act. For make no mistake, if they did this once, what is to stop them doing so again!? It could be the order of Tyche next, or Nim or even Oldoth.' He knew that he had their attention now. 'We have not lost an avatar since the War in Heaven more than six thousand cycles past!' He knew that he did not need to mention the ninety-one fallen gods that those avatars had also served.

Aegon rose then from his seat, his voice like the rumble of stone, the moonlight glittering ominously off the rocks and gems embedded in his skin. 'Your words are wise, Aolandar. All the gods know that the divine pantheon is sorely diminished and we can ill afford to lose an avatar. And yet... none of us were there, my friend. The Crystal Wood is a sacred place and much that happens there is closed, even to our eyes. And even we cannot turn back time. How can we reveal the face of our foe?'

'We must be alert, as we were not before,' said Imdalla, most beloved daughter of Eli-shar, in a clear, ringing voice. Her posture erect and flowing red dress immaculately arranged about her, she continued, 'We must alert all of our brethren in all the lands of this world. We will use the creatures of this world and others if necessary to help us too. It may take time, but doing so we *will* find this foe.'

'But do we have the time?' rumbled Aegon, suggesting what no one else wanted to. 'While we seek them out, where will our enemy go next? We were caught completely off guard. While we stumble around in ignorance and seeking knowledge, where will that twisted blade strike next?'

'But what nonsense is this?' snapped Sorbek. 'We must all realise that Ione´ the dragon goddess is responsible for this atrocity.'

'What evidence do you have for this' said Aolandar softly, dreading to hear the answer.

'Events themselves Aolandar' returned Sorbek. 'Tragic history! She will be seeking to avenge the imprisonment of her mate gorGoroth! And this time the dragons will not halt their war until all of the younger gods are destroyed!'

There were murmurs of agreement from many of those present.

Aolandar, though, dared to breathe a slight sigh of relief. 'So, in fact, you have no evidence for this renewal of the war in heaven Sorbek….it is in fact just conjecture.'

Sorbek scowled thunderously.

'There may be another way… perhaps.' The voice was soft and slightly mocking. All eyes turned to where Anemon, Arch-Mage Primus, was rising from the shadow of his seat.

'Go on,' said Aolandar wearily.

Plucking at his costly embroidered robes, the arch-mage did not look up. 'The powers of the magi are not linked directly to the whims of the gods, like your own.'

There was some slight muttering at this obvious jibe.

Aolandar scowled and wondered whether to cut off Anemon now, before things got heated.

'We draw on our own spiritual energy and on that of the wider universe. By this I mean no slight.' His smile was thin at this, suggesting that in fact he did. 'Rather, the magi are capable of manipulating life-energy in diverse and indeed curious ways… ways that are different from your own powers. Theoretically, it's possible that I could reveal the enemy that slew the fallen avatar.'

Voices exploded at this, many immediately raised. The valley echoed with the din.

It took Aolandar several minutes to restore a semblance of order, during which time Anemon leant patiently on his staff of twisted gold wire, a sardonic smile on his face.

Aegon rumbled from his seat. 'But is this a good thing? If the Arch-Mage Primus can do as he suggests,' – his dark glance clearly said that he did not believe it – 'will it not alert our foe? Should we not now marshal our forces and be prepared to strike first?'

Dynnari's voice was laced with acid when she replied, 'And where would you have us marshal them, son of Ondalla? In Athel-Loria or at the other end of Rune perhaps, in the jungles of Ylith?! This enemy could be any creature, on Rune or another world. Where is it that you would direct your vaunted armies?!'

Valeya, daughter of Sha, the war god, had remained silent until now, and when she stood, her golden armour and height, emphasised by her plumed headdress, were a fantastic spectacle. In an oddly sultry voice she said, 'Aegon is right. Marshalling armies and forces takes time. We should delay and reconvene when we are ready to strike.'

Aolandar sighed. He knew that he must act before the assembly became bogged down in debate for hours, if not days. 'We will vote.'

The clamour slowly halted and Balthazar spied a number of relieved faces. Sorbek and Valeya did not look pleased, but he knew that they had to agree. It was the will of the younger gods that the directive of the collective assembly, if called on, should be obeyed by all of the divine orders, and without question.

Aolandar continued, resisting the urge to smile at Sorbek's thunderous scowl. 'The vote is to ask the Arch-Mage Primus to use his skills to reveal our enemy now or later; when our combined forces are fully marshalled. Please use a white light for now and a red for later.'

Sons and daughters slowly illuminated themselves in columns of downy light, casting flickering rainbow lights across the lake waters. After a few moments there were five white and three red columns, the latter being Valeya, Sorbek and Aegon. The Arch-Mage Primus, Aolandar noted, had decided to abstain.

'Very well, we will reveal our enemy now,' said Aolandar firmly.

No son or daughter said anything to that, although certain expressions spoke volumes. All knew that they were now bound to the collective will of the assembly.

Anemon stepped forward with a rustle of velvet robes. He took the centre of the circle. If anyone objected they said nothing, although the assembly had been set out specifically in a wide circle so that all divine orders were perceived as equal, this being why the heads generally spoke from their seats rather than taking to the centre.

'Unfortunately this incantation is not entirely straightforward. I'll need something that was directly connected to the fallen avatar in order to weave the incantation. Anything at all would suffice: a belonging or even just a scrap of fingernail would do. Though, as we know,' he smiled, 'avatars do not normally bear material possessions.'

This naturally caused something of an outburst. Aolandar could personally have throttled the Arch-Mage Primus at that point. Sorbek and Valeya were openly laughing.

'Oddly, none of us have such a thing!' the normally controlled Dynnari shouted from her seat, her beautiful face flushed with anger.

Balthazar had been listening intently from his seat at the edge of the lake. Hearing the sudden turn of the conversation, he'd quickly made his decision, and rising from his seat he walked across the stone bridge to stand respectfully at the edge of the circle. One by one the voices quieted, as the most beloved sons and daughters turned to look at him.

Aolandar sighed, his shoulders dropping with fatigue. 'I assume, my son, that you have a good reason for stepping onto this island.' He did not say that Balthazar would almost certainly be punished for his transgression. Endeavouring to smile, he said, 'If you can help us, Balthazar, please speak, quickly.'

Balthazar met Dynnari's liquid eyes for a moment and she smiled mischievously. Trying hard not to return the smile, he took a deep breath and replied, 'After receiving Aolandar's message concerning the fall of an avatar, I sought and found the glade where the unknown avatar was slain. I carry some dust from its immortal remains with me now.'

Aegon asked gently in his deep voice, 'And would this be enough, Anemon, for you to cast your incantation?'

The Arch-Mage Primus looked about him, violet eyes glittering, and smiled, but there was no warmth in it. 'Yes, I believe that it would.'

Silence followed that statement.

Though he felt dread coiling in his ancient stomach like a nest of vipers, Aolandar said, 'Continue, Anemon. You may cast your spell.' He had no idea yet how they'd counter this enemy, but counter it they certainly would. The strength of the divine orders was absolutely without question, but he wondered what terrible enemy that strength would be pitted against… one with the strength to slay an avatar.

Anemon took the offered pouch of dust from Balthazar and moved back to the centre of the circle. For a moment he stood in absolute silence, his eyes closed, plated grey hair shifting slightly in the wind. Then slowly what appeared to be strands began to appear about Anemon, hundreds or perhaps thousands of them trailing from his body into the air about him. They writhed as if alive and each pulsed with a golden light. Sons and daughters gasped in surprise.

Anemon was now whispering softly and his hands wove gentle patterns in the air, sending the golden strands spilling and moving in countless directions, as if he conducted the movement of thousands of arms. Then he stopped. The entire area around him was alight with the deep golden hue of the strands, and he threw the dust into the air, where it glittered and sparkled blue. Rather than fall, though, the blue dust hung suspended in the air like a small cloud.

The cloud ebbed and shifted, but did little else.

A flicker of uncertainty appeared to pass across Anemon's face for a moment and then he whispered more words. Light coursed down the pulsing golden cords, so bright that the assembled sons and daughters could hardly look, and the circle became almost as bright as day. Anemon pointed at the blue cloud, whispering strong words, and the cloud began to move, slowly, sluggishly, reluctantly.

The Arch-Mage Primus ceased his chant and the dust fell to the earth. It left a single dusty sigil suspended in the air before the exhausted Anemon.

Anemon's next words were a croak, as if he were parched. 'There is your assassin.'

A sparkling blue sword was suspended in the air.

There was a collective gasp from those assembled. It was the sigil of Sha, god of war.

- CHAPTER 7 -
The Retreat of the Magi

The Spire of Arcanum in the ancient city of Loria was a frenzy of activity. Relations between the divine order of Sha and Arcanum had seriously deteriorated and all magi and their apprentices in the empire of Athel-Loria had been called home.

Agastalen and Heath, clad in the simple brown robes of apprentice magi, looked in concern at the angry crowd outside the light silver filigree gates about the grounds of the Spire. Although they might seem stronger than they appeared, both knew with a worried glance at the other that the gates would certainly not withstand the sheer mass of city folk now outside.

This morning the mood of the crowd, composed mainly of normal city folk, from merchants to market vendors and scholars, had been antagonistic. It was common knowledge that all diplomatic relations between the empire of Athel-Loria and Arcanum had ceased, although opinion ranged as to exactly why. The most commonly held story was that there had been some form of formal slur by the magi upon Sha, god of war, and patron deity of Athel-Loria. The other seven divine orders were presently, however, declaring their absolute neutrality.

The crowd had jeered and rattled the gates, and screamed insults, which did very little to upset the composed magi themselves, although the same could certainly not be said for their wide-eyed apprentices.

However, the mood of the crowd had swung when they'd unexpectedly been joined by Loria city guards. There was now a menace about the crowd that had not been there before. Weapons were beginning to appear, raised above heads, and those within had seen various mage-like mannequins burned and hurled over the gates.

However, it was also the presence of the guards that caused Agastalen concern, not just the changing mood of the crowd. The officers of the city garrison must certainly be aware that a fairly large number of their troops were here, and were just as clearly doing nothing about it. As Agastalen thought this through, he realised that this effectively meant that the senior authority in the city was now informally endorsing the action outside the Spire gates.

Agastalen and Heath struggled together with a moonberry bush that they'd rather unceremoniously just dug up from the small gardens about the Spire of Arcanum. The bush, it's fair to say, had been rather less impressed about the whole affair than either of the two apprentice gardeners and had spat and shrieked, casting a barrage of thorns at the two of them, as they attempted to remove the precious horticultural burden. Carrying the bush, which was now just wailing quietly, they felt its jagged red leaves busily cutting wherever possible into their skin.

Heath, Agastalen noted, his usually smiling face grim, had plucked a few immature yellow moonberries from the bush and tucked them into one of the many pouches about his belt.

'Any particular plans for those moonberries then?' asked Agastalen quizzically. His face was almost straight when he said it.

Heath frowned as he tried to keep his hands away from the weaving red leaves. 'Well I'm not going to plant them, if that's what you think.' He stooped closer to the bush. 'Might make soup out of them – it's apparently quite tasty.'

The bush shuddered.

Agastalen just smiled, knowing that if Heath ate a moonberry soup, it would likely be the last, though perhaps most delicious, repast he ever ate. Heath of course knew that too, but the bush did seem to quieten down a little.

Avoiding as best they could the stones and other hurled missiles from the screaming crowd, they shuffled towards the Spire, which looked like nothing so much as an enormous pile of golden rope, heaped upon itself until it rose to over three hundred spans, leaning somewhat haphazardly to one side.

'You throw like girls!' shouted Heath to the mob as they made it into the halls.

Agastalen shook his head. 'Excellent idea. A little provocation should excite them just a little bit further, don't you think?'

'What, and you think they'd really be so stupid as to come in here with a full complement of magi present?' Heath replied.

'Oh, and I suppose you also expected a mob to turn up at the gates genius, did you? It's not like that's never happened in the entire history of Arcanum or anything,' said Agastalen. The accent of his native Athel-Loria was a broad brogue.

Agastalen did not hear Heath's reply, and if the moonberry bush did, it was making no comment.

The Spire halls were abustle with brown-robed figures staggering, often under enormous burdens. Boxes of glittering jewels raced past, sculptures and complex things of such strange shape that Agastalen could find no obvious name for them. There were rare and unique birds in cages, very often politely enquiring where they were going, enormous lizards on chains getting in everyone's way, and armloads of dusty books and scrolls. Agastalen and Heath carried their muttering moonberry bush into the midst of this turmoil.

Making their way cautiously through the shouting, squawking throng, they followed the flow of brown robes towards the dining hall, from where the exit to Arcanum was being coordinated. Agastalen was now sweating profusely and beginning to think inappropriate but really happy thoughts about a moonberry bush bonfire. Smiling to himself, he failed to notice the mottled octopus-like creature making its own way down the steps, carrying something that looked like a large number of family portraits.

Agastalen felt his legs tangle. There then followed a slight sense of motionless and he was airborne. He struck the steps several times on the way down before landing sprawled at the bottom, somewhat stunned. Aware of shouting, he tried to sit up groggily and was hit in the side of the head by the moonberry bush and Heath. Sprawling again, with the bush covering most of him but unable to move, he waited for assistance. The bush was now taking great delight in sawing into him with its razor-sharp leaves.

Moments later the bush was lifted off him and a rather bruised Heath helped him to his feet. The octopus-like creature sauntered past with slightly dull squelching noises. It deigned to give them what Agastalen assumed was a haughty look from several of its eye-stalks and whistled insults at them through its beak-like mouth.

'Damn me, but I swear I'll never get used to this place,' said Agastalen.

Shaking his dark locks, Heath laughed. 'Well, be that as it may, my friend, you look like you've just done ten rounds with a troll. Now as for me, of course, it would take more than a mere tangle with a decapod to damage my winning looks. Unless, that is, of course, it was warrior-cast. Wouldn't like to see one of those things waving half a dozen weapons at me now!'

Agastalen laughed, his mood already improving, and was beginning to reply when a stern voice interrupted them.

'If you two have quite finished?!'

Turning, they saw a female figure in lush dark blue robes. Lei-Weya cut a striking figure despite her age. The waist of her robe was bound by a blue cord, and dozens of circling stitched golden bands rose from the hem and about the cuffs. Her grey hair was woven into an intricate style, held with pins atop her head. Her blue eyes sparkled at them, despite her tone.

'Enchantress,' they both replied as one, bowing with no considerable degree of pain.

Lei-Weya was a highly respected and senior mage in the Lorian Spire of Arcanum. She was also known to be one of the most approachable. Happily for Heath, he was apprenticed to her. Less fortunately for Agastalen, he was not, but rather to one Mage Winfod, who, although a very competent mage, genuinely loved the sound of his own voice above all others. Lei-Weya, knowing the two to be good friends, had helped Agastalen out with Winfod once or twice, to the extent that the elderly Winfod now did his best to avoid her.

'You two really must concentrate on the task at hand,' Lei-Weya said, doing her best not to smile as the pair looked rather chagrined. 'Sometimes you really do make me despair. I swear, if you both weren't so talented, Mage Winfod and I would have had you sent back to your families long ago.'

Agastalen looked sheepishly at Heath, who was now grinning with open fondness at his teacher.

'I honestly don't know if you two actually realise how serious this is! For the first time in history, it's a very real possibility that a country may actually declare war on Arcanum. We must flee and save all we can,' she said, pointedly looking at the rather bedraggled moonberry bush, which was now weeping quietly to itself on the floor.

'Come,' she said, clapping her hands briskly, 'pick up that poor bush and take it to the exit over there. After that I want you to go to the museum and ensure that all enchanted exhibits have been removed.'

With a final smile Lei-Weya then turned and walked towards another small crisis involving the clacking decapod again and what looked to be pack of upset chittering green rats.

The Dining Hall was long and slightly tubular and illuminated by numerous external windows. Curving columns carved into the side of the hall, rather like the rib bones of some giant beast, rose up to meet at the ceiling apex. The old wooden dining tables had been hurled aside in haste and now lay propped or fallen against the external walls.

Over the heads of the seething masses, at the very tubular end of the hall, was the exit. Where the wall should have been there was simply now a circular golden hole, casting an eerie glow which sent clawing shadows reaching from the rib-like pillars. Beyond the hole, impossibly, was a tunnel, which rather than appearing in the gardens outside the spire, simply ran into some infinite golden distance.

As Agastalen and Heath approached with their burden, they could see that carts pulled by horses rumbled to and from the tunnel, rather like some giant road. Stationary carts were waiting on this side of the hole and it was onto one of these that they placed the bush.

Agastalen marvelled at the strength and skill exhibited by Arch-Mage Castigorn to cast such a wonder. He was disappointed that he'd not been there to witness it, but like all of the apprentices he had already been set to his removal tasks. The arch-mage, at the moment, was nowhere in sight.

'Lob it on, then?' said Agastalen cheerfully.

'Absolutely,' replied Heath.

With a couple of trial swings to gather momentum, they launched the moonberry bush up into the air.

There was a shriek from the bush, which clearly had never been airborne before, but by the time it landed in the cart the two apprentices were nowhere to be seen.

Agastalen and Heath hustled through the masses towards the museum, making the best haste they could.

The museum in the Lorian spire was apparently quite small when compared to that in Arcanum itself, but nonetheless displayed some priceless pieces. It was therefore not surprising that Lei-Weya required it to be double-checked, knowing what apprentices could be like. Agastalen took a certain pride in knowing that it was a sign of great trust for her to have asked them to perform this task. All of the arcane exhibits, even if old, were still potent and could prove disastrous should they fall into the wrong hands.

It took Agastalen and Heath some ten minutes to climb the singular spiral staircase through the centre of the tower almost to its top, since they lacked the less conventional methods of transport available to the tower's trained mages. When they reached the small landing and its adjacent door, they were slightly out of wind. Agastalen approached the solid-looking oaken door, and immediately began to wonder how they were going to open it, since he knew from experience that no door opened in the spire unless you were meant to open it. However, happily, the door swung open on silent hinges as he approached.

'How your power has grown, oh great magi,' Heath laughed from behind him.

Agastalen grinned and stepped into the museum.

Steps led down before him into a sunken circular chamber, which had about it the sense of unnatural quiet and stillness that pervades only certain aged places. The hazy late afternoon sun pierced the small windows, sending dust motes dancing in streams of sunlight. With a degree of reverence Agastalen descended, Heath following.

Arrayed about the edge of the chamber were the robes of Lorian arch-mages past. Their deep purple hue was covered in caressing layers of dust. In most cases the golden bands woven about them covered almost the entirety of the robe, so that they appeared almost as much gold as purple, the gold now fading to less precious silver with the cycles.

Within the circle of robes were numerous small plinths of varying height, but none taller than the human eye. The plinths were of various colours, from rose quartz to obsidian, and etched into the top of each was a brief collection of runes. All of the plinths appeared to be empty.

'For once in their lives the other apprentices appear to have been quite thorough,' said Heath.

Nodding, Agastalen replied, 'Seems you're right, Heath. Let's just double-check in case, though, eh?'

Heath nodded his agreement.

Agastalen circled the plinths. He noted how each of the items removed had left a dust-free outline, here a square, there a circle, and in other places no dust at all. Heath, pushing back his long dark hair, his tanned face screwed up in concentration, was trying to read the runic inscriptions on one such plinth.

After running his hands over many of the plinths and finding nothing but dust, Agastalen decided to turn his attention to the arch-mage's robes. He reminded himself that this was the closest he'd ever been to such items.

Whilst regarding the staff indent made in the shoulder of one such robe, Agastalen noticed a small metal brooch pinned to it. The brooch was fitted with a clouded red stone. His interest piqued, he peered at it more closely, and reaching out, he laid his fingertips upon it as he had been taught and then brushed it with the fabric of his mind. A moment later a slight and tingling warmth ran up his fingertips and into his arm. Agastalen smiled.

At his shoulder a voice said, 'See you've found something, then.'

Agastalen jumped and turned. Heath, grinning, was holding up a small feather carved out of bronze. 'Someone must have dropped it. Found it by the door.'

Agastalen did not have the heart to berate his cheerful friend for making him jump, even though he had no doubt it'd been on purpose.

'Any idea what it does?' asked Heath, thrusting the bronze feather into Agastalen's face.

Stepping back, Agastalen laughed. 'Do you think I'd still be wearing apprentice robes if I could tell you something like that at a glance?!'

'Good point,' said Heath. 'You always were a slow learner.' Of course they both knew that wasn't true, and in regard to both of them too, but they both enjoyed such occasional needling.

Removing the brooch from the robe, Agastalen tucked it into a pouch at his belt.

It seemed then as if the crowd noise in the distance had taken on a slightly different tone.

Frowning, Agastalen said, 'Do you hear that?'

'Hear what?' replied Heath.

'The crowd noise: it's different somehow,' said Agastalen.

'So?' said Heath, turning to look at the plinths again. 'Do you want to have another look around? Don't get much chance to be in here, after all. Or shall we get these back to the dining hall? You know we might find something we can keep, something small that they wouldn't miss, maybe.'

'Right, like you want to get tossed out of Arcanum for keeping something which you later find out aids in curing constipation,' said Agastalen as he proceeded to the nearest window and looked out.

It was difficult to see directly down below from the window, since the angle of the Spire swayed outward, rather like a piled rope, at a highly precarious angle. Agastalen could see about half of the outer garden from his vantage point, at the farthest edge of which was the ornamental outer fence. What he saw made his stomach drop. The fence had been thrown down and the ground within the garden was trampled, precious trees and plants broken or torn out. Of the crowd, or the mob, Agastalen corrected himself, there was no sight, but he could hear their roaring like some huge maddened beast. He knew that the mob must be at the base of the tower, or worse, within it. As he watched, from the base of the tower there came a whooshing noise, followed by the sooty billow of black smoke rolling across the garden, accompanied by a flicker of angry flame.

'By the nine gods,' said Agastalen.

'What is it?' replied Heath, the alarm in Agastalen's tone making him look up from his industrious hunt.

'We've got to get out of here,' Agastalen said. 'They're in the tower.'

'Not a chance,' said Heath, and he continued to look around. 'They'd never be that stupid.'

Agastalen marched over and grabbed his fellow by the robe and thrust him at the window.

'My imagination, do you *think*?' said Agastalen.

'Right, get your point. Damn it, that's us buggered good and proper,' said Heath in typical understatement.

'We couldn't be much farther from the exit if we were on the other side of the city,' barked Agastalen angrily.

'Guess we're just going to have to run faster than a gofer chased by a fox, then. Don't know any good spells, *do* you Agastalen?' Heath said, laying his hand on his friend's shoulder. 'You know, the sort you can use to get yourself out of the crap. Magic chariot right now would be good, for example. You know, fly out of the window or maybe even some form of earthquake: we could drop the tower on the buggers then, or even –'

'Oh, just shut up,' Agastalen interrupted him, with only a little acidity in his voice. 'Any *helpful* suggestions?'

'Well,' Heath said, grinning, 'I'm all up for legging it to Arch-Mage Castigorn's rather inviting exit right now!'

'Oddly enough, me too,' replied Agastalen.

With that they bolted for the door, which obligingly opened itself as they careered through it and started bounding down the spiral steps two and three at a time. The descent was not pleasant and on several occasions they almost lost their footing, but they had little time to worry about it.

Brown robes flapping about his legs, Agastalen briefly wondered if they were setting a time record for descending the steps as they hurtled downward. As they got farther towards the base of the stairs the sounds of the rioting mob below became increasingly loud, amplified by the stairwell. The shouting Agastalen could deal with, but the accompanying screams made the hairs on his neck stand up. Smoke too began to funnel up the stairway, making breathing difficult, and by the time they reached the bottom of the stairs they were both coughing, tears streaking their faces.

Gasping at the base of the stairs, Agastalen held out his arm and prevented Heath from hurtling past him and straight into the corridor beyond. Peering cautiously round the corner, he felt tears spring to his eyes anew. The Spire had been his home for ten cycles and now it was burning. Tapestries had been torn down or flickered in flame where they hung from the walls. Ornaments lay smashed on the floor, ceramic tears beside two brown-robed figures lying in spreading pools of blood. The faces were transfixed in horror and pain. One still had a short sword impaled through his gut, which he was pitifully curled around, as if nursing it.

'May Nim protect us,' Heath choked beside him, sudden tears coursing down his face. 'I hope those heathen bastards burn for this.'

'They will,' said Agastalen, the pitiful figures on the floor seeming somehow unreal and distant to him. 'Castigorn can't stand for this. He'll burn them to ash.'

They staggered onward through the curling smoke, but it became quickly apparent that the mob was everywhere. Twice they ducked into shadows as scores of screaming Lorian citizens raced past. Agastalen was sickened to see that many of them were also women, and there were even a few older children. On each occasion the groups were led by several chain mail-clad soldiers in the blue livery of the empire, the sword sigil of Sha bold upon their surcoats and shields.

They stepped out of the dormitory as the final group had passed, and then realised too late that there was a straggler. He appeared to be no more than a normal city man, balding and clad in regular daily clothing; he even wore an apron. However, city folk did not normally carry weapons, which he did. The club in his hand was bloodied and his white apron had the blood-spattered appearance of one that a butcher might wear.

The man turned slowly and grinned. He spat at their feet. 'Well, well, looks like I've got myself a couple more Nimish cubs. Stamp you out while you're young and stop your vile arcanish plague from spreading, that's what I'll do.'

By Nim, what have we done to deserve such anger, thought Agastalen, as he and Heath began to back down the corridor.

'Please, we only want to leave. Let us pass. We wish to harm no one,' said Agastalen.

Stalking forward, the man licked his lips as he said, 'You've got to be joking, young 'un, this'll make four for my tally. Talk o' the street I'll be!' With that he leapt towards them, levelling a wicked blow with his club.

Agastalen and Heath were both agile and easily avoided the clumsy blow. The return blow, however, caught Agastalen a glancing blow to the shoulder, sending him sprawling across the floor. The man stepped over him, grinning.

Eyes riveted to the club rising above him, Agastalen heard Heath's shout behind him. 'Merge and strike, Agastalen.'

The well within Agastalen opened easily as his thoughts touched it, blossoming outward like a flower to the spring dawn. Energy flooded through him, light and pure as rain water, and though he knew that afterwards he would be exhausted, the sensation at the moment was utterly intoxicating. He felt Heath's hand touch his, followed swiftly by the familiar flow from Heath's own well. Then their energies merged to form a greater flow.

The club swung down towards Agastalen as if slowed by some strange force, its wielder's face twisted into something almost lustful.

Agastalen's training came to the fore and he paused only for a moment for the correct form and then lashed out with their combined energies. The force struck the man, but rather than hurl him bodily away from them as Agastalen had intended, it launched him with massive force directly upward. With a shout of surprise the man struck the ceiling some thirty spans above, and his skull shattered. Gore rained down for a moment on the two stunned apprentices, and then the body crashed to the stone floor, taking with it a burning tapestry.

Heath slumped down wearily beside Agastalen, heedless for a moment of their continued peril as they both stared at the twitching, immolated body, within its impromptu pyre.

'Well, that's a surprise and no mistake,' Heath said. 'Next time at least try and leave us enough in our wells to breathe and walk, please, Agastalen.'

Heath stood up and pulled a sagging Agastalen with him.

Agastalen felt quite simply empty, as if everything that he'd ever had inside him had been taken out and thrown down the corridor. He'd never become used to the feeling, he thought. But that was the woe of the apprentice: to experiment, to learn and to make mistakes with their own life energy before they ever gained their first threads linking them to the Nexus. In this way they learned a healthy respect for power, its use and its price. Feeling the way he felt now, Agastalen really couldn't disagree.

Turning to Heath, he said, 'You know, we're never going to make it like this. If we run into any more trouble, we've got about as much strength left in us as two newborn pups.'

Heath nodded wearily in agreement. 'I say we go back and grab the clothing of a couple of those looters' bodies we've passed and try to blend in.'

Agastalen saw the immediate sense of the idea. 'Right, let's go. We'd better be quick.'

They tottered off.

Thinking it through, Agastalen realised that out here there were very few places where the magi appeared to have offered any real resistance, perhaps only where they'd been cornered. He surmised that they must all be falling back as fast as possible to the dining area where the exit was.

They found a small group of half a dozen bodies of city folk, which included a guardsman. They all appeared to have blackened holes about a hands-span in width burned straight through them, the holes still smouldering, as if hot.

'This lot must have run into one of the magi,' quipped Heath. 'Real bad day for them, that.'

Agastalen joined Heath in pulling a male figure into an adjacent room. Quickly they stripped the bodies of their clothes and donned them after taking off their brown apprentice robes. Both made sure they kept their own pouches and meagre collection of personal possessions.

'Most fetching,' said Heath, looking at Agastalen's orange smock and brown leggings. I especially like the burn hole. That style is so you.'

'I think you're right,' replied Agastalen, looking out into the corridor. 'I can definitely see the nobles wearing this style next spring. Right, let's go.'

They stepped into the corridor, Agastalen taking a deep breath and forcing himself to be calm. On impulse, he stopped and took off the fallen guard's short sword and strapped it on. Heath looked at him questioningly – Agastalen just shrugged.

They raced towards the dining hall, endeavouring to make up the time they had lost. They passed several groups of city folk along the way, none of whom more than glanced at them. Agastalen was slightly alarmed to notice that some of the soldiers now appeared to be organising the groups into cohesive search parties, to flush out magi pockets that might have gone into hiding. They were heartened, however, as they began to near their destination, to hear the sounds of fighting. Encouraged, Agastalen flashed Heath a smile, to which Heath returned a brief nod.

Moments later the pair reached a set of steps, which was heaving with armed city folk. Below the steps in the dining area a battle ensued, or more accurately appeared to have reached a stand-off. At the farthest end of the tubular dining hall stood the exit: a flat and inviting golden glow. In the centre of the gold disc stood Arch-Mage Castigorn, arms crossed on his chest, resplendent in his purple and gold robes. His flat blue-eyed gaze was like that of a hawk. Over a prominent nose, long ebony black hair streamed about him, as if on some mad wind. The air about the arch-mage was alive with hundreds or even thousands of threads of weaving and snapping golden energy, connecting him to the Nexus, with Castigorn at the centre, a calm, purposeful, purple-clad spider. Many of these golden threads appeared to sink into the golden exit in which he stood; others simply wove in the air about him.

Between the arch-mage and the apprentices stood a mob of city folk, possibly several hundred strong. Fronting the mob was a large contingent of chain mail-clad Lorian city guards, perhaps sixty in total and three ranks deep across the hall. The guards had pulled the overturned dining tables across the hall's width and were using them as improvised barricades. Those with crossbows were in the front ranks.

The area between the table barricades and the circular exit was marked by the ranks of the fallen, somehow cut down as they ran towards the exit gate. Nearly all of the bodies, Agastalen noted, were Lorian soldiers, and a few were city folk. Occasionally, amongst the fallen could be seen a pitiful brown-clad body.

Standing calmly before the glowing gate and Castigorn were two other figures; both clad in deep blue robes with golden threads twisting and rising up the hem and cuffs. The air about them also appeared alive with golden strands, moving and snapping. One figure Agastalen recognised immediately as his master, Mage Winfod, and the other was Lei-Weya. Winfod looked for all the world as if he was wondering what was going on, his wispy grey hair waving about his head, rheumy eyes peering at the crowd, palsied hands trembling upon a gnarled oaken staff. Lei-Weya's face was one of deep concern. She appeared to be saying something to Winfod, while for emphasis pointing to the various stairs down into the dining hall. Occasionally crossbow bolts would whip out from the soldiers behind the wooden barricades, but they came nowhere near the two unconcerned magi, just seeming to slow in mid-air and then clatter harmlessly to the ground, several feet from them. Despite this, the magi seemed content not to fight back and continued to converse.

Cursing, Agastalen realised that the entire shrieking mob, including barricades and ranks of soldiers, was between them and the gate. There were three sets of stairs into the dining area and they'd chosen the set that led directly down into the mob. The other two stairways, however, came out beyond the barricades.

He pulled Heath back against the wall, leaning wearily against it. 'What are we going to do, Heath? We'll never get through that mob. If we circle round to the other stairs, though, that's going to take time.'

Heath nodded his head grimly in agreement, scratching his chin. 'How about we work our way through the mob, leap the barricade and then pretend to charge the gate? Be a lot quicker.'

Agastalen goggled at his friend, thinking he was joking, but when Heath didn't smile he said, 'Well, I suppose the worst that could happen is that we get cut down by good old Winfod. His eyesight is pretty crap, you know!'

'Exactly,' replied Heath, grinning. 'I'd be amazed if he could hit us, quite frankly, although he's more likely to try if he sees it's you!'

Agastalen couldn't help but chuckle at his friend's irrepressible humour.

With a final glance to Heath for confirmation, Agastalen stepped into the throng, pushing his way down the steps. Jostling their way through was not difficult amidst the screaming tumult, and no one appeared to think it was odd that they wanted to be closer to the action.

Minutes later, Heath having managed to appropriate a small club along the way, they had reached the armoured backs of the Lorian soldiers. Steel helms occasionally obscured the view beyond: a tantalizing clear view of the hall and golden exit, before which Lei-Weya and Winfod stood, talking heatedly. Winfod was gesturing directly at the glowing exit and Lei-Weya appeared to be shaking her head. Arch-Mage Castigorn appeared to step forward slightly from his glowing web, perhaps saying something, and Lei-Weya's head dropped, nodding.

Agastalen realised with horror that the mages were about to leave. Grabbing Heath's arm, he saw from his horrified expression that Heath too had realised what was happening. They began to push their way frantically through the crowding soldiers. Soldiers' faces turned in surprise as they moved through their ranks. One with an officer's rank on his surcoat reached out and grabbed Agastalen's arm in a tight grip, halting him.

'Here now,' grinned the officer, 'where are you so keen to be going?'

Agastalen attempted to pull himself free, but the grip was just too strong. His mind scrambled frantically and he blurted out the first thing that came to mind. 'We're going to cut that scum down, sir,' and he pointed towards the talking mages.

The officer did not release his grip.

'They killed my brother, sir, he's out there,' Agastalen said, continuing his ruse and pointing to the carnage across the hall floor.

The officer's face relaxed slightly, softening into a look of understanding, and he nodded. 'All right, lad, go on, and may Sha watch over you.'

Not waiting to thank him, Agastalen raced after Heath.

They were both at the table barricade now, the ancient tables seeing a use which their maker had certainly never expected. Soldiers were all about them and the smell of armour and sweat was thick in the air. Agastalen's pulse drummed and he felt energy flow back into his tired body. He knew it would not last, but was grateful. All he needed was a single burst of speed and they'd be through the gate. He was dimly aware of a few soldiers clapping them on the back, wishing them luck, and an officer shouting orders to give them cover.

This is it, then, he thought. Agastalen drew his short sword and glanced at Heath, who was fiercely clutching his appropriated club. Their eyes met briefly in acknowledgement and as one they leapt over the table.

Screaming not in rage and anger, but certainly in fear, Agastalen and Heath raced towards Lei-Weya and Winfod, who were already moving towards the glowing gate. Arrow and bolts began to zip through the air from behind them towards the mages.

Screaming their battle cries, they were vaguely aware of others running beside and behind them. Inspired by the two, city folk shouted eager cries: 'Follow them!', 'For Loria!', 'For Sha!.'

Winfod and Lei Weya spun to regard the sudden attack as crossbow bolts hummed past them. But as they did so, a small group of brown-robed figures lurched into view at the top of the farthest stairs, into the hall. The mages' gaze swung to the group of six apprentices, many of whom appeared to be wounded, sagging against each other for support.

The gaze of the magi became then hard as granite and they turned an icy regard on the rabble racing towards them. They said something briefly to each other and Lei-Weya, hefting her robes around her knees, ran towards the group of apprentices, who were now staggering and falling down the stairs, scattering scarlet blood trails in their wake.

Winfod turned towards the racing mob, and as he did so Agastalen noticed in sharp recognition the gaze he had seen so many times. No longer was it rheumy or clouded, but it was purposeful, empowered by his art. Golden threads snapped and spat about Winfod, yet he didn't move a hand, or even utter a word; he simply stared hard at the howling mob. About Winfod small sparks began to glow and flicker in the air, slowly materialising into hundreds of small golden discs, gently orbiting him like some ancient and dying sun.

Agastalen saw what was happening in horror. The magi would do anything to protect their apprentices, as a mother would a child. And here he was, now, part of a mob, baying and charging at them, waving a sword.

Not knowing what else to do, he continued running towards Winfod and screamed at the top of his lungs. He didn't care who heard him now, for he knew that his very life was in peril. 'Master Winfod. It's me. It's Agastalen, Heath and Agastalen. Winfooood!'

Running beside him, Heath was aware of Agastalen shouting. Heath watched his Mistress Lei-Weya reach the bottom of the stairs and hold out her arms for the staggering apprentices, their faces grey and ashen. As she did so, crossbow bolts thrummed past her, many simply dropping from the air a few spans from her. One bolt though, made it through and struck an apprentice clean through the neck. Heath saw the look of shock on the young apprentice's face, her golden hair falling forward as she fell, and Heath recognised his friend Iri as the spark of life went out in her blue eyes. Blood fountained over Lei-Weya's outstretched hands as she cried out in shock, catching Iri's body to her breast as she fell.

Lei-Weya knelt and placed Iri's body gently upon the ground. Without looking up she gestured forcefully towards the gate to the ashen apprentices, who, nodding, lurched towards it. When Lei-Weya lifted her face from Iri, it was mottled red with rage.

Rising, Lei-Weya raised her arms, palms pointed outward, and scores and even hundreds of golden threads exploded into view about her. A moment of concentration passed her face and then a circular column of golden light ten hand-spans wide exploded out from her palms. The column of light howled straight down the hall with a reverberation that shook the very foundations. When it struck the mob immediately before the mage it sliced straight through, cutting a swathe ten spans wide. Blood spattered and body parts fell to the floor, twitching in its wake, and then it slammed into the table barricade behind which the archers sheltered. Where the column struck, the barricade simply vanished. The archers did not even have time to cry out as they were neatly spliced, crossbows and swords falling clattering to the earth, from lifeless hands.

With a grim nod, Lei-Weya turned back to shepherding her remaining apprentices towards the gate, where the Arch-Mage Castigorn, apparently unconcerned, awaited them.

Almost there, Agastalen thought: just fourty spans from Winfod now. Agastalen silently cursed Winfod's poor eyesight, eyesight that had been the butt of many an apprentice joke but that now placed them in mortal danger. 'Winfod,' he shouted again. 'Winfooood,' waving his sword in the air.

'Drop the sword, dammit,' shrieked Heath. 'Drop the damn sword. He'll think we're one of them!!'

Agastalen immediately saw the truth of Heath's words and dropped the sword with a clang. He also then saw the slight hand-gestures indicating that Winfod was almost ready to unleash the forming.

'Nooo. Winfoood. Masteeer,' they both shouted as they raced.

As they ran, Agastalen's mind was captured by the minute hand gestures with which Winfod created the form. They seemed magnified in his mind, and his consciousness scrambled to unravel them. Minute golden discs began to pop into existence about the old mage, and then he could see it in his mind's eye described on a page before him: 'binding-breaker'. By all the nine, no, he thought.

Looking over his shoulder to where Heath ran beside him, he caught his friend's eye and shouted 'binding-breaker' just as Winfod unleashed the forming. The look of horror on his friend's face must also have been mirrored in his own.

Both apprentices knew, beyond any hope, that defence against this form was far beyond them. Agastalen made to turn and run, but the screaming mob was at his back like some heaving animal, driving him forward. Knowing that it was his only chance, he dropped to the floor as if struck and let them race over him. Boots battered his body and struck him about the face as the mob ran over him, regardless in their lust to reach and rend the old mage.

Agastalen, bloodied, looked up and dazedly watched as they struck the unmoving Winfod like an angry tide. The discs about Winfod suddenly rose whickering into the air above them all. Agastalen could see weapons beginning to rise and fall in the heart of the mob, but the discs moved above with an almost lethargic pace, weaving from side to side, and then softly began to drop in the masses.

A spinning disc struck a young woman; she could have been no more than twenty cycles old. It vanished into her chest and then emerged from the other side briefly, where it vanished with a slight pop. The woman had an astonished look on her face as she simply collapsed to the ground, like a marionette whose strings had just been severed.

The first to fall were not noticed, but as more discs began to drop, humming, into the mob the screaming began and they started to push back from the old mage who stood untouched at the heart of the mob. Those closest to Winfod were dropping their weapons now, scrambling over each other in their haste to get away, mindless of the injury they caused to each other.

Crumpled and barely clinging to consciousness, Agastalen saw Winfod, still surrounded by spinning discs, serenely totter away from the retreating mob towards the winking gate. Lie-Weya now calmly awaited the old mage before the gate. As one they then stepped into the golden light.

Almost like the shutting of an eye, the gate slowly diminished as Arch-Mage Castigorn released his holding spell. As the gate shut and the retreating mages were lost from view, so did Agastalen's consciousness fade.

- CHAPTER 8 -

Refugees

The wagon creaked and bounced.

Agastalen curled up deeper under the hessian sack and tried very hard to find a more comfortable place to nestle amongst the parsnips. Try as he might, though, the parsnips were just not very accommodating bedmates; their idea of comfortable was apparently just not his. Why could whatever god had dreamt up the parsnip not have made them round and soft, rather than long and with a pointed determination to dig into everything?! Another bounce of the wagon made Agastalen finally give up, and pulling his cloak aside, he sat up in the wagon back feeling very out of sorts.

He stretched in an attempt to get the crick out of his neck and felt little better. It was well into the afternoon of their fourth day since fleeing the city of Loria and Agastalen was still feeling morose. Their miraculous survival of Mage Winfod's attack on the mob had ironically made them both heroes to the city folk and they'd had quite a job extricating themselves from congratulations and invitations to celebrations concerning the fall of the Lorian Spire of Arcanum. They'd obviously felt it singularly inappropriate to attend, despite the irony, and knew too that it was only a matter of time until their true identities were discovered.

Their would-be friends in Loria had eventually come to understand that the two young men were apparently so 'harrowed' by their experience of the magi attack that they needed to leave the city, to spend time recuperating with family and friends in the provinces. So, they'd seen their charges equipped with warm clothing and a few copper coins. Heath and Agastalen had realised the wisdom of taking help, even if offered by the hand that would also strike them, and so they'd not refused.

When they had left Loria, hitching a ride in a small merchant caravan headed to Torin, a large town south of Loria, and from there on the wagon of a farmer heading south, all the talk had been of war and the terrible fate that the magi would suffer for the slur cast against the Athel-Lorians' beloved deity Sha. The god of war held almost total dominion in the empire of Athel-Loria, an unusual situation for any country, most of which tended to be more multi-faith in their worship of the full pantheon of nine younger gods.

Agastalen reflected that the might of Athel-Loria was almost unchallenged in the entire world. Their armies were vast, and undefeated, since the time four hundred cycles past when the two original countries of Athel and Loria had met in a war in which they almost exterminated each other. Both sides were left so weakened from the conflict that smaller and opportunistic neighbours were able to prey upon them. This included the vociferous Duke of Taed, who declared independence for his small fiefdom, as then did the Barons of Peldane, all of whose territories remained independent to this very day.

It was Agastalen's recollection of numerous geographical maps that had allowed him and Heath, who had always been a fairly indifferent student of the mundane things in life, to plot a route for them to return to Arcanum, the heart of magic on Rune and site of the Mother Temple of Nim, god of magic. Lacking any magical or even mundane means to contact Arcanum concerning their plight, their sole solution was to make their own way to the magical city. Arcanum was located in its own province far to the east of Athel-Loria on the southernmost tip of the Immiriel peninsula. This meant either traversing the Heaven's Reach mountains, a prospect that appealed to neither of them, or making to Limfrost, capital city of Shael, and from there taking a ship to Arcanum. This latter course had seemed the most achievable and likely the swiftest, and so they'd agreed on it.

Heath stretched, rubbing wearily at tired eyes. He cracked them open and scrubbed his wavy dark hair back, peering at his friend. 'Is the cooked breakfast ready?' he asked, sitting up. Despite his morose ponderings of their predicament, Agastalen's scowl faded, and he tossed Heath a parsnip. 'Just like mum cooks,' he replied.

The farmer's deep rumble interrupted them from the wagon's front bench. He peered at them both from beneath a broad hat, his complexion stern. 'Got some bread n cheese if you young 'uns want it.'

With a nod and thanks from Agastalen he tossed an almost fresh loaf and a block of cheese to them, followed by a water skin.

Heath scooted forward from his makeshift parsnip bed as Agastalen set to dividing up their small feast.

Between mouthfuls of bread and cheese Agastalen turned to the farmer and asked, 'When do you expect to cross the border, sir?'

The farmer seemed to take the question in for a moment and replied over his shoulder, while keeping his eyes on the horse and road, 'Strange way of putting it, young sir, but if by that you mean when will we reach the town of Firs Deep, well that should be about three hours from now, about lunch time.' He paused, and set a half-eye on Agastalen. 'But if it's the border you're interested in, well, we crossed that just over an hour ago.'

Agastalen and Heath locked eyes, trying hard not to smile around mouthfuls of bread.

Agastalen huddled in closer to Heath. 'If memory serves,' he said, 'Firs Deep is a small town in the Barony of Croft. As I recall, Croft is landlocked, so we'll have to make our way east to Shael, passing through the other baronies. I think they're all fairly peaceful these days, though, so as long as we don't get lost we shouldn't have too much trouble.'

Finishing a mouthful, Heath asked, 'But if we've got to traverse the other baronies, mightn't one of them have a port where we can get a ship? Must be closer than hiking to Shael, from what you've said.'

Shaking his head, Agastalen replied, 'I'm guessing not. The baronies are all fairly small and a bit rustic. They're not likely to support ports of any real size and we need a deep-water vessel to get us to Arcanum, it's a long way. I still think we'd be better off headed straight to Shael. The capital, Limfrost, is a major trading centre and port; it's going to have the type of ship we need.'

Heath stuffed the remains of their breakfast into a crude sack with their other meagre possessions, including the bronze feather and brooch they'd rescued from the museum in the Spire of Arcanum. On a whim, he pulled out the red stone brooch, from the museum and clipped it to his cloak.

A few hours later the wagon rumbled into Firs Deep. Cresting a small rise, as per its namesake, the town of Firs Deep was set into a small valley with fir woodland carpeting both sides of the vale. The vale floor itself was largely given over to farmland, and with it being late summer most of the harvest appeared to be in. The town was not large and was centred on a small thoroughfare, appearing simple and unsophisticated, with all of the buildings looking to be built from wood.

'You take me to all the best places,' murmured Heath.

Agastalen did not reply.

Approaching the town, it seemed their initial assessment of it being slightly backward was proved correct, being two young men used to the cosmopolitan feel of city life. Folk they passed on the road wore crudely spun practical clothing, with not a silk shirt or velvet doublet in sight. They did not appear unfriendly, though, often giving their impromptu driver a wave as they rumbled past.

They drew up before reaching the main thoroughfare, at a large wooden building appearing to be a warehouse of sorts. With the farmer drawing on the reins the plodding old horse happily stopped.

A stocky man stepped out of a small office on the side of the warehouse, a smile splitting his face. 'Dack, good to see you,' he said.

The farmer dropped from the driver's bench to grip the merchant's hand in a meaty paw.

Agastalen and Heath scrambled down from the back of the wagon and shouted their thanks to Dack the farmer, who waved briefly at them and turned his attention back to the merchant, who although friendly seemed to have already started haggling.

The thoroughfare was not large, comprising a few wooden-built shops, which, as with all the buildings here, were apparently treated with a caustic substance to prevent rot, leaving them all looking blackened and decrepit. It certainly did not lend the place a cheery feel, Agastalen decided.

A couple of horse-pulled carts negotiated the rutted mud street. They stepped aside and received cheery waves from the drivers for their trouble.

'Certainly not Loria, is it?' said Heath, smiling. 'I just love what they've done with the buildings.'

'City boy,' replied Agastalen with a chuckle. 'You should try being brought up in Immiriel: parts of it are so remote as to make this look chique.'

'Exactly,' replied Heath. 'That's why I just love the city. Not that we'd find much welcome in any Athel-Lorian city right now,' he concluded somewhat lamely.

Agastalen scratched at his long black hair, reflecting briefly how much he'd like a nice hot bath. Putting such idle thoughts aside, he tied his hair back at the nape of his neck and said, 'I'm thinking that we need another ride down to the coast, or at least more supplies if we're going to have to walk it. What do you think?'

'Seems like a plan,' replied Heath, slightly morosely, 'particularly seeing as I don't have a better one. That bloody Winfod!' he said with venom. 'If his eyesight wasn't so bad he'd have seen us instead of trying to butcher us! And he's your master – can't believe he didn't even recognise you from just a few spans away,' he said, striking Agastalen in the shoulder with a fair amount of force.

Agastalen scowled at his friend. 'Yeah, like this is my fault,' he replied, hitting Heath back, in the stomach.

The two tussled for a moment and ended up in the dirt, laughing to themselves. 'Bloody Winfod!' they both shouted in unison, and burst out laughing.

Realising that they were drawing a few strange stares, they clambered back to their feet, dusting off their plain but serviceable clothing. Heath picked up the sack containing their few meagre supplies. 'General Store, then?' he said, pointing to a painted sign depicting a sheaf of wheat and a shirt.

'Absolutely,' Agastalen replied, starting off across the street.

The door bell chimed gently as they stepped inside the general store. It was a small shop, stuffed to overflowing with commodities of all sorts, from loaves of fresh bread, to spices in earthen pots, bales of cloth and simple shirts and trousers folded neatly on shelves. The smell of spices and flour hung thick in the air. A diminutive lady popped up from behind a sack of potatoes as they walked into the small section of well-trodden, available floor space. Her greying hair was scrunched up wildly atop her head and her glasses were slightly askew upon her nose. She wiped her hands on her apron.

'Good day, sirs,' she said in a surprisingly stern voice. 'What can we be doing for you?'

Agastalen and Heath paused and looked at each other. Agastalen knew that Heath was waiting for him to take the lead, so he said,

'Well, we've just arrived and were hoping that you could give us some directions,' and as an afterthought added, 'and we may also need to buy supplies... whatever we can afford, that is.'

'I see,' said replied, stepping out from behind the potatoes.

'We've just come in from Loria, ma'am' added Heath.

Agastalen cast him a sharp glance.

At this as the shopkeeper said in surprise, her eyes slightly wide, 'Well, is that so, now?' she said with relish. 'So you must have seen all that going on there, then. Terrible business, that. Is it true that the Spires of Arcanum have been cast down and the magi forced to flee?'

'It is,' said Agastalen, trying very hard not to be drawn on the subject, while giving Heath another acidic glance for good measure.

'And what is the Warlord going to do next?' she asked. 'Arcanum is a long way from Athel-Loria, isn't it? The Warlord's arm is long but he's going to have a heck of a job reaching all that way.'

Trying to keep his responses to information that he believed to be well known, Agastalen replied, 'Word has it that the Warlord has written to the heads of all the nations in Rune, demanding the destruction of all Spires of Arcanum within their kingdoms.'

The shopkeeper gasped, unconsciously still wiping her hands on her apron. 'I didn't know that, and no mistake, my, my. So what of the talk of war, then? What does the Warlord intend to do? Will he march on Arcanum?'

'Ma'am, I really don't know,' said Agastalen, trying to bring the subject to a close. 'We left Loria several days ago and events were still developing, rapidly. Much could have happened since then.'

Endeavouring to change the subject, Agastalen then said, 'We need to reach the south coast of the Baronies. Would you happen to know if there are any caravans or wagons passing that way? We'd like to hitch a ride, you see.'

Seeming disappointed by the change of topic, the shopkeeper replied, 'There are a few wagons that go south from here into the Barony of Wren, but they're mostly finished now, since the harvests are over. Certainly none would go as far down as the coast. Why is it you need to go all that way?'

Agastalen, gloomily considering the long walk that apparently now lay ahead of them, almost did not hear the question. With a start and a slight pause he said, 'Oh, um, we want to get as far from Loria as possible, with war likely and all.'

The shopkeeper nodded sagely when she heard this.

Elaborating slightly, he continued, 'We're headed to stay with my family in Limfrost and thought to follow the coast eastwards.'

After a pause, and staring quite hard at the two, who shifted slightly uncomfortably under her scrutiny, she said, 'That's a long journey now, from here down through the Barony of Wren and then following the coast east to Shael. You must have felt the need to get out of there quite badly indeed. But there are quicker routes to Shael from the city of Loria. Coming down through the Barony of Croft seems a bit out of the way to me… though it is the nearest border, mind.'

Agastalen and Heath both shifted but made no reply.

'Well, that's up to you, of course. The baronies are mostly peaceful these days,' and with that she began to bustle about gathering up a few things, continuing as she went. 'There's been some talk, mind, of trouble to the west. Something going on between the Duke of Taed and that pompous old fool the Baron of Lont.' Pausing and peering hard at them, she began to cluck. 'That clothing surely won't do, now. You're going to need stout wool cloaks, bedrolls, flint and steel, foods that won't moulder…' The rest they lost under her muttered breath as she bustled about.

'Well done, Heath,' hissed Agastalen with a fair degree of venom in his voice.

Heath had the good grace to blush.

'How are we going to afford all that stuff she's gathering?' said Heath, perhaps keen to change the subject. 'We've only got a few coppers!'

Agastalen saw that his friend was right. The shopkeeper had already gathered a veritable armload and was still going. Taking a breath, he said, 'Excuse me, ma'am, but I really don't think that we have enough money for all of that.'

The shopkeeper stopped with her armload and walked over to them. 'You two do seem to be in a bit of a fix now, don't you? All those leagues to travel and no money?!'

Agastalen dug into his belt pouch and pulled out their coins. Opening his palm towards the shopkeeper, he revealed ten copper pieces.

She laughed. 'That should get you the cloaks at least,' she said, smiling. 'Look, you're obviously in a bit of a fix... Go on, take it all and just give me five.'

Heath and Agastalen looked at each other, surprise etched on their faces.

'Well, go on,' she snapped. 'Don't just stand there like a couple of landed carp, give me my money and get out of here!'

Surprise still showing on his face, Agastalen handed over the coins and took the proffered armload. 'Thank you,' he said simply, 'I don't know what else to say, but thank you and may Nim bless you.'

The shopkeeper smiled and showed them to the door. 'And may *Sha* protect you both,' she said quietly, shaking her head as they left.

They made camp that night several leagues south of Firs Deep. Using the flint and steel the kindly shopkeeper had provided, they managed to get a small fire going under the sparse canopy of an abandoned apple orchard. They dined on overripe apples and salted meat. The fire popped gently and the feeling in the orchard was peaceful, broken only by the occasional hoot of an owl seeking his nightly repast.

Finished with his fourth apple, Heath threw the core into the flames and sat back, pulling his new grey woollen cloak about him. His mien to Agastalen seemed slightly more sombre and reflective than usual.

'What are you thinking?' Agastalen asked his friend after a few moments.

Heath paused before replying and looked up, the firelight catching in his eyes like a mirror. 'Mainly about my family – Mum, Dad and Riana,' he said, referring to his young sister.

Agastalen knew that before Heath had been accepted into the magi, he'd been very close to his family. Older than most before being taken into the order, Heath had actually been spotted using his arcane talent to cheat at dice by Lei-Weya.

Agastalen himself had been offered to, and then accepted by, the order when he was just five and so had had little time to develop lasting bonds with his family. Heath, however, had been twice that age.

'Do you think they'll be okay, Agastalen? It's common knowledge that I'm an apprentice mage. You don't think that they'll take it out on my family, do you?'

Not being sure of the answer himself, but also understanding that his friend needed reassurance, Agastalen said, 'I really doubt it, Heath. The Warlord would never stand for anyone targeting Lorian families. Nim knows, your family is one of many. The magi themselves are a different matter, though.'

'Yeah, I expect you're right,' Heath replied and, turning into his cloak, said, 'Good night, Agastalen.'

Agastalen watched the fire burn down to embers as he considered the fate of Athel-Lorian families with magi sons and daughters.

- Chapter 9 -

The Gift

It was their fifth day travelling and they'd encountered only one woodsman, headed north towards Firs Deep. However, he had not replied to their greetings and had kept his head down as his cart rumbled past in apparent haste. The only acknowledgement of their existence was the snarling and barking of his large black dog from the back of his cart.

They were surprised later that day when they came across the hamlet. It was set in a small and lightly wooded glade, and they had neither seen smoke nor heard any noise to alert them to its existence.

By unspoken agreement Agastalen and Heath halted at the edge of the glade. There were just a half-dozen thatched dwellings in the community, set into an approximate circle about a small totem of some form. Small piles of chopped lumber rested outside those houses that they could see. There were no apparent signs of life.

Heath shrugged to Agastalen and left the cover of the wood, walking out towards the hamlet. Agastalen stepped out and followed. He was acutely aware of the silence of the glade and wood as he followed his friend. As they drew near, he noticed that much of the grass in the clearing appeared churned. Kneeling down, he noted the U-shaped imprint of horses' hooves.

Looking up, Agastalen saw that Heath had halted at the edge of the hamlet. Arising from his crouch, he approached, curious. Heath was staring straight ahead, ashen-faced.

The totem in the centre of the hamlet was carved into a crude likeness of a smiling female face, the features bark and the hair wheat; it was not an uncommon representation of Ondalla, goddess of nature and the harvest. Impaled on the totem was a young boy. A spear had struck his torso with such force that it had split the wooden totem. The youthful countenance that could have seen no more than ten cycles was transfixed in horror, eyes staring sightlessly ahead. His sundered chest was matted thick with the lifeblood that had run down his legs to pool in the wooden offering bowl to Ondalla below; becoming a dark and unwanted offering to the goddess of nature.

About the totem lay other crumpled forms. The bodies lay in angles of unnatural repose. Some lay beside the limbs that had been brutally hewn from them and there they had died, futilely clutching at the stump of a leg or arm, their departing life running in measured beats onto the mud. Others appeared to have been run through, sword and spear rising from backs or gut like some strange salute to the sky.

Heath stared aghast at the carnage. Gasping, Agastalen dropped to his knees and vomited.

Heath barely whispered, 'Who could have done this? Why? The baronies are at peace, aren't they?'

Retching, Agastalen barely managed a nod.

'Where are we?' asked Heath. 'Are we still in the Barony of Croft?'

Agastalen wiped his mouth with his hand and, taking a breath, said quietly, 'No, we couldn't be. Croft is one of the smaller baronies, we must have crossed into Wren at least a day, if not two days ago.'

Heath nodded and said firmly, 'Right, we should get out of here. That blood has barely congealed: this happened within the past few hours.'

'All right,' replied Agastalen, getting back to his feet, 'but we should check to make sure that no one is still alive first.'

'You've got to be joking,' Heath replied, incredulous and without humour. 'That looks like a pretty thorough job to me.'

Agastalen, however, was already moving towards the pitiful fallen forms.

Moving from one body to another proved to be a grisly task. Heath was right about the time of this, though, thought Agastalen: this had happened within the past few hours. He tried to ignore the agony frozen in the faces of the victims, their mouths often gaping in one last silent scream of pain or perhaps to some unhearing god, beseeching mercy. There wasn't one weapon among them, Agastalen noticed with burning anger: these villagers had either not known the attack was coming or they simply didn't possess a single weapon.

His fingers placed upon the withered neck of an old lady, Agastalen started back in surprise to find a soft, irregular heartbeat. Her face was deadly pale against her iron grey hair, the lips almost blue. This grandmother's got strength in her, thought Agastalen with a slight surge of hope. He gently pulled aside her coarse wool smock to inspect her wound and gasped at the dark glitter of entrails showing clear through the belly wound. He gagged and called softly to Heath, who was crouched beside him in a moment.

'She's alive,' said Agastalen.

Heath blanched when he saw the grievous wound that she had taken, and looked at his friend. Understanding the determination he saw etched there and feeling akin himself, Heath said, 'Right, but we can't stay here. Whoever did this could be back any time. We'll have to take her with us.' Agastalen nodded in agreement.

Agastalen lifted the old lady as gently as he could, cradling her in his arms as he would a child. They walked towards the wood and neither of them looked back.

They carried her as far as they could until they were both almost exhausted, halting eventually in a small gully, no more than thirty spans across. Gently laying the old lady down on the woodland floor, Agastalen collapsed onto the damp earth, his feet almost in the small stream that bubbled cheerfully through the the gully.

As the sun began to set, Heath set about getting wood for a fire and Agastalen turned his attention to the old lady's belly wound. The wound was deep; almost half the width of her torso. The flesh around it was puckered and angry. Already it was beginning to smell. Having little real medical skill, Agastalen knew that there was little he could do for such a grievous injury, so he set about cleaning it as best he could with fresh water from the stream and then bound it with strips torn from their only spare shirts.

Heath had got a small but warm blaze going by this time, and noticing the diminution of their only spare shirts, he said, 'Looks like we're both going short-sleeved, then.'

Agastalen laughed softly and covered the lady's recumbent form with his cloak. Her face appeared haggard and deathly, even in the warming glow from the fire. Sitting himself next to his friend in the fading light, he said, 'There is little we can do for her, I fear. She needs the skill of a true healer or possibly even a daughter of Eli-shar, the goddess of healing.'

Heath did not reply and stared into the flames, face hidden by his curling hair.

'Does this change anything?' Heath asked eventually, keeping his gaze on the fire.

Agastalen thought for a moment and reached into their sack, retrieving some salted pork, part of which he handed across to Heath. 'I don't see that we have much choice but to continue on as we were. If we knew the geography of the area, we could alert a local garrison and perhaps even find a healer, but without that knowledge we've got as much chance of stumbling across both as we have of finding them by intent.'

'Those chances both being remote,' said Heath.

Agastalen nodded gently.

'I wouldn't worry,' said a soft and frail voice. 'I'm tougher than I look, you know.' The old lady was watching the two of them from watery, half-open eyes.

'How are you feeling?' said Agastalen, after recovering from his surprise.

'I've certainly felt better,' she replied, managing a small smile. 'My name is Rosie. So, might I know the names of my rescuers?'

Agastalen and Heath stumbled over each other trying to introduce themselves.

Rosie laughed quietly, which swiftly turned into a hacking cough, during which time they both waited solicitously.

Agastalen asked, 'May I get you anything, Rosie?'

Rosie replied, 'Unless you've got a daughter of Eli-shar hidden in that old bag of yours, no thanks.'

Walking around the fire, Agastalen knelt beside Rosie and gently stroked the grey hair from her face. 'Can you tell us what happened, Rosie?'

'What, and you're going to gallop off and sort it all out, are you, like some knight of Athel-Loria?' Rosie chuckled weakly. She smiled and Agastalen noticed dark blood rimming her teeth. 'Sorry,' she coughed, 'I'm a caustic old girl. You get to be when you've seen as much of life as I have.'

Agastalen nodded, waiting for her to continue.

'Didn't recognise them,' Rosie said, 'not that I know many warriors mind you. It was all so quick, so brutal. We didn't even hear them coming. One minute it was quiet, the next they were galloping among us, hacking and slaughtering. They were laughing, Agastalen; by the nine gods, they were laughing.' She paused a moment and then whispered, 'Am I the only one left?'

Agastalen hung his head and replied, 'I'm sorry, Rosie.' She nodded resignedly and her eyes closed.

Sleep did not come easily to either of them that night. Agastalen eventually settled for sitting and staring into the fading fire embers, trying to make sense of what he had seen. Heath tossed and thrashed in his sleep, calling out unintelligible things. Occasionally Agastalen got up to check on Rosie. Her face was cold, colder than it had been, he thought, so he appropriated Heath's cloak as well, causing him to cry out in his disturbed slumber, and gently draped it over the old lady.

Agastalen racked his brains for an answer as to what they had seen, but try as he might, he could come up with none. Excluding an occasional border dispute, the baronies had been at peace for four hundred cycles. They were each fiercely independent and would suffer none other to rule them. The larger Dukedom of Taed to their west had from time to time attempted to annex either Lont or Mytle but had always been beaten back by combined forces from the baronies. Although barony relations with Taed remained terse, the last such battle had been more than a hundred cycles past. Certainly Agastalen knew that his knowledge of Runic history was not exhaustive, but was sure that he would have taken note of the existence of such a brutal regime or force as the one evidenced in the village.

'You're magi, aren't you?' Agastalen turned at the sound of Rosie's soft voice. Her face within the nest of cloaks was angled towards him, and the fire having largely died out, it was outlined only by the faint silver moonlight. It made her seem more frail even than before, almost translucent, like the finest china.

Agastalen nodded. 'I am, but not much of one, I'm afraid. I'm just an apprentice.'

'No such thing as *just* an apprentice when it comes to,' she coughed, 'Magi.'

'How did you know?' Agastalen asked.

'My life is slipping away,' Rosie replied. 'I can feel it ebbing with every beat of my heart. With death's cold hand closing about me, I can see the very life-force glowing within you. Only a mage could have such an affinity for the force of life. It's beautiful.'

Moving closer to her, Agastalen said, 'We're going to get you to a healer, Rosie. You just need to hold on.'

Taking a rattling breath, Rosie said, 'I'm old, Agastalen, and if you ever see as much of life as I have, you'll be lucky indeed.'

Agastalen smiled at this, admiring the strength and courage in her.

'So, don't delude yourself or try to lie to me, young mage! My life's breath is measured in hours now.'

Agastalen took a breath to raise protest, but seeing the steely look in Rosie's rheumy eyes, he chose not to say anything but instead took her hand in his. He was startled at how cold it was.

Minutes passed while Agastalen sat holding Rosie's hand, when she softly said, 'Did you know that once the magi were the preservers of life? They did not always manipulate their links to the Nexus in the ways they do now, ways that they so elegantly call "forms".'

Agastalen shook his head at a loss for words, as Rosie continued. 'That's right, the Nexus is the heart of all life and that to which all mages are attached through bindings.' Looking fondly at Agastalen, she said, 'Save their apprentices, that is. Using their bindings, the magi once simply nurtured and preserved life for the love of doing, so you know.'

'Rosie, how do you know all this?' Agastalen asked. Out of the corner of his eye he noticed that Heath had sat up, apparently having given up on sleep.

'Let's just say that there is mage blood in the family,' she replied.

Agastalen started to ask another question but a soft squeeze of her hand forestalled him. 'I would give you my binding, Agastalen, that which links me, as it does all living creatures, to the Nexus.'

Agastalen rocked back on his heels, vaguely aware of Heath's gasp across the dormant fire. His mind whirled at the implications. As an apprentice, he had no bindings of his own save one, as was held by all livings creatures, through which life flowed into him from the Nexus, the source of all life in the universe and the heart of the power manipulated by the magi. Certainly in ancient history it was not unheard of for a binding to be "gifted" from one human being to another, but since that always resulted in the death of the person bequeathing the gift, those instances had been rare. In present times bindings were usually handed from one mage to another to allow elevation within the magi's ranks, or more rarely they were seized during, or as a result of, combat. Thus, an apprentice's first binding was always now gifted from their master or mistress, when the apprentice was deemed ready for elevation to the rank of Demi-Mage. This also ensured that the first binding, a highly delicate process, was conducted with success.

At last Agastalen replied, 'Your gift humbles me, Rosie, but I cannot take it. I am not worthy to receive it. In ages past I know that such gifts were not unheard of, but no longer. That time is done now. A binding has not been taken from outside the mage order for more than three centuries.'

Rosie's eyes twinkled as she said, patting his hand softly, 'And that, my young saviour, is exactly why you are the right person to take it.'

Shaking his head even more firmly now, Agastalen set his mouth in the firm line that Heath knew would take no rebuke. 'Even should I want to, Rosie, and your gift overwhelms me, I could not. There are edicts concerning such things, since during previous ages they were sometimes taken from people by force. It would have to be witnessed and assisted by another mage.'

'I'll do it,' said Heath quietly.

Agastalen turned to look at his friend, whose eyes were shining brightly with fervour in the moonlight.

'Agastalen, I know I'm just an apprentice, but that still means I'm of the mage order. I could witness the gift for you and help, if you need me to, that is.'

'You see,' said Rosie, coughing and wiping at her mouth with a withered hand; it came away dark with blood. 'Even your fellow apprentice agrees with me.'

Agastalen looked somewhat hopefully between the faces of Rosie and his friend, but saw little to help him extricate himself.

'Never forget,' continued Rosie, 'it is mine to give to whom I choose, as is the right of any living creature. And I choose to give it to you.'

Agastalen bowed his head, humbled. His hair had fallen free from its clasp and when he finally raised his face to meet Rosie's eyes, it was wet with tears. 'Very well, dear Rosie… I accept your gift.'

'Good,' said Rosie, her voice remaining firm. 'Now let's get a move on. I'm getting cold, I'm afraid that my passing is almost upon us. Can't help you when I'm gone, now.' With an almost childlike quality to her voice she then said, 'Will it hurt?'

Agastalen shook his head. 'I have witnessed many such ceremonies. The process, I believe, is brief and painless. But before we do this, is there anything that you would like us to do for you, or perhaps pass a message to someone when you are gone?' He finished the last word softly.

Rosie shook her head. 'All the ones I loved passed yesterday, and the others round about, well they're not really worth worrying about,' she grinned. Her breath was now coming in shallow gasps and she feebly gripped at Agastalen. 'Now stop fretting. Get on with it, please.'

Agastalen sighed a brief assent and looked to Heath, who also nodded, his face deadly serious.

The glade seemed unnaturally quiet as Agastalen placed a trembling hand upon Rosie's breast, directly over her heart. She smiled reassuringly at him, but Agastalen did not see as he reached within himself and opened his well, the place which also harboured the anchor of his own personal binding to the Nexus. His innermost self blossomed open with the slightest whispered touch of his mind and warmth suffused him. Watching quietly, prepared to help if needs be, Heath saw a soft golden light suffuse his friend, illuminating Rosie's pale skin and drawing a slight gasp of wonderment from her.

Opening his inner mind, Agastalen saw the woodland glade anew. No longer was it a place of damp, moss and silver moonlight but now it was suffused by life. The trees quivered with it; soft silver light pulsed in soft steady beats from their roots deep in the earth, throbbing to the tips of their leaves. The insects that crawled across their bark and lived in the forest floor were alive with it; and glowed a thousand different shades, racing motes of movement in the night. The very air and earth were alive, writhing with bindings, tubular vein-like conduits, connecting every living creature to the Nexus.

Agastalen's gaze dropped from this wonder to Rosie. The golden cord that bound Rosie to the Nexus blazed with a pure and golden light but the pulse along it was faint and sluggish. The binding disappeared into her sternum, where Agastalen knew that it fed her inner well. Her flesh seemed pale and almost translucent to his inner mind.

Opening his hand, he gently placed it around the binding which shimmered gently in his grasp. Rosie gasped softly as he did so. Agastalen looked at her in concern.

'I see it,' said Rosie, 'I had no idea: it's so beautiful.'

Agastalen could only nod, tears standing in his eyes, struggling to bring to mind the ritual words. He'd never spoken them before, but only witnessed them used in ceremony with others. Yet they were emblazoned on the mind of every apprentice, as he or she hoped one day to speak them to their master and be bequeathed their first binding.

Agastalen drew comfort from Heath's presence beside him. Taking a deep breath, he looked into Rosie's eyes and brought to mind the ritual words. 'I am a disciple of Nim, father of magic and bringer of life. I hold now this sacred binding, your connection to the beloved Nexus, which is the heart of our father Nim. Do you give this binding willingly and for the betterment of the order of Arcanum?'

Rosie, looking directly into Agastalen's eyes, said softly, 'Yes, Agastalen, I do. And may Nim guide you and protect you. Use it well.' Then, smiling gently, she closed her eyes.

Suddenly the binding in Agastalen's hand gave slightly and came away from Rosie's sternum, the slim end pulsing golden light that flowed into the air to scatter like fireflies.

Smiling, Rosie breathed her last breath.

Agastalen looked at the pulsing binding clutched in his hand and then at the recumbent form of Rosie before him. Emotions tumbled through him. What right did he have to do this? He had just taken the life of an old lady. This was wrong. No mage had taken a gifted binding for centuries and there was a reason for that.

Agastalen gasped, clawing air into his lungs, and shuddered.

He was aware then of Heath shaking him. 'Quickly, Agastalen, it's fading.'

Agastalen shook his head and gasped, 'I can't. What right did I have?!' Tears coursed down his face.

Clutching Agastalen's shoulders and placing his head against his friend's, Heath whispered urgently, 'She was dying, Agastalen, and wanted to repay your kindness. Don't let her gift be in vain.'

The binding was beginning to fade in his hand; the binding that was Rosie's gift, as Heath had said. Within, Agastalen understood that Heath was right and that the gift was freely given.

Summoning his courage, he spoke the final words. 'Rosie, I accept your gift on behalf of Nim and the order of Arcanum.' His inner well reached out and the binding came free of his hand and floated through the air, drawn towards him and his own single binding. Where it touched his own binding at the point at which it touched his sternum, it simply vanished. Agastalen gasped and the pulsing of his own binding grew stronger, as if with a double beat.

From beside him he was vaguely aware of Heath completing the ritual words. 'Nim embraces you, Agastalen, as you grow now, becoming our beloved demi-mage.'

- CHAPTER 10 -

Immortal Veylistra

'He must be corrupted.'

'I am aware of that' replied the silky voice.

'How will you do this? If the seed blossoms before he is corrupt, even we could not control him.'

'The human heart is weak, he will seek revenge; it is inevitable.'

'Remember our bargain.'

'How could I forget?! Now go, the boy is waking!'

One of the figures vanished.

'Where am I?' asked Thorn, his voice barely a hiss through the band of grief bound tight about this throat and heart.

'My home.'

'What kind of place is this?' Thorn croaked as he pushed himself to his knees. The sky was laced with purple fire and broken bronze ruins thrust up like rotten teeth from a tortured mountaintop.

'I know; it's not much.' The feminine voice laughed, sultry, almost a purr.

Thorn's gaze looked upon bare feet laced with tiny silver charms, and traced upward to where whispering translucent silk hinted at the softest of skins. A carven sliver breast plate highlighted a lush and female form and raven hair framed a face, where wide eyes of deepest mauve were flecked with gold. A rune; two dark lines slashed by a third marked one cheek, at odds with such apparent perfection.

Heat rose in Thorns' face as his gaze traced her ripe body. He gasped at the heat of the desire that suddenly began to course through him.

Thorn thrust himself angrily to his feet. 'Are you my captor?'

'Yes darling, I suppose that I am.'

'Then you killed my Mum!' Visions of the dreadful sweeping axe blade raced through his mind, his mums' body suspended motionless for a moment before it fell limp beside him, unheeding as he screamed in despair.

Unthinking he launched himself at her with a shriek, his hands outstretched like claws.

The lady smiled, though it was without warmth, and stepped away from him with an astonishing speed.

Thorn plunged into a decrepit bronze wall, which burst apart as he struck it, and for a moment he teetered at the edge of a cliff. Winds shrieked and plucked at him, seeking to cast him onto the empty ragged land beneath. His arms flailed desperately, seeking a hold and found none.

Strong arms dragged him back and he fell to the ground panting. He lay for long moments clawing breath into his lungs in deep uncontrollable shudders, and with each breath his wracking sobs grew deeper. Images flashed into his mind; the axe, the red mailed chieftain and the twisted face upon his helm, his mothers last words 'please, do not take the life of my son.' It played over and over. She couldn't be gone. It made no sense. His Mum dead. Alazla, gone. Nothing made sense.

Thorn didn't realise that he wept in her lap. In those mighty bronze ruins, that lay like the ancient bones of some giant upon a mountaintop, where they seemed to be the only two people on the world, he wept in the arms of a stranger, and she stroked his hair as if she had known him his entire life. His tears spilled across priceless silks, and he screamed his mothers name until the stars became beads of silver in a twisted violet sky.

When he finally opened his eyes, the world of Rune hung above him, fat and blue in the night sky. The stars hung about it, as if seeking to create some heavenly crown.

He rubbed at his eyes. 'By the nine gods' he hissed to himself 'that's Rune.'

'Yes, yes it is. And this is my world.'

The lithe figure hopped down from the embrace of a bronze wall and strolled toward him, a gentle smile upon her face.

'If that is, you can call it such' she added bitterly.

'You're a god' Thorn stated.

The lady laughed, though the smile on her face seemed mocking. 'No, I'm no god.'

Thorn took in then the mauve landscape and his world that floated far above and his mind moving as quickly as ever said 'we're on the Violet Moon; Veylistras' face. And that means you must be Veylistra, daughter of the god of Magic.'

She stopped then and smiled at him, and this time, it seemed genuine. 'You're right, on both counts Thorn. This 'world' was a gift from my mocking father. I asked for a place to rule, to call my own, and he gave me this; a world of dust, ash and tortured skies.'

'So you're just an immortal then?'

Veylistra stepped closer, and there seemed to be some menace about her as she replied 'yes…I'm *just* an immortal Thorn. Daughter of a god….but not, in fact, a god.'

Thorn had no idea how he was going to do it, but he became utterly resolved even as he stood up. There was a rage in him, and rage was not something that Thorn was used to. It replaced the fear that he normally felt, and it was good, deep and cold, coiled within, right in the pit of his stomach. 'Well, immortal or not, you'll pay for killing my mum you immortal bitch. I'll hunt down your followers and burn every temple of yours to ash. Every day of my life, will be dedicated to your destruction.' As he stood upon the violet moon, his own world literally as far from him as the stars, his words sounded utterly hollow, even to his own ears.

Her reaction was not what he had expected.

Veylistra sauntered closer and Thorn felt his breath catch, intoxicated by her very presence. He swam in the golden sparks in her eyes as her honeyed voice replied 'but it was not me Thorn. *I* did not kill your mother.'

Thorn snarled as he struggled to hold onto his anger 'I, I, know it wasn't you, but, but, I'm here and that means that whoever did it serves you!'

An elegant hand rested softly on his burning cheek. 'Things are never as they seem Thorn. You must believe me when I say that I did not order the death of your mother. I'm sorry that she died. Truly.'

Struggling through the heady intoxication of her presence Thorn fought to continue. 'But it *was* your order that brought me here – it must've been! It was your order that killed dozens of sons and daughters of Oldoth! Whether or not you ordered it, my Mum is dead, dead – because of you!!'

Veylistra hung her head, raven hair hiding her clouded eyes 'I'm sorry Thorn, I never meant for us to meet on these terms.'

Thorn did something then that he'd never done before today, he hit out. His hand lashed out, almost of its own volition, and unnoticed, motes of blue light blazed about his fist. Her eyes widened slightly in surprise as he struck her square on the cheek, with as much force as he could muster. Veyilstras' head moved only slightly with the impact, but a shudder went through the earth and the bronze ruins groaned as if tortured.

A trickle of ruby blood traced Veylistras' cheek, where it followed for a moment the line of the rune that marred her perfect features.

Velylistra said nothing as she lifted a single finger to her cheek and scooped the drop of blood onto it, where it hung as if frozen for a moment, before she licked it with the tip of her tongue.

She laughed and scampered away from him, where she leapt into the air and landed with a swirl of silk and silver. 'Your power begs to be awakened boy and *that* it why you are here!'

'Send me home Veylistra. Send me home so I can burn your temples until your name is nothing but a faded memory and all that's left is this broken rock hanging in the sky.'

'He's here you know.'

'Who?'

'The one who killed your mother.' She smiled, and it was that of a predator.

Thorn reeled. Fear and rage raced through him like a torrent; a mixture of fire and ice. He was here – the red armoured giant! Was he, Thorn, next? Would his blood drip next from that same axe blade to mingle with his mothers? His very limbs felt sick with the fear of it. And yet… there it was again, within him, that throbbing insistence and he felt it welling, rising up, to smother the fear - rage. Rage boiled within him thick and heated as molten lava.

Veylistra must have seen it, for the smile on her face was rapturous.

'I can…introduce you, if you wish.' Her coy understatement was lost on Thorn.

Thorns' fists clenched. 'Yes, I think I'd like that.'

Taking Thorns' hand in hers Veylistra led him through a cut in the jagged rocks. Long before they reached their destination, deep voices and laughter echoed up to reach them. Thorn had never felt rage before and he embraced it. He had no idea what he was going to do, and seemed numb, almost incapable of any thought, other than he had to meet his mother's murderer again. He had to look on that twisted helm, somehow even to remove it and see the face beneath. To look into the murderers' eyes.

They descended down a narrow ravine to emerge upon a small plateau that hung precariously out from the mountain, above a landscape torn with rivers of fire and utterly empty of life. Encircling the plateau were seven bronze thrones, precariously close to the cliff edge. Each throne, except one, was occupied by a figure. All were elegantly dressed, in a variety of expensive robes, gowns, or armour rich enough for any court in the land. Each also bore the same Rune of two lines slashed by a third upon their cheek. In the centre of the circle stood, the red armoured chieftain.

All talking stopped as Thorn emerged from the ravine, hand in hand with Veylistra.

The chieftain turned. He was as huge as Thorn remembered. The handsome face upon his carven helm seemed to leer at Thorn, as his eyes gravitated to the double bladed axe slung across his back.

'Mistress' the armoured giant boomed from the centre of the circle and bowed to Veylistra. 'I was just apprising the Council of our plans for the annexing of the Peldane Baronies.'

'Very good Pyrus. However, we have a little something that we need to discuss first.'

With those words, something within Thorn broke, all the fear that he had felt during his life evaporated and became white hot. That he should see his mother's murderer here before his eyes, and be powerless, as always, to do anything, was too much.

He screamed. It was a primal thing full of rage, pain and despair. It echoed through the mountains like the piercing cry of an eagle.

And with that scream still breaking from him, Thorn charged. He had no idea what he was going to do, other than he had to so something.

'Oh my' said one of the figures, on a throne, a plump lady in red satin brocade.

'Don't worry' chuckled an aged man in a long scaled leather coat. 'She's just trying to goad him. It's going to take more than this for him to become ours though.'

The giant Pyrus took a step back in surprise, and looked to Veylistra as if asking what to do.

Thorn did not see Veylistra shrug and wave a nonchalant hand.

Pyrus did not draw his axe, apparently unconcerned as Thorn ran at him.

Rage and despair raced through Thorn as he churned towards Pyrus. His mothers' decapitated head hung before his eyes, the eyes wide and sightless, the mouth still moving reflexively. Tears chased his cheeks unheeded and he barrelled into Pyrus.

The crack as Thorn struck Pyrus shook the plateau, and it seemed to tilt. Rocks tumbled from the mountainside and Pyrus was lifted clear off his feet, to crash against the base of one of the bronze thrones.

The gasps from the thrones were audible.

Thorn barely paused, and then he was on the dazed Pyrus like a rabid wolf.

He landed atop Pyrus and began to pummel him, and all he knew was white hot fury. He rained blows with a bone cracking strength, as the armoured giant battled to fend him off.

With a roar of pain and a massive thrust Pyrus sent Thorn tumbling away from him, where he rolled fluidly to his feet in the centre of the throne circle.

'Oh bravo' shouted a voice.

'Quiet you fool' hissed another, 'this is no game – at least, not now.'

It seemed that Pyrus had realised the same, for without even a glance at his immortal mistress he drew his giant axe.

'Come' boomed Pyrus' grating, metallic voice, the face on the helm twisting the words obscenely. 'Die upon the same blade that slew your mother. The demon in this blade fed upon her soul…. you should know this. Or did not the order of Oldoth tell you – even as they cast her body from the cliff in their precious and false ceremony?'

'No!' Thorn staggered.

'In Oldoths' name no….please.'

'Ah, they did not tell you I see. Demon blades child; they need to be fed and souls are their meat.'

Thorns' world span as he remembered his mothers' laughter, and the endless love reflected in her eyes. The times when she'd held him when he was ill and sung him to sleep. She did not deserve this fate, or any such fate. She deserved life, but it was not his to give.

He dropped to his knees. It was too much. That she was gone was enough, but to have been consumed, her very soul eaten. What was he to think? He was numb. It was all gone – his mother dead, his father lost, Alazla lost. It was over.

Pyrus was beside him now and raised the axe.

An expectant hush dropped across the plateau. Pyrus looked for a moment to Veylistra who nodded.

'Die by the same blade child….fitting' he grated.

He was numb and through that haze he could hear the heart beat of the giant as he loomed over Thorn. Somehow it seemed slow. But what right did that giant have to a heart beat, to life, when all that Thorn knew was dust?

The axe swung and Thorn looked up.

He saw the demon in the blade smiling at him as the blade descended; its massive maw filled with razor sharp teeth was opened wide, as its roar joined that of Pyrus.

To him, the blade moved slowly. What right did Pyrus have to life!?

Thorn reached up and stopped the blade a span from his face. Its blade rested quivering upon the palm of his hand.

Pyrus staggered with the force of the blow. It was as if he had struck solid rock.

Thorn wrenched the axe blade from Pyrus, and swung it upwards. Pyrus' head span away from his body, and blood fountained into the air, as the corpse tottered before collapsing.

'Feed while you can demon' said Thorn and then cast the blade at the mountain where it exploded with a wail, in a flash of green fire.

- CHAPTER 11 -

Corruption

The faltering heart within the giant Pyrus' body pumped the remnants of his blood across the violet rock, from where it created tiny scarlet rivers.

Thorn felt nothing as he stared at the headless corpse. He was as empty as this desolate world, this mockery of a realm, beholden to the child of a god. Why did he not feel elated? Why did he not feel sated, somehow? Justice had been done; he had avenged his mother. Instead, there was just this emptiness. For the first time in his life he had been able to stand up for himself, he'd put something right and he felt – nothing.

And yet, how had he done this thing? What he had just done would have been beyond even Alazla, beyond.....anyone.

'I'm changing' he said simply, rubbing at the blue stain in the palm of his right hand. The tiny stars within it were bright this morning.

'Of course, you are.'

Thorn had not heard Veylistra walk up beside him. Here eyes were wide with compassion, the golden flecks within bright as fireflies.

'You carry the seed, of a fallen avatar within you Thorn. You must embrace your destiny now; become so much more than you ever were!'

A sudden understanding struck Thorn then as he watched the orbiting stars within his palm. 'It was you that night wasn't it? It was you who killed the Avatar.'

The change of topic appeared to catch Veylistra off guard for a moment and she just shrugged delicately.

It was another, though who replied to Thorn. An aged man with frosty white skin and wearing a long scaled grey coat that shimmered like fish scales arose from his throne. His voice was soft, barely above a whisper as he walked toward Thorn, with deliberate slowness, but surprising fluidity for his age. 'You cannot fool this one Veylistra and you are the fool, if you think to. His mind it seems is likely the equal of any here.'

'Keep out of this Rivadus-Hex' spat Veylistra.

'No, I don't believe that I shall' returned Rivadus-Hex, and he closed the distance to Thorn, with barely seeming to move. His voice was close now, but still little more than a whisper. 'What happens now concerns us all, concerns all of the council of seven.' He said this last louder and swept his arm about, encompassing all of those seated on the thrones.

'To answer your question Thorn, yes it was Veylistra who slew the avatar and She did so at the behest of *this* council.'

Rivadus turned white eyes upon Veylistra then. 'This boy is not your play thing, Veylistra – Queen of a broken world. He belongs to all of us.'

This last brought murmurs of assent from all on the thrones.

'I don't belong to anyone' said Thorn, surprised at the strength in his own voice.

'Of course you don't' responded Veylistra lightly, and touched his cheek softly. Thorn felt passion flush his face at her slightest touch, and his gaze lingered for a moment on her ripe form, hidden only beneath gossamer silk and silver armour.

Veylistra returned his gaze with a smile. Embarrassed, Thorn looked away to Rivadus-Hex.

However, Rivadus' returning smile was filled with black fangs, and Thorn took an involuntary step back.

'I want to go home' said Thorn weakly. It sounded pathetic, even to his own ears. He just wanted to return to his father, to hold him and see Alazla again.

'Your fate, lies on a different path now, boy' said a plump lady, with bright rouge on her cheeks and a voluminous pink dress to match, that made her look to Thorn like a fat pink balloon. It should have made her appear slightly comical, but when Thorn looked into her eyes; it was like looking into those of a snake; dark and empty of life.

The plump lady had a tray of sweets on the arm of her bronze throne, from which she grazed continually. As she crammed sweets into her mouth she said, 'there is no way back for you boy. You carry the seed of an Avatar within you now….and there are few of those left. And of course, we won't let you go anyway.'

Thorn felt his new anger flare and he stepped towards her, his fists clenched. 'You're going to send me home lady.'

Her chuckle was light, though it never reached her eyes. 'You are deluded child. You're corruption has already begun' and she gestured to the headless corpse at his feet, as she dabbed at her mouth with a floral napkin. 'Have you killed many people before Thorn?'

Thorn was not prepared for that and stared at the headless corpse, as if for the first time. The world blurred and he sank to his knees.

'Heh. Pathetic' laughed Rivadus-Hex.

'Enough!' snapped Veylistra.

Thorn was aware of her presence kneeling beside him, and she wiped his mouth with a cloth as he hung his head.

There was steel undertone in Veylitras' voice. 'He has had enough for now brethren. This session is at an end. Leave me.'

'Leave you?' Rivadus-Hexs' soft voice was laced with menace. 'This is a Council Veylistra and just that. You are not a Queen. We go where we please.'

Thorn looked up weakly, coughing, as Veylistra surged to her feet. Her armour flashed bright, and her raven hair streamed out behind her, as a sudden wind moaned across the plateau. 'Equal we may be Rivadus-Hex, and broken though it is, this *is* my world, my power here is absolute. You will all leave and leave now.' Her gaze swept about the bronze thrones.

Stony faces regarded Veylistra, though one-by-one they all arose from their thrones and walked to a circular bronze disk in the centre of the plateau, where they were vanished into a column of blossoming green fire.

As Rivadus-Hex proceeded to the disk, he never took his white eyes from Veylistra. 'Do not seek to betray us Veylistra. The Council would not forgive you. *I* would not forgive you.'

He turned, and pulling his rippling scaled coat about him stepped into the column of green fire, where he vanished.

'They're gone, Thorn.' Veylistras' voice was soft and compassionate. 'You and I are alone now. It is just us - on this entire world. You are safe.'

Safe, those words resonated with Thorn. How he had always longed to be safe, safe and protected.

'I won't let them back, if you don't want me to.'

'I don't know what I want' mumbled Thorn. 'There's nowhere left for me to go.'

He looked then directly into her eyes, and the look she returned was solemn. 'Why did you kill the Avatar Veylistra?'

She sighed, and knelt beside him. It was, he thought, an oddly submissive gesture. 'Though immortal Thorn, I'm also a prisoner. This Rune upon my cheek and those of all immortals (and there are hundreds of us), chains us to the world of Rune and its moons. We can go no further. We should be able to roam the stars. The universe should be our playground. But, instead, we must live out the countless ages of our lives here, and only here.'

'But why' whispered Thorn, his heart in his throat as he thought of Veylistra a prisoner.

'Because the younger gods are capricious!' hissed Veylistra and for a moment her beautiful face contorted with anger.

The immensity of it was threatening to overwhelm Thorn again, and he struggled with his words. 'Why, why do you need me?'

'You carry power now Thorn. You have it within you to open the door to great power, power that can set me.....set us, free!'

He shook his head. 'How? Why me? I...'

'Enough' She replied and the look in her eyes caught the breath in Thorns' throat. Veylistra lips parted and she leaned into him. The heat of her breath was on his face. The scent of her was intoxicating, it was around him and within him. He could think of nothing else.

Heat swelled within his loins, even as fear and confusion worried the edges of his mind. 'But I've never....I, I don't know how.'

Her lips descended onto his and all confusion and uncertainty was swept aware on a river of passion.

They made love upon a mountain plateau, on a desolate world, where the moaning wind whisked away their cries of pleasure.

And as Thorn lay atop her, Veylistra cried out in ecstasy as the fire of his innocence spilled into her and unknown to Thorn, she consumed it.

Later when Thorn slept, Veylistra stood alone and naked upon the edge of the plateau, the toes of her bare feet curled upon the very edge of the cliff, making their silver charms chime in the breeze. She ran her hand thoughtfully through her thick hair. His innocence burned in her, She could feel it like a fire in her belly, adding to her strength. He was bound to her now.

Veylistra had felt him approach; none could enter this world without her consent.

'What have you done?!'

'Only what I needed to Cinder' she replied turning, though still balanced lightly on the cliff edge.

The immortal son of Oldoth, god of sun and storms, stood smouldering before her. His eyes were like fiery coals, and his ebony plate mail steamed with the heat from his body, setting the fiery whorls and patterns on it ablaze. His great flaming sword Kalak-Dade was sheathed across his back.

Cinders' glowing eyes roamed freely over Veylistras' nakedness. She scowled and a simple woollen dress appeared to cover her.

Concealing her irritation further she took Cinders' arm, ignoring the tremendous heat from his body. 'In my position, would you have done any different?'

Cinder laughed and disengaged his arm. 'No probably not, but the other Council members will not think it as amusing as I.'

'He is bound to me now Cinder and only to me. I can feel him where he sleeps and feel the heart that drives the blood about his body. I can see the childhood dreams that chase through his sleeping mind.'

Cinder did not reply immediately, his craggy black face deepening in thought, his mane of yellowed hair, making him appear somewhat feline. He stared far out across the barren plains below. Finally, he replied. 'The others may not be as understanding as I. You and I, we have always been…...close.'

Veylistra took a step away from him as she said. 'They will have little choice but to support me. They cannot undo this.'

'It seems that none of us has much choice' grated Cinder. 'But he is not yet yours, or ours. He is bound by ties of love to his home and to his friends, especially Alazla. This remains and you must break him of it.'

'Alazla holds a demon blade Cinder. You forget. That blade will eventually drive him to evil, unless it consumes him first.'

'We don't have time Veylistra.' Cinder clenched a gauntleted fist for emphasis, which promptly burst into rippling flame. 'The divine orders could uncover this at any time! And, if they know, then the gods know.....at which point being chained only to Rune will be the least of all our problems!'

Veylistra turned away from him, and sighed, hugging her shoulders. 'You are right Cinder. I will do what I must.'

Later, when Thorn awoke from a deep and untroubled sleep, he saw Veylistra sitting in a simple woollen dress near the cliff edge. Her knees were drawn up to her chin, and somehow against the mountains and towering bronze ruins, she looked very small and vulnerable.

He threw off a blanket and realising he was naked hastily drew on his clothes, barely noticing how torn they were, and covered in dirt and blood.

Veylistra looked up, as he approached, a welcoming smile on her face. 'That my handsome prince will never do, and with a wave of her hand his dirty clothes vanished, to be replaced with an emerald silken shirt, woollen trousers and bright black boots. Running a hand through his hair, he realised that it had even been combed.

Grinning a little self consciously, he sat beside Veylistra at the cliff edge, but did not touch her. He felt a little unsure of himself, as if she was a precious object that he didn't know if he was allowed to touch again, when all he wanted to do was reach out and hold her.

'Don't I get a kiss then? Or have you gone off me already?' She quipped.

Thorn grinned and leaned in to kiss her. Her lips were warm and parted hungrily beneath his. He felt his ardour stir again, like a stoked fire, and he reached out clumsily for her.

Veylistra pulled back and placed her head upon his shoulder instead. 'There are things that we still need to discuss, Thorn.'

'Can't it wait?' said Thorn, not so easily deflected.

'No, there are things happening in the world, even as we sit here. This cannot wait.'

'Fine, what is it?!' he grouched.

'You must embrace the seed within you Thorn, accept what you could be. Only then will you realise your potential.'

'What?!' said Thorn, so shocked for a moment that his hand slipped on the cliff edge. 'You want me to accept the seed of an Avatar. That's ridiculous! How can I, I'm just Thorn! I can't even comprehend what that even means!'

'No! You are so much more than that already. Look at what you did yesterday. Pyrus was a trained warrior from Zamad-Dun, part of a warrior cast and bound with magic. You slew him Thorn….and in doing so, righted a great wrong.'

Thorn knew that she was right. He felt different. There was a strength in him now, and he found that he liked it; strength had replaced the fear, fear that he had carried his entire life, a fear that had always forced him to hide behind Alazla. 'It's good not to be afraid Veylistra, but that's it, I'm still just Thorn. I think I always will be.'

'I know, and that is why there is more that you must do.'

'What?' Thorn replied cautiously.

'You must avenge yourself! Cut your ties with your past and overcome it. Become what you were destined to be. Those that picked on you Thorn, where you once lived, they are nothing more than worms! Yes, I know of this, I see the fear rise in your eyes once again. You must visit them Thorn and repay them. Alazla too, yes, your friend, were it not for him, you would not have had to hide your entire life!'

The very thought of Lorm and his pack of college bullies made butterflies dance in Thorn's stomach. His heart began to hammer. And Alazla was his friend, a lifetime friend, were it not for him Thorn knew that his life, such as it had been, would have been an utter misery. 'No. I won't do it. And Alazla is like a brother to me. Can't I just stay here with you?'

'You must do this thing Thorn. Avenge yourself! Overcome your fear, overcome your past and then do, do…what you think is right.'

'No, I won't hurt them and I won't betray Alazla!'

'The strong take from the weak Thorn, it is the way of things, but you don't need to hurt them Thorn, not if you don't want to.'

'Why can't we just stay here Veylistra, you don't need those others….you've got me now.'

Veylistra sighed, and took his hand in hers. He decided that it was a nice feeling, her holding his hand.

'Please Thorn, do this for me. I need your help. Without what you could become I'll never be free of this world, or of this cursed Rune that scars my face. None of the Council will be free. Only if you awaken the power within you can this be done Thorn, my love, please.' Her eyes were wide and with her head on his shoulder he felt her presence like a heat, and he understood then, that he would do anything for her.

He raised her head from his shoulder and gazed into the golden sparks that orbited with her wide eyes, and though he knew that it was wrong, Thorns' resistance utterly crumbled. 'Okay.'

Veylistra smiled, and the heat of her lips met his.

- CHAPTER 12 -

The Axe

The house was unremarkable. Certainly it could not be called a slum, for there were no such dwellings in 'radiant' Korth, yet it was assuredly poor. Sited in the Stone District it had once been lovingly painted a soft green, which was now only slightly peeling.

Liandra bustled inside. Once lustrous golden hair was pulled back into a ponytail, now streaked with grey. Her apron bore the dust of cleaning, and the stout straw broom swept relentlessly in brisk motions across the already spotless stone floor. Normally a gently hummed song would have graced the air, often heard by passers-by who would smile at the familiar sound. Today there was no song, just the harsh swish of the beleaguered broom.

She paused to wipe a dusty hand across her face and unbeknownst left a trace of dirt across her high cheekbones. Glittering blue eyes which had captured the heart of many a would-be suitor were clouded and worried. Pausing for a moment, Liandra glanced towards the door of the only bedroom in the house. Seeming to make a decision, she propped the broom against a wall and moved towards the bedroom door. Cautiously she opened it.

In the ancient rocking chair beside the bed sat Alazla. He sat there as he had sat for a week now; scarcely moving, with that axe in his lap.

When he had first brought the axe home, Liandra had not commented, since it was not entirely unknown for senior students to practise combat with real weapons and certainly Alazla had been keen to pursue a military career, possibly in the Korthian Fist. As the days had passed, though, Alazla had not even moved from the chair. Liandra then not only became concerned about him, but also about the axe. She was not sure why, but the blade gave her an uneasy feeling. When she tried to look at it, her gaze would seem to slide off it, as if it were somehow greased.

Her son's only movement was when from time to time he would run his hand across the blade, muttering unintelligibly. He'd not said a word to his mother for days, and had eaten hardly anything. His face was gaunt, cheekbones hollow, eyes shadowed pits. Liandra could get him to eat nothing now and she feared deeply for her son.

What had happened to shatter her beautiful, robust son so, Liandra could not even guess, and neither could she seem to find out any information. She had gone to the Three Barrels Inn to seek out Thorn, initially suspecting that it was the result of yet another disastrous prank that the two had managed to concoct. But the inn was closed and there was no sign of either Thorn or his parents.

An awful feeling of dread had settled on Liandra then. Not knowing what else to do, she had run all the way from the inn to the Square of Knowledge, drawing startled looks as she went. In despair she had found the school gates locked for the Seventy Seven festivities. Asking about, she had managed to track down the old troll Master Fafner, the boys' (as she thought of them) teacher in ancient lore, to his home.

After recovering from the initial shock of seeing such a distressed mother on his doorstep, with his ears seeming to wilt, the old troll had regretfully told her that he had no idea where either Thorn or his parents were, or indeed why Alazla appeared to be in such a condition. After tending to Liandra with an assortment of strange teas and cakes, which largely tasted like so much rock, he promised to find out what he could. He had contacts in the Fist, and would be sure to make enquiries. With the troll's rumbled reassurances in her ears, Liandra had gone on her way.

Four days had passed and Alazla still sat in his chair. It had been just the two of them now for almost as long as Liandra could remember, and she had no one else to turn to.

The knock at the door made Liandra almost jump out of her skin with fright. Hoping to see the wizened face of Master Fafner on the other side of the door, she practically flung it open. A beloved son of Oldoth stood upon her doorstep, his golden hair flaring about his head like some form of halo.

'Oh,' gasped Liandra, as she gaped in both surprise and disappointment.

The beloved son's handsome face creased in concern as he spoke. 'I'm sorry, I did not mean to startle you. I am Brother Balthazar of the divine order of Oldoth. I would like to talk to you. If this is a bad time, though, I would be happy to come back.'

Liandra clutched feebly at her skirts, hands clenching and unclenching, her thoughts racing. Could this be connected to Alazla's condition, she wondered? Certainly sons of Oldoth did not usually just present themselves upon her meagre doorstep, and she feared that the timing was no coincidence.

'No, please come in,' she said with a frown, opening the door for the son. Balthazar stepped inside, noticing the immaculate though painfully plain interior of the house.

Liandra offered the son a drink, which he politely declined. Cursing herself inwardly, she realised that sons and daughters of Oldoth drank nothing but natural rainwater. Colour rose in her cheeks.

Feigning not to notice, Balthazar said, 'Thank you for you time, Liandra. I have come to talk to you about your son, Alazla.'

Liandra swallowed as a sinking feeling started in her stomach.

'I know that your son has not left the house for a week now and I am sorry that you have worried and fretted. We would have come to you sooner, but highly urgent matters drew our full attention elsewhere.' At that, he seemed distant for a moment. 'But I am here now,' he said kindly, and leaned forward to take her hands.

'This will be hard for you, Liandra, but you need to know what happened a few days ago. Before I tell you, though, I must ask that you repeat this to no one.'

Worry overriding what the son had asked, Liandra simply nodded.

With that, Balthazar began Thorn's tale.

****

In the adjacent room, Alazla caressed the axe. Its touch both thrilled and revolted him. The steel of the blade had a slight greenish hue, and from time to time shadows and ripples would chase across its oily surface. It was enchanting. Alazla knew that the blade's very presence was an obscenity to the world. He knew that, but he did not care.

The axe was all he had left.

Thorn was gone, carried into darkness by the giant warrior. The friend, as much a brother, with whom he had grown up and shared so much laughter and pain, had been ripped from him. It seemed impossible. Without Thorn, his brother, he was simply incomplete.

What Alazla had seen with his own eyes contradicted so much that he knew, so much that he had been taught! The values that the kingdom of Korth represented, where were they now? And now his friend was dead! Didn't they teach that true evil did not exist? That lie had been exposed for the sham that it was.

Evil had broken into the House of Oldoth, and the sacred blood of sons and daughters had then anointed the soil of their so damned holy house. The blood of Thorn's mother Catherine had joined theirs to blacken the earth, as she'd sought to protect her only son with her own frail mortality.

Alazla rubbed the axe-blade; hatred and anger coiled through him like a living thing. The muscles of his forearms twisted as he clenched and unclenched his fists.

He had sworn to protect Thorn, to always be there. Although not born of the same flesh, they were brothers in spirit. Alazla had protected Thorn with his body. Thorn had always protected Alazla with his mind. The two were one. Without his friend he was empty.

No, he was not empty. He had hate. Hate was a hollow thing, a hollow thing that gnawed inside you. But it was better than the emptiness. Like the curling green shadows within the blade, Alazla embraced the hatred within him. He fed it the cherished memories of his friend. He stoked it until the fire within him roared with an unearthly howl.

He had not noticed his mother's ministrations as she tried to talk to him and even feed him. The reasoning, the touching, the crying, none of it reached him. It was meaningless. The axe had meaning, though; it could bring him revenge.

Alazla's consciousness became slowly aware of murmured voices in the next room. He recognised one voice; Balthazar, the divine fool, who had done so little to save his friend. Without him and his meddling Thorn would still be alive. The concerned voices rose and fell in conversation. Somewhere he was aware that his mother was crying, deep racking sobs. He knew that he should go to her. Alazla loved his mother deeply. They had survived together. But he could not. Where his love had dwelt, now there was only hate. Though he knew that hate would not sustain him, at least he felt alive.

Instead, he slid smoothly to his mother's single pallet bed, and placed the axe under the stuffed straw mattress. As he sat back down in the chair, the door opened.

Alazla was aware of Balthazar leaning over him, but did not even look up. He heard his mother crying. He did not react as the beloved son placed a gentle hand under his chin and lifted his head. As his head rose, Alazla allowed himself to look at Balthazar and the hate roared behind his eyes like a furnace. Alazla's eyes bored into that weak and gentle face, the eyes so clouded with a false concern.

'Abomination!' shouted Balthazar, involuntarily taking a step back.

Reacting with the speed of a striking snake, Balthazar slammed his hand onto Alazla's chest, above his heart.

Alazla tried to recoil, but he could not: Balthazar was too strong. He struck out with his fist and heard it connect, but to no visible effect. He heard strong words chanted and the name of Oldoth spoken.

'Mum, help me!' Alazla shrieked.

'Let him go! Let him go, bastard!' shouted Liandra as she pulled futilely at Balthazar.

Suddenly a deep calm settled over Alazla and the hatred receded like black clouds scattered before a fierce wind.

Chest heaving as if he had just run a league, Balthazar gasped, 'Child, look at me. Are you well? Alazla? Look at me, child.'

Eyes swimming back into focus, Alazla looked into the concerned face of Balthazar. 'Yes, yes. Thank you. I think so,' he replied.

His mother flung her arms around his neck. 'Oh, my child,' she sobbed, 'I'm so very sorry. I know Thorn's gone now. I'm so very sorry.'

Tears came unbidden to Alazla's eyes at last and he let them run down his face without shame. Grimly he replied, 'I know, mum. Don't worry, though, we'll see him again. I'll have my brother back.'

Alazla didn't notice Balthazar watching him intently as he said those words.

'I will leave you both now,' said Balthazar. 'Oldoth's blessing protects you now, Alazla. I do not think that you will face that darkness again. I should have foreseen that other enchantments may have been at work that day… it seems that there was much that I missed.'

The beloved son paused in the doorway, though his gaze was distant. 'I know that it is not easy, but try not to fear for your friend. Thorn's spirit will reside with Oldoth now. He dwells within the aerial host and his name will be in our prayers. The Order will see that your immediate needs are cared for, Liandra. You have my word.'

With that Balthazar turned and left, leaving behind only his lingering words and the gentlest hint of a summer breeze.

Weeping, Liandra clung to her son. Alazla buried his face in his mother's shoulder and wept for his lost brother and friend.

Later that night, when the tears had dried and Alazla stared unseeing at his bedroom ceiling he heard the sultry whispered calls of the axe. He did not hesitate and retrieved it from beneath the mattress and listened to its whispered promises of revenge.

- CHAPTER 13 -

Home Sweet Home

Thorn appeared in the courtyard of the Three Barrels Inn, although nobody could have seen him, steeped as he was within coiling shadows.

It was evening and Veylistras' face in the heavens above was covered in cloud, as if his immortal lover had become suddenly coy. The ivory Solstice Moon cast at best a half-hearted light across a gate that creaked harshly on broken hinges, and crude boards nailed in haste across lovingly painted shutters.

It took Thorn a moment to recognise his family home.

'What am I doing here?' he whispered. Thorn didn't understand; this was not what Veylistra had asked him to do. Those he sought wouldn't be here.

'But what's happened here?' he said to himself as he stepped out of the shadows of the outhouse. He recalled a fleeting memory of when he'd raided that same outhouse for a bottle of black spite that he'd drunk with Alazla. The memory felt like it belonged to someone else.

He walked to the backdoor that led directly into the kitchens. The lock had been kicked in and the stout oak had broken, so that the door hung mournfully askance on its hinges.

Stepping into the kitchen with its thick oak work tops and giant iron ovens, the smells of roast dinners, the crash of pans and his mother shouting at her assistant Lisa, all washed over him and his grief returned welling up, thick and cloying inside him.

He stepped around copper pans that had once been so lovingly burnished and had hung in orderly ranks from the walls. Noticing a small iron pan, he reached down and retrieved it from under a counter, remembering when his mother had let him play with it, pretending it was a shield in his fights against dragons. He placed it gently back on the hook where it usually hung, beside its fellow.

But where was his father? Thorn didn't understand why he wasn't here. They didn't have any other homes, this was it. His parents had worked their whole lives to build up this inn.

'Dad' Thorn shouted, 'Dad, are you here?'

The only answer to his call was the mournful creak of the broken gate from the courtyard outside.

Thorn pushed open a dark pine door whose surface was worn smooth by the passage of his parents hand over the cycles and moved into the main bar.

The bar, whose surface had once gleamed with oil, now lay under a layer of dirt and dust. The trace of mice feet could be seen across its surface. There was no sign of any stock behind the bar, everything from the bottles of Spite to barrels of mead and ale had all gone.

'Dad' Thorn shouted again, 'Dad where are you? Dad?'

Most of the chairs and tables were overturned. He recalled helping his father to make those tables and chairs, when they had first bought the inn. Desperately short of money, his parents had done anything that they could to economise, and that included everything; from making their own bar furniture, to building an outhouse and fitting bottled glass in the windows, to help keep out the chill.

Not quite sure why he moved around the bar room picking up the tables and chairs. He recalled where each one went, placing it carefully, noting as he did so, the firm plane and chisel strokes from his fathers hand that still marked many of them.

He had decided to go upstairs and check the bedrooms when a crashing noise stopped him in his tracks.

That came from the cellar he thought. He started to move towards the cellar door located behind the bar, when it opened.

Two young men stepped into the room, their arms full of bottles of wine and ale. Thorn recognised them immediately and his stomach clenched in fear; Ralf and Mika; Lorms' lieutenants and ring leaders in the pack that had often bullied Thorn.

Ralf and Mika both halted in the cellar doorway, shock evident on both their faces. Ralf appeared sheepish, a ruddy blush creeping up his thin face until it reached his close cropped hair. Mika, more rotund than his friend, and carrying even more, flapped his mouth for a moment before speaking. 'You're meant to've gone!'

Thorn didn't know what to say. He was caught between his instinctive fear of these two, the fact that they were obviously stealing from his parents' inn and frantic concern about where his father could be.

Somewhere within him, Thorn hoped that they'd have a spark of decency and croaked. 'Do you know where my Dad is?'

This was obviously not what they'd expected him to say and depositing their armloads on the floor, they stepped round the bar.

Both were grinning as they approached, apparently having got over their shock.

Thorn smelt Mika before he even reached him. He'd forgotten that he smelt almost as bad as he looked. Had it not been for the fact that his personality matched his odour, it's just possible that Mika would have been bullied in the same way Thorn had been.

Stopping a few spans from Thorn Mika wiped a dirty hand across his already filthy shirt. 'You're meant to be wiv your Dad stupid! Meant to av gone some place else! What yo doin ere?'

'Agghhh, poor thing, Daddy left and lost you did he?' said Ralf, scratching at the half stubble that he affected.

Trying to keep the quiver out of his voice Thorn said 'look, you can keep what you were taking if you want. Just tell me if you've seen my Dad....please.'

'Oh that's generous. But we're gonna to keep it anyway, cos there's nothin you can do' said Mika.

'I'm thinking that if he's here and asking us questions about where his folks are, that means no one knows he's here,' said Ralf, with a feral glint in his eyes.

Thorn did not miss the way his fist clenched.

Mika grinned.

'Oh dear' said Ralf 'looks like it's another bad day for poor old Thorny. Lost his daddy, he gets a beating and we take all his stuff.'

'Good day for us dou.' Mika laughed.

Thorn backed away and held up his hands, he was ashamed to see that they were shaking. 'Look, we don't need to do this. Go. Please.'

'You wish' said Ralph, as he shoved Thorn in the chest.

Trying to back away, Thorn bumped into one of the tables he'd righted and started to back around it.

Mikas' face twisted in pleasure as he launched his first blow, which took Thorn straight in the stomach. The air exploded out of Thorn and he almost doubled over, where he met an upper cut that launched him from his feet, catapulting him across the table behind him and then onto the floor.

Before Thorn could get to his feet they were on him like dogs savaging a kitten. Blows rained down and he attempted to cover his head but still they came. He curled into the foetal position getting smaller and smaller and still the blows came. 'Please' he croaked, 'please stop.' Whether they heard him or not he couldn't tell, it was all becoming numb. He was vaguely aware of something breaking, his ribs he wondered, it all seemed oddly distant, as if it were happening to someone else.

At what point the fear finally left him, he never knew. He was aware of the blows, still coming, though by all rights they must now know that he was apparently unconscious. The anger was a tight thing, bound with wire in the pit of his stomach and it fed him. As he focused, he was aware of his ribs popping back into place and the bruising to his inner organs receding.

Thorn stood up.

The young men stepped back astonished.

'Wh, what?' managed Ralf, his eyes wide in amazement.

'You need to leave' said Thorn. The anger within him heaved at the wires that bound it. 'Please…just go.'

'Not bloody likely' snarled Mika, and he picked up a broken chair leg from the floor. 'Looks like you've learned how to take a beating. Means we just gunna have to hit ya harda.'

Thorn backed away, something made his voice boom unnaturally across the room. 'No!' His chest was heaving now with the effort of maintaining control. Sweat beaded his brow. 'Please, go now. I can't, I can't….'

'He can take a beating' said Ralph 'but he's still scared, common give me that.' And he grabbed the chair leg from Mika and swung at Thorns' head.

Thorn watched the blow calmly as it came aimed directly at his temple, and he unleashed the anger. The chair leg never even reached him. His fist shot out and struck Ralf in the sternum, there was a reverberating crack as the sternum broke and Ralf shot across the room where he struck the wall opposite, to slide down to the floor still clutching the chair leg.

Mika watched on, his jaw moving up and down but making no noise, as Thorn stalked across the room. He did not notice that the floorboards creaked under his weight.

He felt no pity as he looked down on Ralf, noting how though half conscious his hand was trying to reach into his jacket, presumably to find a knife. Thorn reached down and casually tore the chair leg from Ralfs' hand and without a thought drove it straight into his chest and with such force that it sank into the floorboards beneath. Ralfs' scream was piteous and blood burst from his mouth as he thrashed.

It seemed that Mika had found his voice and feet, for when Thorn turned, the sweating bully was backing away. He blubbered and made little sense. Thorn noted with amusement that he appeared to have soiled himself, no doubt adding to the stench.

What Thorn did not know, was what Mika saw, and that was a young man with eyes of darkness surrounded by tendrils of shadow that whipped and struck like vipers.

'Pppplease, av mercy…don't hurt me.'

The shadow vipers spat at Mika.

'That would be the same mercy that you showed me, I expect?' said Thorn smiling.

Thorn picked up another broken chair leg and strode across the room. Mika whimpered and tried to flee, but he had not taken one step before Thorn had him by the throat. Mika looked into those dark eyes then and saw his death.

He screamed piteously as Thorn drove the chair leg into his chest and pinned him to the wall.

Thorn did not move until Mika had stopped thrashing.

Thorn shook his head as he looked about him. 'Huh, home sweet home.'

'Now, it's time to have a *chat* with Alazla.'

- CHAPTER 14 -

Revenge

Alazla had finally returned to college two weeks later. His mum had felt that it was the right thing to do. She was probably right: life had to go on, but that didn't make it easy.

Alazla had always been popular and been blessed with many friends. Yet he'd never felt the twisting agony of bereavement before and it left him desolate. He was moving in a world that was painted in ash and dust. Nothing seemed important any more, and certainly not college or any of his other friends. Anything people said to comfort him seemed meaningless and empty. Thorn had been his brother in spirit, coaching and supporting Alazla in more ways than Thorn ever really knew.

Would this feeling of emptiness ever leave him he wondered? And yet, he didn't want it to, because that would be to accept that Thorn had gone, that he had been lost. This might be true, but Alazla had not seen Thorn die, so he would always hold on to hope. He would never forget him. He would always believe. That thought helped.

He had attended Thorns' Mums' funeral atop a hill outside Korth. It had been a lovely ceremony conducted with great compassion by brother Balthazar. According to tradition, Catherine's body had been cast from a cliff at the penultimate moment of the ceremony. Of course it never struck the base; it simply vanished in mid-air as the aerial hosts claimed it and ensured a place for her soul in Oldoth's realm.

Thorn's father Jouran had been there. The usually trim and hearty man seemed grey and withered, almost as if he were shrinking. He had watched seemingly without emotion as his wife's body had been cast from the hillside.

Some days later Alazla, leaving college early, had gone to the Three Barrels Inn, Thorn's family home, hoping to talk to Jouran and find out if he'd heard any further news. He had found the inn locked. A sign nailed to the door simply said 'Closed until further notice.' Passing by again on several occasions, he found it still the same. Some days later he was able to find out that Jouran had left the city to stay with close family. No one knew where he was, or were not telling if they did, including Alazla's mother.

Alazla thought all of this through as he walked to school again. He really didn't want to go. There seemed so little point. Yet his mother would be disappointed in him if he didn't go, so he went, even if he did cut every day short. Liandra had been to see the compassionate Master Fafner and told the old troll only what he needed to know: urgent family business had taken Thorn and his family away and they might not return, for a long time. They sent their deepest apologies to the college. The wrinkled old troll had listened with concern, peering intently at Liandra over the top of his half-moon glasses, and gently patted her hand. He assured her that he would let the other teachers know, and that although Alazla would miss his closest friend, he was a popular lad and should not suffer too badly in the long run. It had been almost as easy as that to explain away the disappearance of an entire family.

Alazla's mind was simply not on the military studies class, which was normally one of his favourites. Mistress Mimb was an eccentric at best and a diminutive creature, standing not more than eight spans tall, with coarse black hair atop her withered skull perpetually sticking out at precarious angles. She was presently enthusing about the Blue Cinder War, waving her little arms around like a miniature windmill.

'And does anyone know how Korth discovered the deceit of the Bordish emperor?' asked Mimb brightly.

Alazla knew that Thorn would have known the answer immediately, but equally might have chosen not to answer it for fear of appearing too studious. Looking about the class, Alazla noted that no one appeared to know the answer. So Mistress Mimb commenced again: 'Well, it was of course due to the departure of the order of Aevarnia. A son of Aevarnia, an advisor to the then emperor, overheard of the deceit…'

Alazla though was finding it far more interesting to observe his classmates, although he thought to himself that he used the word 'mate' very loosely indeed. His gaze came to rest eventually on Lorm, where he sat with his sycophants, and as he did so he felt his anger begin to rise. Lorm's round and ruddy face appeared content, if somewhat bored; head resting in one hand, he was watching the antics in the courtyard below with interest.

Lorm was a tall, thickset, chubby lad who professed little interest in academics. On many occasions Alazla had met him head-on on the sports field, at least as often defending Thorn from his oppressors, including the fairly recent incident in the courtyard when Lorm had broken Thorn's nose. Though a difficult time, at least Thorn had been around then, though it seemed a lifetime ago.

Lorm turned to nudge his friend, pointing at something in the courtyard that amused him. Mistress Mimb ignored their coarse laughter.

Alazla scowled and realised that he actually hated Lorm with a passion. He was ignorant and brutal, and his bullying had brought wretchedness into the lives of many a student. One of his favourite occupations had been making Thorn unhappy. Why should an animal like Lorm be allowed to live and enjoy life, when such a good and kind person as Thorn, who had endured bullying for much of his life, had been thrust into such undeserved darkness and terror?

Alazla studied Lorm intently, noting the heavy jowls and the apparent lack of intelligence displayed in the eyes. Lorm noticed him looking and held Alazla's stare with a provocative leer. It was then that Alazla made a decision. He might not be able to change what had happened to Thorn, but he *could* do something to correct the wrongs of the past. He smiled at Lorm. Lorm's sneer faltered at Alazla's smile: he did not know how to handle the unexpected response.

Alazla promptly packed his things into his backpack and made his excuses to Mistress Mimb. Mimb, understanding the problems that Alazla was going through, simply replied, 'Of course, my dear, hurry home. We'll hope to see you tomorrow.' She then returned to boring most of the students.

Alazla hurried home. He didn't notice the occasional greeting or the beautiful crystal buildings about him that cast dancing rainbow lights across the street. He reached the Stone District of Korth and a moment later was at his house. Entering, he was pleased to see that his mother was not home.

He moved into the single bedroom. Now that he was well again his mother had returned to using it and he'd gone back to his trusty straw mattress on the floor in the living area. Reaching under the mattress, he removed the axe. His gaze lingered on the weapon, tracing it with affection, noting the greenish ripples that swam across its surface. Though he'd only had it a short time, somehow it felt like a part of him, like, an old friend. Things always felt better when he held the axe, he felt more confident, though the pain of Thorns loss roared through him again, but strangely it felt as if the axe understood that anger.

Reluctant to set it down, Alazla nevertheless wrapped the axe carefully in a loose sheet, to conceal its shape, taking care to place extra wadding around the head. Slinging it carefully over his shoulder, he slipped out of the door.

Noting that the day was becoming a little grey as the afternoon gave way to evening, he increased his pace. The students would have left college by now and there were very few places where he could enact his plan successfully.

Walking swiftly, Alazla played over his hasty plan in his mind. He knew that he could give Lorm the biggest fright of his life. It was a real opportunity to make him cringe and beg forgiveness for everything that he had done to Thorn. Lorm would pay, he would grovel, and if he didn't he would get very hurt indeed. The axe was reassuring, and warm, against his back.

Alazla did not know exactly where Lorm lived, but he knew that it was somewhere in the merchant district. Lorm's father was by all accounts a very wealthy man, which was almost certainly why Lorm never bothered to study, relying on the fact that he and his two brothers, who were equally stupid in Alazla's mind, would inherit the entire estate and extensive mercantile network.

The houses in the merchant district were not as large as some in newer parts of the city, since they were crystal-sung. Many were like miniature castles, with sparkling spires and minarets. Such a house coming up for sale was rare indeed, since most were passed down from generation to generation. Lorm's father, however, had somehow managed to buy one.

Alazla reached the corner of a quiet street that he knew Lorm would walk down on his way home. There were few folk presently about, indeed most of the residents would be still be working in their offices near the docks or warehouses.

Waiting patiently, Alazla did not yet unwrap the axe. The occasional person walked past, but either did not see Alazla or decided that he warranted no major notice. As he waited, Alazla began to construct an image of the look of terror on Lorm's face when he saw Alazla and his apparent intent.

Coming out of his daydream, Alazla heard heavy footsteps coming down the cobbled street. Peering carefully around the corner, he saw Lorm's bulk huffing down the street.

Alazla slipped back round the corner, withdrawing beneath a rose-coloured crystal arch. Checking that no one was in sight, he unwrapped the axe. Liquid green swam across its surface and momentarily Alazla saw his face reflected in the blade, contorted and grinning wickedly. He gripped the haft of the axe tightly and confidence flowing into him.

Lorm walked past. His face was flushed from the exertion of his walk; beads of sweat covered his forehead and jowls and stained his tunic.

Alazla stepped out behind him, the axe glittering in his hand.

'Lorm,' Alazla called, 'A word with you.'

Lorm spun round with a speed that belied his size. Alazla was not surprised; he knew that thinking Lorm ignorant and slow was a common mistake. Lorm's fists were clenched at his sides and his beady eyes widened as they came to rest on the axe in Alazla's hand.

The anger within Alazla was coiled tight as a spring, but his words were clear. 'You and I have something to talk about.'

Lorm didn't reply. He stared instead, transfixed by the twin-bladed axe, a look of unabridged lust now upon his face.

'You and I've never liked each other, Lorm, but that's not the problem. What I do care about is that you've targeted people weaker than you, bullied them and done your best to make their lives a complete misery. And most importantly to me, until recently that included my friend Thorn. It's going to stop - now.'

Tearing his gaze from the axe, Lorm looked into Alazla's eyes and mopped his forehead with his sleeve. A sweat stain was spreading across the front of his loose tunic and his high voice was somewhat more squeaky than normal, but he replied steadily, 'Who do you think you are, idiot, some holier-than-thou son of Lorethian?! Who made you the people's champion?' He said the last with a sneer.

Alazla stared at Lorm steadily, and gritting his teeth in anger he replied, 'You may be big Lorm but your brain's small. You only prey on those weaker than you, to make your petty and spoiled life richer. You picked on my best friend, and I should've done more to stop you. I'm putting that right. You'll apologise to me for the misery you caused Thorn and then you'll promise to stop picking on people weaker than you.'

Lorm laughed, an unpleasant high-pitched squeaking. 'Did you prepare that speech in advance, poor boy? Sounds like something that puppy Thorn would come up with.'

Alazla waited, his anger coiling tighter like a spring, and the axe began to throb in his hand as if responding to his anger. He was unaware of the green light spilling from the blade.

'Your friend was pathetic, Alazla, and deserved every beating I gave him. I even hear that his mother died recently, no doubt from a broken heart that she'd birthed such a loser.' Smiling, Lorm moved a step closer, his gaze flicking to the axe in Alazla's hand. 'You need to watch your back, Alazla. Keep your friends with you, because when you're alone I'll be there and I'll make sure that your sporting days are over this time, slum-dweller.'

Alazla's rage was now something physical and his normally jovial face was mottled with it. Anger thrummed through his every fibre. His grip on the haft of the axe was so tight that his knuckles whitened. Thoughts blazed white hot in his mind – 'beat him! Cut him down! Hurt him! The world will thank you for it.' The axe quivered in his hand eager to do his bidding. Alazla fought desperately for control.

Lorm grinned at the look on Alazla's face. 'You've not got the courage to use that,' he said, pointing at the axe. 'Belonged to your dad, did it? Oh, I forgot, you don't know who your dad is, do you, bastard?'

Oddly, Lorms words allowed Alazla to regain a semblance of control, and his breathing slowed. The anger slowly began to fade; he'd heard words like that his entire life, and whereas once they would have wounded him, now they were just that – only words and they gave him focus. 'You can't provoke me, Lorm, but are you really so stupid that you think I won't cut you down?'

Again Lorm laughed. 'You are all words, bastard. Your friend was pathetic, as are you. If he were here I'd beat him just for the joy of hearing his pathetic whimpers and to piss you off.'

Rage thrummed again in Alazla now and he physically shook with it. Green light from the axe-blade bathed his face and unknown to him that face was now reflected in blade, and it was something twisted and hateful.

'Slice him. Dice him. Tear open his corpulent belly. Avenge your friend!' Were these his thoughts, his words? He could no longer tell. His vision was clouded with the white hot fire of anger.

And then, with a momentary flash of insight, he thought, this is not me. This rage, this anger, this….lust, it is not…. Me. Revenge yes, but death, no death, that is….wrong….too much. No.

Though his body seemed to fight the will of his mind, Alazla focused on opening his hand. His jaw clenched with the effort, and veins began to throb in his temples and then the axe fell to the cobbles with a metallic clang.

His vision cleared and he took a steadying breath.

Lorm grinned.

It was then that Thorn arrived. The shadows at the edge of the alley moved of their own accord, and welcomed him. Had Thorn heard what Alazla had said about him, things might have turned out differently but, he didn't. Instead he saw the two people that he most wanted to see in one place, and it seemed, about to fight. He would observe the outcome. Things had turned out rather well.

For a fleeting moment, joy at seeing his friends' face had again filled Thorn, but the rage within him swiftly consumed it. There was only one thing that mattered now; his mistress and her love for him. He would see her freed from her bonds, no matter the cost.

Calm settled across Alazla, and he was utterly unaware that the best friend he thought lost or dead calmly watched him from the shadows.

Alazla launched himself at Lorm, crashing into his mid-section. Most young men would have been swept off their feet by the attack, but Lorm had vast bulk, and though slightly winded he brought his knee up into Alazla's face. Falling back with blood running from his eye, Alazla struck out with a swift horizontal punch, taking Lorm straight in his pudgy mouth. He was rewarded as Lorm staggered back and spat out several teeth.

'You'll pay for that, poor boy,' Lorm spat with a spray of blood.

Alazla smiled and retorted, 'I'll not pay the price; you will.'

Lorm took no notice and levelled a series of wild windmill punches at Alazla's head. Familiar with this strategy and knowing that if one of those punches connected it was probably over, Alazla dropped and rolled into Lorm's legs. Lorm stumbled, falling over the top of Alazla, his arm twisting under him as he fell. An audible crack of bone followed as he landed. Lorm cried out but kicked out with his leg, taking a prone Alazla in the ear. Alazla's ear rang with the blow and he crawled away, staggering disorientated to his feet.

Clutching his arm, Lorm clambered up and then saw the axe before him. An unholy green glow limned its outline in the fading light. Grinning, a bloody smile, he picked the axe up with his good hand.

Within the shadows, Thorn started. He recognised the demon-blade immediately, and even perceived the twisted and horned creature that raged for blood within it, as it threw itself against the glowing chains that bound it within the cursed metal. He'd not been aware of its presence. Fear for Alazla suddenly thrummed through him, whatever, the outcome of today, he was not going to see his best friend killed, and worse, his soul consumed.

Thorn began to step from the shadows, but oddly found himself constrained. Viperous shadows chased about him, and seemed to pull him back into the darkness.

Thorn strained. 'No' he hissed 'I won't let him be hurt.'

The weaving shadows tightened, and began to bite at his flesh. Thorn cried out in pain, and his rage began to burn within him and he strained at his bonds.

The moon Veylistras' Face came scudding from behind a bank of clouds, casting a sickly mauve, otherwordly light, across the alley. Her whispered voice was clear to Thorn. 'Be calm my love. Your friend may yet still win. Do not interfere….not yet.'

Thorn felt himself calm, and his love for his mistress drew him back into the shadows.

'Stupid thing to do, leaving a good weapon like this lying around' said Lorm. 'Never know what might happen if it falls into the wrong hands!' Hefting the axe, he advanced on Alazla.

Alazla suddenly knew that this had gone too far. In anger at his friend's terrible treatment by Lorm in the past, he'd sought an unconditional apology. He'd thought that perhaps this would help him to reconcile Thorn's loss. This was not going as planned; Lorm was even more malicious and brutal than he could ever have known.

Backing up carefully, Alazla held his hands up before him. 'Put it down, Lorm. Neither of us wants this….let's just both walk away.'

Lorm did not reply; he was pleased at how the axe felt in his hands, if felt right. Its weight was perfect and he could also see his handsome face reflected in the blade. He now looked forward to splitting the self-righteous Alazla open with it. Certainly he had never done anything like it before, but his father had often covered things up for him and his brothers before, by placing gold in the right hands. Lorm was certain that this would be no exception. He was going to keep this axe too: he could use it again. The axe whispered encouragement to him.

Alazla looked around desperately for help, but could see no one, though for a strange moment, he thought he glimpsed Thorns' pale face within the shadows at the edge of the street. He rubbed desperately at his eyes and the illusion, or memory, vanished. There was nothing that he could even grab to defend himself: the streets were immaculately clean, with not even a stick in sight. Great planning, he thought wryly, caught in the snare of my own plan.

Despite Lorm looming, bearing down with impending doom, Alazla managed to think calmly. Brute that he is, he'll likely go for the big strike: I'll need to dodge it and then take him when he's off balance, he thought. Alazla balanced on his toes and waited.

Sure enough, a grinning Lorm raised the axe directly over his head and swung downward at Alazla's head, seeking to split it open like a fruit.

To Alazla it seemed that Lorm's blow was slow and clumsy. Waiting until the last moment that he dared, he stepped nimbly to his left, and the blade swept down through where he'd just been standing. Grabbing at Lorm's outstretched arm, he encouraged the blow to carry on downward, thinking the axe would strike the cobbles. It didn't, because at that moment Thorn recognised his chance for revenge.

Shadow vipers dark as smoke, and faster than the eye, struck out from Thorn with gleeful malice toward the battle. Swiftly ensnaring the axe blade they tugged it slightly inward and instead of striking the cobbles, the axe struck Lorms' leg and sheared it straight off above the ankle.

Lorm collapsed with a scream, the axe falling to the street with a clang. He clutched futilely at his sheared leg stump.

Thorn hissed with glee.

'Aiiieee. Help me!' Lorm screeched to a frozen Alazla, clutching at the stump of his ruined leg, as blood pumped in great scarlet gouts onto the street.

Alazla felt no pity as Lorm thrashed. He'd brought this upon himself. Lorethian god of justice, it seemed, had delivered his verdict.

Leaning down, he picked up the axe, looking with little trace of interest at the blood on the blade. He swiftly wrapped it, not wanting to touch it more than he had too.

Lorm continued to thrash and wail, awash now in his own blood.

Looking about, Alazla noted that there was still no one in sight, his eyes slid straight over where Thorn stood within the shadows. 'Good bye, Lorm.'

He turned and walked away.

Thorn watched him go and as he did so realised that though he had achieved absolute revenge this day, he had just turned his best friend into a murderer. The realisation struck him like a blow. 'What have I done?' he whispered. 'What have I done?' He slumped to the cobbles and wept within the shadows.

- CHAPTER 15 -

The Dispensary

The triple murders were greeted with stunned shock and dismay by the city and college. There had not been a single murder in the city of Korth for scores of cycles and many citizens would now not leave their homes. The Fist had doubled its patrols.

The college had closed for the day of Lorm, Mika and Ralf's funerals, although Alazla couldn't help but notice that just two pupils actually went to them; most just treated it like a day's holiday.

College had finished for the day and several of his friends were loitering in the courtyard, discussing the murders and doing their very best to draw a reluctant Alazla into the conversation.

Ash, a fit and bright young man with a dry sense of humour, was laughing. 'If Lorm was cut clean in two as you say, Pell, then it must have been a mighty big sword. Anything smaller would probably just have bounced off his stomach.'

His friends laughed.

'Not caught the killer, though. They say that nothing was stolen from any of them, which is wierd. Apparently the Fist are looking at other motives. Doesn't make sense, if you ask me.'

Pell, a small, wiry lad, replied, 'I heard that they're going to interview everyone at the college, see if they know anything.'

Alazla looked up at this. He felt regret that Lorm had died, but surprisingly no remorse. He'd come to believe that the bully had brought his demise on himself, and frankly Korth was actually better off without him. Alazla was pragmatic about it and was not wasting any time with guilt. However, he knew that the Fist certainly wouldn't see it that way. It was also very strange about the other murders of Mika and Ralph and deeply worrying for him. Though he knew he'd had nothing to do with them, even to Alazla is seemed beyond co-incidence that both of Lorms' closest sycophants should die the same day as him. The gods knew, enough people hated them all though.

Turning to Pell, Alazla said, 'Where did you hear that?'

'Well, my uncle's in the Fist and they're not talking about much else at the moment. Want to know if they had any enemies, anyone who bore them any grudges, that sort of thing.'

Alazla's stomach sank.

Ash laughed again, elbowing Alazla. 'Well, that's going to be a long list. The three of them were about as popular as yellow fever.'

Alazla knew that Pell was right.

'Right, I'm off, guys,' Alazla said. 'See you all tomorrow?'

'What? You not coming for a game of Tyche's run?' Pell replied, referring to a game played in woods, in which someone was picked and had to make it from one point to another without getting caught by his friends. (Getting caught usually resulted in a thorough dunking in the pond.)

Alazla smiled, replying, 'No thanks, got to help my mother with the chores.'

His friends nodded and waved, respecting his wishes, knowing that he lived alone with his mother.

Alazla walked home alone, with just his thoughts for company. He didn't dwell much on Lorm, though, since in his view the dead bully was largely irrelevant now. His thoughts returned, as they often did, to his lost friend Thorn, to where he might be and whether he was he still alive or dead. It was odd that he'd heard nothing from the order of Oldoth for several weeks now. They said they cared about Thorn, and Balthazar had clearly said that he would do all he could to help, but Alazla had heard nothing from them. Perhaps, he mused, Balthazar's words had been just another set of well-meant intentions that, like so many, often simply resulted in nothing.

He worried too for Thorn's father Jouran, who in just a single day had lost both a wife and a son. The mere thought of losing his own mother left Alazla cold.

Lost in thought, Alazla found himself at his house. Opening the door he stepped inside and his heart leapt into his throat. His mother sat in one of the two chairs in the main room, her face grey. In her lap was the axe, blood still staining the blade. In the other chair beside her, the one usually occupied by Alazla, sat beloved son Balthazar, his eyes dark and unreadable.

Balthazar rose from his chair, the toned muscles rippling across his bared golden chest. 'Come in, child, and close the door behind you.'

Numbly Alazla did so. Thoughts of flight did not even enter his mind. His mother did not rise to greet him, but just stared sightlessly at the blood-covered axe. Balthazar moved to Alazla and guided him to his chair. Seating him, he remained standing himself.

'Alazla, your mother discovered this axe under your straw pallet. Not knowing what else to do, she sent for me. She can take no blame in this, son.'

Taking the blade from Liandra, he held it up before Alazla, its metallic surface rippling green. 'This is a fell blade, Alazla, and one that I am sure was carried by one of the dark warriors who attacked Oldoths' House. No doubt it was this that originally caused your subsequent illness, when the goodness within you fought the corrupting power of this blade.'

When Alazla said nothing Balthazar continued: 'I should have realised that there was something else involved in your illness after we lost Thorn, but my mind was clouded, with other concerns, and for that I am sorry. It seems that I am getting used to failure and others are paying the price for it.'

He then threw the axe to the floor with a contemptible cast, where it landed with a metallic chime, making Liandra jump. 'The question now, though, Alazla, is what are you doing with this fell weapon, and more importantly what have you *done* with it?'

Silence followed and Alazla stared forlornly at his mother. Liandra though, would not look at her son.

It was not for himself now that Alazla was concerned but for his mother; he loved her dearly and had never wanted to let her down. And yet whatever his intentions had been, it seemed that he had failed her and now she had no one else to turn to. As he reached for her hand she recoiled from his touch.

Alazla sighed and reached deep within himself. Steeling himself for the outcome, he told the truth, without blemish or omission. He recounted his finding the blade on the battlefield, taking it with him in the confusion afterwards and even knowing in his heart of its corrupting influence, yet not caring. He watched the grief in his mother's eyes as he recounted how deeply he had mourned his lost friend and how finally he had taken Thorn's revenge on Lorm.

Silence ensued and tears ran unchecked down his mother's cheeks.

Balthazar regarded him steadily. His eyes, now blue and bright, seemed to bore into Alazla's heart. Alazla met that gaze unflinching.

'And how did Mika and Ralf die Alazla? What of them?' asked Balthazar.

'I don't know' replied Alazla, as honestly as he knew how. 'I had nothing to do with that.'

The silence between them seemed to stretch out as Balthazar searched his face. Finally, he nodded.

'You must be judged, of course,' Balthazar said with a heavy sadness in his voice.

Liandra cried out, 'But he didn't kill Lorm, they just brawled; he only tried to put right wrongs of the past! No one's ever been judged for brawling. From what Alazlas' said, Lorm mortally wounded himself: it was him who picked up the axe and attacked Alazla.'

'That may be so, Liandra,' Balthazar replied with a sigh, 'but Lorm has been killed, and a triple murder has taken place, however it all happened. The Loremaster will need to make a judgement on this. Perhaps, though,' he said as an afterthought, 'there is a slim chance that Alazla may walk free.'

'But you don't think so, do you,' cried Liandra, rising to her feet. 'You think he's going to be punished, don't you?'

Balthazar hung his head, his gold hair falling across his face. When he looked up his face was calm and resolute. 'I *must* inform the Loremasters, Liandra. I'm sorry. But know this: I believe you, Alazla, although this judgement is not mine to give. The Loremasters will ascertain now whether you are telling the truth. Seek to hide nothing and you will persevere. The divine order of Oldoth will stand behind you both in this: that I pledge. We do, after all, bear great responsibility in this matter,' he added sadly.

He placed a hand upon Alazla's shoulder and said, 'I must arrange for you to be taken for judgement, son. If I go now, can I trust you to remain here until they come for you?'

Alazla nodded, taking a little solace in the beloved son's trust in him. 'You can, Balthazar.'

'Very well,' Balthazar replied, and left the house with no further word.

As soon as Balthazar had left, Liandra grabbed her son, her features contorted in panic, and pulled him up from the chair. 'You must flee, child. I have a little money; take it and go. Leave the city or get down to the port and stow away on a ship. But you must go at once: they'll be here soon. Quickly now.'

Alazla looked into his mother's brown eyes and smiled sadly. 'I won't run, mum. I stand by what I did. Although I'd not have wished that harm on him, Lorm was a menace that this city is best off without. He did us all a favour by killing himself. Wherever Thorn is now, he'll be smiling at this.'

'No, Alazla,' Liandra replied, her voice rising, 'you can't do this. The last person to be judged for murder was hanged. You must run!'

'I won't run!' Alazla's face was set in firm resolve. 'You heard what Balthazar said: they have ways of seeing the truth. I'll be proved innocent Mum– the worst I'll get is a fine for brawling.'

Liandra recognised the resolve in Alazla's face, the stubbornness and integrity that had seen him end up in so many scrapes in the past. Smiling fondly at her son, knowing that she couldn't change his mind, she finally said, 'Very well, then, let's wait.'

They did not have to do so for long. Just minutes later there was a forceful knock at the door, shaking its flimsy assembly on its hinges. Liandra's eyes shot to her son's face, which remained resolute.

Alazla opened the door. Two members of the Diamond Fist, Korth's elite, stood waiting for him, one by the door and another directly behind, holding the reins of three enormous warhorses.

The Knight's plate-mail was burnished so that it shone like silver; Korth's coat of arms, a crystal shining like the sun, was engraved into the breastplates. Their helms were visored with bars covering the eye-slits, the visors down, as if they went into battle. Each Knight carried a gleaming long-sword, unsheathed and deadly in his hand.

The Knight by the door inclined his head briefly and spoke, his voice echoing slightly. 'Alazla El-Vanium, you will come with us.'

****

Alazla was beyond bored and had already decided that prison was really not for him. The quicker they got what he was now viewing as a charade over, the better. He wanted to take his punishment and just go home.

However, things did not seem quite as simple as he'd expected – perhaps naively. They were treating him like some form of criminal mastermind. He'd been locked up in the very highest tower of 'the Dispensary', so called for that was where justice was meted out in Korth. In the past three days he'd only been allowed to see his mother once.

The Dispensary was one of the oldest buildings in Korth, built of unyielding rock, both grey and uninteresting. The crystal singers had decided not to offer the sight of true crystal beauty to criminals and had instead forced the criminals of the time to labour and build their own Dispensary: certainly ironic at the least. Alazla, now in its highest tower, would have thought that the height alone would afford a nice view of the city, at the very least. However, it was not nearly so accommodating and the slitted windows a good twenty spans above him allowed only a slight and dismal light.

All things considered, he decided that he'd had much better days; that was until the guard informed him that he had visitors. The clanging of iron doors announced that they were on their way, and then his friends Pell and Ash were escorted into his temporary home.

Alazla, overjoyed to see his friends, leapt off his wooden bunk and grasped them both in hugs which they returned in kind, even the diminutive Pell.

'Gods, it's good to see you both,' said Alazla, taking comfort in the closeness of his friends. 'And before you both ask, yes I was there and *no* I didn't kill Lorm, Mika or Ralf!'

His two friends looked at each other and breathed an obvious sigh of relief.

'So, what news?' asked Alazla. 'No doubt it's the talk of the college?'

'You're not joking there,' said Ash, so called for the early smattering of grey in his thick dark hair, smiling in a way that most people found so infectious. 'Lessons have practically halted. People are divided as to whether or not you could've done it. Those who know you have never had any doubt... or very little, anyway,' he added with an embarrassed smile.

'Listen,' interrupted Pell, his freckled complexion showing a rare concern. 'We've been told that we haven't got much time and there's something you need to know.'

Alazla quieted, concerned at what he saw in Pell's expression.

'You know my uncle's in the Fist. Well, I was round there for dinner last night and heard him talking. Obviously, Lorm's parents blame you for the death of their son and it seems that Lorm's dad's been spreading a lot of gold coin around.'

Pell paused, and taking a breath he plunged on. 'They want you hanged, Alazla, and they're paying people to make sure that it happens.'

Alazla went cold. 'Wh, what do you mean?' he asked, confused. He couldn't seem to grasp exactly what Pell was trying to say.

Pell shrugged apologetically, pushing his carrot-coloured hair back from his forehead. 'I'm sorry, Alazla, the only other thing I heard was that they'd tried to bribe their way into the Diamond Fist. Wanted to ensure you met with an accident in your cell, that you never even made it to judgement! Anyway, apparently the Knights of the Diamond Fist didn't take it too well and Lorm's dads' "representatives" spent the night in the cells.'

Alazla sat down on his bench, stunned, and was only vaguely aware of his friends being escorted from his cell and of their promises to return and muted goodbyes.

This was a worrying twist and no mistake. Alazla knew that he shouldn't have done what he had, but he'd committed no major crime in his view and had ultimately acted only in self-defence. That he could end up with Lorms' or even a triple murder pinned to him seemed utterly beyond comprehension. Muscles spasmed in his jaw and he thumped his bunk in frustration.

'Damn. How can this be happening?' he swore.

'Korth's meant to be a civilised kingdom. Damn and damn again.'

Alazla had believed in Balthazar and in the Korth system of justice, and yet here he was, being engineered as the target for the rage of a bereaved parent. Whilst he could understand their viewpoint, sympathy was still beyond him, despite his predicament. Deeper consideration allowed Alazla to realise that the facts likely made little difference to Lorm's family. What they wanted now was a target for their wrath and it seemed that he was it.

Sleep eluded Alazla that night. Each time he closed his eyes he had visions of Lorm's bloody face laughing at him as he pointed to the gallows. So he lay there with his eyes open until the grey light filtering through the window slits above announced that dawn had at last arrived.

Some time later a key rattled in the lock to his cell and a plate-mail-armoured guard announced in a hollow voice that it was time. A lump welled in Alazla's throat but he forced himself to take a deep breath and deliberately stepped out after the guard.

Their route took them down the long stairs from the tower and then through a complex of grey corridors, guttering torches and guards clad in glittering white plate-mail. None moved as he passed. Good job I didn't try to escape, he thought wryly, I'm not sure that I could have made it down from the highest tower in Korth *and* fought my way past this lot with just my bare hands. Morosely, Alazla chuckled to himself, eliciting a sharp glance from his guard.

Eventually they entered a vast circular grey hall. The ceiling was several hundred spans above, unsupported by pillars, the walls shear and smooth. The only windows were mere slits just below the ceiling. A half-hearted early morning sun cast dusty beams into the hall. One such beam fell onto the only piece of furniture in the room, a large high-backed chair carved intricately in dark wood. Sitting in the chair was an old man, hunched with the rictus of advanced age. He was clad only in a black robe that did little to fill out his frail frame, his hair sticking out in crazy wisps from his bald head. He beckoned Alazla with the barest twitch of a finger, and Alazla found himself pushed gently, but firmly, forward.

As he walked across the hall Alazla's footsteps seemed unnaturally loud and he was very aware of the presence of the guard following him. He stopped before the wizened figure. Alazla now noticed that the old man's skin carried liver spots suggesting great age. In places the skin was so thin as to be almost translucent, stretched taught across ancient and knobbly bones.

Resting on the arm of the carven chair, Alazla noticed chalks of various colours.

In a voice that creaked like old leather the old man spoke. 'I am Loremaster Cantillion, the thirteenth.'

Alazla gasped inwardly; even he'd heard of Cantillion, who sat only for the most heinous of crimes. A ball of ice suddenly seemed to sit in the pit of his stomach. The Cantillions had been Loremasters for hundreds of cycles and were known to be both rich and greedy.

Icy sweat broke out on Alazla's brow. Oddly, he was also aware of a growing warmth behind him, but he dared not turn lest it show even the slightest disrespect.

'Alazla El-Vanium, you are accused of most grievous and abhorrent crimes.'

The Loremaster pointed to a series of three simple chalk marks inscribed on the floor at his feet.

'These crimes have been marked before you so that you may understand them, and then mark your response, in your own hand. You will notice that all three marks are in different colours: this pertains to the gravity of the punishment attached to each crime. The first crime is thrice murder, of which you are accused, and it is scribed in red. The second, thrice mutilation, is marked in blue, and finally thrice theft is marked in yellow. I am sure that I do not need to explain the punishment attached to each.'

Alazla was actually not even remotely sure, although he could guess at that of the red one.

The Loremaster allowed Alazla a moment to look at the markings before him.

Spittle caught on his blue lips as he spoke in a dry wheeze. 'You will mark your response under each; yay or nay. You will not be permitted to change your response once it is scribed, and you will be judged according to it.' He paused for a moment, then before finishing, 'And if you are not already aware… we have ways of seeing the truth of things.'

Trying his best to remain composed, Alazla took the chalks offered to him by the Loremaster. Willing his hands not to tremble as he did so, he bent and wrote 'nay' beneath the mark pertaining to each crime.

The Loremaster glanced at Alazla's marks and held him with a piercing gaze. 'Very well, young one… if that is what you wish.'

Alazla jumped slightly as a hand touched him on the shoulder. Glancing round, he saw that the armoured guard was now at the far side of the hall beside the only exit. Behind Alazla stood Balthazar, his eyes bright and his bare skin glowing a soft gold, despite the oppressive grey light of the hall. His golden hair and earrings seemed quite out of place in this sombre environment. Strength blazed from those eyes.

'Well done, Alazla. Now be strong, child.' These words were spoken softly and for his ears alone.

Alazla allowed himself a moment of hope.

The Loremaster harrumphed and Alazla turned back. 'Bring in the crystal,' he snapped.

At his words a knight stepped through the door into the hall, bearing a small metal cask. His footsteps cracked unnaturally loud upon the flagstones as he marched. Reaching the Loremaster, the knight opened the cask and Cantillion reached inside. Gnarled fingers lifted out a single blue crystal shaped like a tapered spike and about a span in length.

With a crisp salute the knight withdrew.

The Loremaster ran the crystal lovingly between his fingers for a moment, intently watching Alazla. 'A rarely known secret, child, is that crystal remembers what it sees! Whatever is reflected in its surface will reside within the mind of the crystal for all eternity. As long as the crystal lives, so does the memory remain. Crystal lives - it is in fact as alive as you and I.'

'Did you know this, child?' asked the Loremaster.

Alazla shook his head and wondered at the huge implications of this revelation. Korth was thousands of cycles old! Cantillion was apparently saying that the crystal throughout Korth, from the houses to the towers, the dockyards and palaces, remembered it all: every name, every face and every word spoken throughout the ages. Crystal was probably the greatest historical archive in the world of Rune! Yet he had no time to ponder this, as the Loremaster pressed relentlessly on.

'Your little skirmish with Lorm, Alazla, took place within a crystal district, from where we have taken this crystal. Sadly, the same could not be said for the other deaths that took place within the The Barrels Inn. However, this one should be enough to unravel the fabric of your lies.'

Elation filled Alazla. Now the truth would out; they'd never convict him. They'd see that Lorm had killed himself! Ironically, Cantillion's crystal would save him! The Loremaster spun the blue crystal in his fingers and released it into the air. Rather than fall to the ground, though, the crystal hung suspended, spinning with the quietest whisper.

'Remember,' spoke the Loremaster, 'Alazla El-Vanium, remember,' and leaned forward eagerly, licking his blue lips. He blew softly upon the crystal.

Gradually the crystal span faster and faster until it hummed and began to glow with a soft blue nimbus. Light spilled from it, light that wove into distant, hazy azure images, playing out like the shadow puppets so often displayed by entertainers in the markets.

The images commenced in the alley where he and Lorm had fought. He saw Lorm enter the alleyway and halt at the point where he and Alazla had exchanged barbed words. Oddly, however, Alazla could not see himself and he guessed that this would be shown afterwards. Lorm then reeled from the first blow and windmilled punches at the vacant air.

Images flashed and blurred with the mêlée. He could barely make out Lorm and the axe, which one moment was on the ground and then the next was sweeping off Lorm's leg at the ankle. Moments later the image became startlingly clear and he saw Lorm lying there with a bluish cast, his life expiring as blood pooled about him on the street.

The image flickered and faded away.

'What trickery is this?' demanded Cantillion, half rising from his chair.

Alazla was unsure how to reply. Balthazar's hand touched Alazla's shoulder briefly in reassurance. The Loremaster irritably swiped his gnarled hand and the crystal replayed the images again, exactly as before. Cantillion sat as still as a coiled serpent, his eyes dark and hard as agates.

'Never have I seen this before. It was as if you were not even there, Alazla El-Vanium. Crystal memory is infallible!'

Alazla then realised that the Loremaster had expected Alazla's images to be played out with those of Lorm. Knowing that he had no answer to the puzzle, he wisely decided not to anger the Loremaster further and just remained quiet.

Cantillion regarded Alazla, his chin resting on steepled fingers. 'I asked you what trickery this is, child? Do you think to outwit me? And yet....perhaps, you do not even know yourself!'

Not knowing what else to say, Alazla said, 'I've no idea, Loremaster. Could the crystal somehow be uh...broken?'

A yellow smile cracked Cantillion's emaciated face, and either he did not hear Alazla's answer, or perhaps just ignored it. 'Fortunately, however, this changes little. The axe was yours by admission, Alazla, and indeed a daughter of Eli-shar the goddess of life has confirmed that the blood on the blade of the axe was that of Lorm. You admitted to attacking him, although just not to the extent of the crime. It is clear to me that you murdered a defenceless man in cold blood and therefore certainly commited the other two murders by association. You are also a coward, since you have pleaded innocent to crimes that you clearly committed and possibly the most abhorrent criminal that this city has ever seen. You are worthless, Alazla El-Vanium,' he spat.

His blue lips curled back from his yellow teeth as, staring straight into a petrified Alazla's eyes, he finished. 'You will be hanged at dawn tomorrow.'

Alazla reeled; his vision swam and he sank back incoherent. He was aware of strong arms holding him and then of being lowered to the floor. Voices were raised around him but he could not distinguish them.

Gasping for breath, Alazla peered up, trying to focus, searching for something to say, anything that would save him. Words eluded him utterly.

Balthazar loomed over the Loremaster and burned as brightly as a small sun. Shadows fled to the remotest corners of the grey hall that now shone bright as a summers' day. Balthazar's anger rolled off him in waves.

The Loremaster looked insignificant, huddled in his black robe before the son, but Alazla could tell from the glint of anger in his dark eyes that he was not cowed.

'You are a worm, Cantillion, and I shall not suffer for this,' raged Balthazar. 'Your greed has finally gone too far! I am fully aware of the attempts at corruption that have surrounded this judgement and had thought the Loremasters, as the Diamond Fist have proven to be, would be above it. Greed has a firm hold over your withered heart, Cantillion. I should have foreseen this when I found out that you were officiating. That evidence is a mockery and you will rescind the sentence immediately.'

Cantillion spat at the son, 'Your golden bangles and bluster do not cow me, son of Oldoth. I shall not rescind the sentence; it will stand. You would do well to remember that the Loremasters have the full might of Korth behind them and we are not without powers of our own. Do not seek to challenge me in my own hall!'

With that he rose to face Balthazar and looked like nothing so much as a small puff-adder rising to strike.

'I see,' said Balthazar with venom Alazla hadn't realised he could possess. 'You realise, of course, that all the gold in the world will not allow the dark clouds of night to lift from your house, Cantillion and those whom you have sired. Nor will it bring air to your withered lungs or to those of your children. A shortage of breath is a terrible thing and quite debilitating, I am told. It would be unfortunate indeed if the darkest of clouds were to chase your footsteps for the rest of your black days.'

Alazla thought that the Loremaster would strike Balthazar then, his bony hands clenched at his side. The son smiled benignly down at the incandescent Loremaster.

'I concede your point, beloved son Balthazar,' hissed the Loremaster. 'Alazla's sentence is hereby rescinded. He will instead be banished to the slave mines, where he shall labour for no less than a decade - for *each* of the three lives he has taken.' He added the last with a yellowed smile.

Balthazar hung his head.

- CHAPTER 16 -

The Web of War

Agastalen and Heath buried Rosie the next morning. They had no tools, but by unspoken agreement they dug the grave as best they could with their bare hands.

Believing from the totem in the village that Rosie had probably revered Oldamma, goddess of nature and the harvest, they said prayers over her simple grave, asking Oldamma to bear Rosie's spirit to her. Finally they marked the grave with a small sapling from the wood. With little else to say, they said their final farewells to Rosie and left her to the peace of the woods.

Their route was not difficult to find, since in effect they were headed directly south, and thus they took a simple bearing from the sun. Trudging though the dewy grass, Heath was delighted for his friend. Where many would have been jealous of such a great gift and the inherent advancement, Heath knew that Agastalen was more than ready to become a demi-mage and looked forward to the accolades that must surely come Agastalen's way for such an unprecedented first binding – when they eventually managed to get back to Arcanum, he amended.

However, sensing that his friend needed time to sort out his thoughts, Heath left Agastalen in peace for the morning as they trod the sparse woodland and fields, heading south.

Agastalen tried to sort out the riot of emotions that tumbled through his head. He knew that Rosie had been dying and that her life would probably have been measured in just a few hours beyond the brief ritual last night. Yet that did nothing to assuage the feelings of guilt that nevertheless assailed him. A binding was a gift of incalculable worth. Had Agastalen thought a little deeper he would have realised that it was a measure of his gift that he had even been able to take the binding without supervision from a fully trained mage. He worried that there had been pain for Rosie, perhaps, but again searching his recollection of events could find nothing to suggest that had been the case. It was simply that not in his wildest imaginings had he expected his first binding to happen in such a way; as all apprentices he'd assumed that one day he would be gifted his first by his master. Rosie's act was without precedent in recent cycles.

He could not deny that with his first binding he felt stronger. The vibrancy of youth was still on Agastalen, his being only twenty two cycles of age, but this was different: there was a greater strength within him that was undeniable, a spring in his stride. It was almost incomprehensible to him, how a mage with potentially hundreds of bindings must feel.

They halted for a brief lunch when the late summer sun was high in the sky. Propping his back against a craggy old oak tree, Heath waited for his friend to speak first. It was when they had finished lunch and Heath was packing their things away that Agastalen finally said, 'You don't think there was any pain for Rosie, do you, Heath?'

Understanding that his friend was wrestling with a degree of guilt, Heath smiled, and, standing up, said, 'Rosie knew exactly what she was doing, Agastalen, and even if she hadn't it would have made little difference: she was about to die anyway.' He forestalled Agastalen's reply by holding up a hand. 'But she did know, and she wanted you to have that gift. By the all the gods, man, she had to persuade you to take it! I'd have jumped at the chance myself,' he said, and chuckled. 'And stop worrying, there was no pain for Rosie. You handled the ritual flawlessly.'

Agastalen nodded in gratitude just as an arrow hummed straight past his ear and slammed quivering into an unoffending oak tree. They both spun, to be confronted by three burly warriors facing them, two holding bows levelled directly at them. As they stepped out from behind the trees their movements were almost silent and deliberate. They did not wear armour, favouring instead clothing and capes, a motley of greens and browns. The third warrior carried a sword with the ease of one accustomed to its balance. It was his flat gaze that flicked over Agastalen and Heath, taking in their apparel and situation.

Without taking his eyes off them, the leader said, 'Bind and bring them.'

One of the warriors stepped forward, slinging his bow over his back, and unhooked a rope from his belt. The other warrior retained his bead upon them.

Agastalen immediately realised that these were almost certainly part of the warrior contingent that had attacked the hamlet, and rage boiled within him. His well opened immediately inside him and he felt the power of his new binding throb to fill him with life's energy.

Anger mottled his visage as Agastalen stepped forward and snarled, 'If you take one more step I'll burn you where you stand.' He had no idea whether he was capable of such a feat but the tide of his anger cast aside such fragile uncertainties. The confidence of his tone stopped the warrior approaching with the rope, in his tracks.

The leader's eyes narrowed in a weather-worn face as he looked at Agastalen. 'Fine. Shoot him,' he said.

Agastalen frantically drew on his well. Golden energy coursed into his mind as he struggled to recall a form that could help them.

The arrow struck him in the shoulder with a force that spun him around and slammed him into the ground. He lay gasping, clawing at the grass, as the fire of agony raced through him, all thoughts of forms scattered like mist on the wind.

Heath shouted in horror and rough hands dragged Agastalen to his feet, mercilessly wrenching his hands behind his back. He screamed with the pain that bloomed through him and thankfully passed out.

****

Darkness smothered him, and to Agastalen it was a comfort. Within it he could hide from the pain, pain unlike anything he had experienced in his life.

Within the comfortable blanket of the dark he was distantly aware of a voice but he pulled away from it: the closer he got to the voice, the closer became the pain. But the voice would not go away, like a buzzing insect that he could not escape. A part of his consciousness eventually recognised the voice as Heath's. Agastalen began to swim towards the voice through the blackness that was thick as treacle.

Opening his eyes, he heard Heath gasp, 'Thank Nim, you're awake.'

His friend's face slowly swam into view, almost directly above him. Heath's strong-jawed countenance was unusually pale. 'You're not a mage yet, you idiot,' hissed Heath, his breath on Agastalen's face. 'You could've died. What did you think you were doing?'

Agastalen didn't answer, and carefully sat up in what he realised was a bed. Swimming into view came the inside of a red canvas tent. The canvas walls rippled with a light breeze, the interior illuminated only by a solitary oil lamp that was burning with a dull yellow glow on a lopsided table. The tent flap was part open and it was dark outside.

Turning his attention to himself, Agastalen was equally surprised to notice that he was naked from the waist up. The arrow had been removed from his shoulder and it was wrapped thick with wadding, much of it already soaked through with blood.

'Where are we?' said Agastalen groggily.

Heath shook his head and started to reply when he was interrupted by a deep voice from the tent entrance. 'I think that I can answer that for you.'

Pushing aside the tent flap, a tall figure entered. Certainly into his sixties, the man was lean and carried with him a sense of vigour. An intolerant scowl marked his face and his grey hair and beard were close-cropped. His full chain mail armour chimed as he marched over to the bed.

'But first,' said the man, his blue eyes glittering dangerously, 'you're going to tell me exactly what you're doing in my barony.'

Agastalen knew that he was in little position to make demands or threats, but despite the throbbing in his shoulder he was surprised when he found that his anger had still not left him. Meeting the aged warrior's steely gaze, he replied, 'We don't consort with murderers. If you want to add us to your list of dead and conquered as we sit here helpless then go ahead.'

The man's face mottled with rage and he raised a chain mailed fist to strike.

Agastalen waited for the blow, unafraid.

Fist raised, he stared at Agastalen and then slowly lowered it, the colour leaving his cheeks. Unexpectedly he said gruffly, 'Forgive me. You will understand that I had to understand your motives.'

Agastalen exchanged a puzzled look with Heath, who just shrugged. 'I am Baron Wren and I surmise that you must have seen some of the terrors that have suddenly been visited upon my barony. Tell me, what have you seen?'

Agastalen was about to speak and reject Baron Wren's request for information. Heath, however, stepped in first. He quickly recounted that they had been trying to reach Shael heading by way of the south coast when they had stumbled across the hamlet, where they had found Rosie badly injured.

He tried to interrupt once and halt Heath's truthful account, but Heath was not in any mood to be stopped and brushed his friend's interruption aside. He did not, though, explain about Rosie's gift to Agastalen, and neither did he detail their own impolitic background, fleeing Athel-Loria. Baron Wren listened without a word throughout, an armoured giant brooding in silence.

Heath then lapsed into a slightly awkward silence when he finished. Baron Wren looked at Heath with piercing blue eyes as he fidgeted uncomfortably, the silence only broken by the billow of the canvas walls.

Eventually the baron said, 'I appreciate your honesty.' At this he looked pointedly at Heath. 'You will find that your trust is not misplaced. You may be assured that I and my vassals are not the ones to carry out that hideous perpetration. And, I'm sorry to say,' and his face creased thoughtfully, 'that what you have just told me is but one of many such barbaric acts.'

'But who would do such a thing?' asked Heath.

'That,' replied the Baron, now even more sombre, 'you shall find out all too soon,' and with the rustle of chain mail he turned to go.

'Wait,' said Heath. 'What about us? Can we go?'

The baron paused for a moment and shook his head. 'I'm sorry, but while I am inclined to believe your story, I still cannot fully discount the fact that you could still be spies. You may have free rein of this camp. However, you may not leave. We face our foe tomorrow. You may draw arms if you wish and prove your worth.' With that he was gone.

Flummoxed, Heath turned back to Agastalen and dropped onto the bed beside him. 'Great, like I'd know one end of a sword from another,' he said.

'I'm inclined to believe him, though,' said Agastalen.

'Oh, by the way,' said Heath, 'the surgeon said to keep your shoulder immobile so that the stitches don't tear. Said he'd got the arrow out in time to prevent the bone getting infected, or something.'

'Well, that's some good news, I suppose,' replied Agastalen. 'Come on, help me get my shirt on. We should at least check out our host's accommodation.'

'Absolutely,' grinned Heath. The shirt, which after some huffing and no small amount of pain Agastalen finally got on, looked frightful, with an arrow hole in the shoulder surrounded by dried blood.

'Makes you look like a war veteran,' laughed Heath.

'Well, by the sound of it, tomorrow we might be just that,' said Agastalen, promptly wiping the smile off Heath's face.

They stepped out of the tent and into an armed camp. Their tent was part of a small circle of small deep-red pavilions. Pennants snapped atop the pavilions in the night wind, displaying the Wren Barony coat of arms: a small bird sitting upon the pommel of a sword. Beside these sat a second circle of green pavilions from which flew pennants with a boar-and-tree coat of arms. Hundreds of men sprawled out from the tents, sitting about campfires. A young squire in a green tabard with the boar-and-tree crest stared at them as he led a white charger past.

They both jumped when a voice behind them said, 'You can get food at any of the campfires if you're hungry.'

They turned to see a guard. Apparently he'd been at their tent entrance all the time and they'd just not seen him. He wore a Wren surcoat over chain mail armour and held a spear at attention.

'Thanks, we would certainly use some,' said Agastalen.

Calling to them as they walked away, the guard said, 'Don't try to leave the camp, though. The sentries are likely to shoot anyone they're not expecting first and ask questions later.'

'Sounds familiar,' murmured Agastalen as they walked away.

Weaving amongst the campfires, they picked their way through lounging soldiers, looking hopefully for some edible remains in a pot that the soldiers had already not wolfed down.

Despite the huge number of soldiers present, there was a slight hush about the camp. Men sharpened swords on whetstones and oiled their armour; others ate or joked and diced quietly with comrades, but their voices were low and hushed, almost reverent and expectant. Occasionally Agastalen would hear the name of Sha spoken reverently, the god of war no doubt being called upon to give them swift victory in battle and see them home safely to loved ones.

Agastalen noticed, as they picked their way amongst the sprawled army, that it was only a minority, those closest to the pitched command pavilions, that appeared to be regular soldiers. The bulk of the troops here were apparently militia, and some perhaps even levies. The armour of these militia and levies wasn't the glittering chain mail of the regular troops but usually hardened leather or sometimes just heavily padded jackets. Swords and arms had the look of aged weapons that perhaps had been lovingly handed down from generation to generation.

Agastalen stopped at one such fire, around which five men sprawled, three of whom were engaged in a game of dice. 'Mind if we join you? We could use some food,' he asked.

Those dicing didn't even look up. One slim middle-aged man, oiling a well-used boiled leather breast-plate, glanced at them with a welcoming smile and gestured at the pot hanging over the fire. 'Sure. Help yourselves. Like as not, we'll not need it tomorrow.'

Agastalen and Heath smiled gratefully and sat down by the fire. Grabbing a bowl for each of them, Heath spooned out a generous helping of some form of stew.

'Name's Spots,' said the militia man, 'and them over there's Lynt, Ulo and Daydle,' he said, pointing to the men dicing, who looked up and nodded as they heard their names mentioned. 'One asleep there is Riz: swear he could sleep through the wrath of the gods, that one.'

Agastalen introduced himself and Heath between mouthfuls of the stew.

'You been involved in some of the skirmishes already, then?' asked Spots, pointing to Agastalen's shoulder wound.

Agastalen stepped in before Heath could be a bit too forthright, replying, 'Not really. We lived north of here and barely escaped with our lives when our village was attacked. Baron Wren agreed to let us stay with the army.'

'Ha, not much of an army,' retorted Spots, the firelight now showing them the rash of acne scars that no doubt had given him his adopted name. 'Mainly militia and levies here. Barons weren't wont to keep much of a standing army in these peaceful times. Bet they regret that now, silly beggars,' he chuckled ruefully.

Agastalen thought that he did not really look especially happy about it, though.

Listening to the exchange avidly, whilst rapidly spooning stew into his mouth, Heath said between mouthfuls, 'We've heard of some appalling atrocities. Is this all concerning the same person that Baron Wren is about to fight tomorrow?'

They were interrupted by the thickset Ulo, who, leaning across from his dice game, rumbled, 'It's not just Baron Wren he's up against here, son. This is the entire muster for both Baron Wren and Baron Mytle. Baronies of Lont and Idon have already fallen to the bastard.' With that he spat in the grass and returned to the dice.

A chill ran down Agastalen's spine. 'What are you saying?' he said incredulously.

For a moment Spots looked weary as he ran his oily hand through already greasy hair. 'It's all happened a bit quick son, not many know yet. Barons Lont and Idon didn't even know what hit them, although Lont was a pompous prat at the best of times, folk say, and not the sharpest sword in the armoury at that. Listened to all the sweet talk about friendship and joint prosperity, they did, then he went through both baronies like fire through the trees. Mounted the barons' heads on lances, I hear.' His voice grew thick as he said, 'His folk didn't deserve what happened to them, though, not that.'

Agastalen said in a voice barely above a whisper, 'What actually happened, Spots?'

'Well,' Spots continued slowly, 'word is he butchered everyone save the womenfolk, and them he's made slaves. We've got Sha to thank that Baron Wren is a wily old buzzard, and not easily fooled by sweet talk and flattery. It was him who bullied Mytle into calling his muster. Hadn't he done that, Mytle would probably already have fallen.'

Silence ensued then, broken only by the crackle and pop of flame from the fire. The soldiers dicing had stopped and they were just staring at the grass.

Finally Heath said, 'Who could do this?'

It was Ulo who answered. 'They say, it's the immortal Cinder, killed the Duke of Taed and took his lands and army.' He shook his head. 'We're up against an immortal.'

- CHAPTER 17 -

Cinder Attacks

The combined army of Wren and Mytle awaited their foe.

The barons had drawn up their forces across a small rise, before which ran a meadow flanked by forest. Formed into units, the militia, perhaps numbering five hundred in total, held a simple line formation across most of the rise's breadth. In the centre of this formation glittered the armoured ranks of a hundred of the two barons' professional footmen, coats of arms displayed proudly on their shields. A contingent of lightly armoured longbowmen, who from their tatty attire looked to Agastalen remarkably like poachers, stood at ease behind these ranks with arrows tucked into the ground before their feet, ready to be easily pulled forth in haste. Having effectively no experience with weapons, Agastalen and Heath had been forced to take position close to the barons' command force, behind the bulk of the troops. They would be called upon as runners, if needs required.

From his advantageous position Agastalen could see that both of the barons were on horseback, presumably to give them the elevation of height to see the unfolding battle. The armoured Baron Wren, his head surmounted by an open-faced helm sporting a Wren crest, appeared quite composed as he calmly discussed the troop disposition with Baron Mytle. The latter of these had squeezed his quite corpulent girth into a shirt of chain mail that perhaps he had worn in his lost youth, and with his rosy cheeks puffing in dismay appeared almost ridiculous within his pot-shaped helm. Mytle would occasionally saw at the reins of his horse as it placidly cropped the grass.

A single unit of combined Wren and Mytle armoured footmen stood beside the two barons' position.

Agastalen heard the song of the enemy long before he saw them. The deep bass of a throbbing war chant carried easily over the forest and field, to the combined barony forces that became quiet as they resolutely awaited the arrival of their foe. Eventually they could hear the dull tramp of hundreds of feet and Taed's forces swung into distant view; a rippling serpentine line wending its way towards the field. Many minutes passed as the churning dark serpent closed on the field, and still Agastalen could not see its farthest end.

At the head of the army rode the immortal known as Cinder in a chariot pulled by twin red chargers. Poles affixed to both sides of the chariot bore the carved emblem of a circle of chains.

The chariot drew up and the distant figure of Cinder raised a gauntletted fist that burst into flame. Horns brayed and officers bellowed orders. Troops swept around the figure like a black tide, deploying onto the field of battle.

Through the din of enemy deployment, Agastalen could hear Baron Mytle's high-pitched voice. 'My goodness, there are so many, Wren, so many. Should we not attack now, though, while they are still confused in their deployment?'

Wren laughed at this, his voice seeming unnaturally loud. 'Your courage as ever is that of a boar, Baron Mytle, and I suspect that you also test me. However, as you know, ours is a defensive position and therein lies *our* advantage. We must let the enemy come to us.'

With the dull jingle of mail, rank after rank of axe-bearing foot soldiers began to take a frontal position on the meadow below. They halted deployment only when they were the entire breadth of the rise upon which the baronies' forces awaited and fully five ranks deep.

Ranks of horsemen took up position upon both flanks; often even the mounts themselves were armoured with mail. Agastalen noticed with a wrench of anger that many of them carried throwing spears. He had no doubt that they were not unlike those that had slain the villagers and Rosie's family.

Only part of the Taed force had deployed onto the battlefield and Agastalen estimated that they must already be outnumbered at least four to one.

Heath tugged on his arm, and turning to his friend he could see the worried expression that he knew was reflected in his own eyes. 'This does not look good,' said Heath, shaking his head. 'When the battle starts the barons' forces are going to get ground up like dog meat. We should try and slip out of here during the fighting. No one's going to miss us then.'

Agastalen thought about it for a moment. He didn't like the idea of running away. But he also knew that there was nothing they could sensibly contribute and they were in service to Arcanum, not to the Barons of Wren and Mytle. 'You're right,' he said to Heath. 'If we can help in any way we will, but we're not going to stay and get slaughtered. When things look like they're turning for the worse, we'll make a swift exit.'

Heath nodded, his expression showing relief, almost as if he'd expected Agastalen to argue.

Returning their attention to the meadow, they saw the Taed front ranks jostling as figures moved through them. Moments later some twenty or thirty women were pushed out in front of the foot troop ranks. They were completely naked and stood shivering and forlorn between the Taed ranks and the forces of the barons upon the rise, clearly unsure what was to come. A hush descended over the battlefield, broken only by an occasional sob from the women.

Cinders' voice came then, borne upon a burning hot wind, its tone like the grinding of rocks. 'Run. This is my gift to the barons, the return of their womenfolk and a demonstration of my good intent that was so poorly rejected by them. Return to your loved ones now. *Run.*'

The women looked momentarily at the ranks of Taed troops as if expecting to be grabbed by them again. However, the black ranks were still. Needing little more encouragement they bolted towards the barony lines. Murmurs swept the barony ranks and a number of soldiers started forward.

Baron Wren spurred his warhorse and galloped around the lines to the front ranks, before the soldiers who were starting to move down the rise. 'Hold, damn it,' he shouted. 'Hold!'

The troops moving forward halted at the baron's words.

The running women closed the distance across the meadow. Many were young, perhaps just in their teens, some perhaps had been wives, but none were old. All could now clearly see the bruising upon their naked flesh. Many had fresh blood between their legs. Shouts of anger and outrage rose from the barony troops, but with Wren atop his pawing warhorse before them they remained in place. Names were shouted by the women in racking sobs as they ran, hoping their calls would find loved ones in the ranks. Some of the soldiers began to shout back in recognition, others just in encouragement.

The cries of longing and hope suddenly became screams of pain, as arrows raced out from the Taed ranks and began to rain down on unprotected flesh. The sound was brutal, wet smacks as arrows pierced flesh. The women fell to the grass like limp white dolls, hands held out in hope before them. Some lay still where they fell, others screamed in pain for moments until they too became quiet. Their blood ebbed onto the damp grass, not a hundred spans from the barony troops.

There was a moment of stunned silence. Baron Wren's head hung in sorrow as his troops stared in disbelief at the unmoving naked forms. The moan of bereaved men shuddered through the ranks. Suddenly, the throaty blast of a solitary horn split the air. The ranks of Taed footmen screamed in tribute, their voices raised into one of inhuman proportions, and the words 'Cinder, Cinder' thundered across the meadow. They raised their weapons into the air and charged.

'But they've not fully deployed yet,' shouted Baron Mytle, rising out of his stirrups. 'Much of their army is still marching!'

Agastalen saw that Mytle was right: more than half the Taed army had not even deployed onto the meadow, still stretching in a dark line beyond. 'They've already made a mistake,' Mytle shouted triumphantly.

'No, my lord,' said a flamboyantly clad aide at his shoulder. 'They just believe that the troops already deployed are more than sufficient to crush us.'

Agastalen and Heath waited somewhat helplessly outside Baron Mytle's circle of advisers, waiting to hear whether they would be needed. Agastalen's heart hammered in his chest. Whilst he had read of battles throughout history many times, he, like most people in what was meant to be quite a peaceful world, had never actually been in one. He fought the urge to flee as the thunder of thousands of charging soldiers shook the earth, faintly wishing that he had a weapon to hand. Perhaps they should have asked Wren for permission to carry one. Even though it was his left arm and not his right that had been wounded by the arrow, Agastalen knew deep down that he would be ineffective, if not a liability, with a sword or any other kind of martial weapon.

'Draw bows and fire at will,' cried the effete Baron Mytle, dabbing at his nose with a scented kerchief. Since he was unable to make himself heard across the roar of charging soldiers, his aide relayed the order.

The archers picked their arrows from the ground, drew and fired in one sinuous motion, with the rich hum of bowstrings. The arrows arched out over the heads of the Barony foot soldiers and hung for the faintest of moments as if suspended, before falling with dull thumps into the charging Taed ranks. Scores fell, but the mass of Taed troops did not falter, heedless feet trampling the unfeeling white flesh of the fallen women, sightless eyes not seeing the enemy offering such disregard. Barony archers continued to fire and reloaded in fluid motion.

Baron Wren remained at the front of his soldiers' ranks as the enemy charged, like some metallic and immovable statue. A small contingent of his professional foot soldiers had formed up about him, including his standard-bearer, proudly displaying the crest of the wren and the sword.

The enemy now could be seen with horrid clarity. Wicked double-bladed axes were raised high, helms were shaped with the snarling visages of wolves, lions and boars, and painted wooden shields bore the emblem of a circle of chains.

'Pikes forward,' carried Wren's voice, and the enemy struck the front ranks with a crash that shook the earth. Pikes ripped through chain mail and flesh as Taed troops threw themselves with savage abandon on their foes. Blood fountained into the air in bursts of scarlet and the first rank of Taed soldiers fell to the earth. Uncaring, their fellow soldiers behind trampled over their dying colleagues, screaming in savage joy as they fell into the militia ranks, swinging their wicked axes. Releasing their pikes, the militia drew swords and battle was fully joined.

Perhaps the Taed forces had expected the ill-equipped militia to fall easily. If so, they had been wrong. Their tactic of slaying the captured women appeared to backfire and the militia, side by side with professional soldiers from the two baronies, fought as if hate were their only fuel. Agastalen watched as militia in the front ranks took blows that would have felled most men, often striking out even in their last breath with a venom that took many of their murderers to death with them.

The brutality of it appalled him, the savage deeds that men could commit upon each other in the name of war. The din and thunder of the battle was a palpable thing, the front ranks a churning mob of dripping red blades rising and falling, dealing death and dismemberment.

Baron Wren seemed to act as a beacon and rallying point for his troops. Whenever the lines began to fall back he would force his kicking and screaming warhorse through the battling throng, and his troops would fight with renewed vigour wherever they saw him. Yet, despite their ferocity, the baronial forces were simply being overwhelmed. Growing gaps began to appear in lines, that there simply weren't the baronial troops left to fill. The warriors with their snarling dog-and-lion helms were getting closer by the moment to Baron Mytle's command position.

Mytle leaned across to his standard-bearer, but Agastalen could no longer hear what was said, the din of battle now being too close. He knew that Heath too was watching the oncoming enemy with increasing alarm. The standard-bearer responded to his lord's command and began waving the baronial crest of the boar and tree high in the air. Moments later a wave of knights burst from the tree line on the farthest flank. Their plate armour shone like silver as they surged in a sparkling river down the hill. Grass churned beneath their chargers' hooves and the Mytle barony pennant snapped from the tip of lances braced under their arms.

The Taed troops were clearly not aware of the charge until it struck the rear of their lines. Lances snapped with the force of the impact and screams filled the air. Taed troops were pinned to the very earth by lances, or disappeared under the churning hooves of warhorses. Lances were then dropped and the thirty knights drew great broadswords and layed into the enemy. Snarling wolf helms were split asunder, shields cracked and shattered under the impact.

The Taed troops sought to pull back from the knights, but the close quarters lent them little chance. When they turned to flee their silver-clad executioners, a militiaman would often strike them, the name of a loved one a song on his lips.

Agastalen and Heath could see that Baron Mytle had a wily look of deep satisfaction on his face as his knights carved through the living ranks of the enemy.

At the farthest end of the meadow, the four harnessed chargers snorted impatiently. A smouldering fist rested elegantly upon the reins, occasionally reaching up to caress the hilt of the fell blade Kalak-Dane, slung across his back. He had not raged as the baronial knights had carved into the rear of the foot troops but merely chuckled, a deep grinding sound devoid of any joy, the coals that were his eyes burning even brighter.

The deep note of a solitary horn sounded across the battlefield. Taed horsemen were drawn up in a rank, fully the entire width of the meadow. Bear and animal skin capes were cast back over shoulders and throwing spears clutched in gauntleted fists. Another blast of the horn and the horses leapt forward, their riders hunching forward over the necks of the beasts. The line stormed across the meadow, the drum of the hooves drawing the attention of the knights whose backs were to the charging force. Baron Wren's powerful voice could be heard calling for the knights to withdraw but they were too enmeshed within the enemy.

'Signal the archers!' screamed Baron Mytle.

Arrows hummed in reply, arcing over the heads of the barony combatants. Charging horses tumbled with shrill screams and riders toppled from saddles, to be churned under the hooves of those racing behind. Yet there were too many: for every arrow that found a target, five horse warriors remained untouched.

Closing now, the horse warriors hurled their short spears with deadly accuracy. Spears punched through plate armour and silver knights toppled from saddles. Where they fell they were hacked apart by the mob of Taed foot soldiers. Some knights managed to turn but the wave of dark warriors rushed over them like a tide and their silver forms slowly folded sinking into the darkness of the churning human river.

'Oh deary me, it seems that's us about done, then,' said Baron Mytle sadly. 'The only question,' he said, 'is should I draw my trusty blade and die beside my troops, or flee and live to fight again another day?' He tapped his plump chin thoughtfully. 'You two,' he said, pointing down from his horse to Agastalen and Heath, who watched the unfolding carnage in horror, 'I require your services.'

Agastalen and Heath approached, fearful that the Taed forces looked like they could break through the ranks at any moment. The final unit of professional foot soldiers had positioned itself between the barons' command position and the battle. The archers had now drawn their short swords.

Mytle's aide, who appeared something of an over-dressed fop in richly embroidered purple velvet tunic and flamboyant lacy cuffs spilling out from a yellow shirt, was looking increasingly nervous as the battle raged closer. Giving a gentle cough, he said, 'My lord baron, we should really think about getting you to safety.'

'Nonsense, Pandim,' said Mytle, batting away his aide's encroaching hand. 'Use these two gentlemen as an example. Do they flee? No, I think not! You really must try to be more robust!'

Agastalen and Heath had the good grace to look slightly sheepish given their earlier agreed plan to depart, which incidentally it now seemed a decidedly good time to execute.

'I would have you lend me a service,' said Mytle to them both, his rotund face flushed with the exertion of command. 'I happen to know, from the presently dreadfully embattled Baron Wren,' he gestured vaguely towards the din of combat, 'that not being the spies he trusted that you were not, you are, as you indeed said, presently headed upon your own volition towards Shael. Would that be correct?'

Wanting to keep this as brief as possible, with Heath hopping anxiously from toe to toe beside him, Agastalen just said, 'Yes, My lord.'

'Good, good,' said Mytle, as if he had all the time in the world. 'Then I hope that I can prevail upon you to carry word of this most unfortunate situation to Queen Iodarii of Shael, of our most delicate predicament herewith. Wren and I have of course sent word to the remaining Peldane baronies, to precipitate a call to arms. Sadly, though, I do not believe that the forces of the remaining baronies will be sufficient to stop this most appalling Cinder. Quite what we have done to precipitate such appalling and unforgivable behaviour on his part I just do not know. And what concerns me equally is, when he's had enough of our little baronies, will Cinder turn his dark attentions upon Shael? Certainly the Queen must be informed of what you have seen here and make her own decision on the matter!'

Mytle looked expectantly at Agastalen and Heath.

Agastalen fervently wished that he had time to discuss this with Heath, or even better that they had not been asked in the first place. However, since, as Mytle had said, they were actually headed towards the port of Limfrost, the capital of Shael, he could see little harm in delivering the message. So with only a slight pause he said, 'We can do that, Baron.'

If Heath disagreed with Agastalen's agreement, he did not say so.

'Excellent,' said Mytle, clapping his hands as if they'd just agreed something substantially more jolly. With that he pulled a jewelled dagger from his belt and passed it down to Agastalen. The dagger was clearly of a ceremonial nature, with a blunt edge, and carried the Mytle barony boar-and-tree crest. 'Show that to Queen Iodarii and she will know that you speak the truth.'

Agastalen nodded and tucked the dagger into his belt. 'Very well. Is there anything else that you'd like us to say Baron?'

'No, no. Goodness me, I think an honest account of what you've seen here should be quite enough for poor Iodarii. What a dreadful shock for her!' said Mytle.

Then, turning to his aide-de-camp, Mytle said, 'Now, Pandim, give them your horse.'

Pandim's face dropped, his hand dropping to rest protectively upon the dappled grey mare.

'My lord, you cannot mean Bella. No, surely not. Could we not get another horse? There are others here, we have but to find one,' he said, looking frantically about.

Mytle scowled and pursed his lips. 'Pandim, I really will not hear this. There's a battle going on here, you know. Give them your horse!'

Sniffling, Pandim climbed down off the mare. As he did so, there was a crash as the reserve troops directly in front of the Barons' position engaged the Taed forces. The screams of the dying were everywhere.

'Now get on,' said Mytle to Agastalen and Heath, 'and ride as if your lives depended on it.'

Agastalen and Heath clambered onto Bella, needing little encouragement and knowing that in fact their lives *did* depend on it.

A despondent and quietly snivelling Pandim watched them without a word.

The mare nickered as Agastalen dug his heels into her, and leapt forward. The last thing they heard as Bella galloped away was Mytle's high-pitched voice shouting, 'Right, now let's see if we can't salvage something from this terrible mess, gentlemen! Inform the standard-bearer, Pandim. Archers to me and full retreat!'

- Chapter 18 -

The Bridge of Mourn

The ebbing wall of light rippled in streams of liquid colour. Its height was unending, seeming to rear to the very heavens, and perhaps it did. Its gentle hum charged the very air. To many it would have been a wonder, to those upon the platform below, it was death.

The vast motionless platform suspended high above the earth, was supported by nothing save the air. It could only be reached by climbing its one hundred steps, each step bigger than a house, and bearing the name in carved runes of a younger god.

'Why are we here, at the edge of the world?' asked Cinder, his hulking presence seeming tiny upon the vast and endless field of shining grey metal that was the platform.

The seven immortals stood about the only feature of the platform, in its very centre a single bronze disk, that bore the same Rune slashed upon each of their faces. Those Runes now burned with a sooty light of their own, giving their faces a hellish cast. All shifted, feeling inadequate and small in this place, despite the fact that each was aged and steeped in power.

'Because we can see' returned Rivadus Hex, his taught skin appeared even more stretched across his face than normal, his smile, peculiarly wide.

'Yes, in fact, we can see everything' added Veylistra smoothly, as she toyed with a lock of raven hair. She, like the other immortals, did her best to ignore the excruciating pain from the Rune that marked her face.

'I don't like it' whined Mahommet. The son of Nim and half-brother to Veylistra affected a scarlet doublet, inset with diamonds and a ruff so big, that it almost covered his chin.

Veylistra barely concealed her scorn. How different they were; he had no strength. In her view Mahommet was the weakest of those on the Council, but his Cult on Rune was enormous, and sadly that necessitated his involvement. They needed numbers for the war.

'If we get any closer to the veil we'll be ashes' Mahommet continued to whine. 'My Rune is burning. I don't want to be any more scarred than I am you know.'

'Enough, of this' snarled Rivadus-Hex, not bothering to conceal his contempt. 'The veil that marks the edge of this world does not move Mahommet. So, go no closer and you shall continue to live – sadly.'

The last addition brought a slight, though nervous ripple of laughter from the other assembled immortals.

'I can see it' said Veylistra softly, the longing rich in her voice. 'If you look, you can see.'

The others turned to the Veil, the ebbing lights within it throwing coloured rivers across their upturned faces. At times, when it dimmed they could just make it out. Within the ebony darkness beyond the edge of the world of Rune, was an ivory bridge, so delicate as to appear fragile, carved in whorls of bass relief. Its end was not in sight.

'The Bridge of Mourn' growled Cinder.

'And beyond it the Hall of the Fallen gods,' said Rivadus-Hex.

'And within the Hall enough divine power to make us all gods' finished Veylistra.

Silence ensued for a while as the immortals all gazed at the Bridge of Mourn. It seemed so close that they could almost reach out and touch it, and yet in doing so their endless lives would, abruptly, cease.

'I'll ask you again though Rivadus – why are we here?' said Cinder, his tongue lolling for a moment across his massive yellowed canines. 'We should be with Thorn. With us at his side, nothing could stop him opening the gate to the Bridge of Mourn.'

Rivadus sighed, and hooked his thumbs behind his belt, from which hung assorted daggers, hooks, darts and other varied short weapons. All were old, though lovingly cared for. His stretched and ancient face took on a condescending look. 'How can a brain as old as yours be so slow Cinder?

Cinder growled ominously and reached for the massive sword strapped across his back.

Rivadus-Hex did not move, but suddenly about him there was an air of readiness, like that of a coiled spring.

'Peace' snapped Velyistra, with a voice that cracked across the platform. She stepped between them and then just as suddenly turned a winsome smile on Cinder.

'Come now, we must all remain friends….at least for now. We are so close to our goal. What Rivadus is trying to say Cinder, is that if we involve ourselves directly at this time, the divine orders could become aware of what we're doing and if they know, then the gods will know too.'

'Hee. Hee. Hee. They'll think it's some plan of the dragon gods – delicious! They'll think they're coming for them at last! Hee. Hee.' Kytheras' voice was unnaturally high, almost sweet. She had a childlike appearance, which she was accentuating today with her hair in bunches.

Veylistra knew that all that Kythera affected was for show, and beneath was one of the most deadly minds of all the hundreds of immortals that roamed Rune. With most of the others on their Council she had a good idea of their motivations and allegiances, but with Kythera she was never sure, and mistakes like that could be fatal.

Almost as if Kythera realised what Veylistra was thinking, her gaze roamed hungrily over her. Veylistra smiled, her memories of their dalliance were fond, but they were just that, memories.

Cinder seemed somewhat mollified and laughed. 'They're fools, they don't even know whose Avatar it was that died yet.….still, I guess we should be careful.'

'Exactly' said Veylistra, the rainbow colours from the Veil splintering into tiny spears of light on her silver breast-plate. 'From here, at the Edge of the World we can see *everything*, we can hear *everything*. We can watch Thorn safely and when he has opened the gate, he will come here and tear down the Veil. *We* will be free and the Hall of the Fallen gods will await our pleasure.'

Seven sets of immortal eyes swung across Rune. The landscape blurred, mountain ranges, forests and cities raced by until at last those undying eyes came to settle expectantly upon a tiny island in the Sea of Korth.

****

Crab Island was remote, but Brother Trib would never tire of the view. He loved it now as much as fifty cycles past, when he had first been sent there to guard the remote sanctuary.

Upon a peninsula of Crab Island, the sanctuary and entrance to the Gate of Mourn was marked to the unknowing eye by just a solitary stone, rising like a lonely hermit from the ragged field. A few haggard trees broke up the featureless flat, hunched over like wizened men in the relentless wind. One tree, some fifty paces distant, seemed almost to hunch for shelter in the modest protection offered by the wall of Brother Trib's meagre stone hut.

Having finished his evening devotions, Trib sat upon the cliff edge in his favourite spot; a small lee beneath the top of the cliff. From here he could see across the small bay to the other peninsula which housed some of the Crab Island's slave mines, where Korth sent some of its more wicked citizens. Often Trib had been to the mines, to offer his gentle ministrations and words of guidance.

He noted with a slight frown the mischievous, wispy grey and black clouds that began to unfurl across Oldoth's Face, as he sank lower into the liquid blue arms of the sea. Indeed this would ruin tonight's display! Sinking for a moment into melancholy, Trib promptly berated himself and duly noted that this display was also Oldoth's will.

Sighing, Trib arose from the lee, with a slight creak in his knees, and began the short walk back to his cottage. He noted sardonically to himself that he was actually looking forward to the welcoming comfort of his wool-stuffed mattress. He was getting soft. Nobody would know, of course, since no one from the order ever came here.

Once a turn, when the world had circled the face of Oldoth, Trib would despatch a wisp with a brief account of the order's progress on Crab Island and to comfirm that all was safe with the Gate. Of course he never heard in return.

Trib's feet came to a halt when he realised, coming out of his reverie, that there was someone standing in front of Oldoth's stone, which since the light had fled so quickly cast no shadow upon the earth. Standing in the lee of the stone was a cloaked figure. Trib squinted, trying to make out the face, but was unable to do so.

'This is a late hour for you to be travelling, my child,' said Trib. 'The village is a good walk from here and the way treacherous; you will almost certainly not make it back before nightfall covers the face of our god.'

Trib paused, but the cloaked figure did not respond. Again Trib spoke into the silence. 'Do I know you, child? Remove your hood, so that I may look upon your face.'

Slowly the figure reached up and cast back the hood. Revealed in the half-light was the face of a young man, perhaps no more than twenty summers old, his face deathly pale.

A slight smile twisted the corners of Thorns' mouth and he stepped towards Trib with an almost cat-like grace. Trib stepped back involuntarily. Thorn's eyes glittered black, reflecting no light from the setting sun. The shadow from the racing clouds above seemed drawn to him, even coiling protectively about.

Trib, never having counted himself a brave man, at that point found courage within himself that he never knew he possessed. Despite his every primal instinct warning him to run and leave this pale young man far behind, he stepped forward and placed a thin hand gently on his shoulder.

'Child, you are clearly unwell. Let me offer you Oldoth's blessing and then we shall share bread together. Tonight you may stay with me. I will see you safely to the village tomorrow.'

Thorn recoiled, shadow weaving about him hungrily now, tendrils reaching out and seeming to snap at Trib. Stepping backward, Thorn stumbled into the sacred stone, and as he turned to look behind him there was a terrified look on his face. He cowered before the stone, hunching down.

Concern and love flowed from brother Trib. It flowed with the gentle force of a mountain stream strong and bright. The waves of compassion washed like sunlight against the curling tendrils of shadow and they recoiled, weaving and snapping like vipers about Trib. Slowly and with palpable rage they retreated until they weaved only about the figure itself, cornered. Trib watched, concern etched upon his face.

Thorn then looked up at Trib and he saw the pain in those ebony eyes. Sorrow abounded there. The eyes called, no, begged, for help and mercy. Tears sparkled there to chase slowly down alabaster cheeks. Glittering blue, with the hue and iridescence of pearls, the tears were such a contrast to the terrible ebony darkness of the eyes that for a moment Trib faltered: he did not understand. As the tears rolled from Thorns' cheeks they fell upon the grass, where they turned to bright, tiny diamonds.

'I do not wish to be here' said Thorn. It was so soft that Trib almost missed it.

'Please you're in great danger. You need to leave.'

Trib's mind whirled, trying to make sense of what he was seeing and hearing. Even as compassion flowed from Trib and kept the snapping shadow at bay, he knew that he had never met this man before, yet was amazed that he felt such an empathy with him. How could this be? Concern overwhelmed him as he suddenly saw how the man actually writhed in agony within the coiling mass of shadow. As much as the shadow would snap at Trib it would also snap at the man himself, biting into his white flesh, yet leaving no physical mark.

'Please help me.' The words were so soft that he almost missed them. They pulled Trib from his study.

He looked down again into the imploring alabaster face cast stark amidst the whipping shadows.

'What is your name child?'

'Thorn' the hunched figure replied, 'my name's Thorn.'

Understanding suddenly dropped into Tribs stomach like a ball of ice. 'You, you're here for the gate child….aren't you?'

Thorn nodded. 'I can't stop it. I've done some terrible, terrible things; my best friend…imprisoned, others…. dead. Go. Please go.'

With a calmness and dignity that he did not feel Trib replied, 'I can't do that my son. This place, it is my sacred duty.'

Suddenly Trib became aware that more time had passed than he'd thought. Oldoth's face had almost fully sunk into the welcoming embrace of the sea and the young man was now lit only by the sunny glow of Trib's holy benediction. But as his god's face sank into the sea, Trib's power faltered. Unable to feel the warming face of his god behind him, he sensed a cold sweat breaking out upon his brow.

Thorn smiled and stood, and the shadow began to thicken and coil about him. Trib took a faltering step back.

'You should have struck me down when you could, brother.' This time the voice was soft and strong in timbre, velvet smooth and laced with menace. 'You're weak. Your god is weak. It'll be your undoing.'

Thorn now seemed almost composed of shadow, and he smiled. 'Poor Oldoth,' he said.

The shadows struck, viper-fast. Trib's benediction faltered under the blow and the sunlight wavered. With the second strike it shattered like the shards of a mirror, scattering pieces of light to rain gently down across the grass.

Trib's head exploded in pain and he fell to his knees, vaguely aware of blood running from his ears and nose. He was aware only of the night as he gasped and fought to draw breath. He couldn't run, he realised, he was in no condition to; his head rang like a struck anvil.

Trying to focus through the haze in his mind, he realised that Thorn now stood before him. Peering through watery eyes, he looked up into that innocent face, so twisted in hatred. Thorn was smiling at him, but it was a bitter thing and utterly without joy.

Trib felt cold as the coiling shadows lifted him from his knees and held him, helpless as a babe in the air, but he spoke with conviction. 'I see your pain, Thorn. Truly I do. I'm sorry. May the face of our god smile upon you.'

The young man's face twisted into a leer as he replied, 'Unlikely. And who will smile upon him, old man?'

Laughing, Thorn turned back towards the sacred stone, now wreathed in almost complete darkness, and gestured. Trib felt himself hurled forward by the coiling shadows. His head struck the stone and simply broke open with a sickening crack. As his body fell lifeless and twitching to the earth and his soul fled into the embrace of Oldoth, Trib's lifeblood flowed down the sacred stone. The stone then broke apart with a crack that shook the earth, a ragged fissure now running directly down the centre. The grass rippled in waves and the trees shook for long moments.

When the shaking had subsided Thorn looked into the darkness within the heart of the stone. A delicate ivory bridge stretched from the stone into the utter darkness of a void.

Smiling and stepping over Trib's corpse, Thorn walked into the heart of the stone.

- CHAPTER 19 -

Rebirth

The gaze of the immortal Council spun from Crab island where a broken Trib lay, to the darkness of the void beyond the veil. It was now split by a slash of light that marred its eternal ebony perfection.

The air on the platform was hushed, and utterly still. It was expectant, nobody spoke, there was no need. They simply watched as a small figure stepped from the slash of light that marred the void, onto the delicate span of the Bridge of Mourn and in doing so changed the fate of the world.

Thorn looked oddly humble there, a single small figure within the enveloping darkness that raged in colossal impotence at his intrusion. He looked about until he apparently found what he sought and began to walk towards them, like a single white candle in the darkness.

'Now we will see the gods undone' hissed Rivadus-Hex into the silence.

Kythera giggled, even for her, it seemed oddly high and shrill.

You are all fools thought Veylistra, nothing is ever as it seems.

As Thorn slowly approached a tiny figure in the distance gradually becoming larger, he appeared to totter like an old man; stooped and uncertain. The light of the Veil cast trembling fingers across him, but it did not penetrate the shadow that writhed protectively about him.

The delicate span of the Bridge of Mourn, named after the fallen god of the dead, touched the base of the Veil and Thorn arrived.

It was like looking at someone below the surface of a lake, his outline was blurred, and indistinct, it rippled with each ebb of the Veil. And yet, there was no mistaking those eyes; eyes that had lost all vestiges of humanity, all vestiges of hope. It was as if Thorn had gone and what was left was just a shell of the young man that had been, a shell that awaited - something else.

'Mistress' called Thorn, as if from miles away, his voice resonated like a struck glass.

Elation filled Veylistra as She looked on the face of Her lover. To have come here, to have achieved this, it was almost unthinkable. She felt like raising her face to the stars and screaming at the gods Her joy, Her defiance. And yet, She knew that She daren't, she must retain control, all could be gained here....or lost. There could be no mistakes.

Veylistras' voice thrummed with power and emotion. 'I am here, beloved.'

Thorn smiled, and it was so full of joy and lost innocence that if Alazla had seen it, it would have broken his heart. He raised a hand to the Veil then and placed it there, as if on a pane of glass, and looked directly at Veylistra in supplication.

She could feel Thorn within Her. She could feel his longing, his lust, his love. Thorn was empty of everything else, he was utterly Hers now. And he throbbed with power. Veylistra almost threw her head back and moaned with ecstasy.

'Break the Veil boy' said Rivadus-Hex, His voice shook with suppressed excitement and His stretched face appeared demonic and unnatural in the twisting light. Veylsistra idly wondered where he had acquired this latest one.

'Mistress' said Thorn again, his hand still pressed up against the Veil, which hissed and spat where he touched it.

All immortal eyes were fixed on Thorn, save those of Cinder. Those burning coals slid slowly between Veylistra and Thorn, and they were narrowed in thought.

'Use your strength boy, break it down…..even you can do that' laughed Mahommet, though no one else laughed. His limpid face shone with sweat, causing His florid make-up to run, giving him an odd, decayed appearance.

'Mistress.' Thorn began to push his hand through the Veil. It thrummed like a taught drum skin, and then there was a sonic crack that shook the platform and perhaps the world, as he slid his hand through, where it seemed to hang like a disembodied member, as if attached to the wall alone. Thorns' body behind it was a rippled blur.

The immortals staggered as the platform swayed.

Veylistra ran.

'Mistress.'

Veylistra ran towards Thorns' hand, and summoned all of Her divine power as She did so. She fed it into herself and held it there, where it raged in a bright, incandescent inferno.

And yet as soon as she stepped beyond the bronze disk, She felt herself unravelling. The Rune upon Her cheek had been painful before, but now it burst into flame, and it seared her body, Her very immortal soul.

Rivadus-Hex, perhaps the first to realise what was happening, screamed. 'Nooo. You bitch!'

Faster than a striking snake Rivadus-Hex drew a blade in each hand and launched himself forwards in a great bound at the fleeing Veylistra. His hands blurred as they swept forward in decapitating strokes and then He rebounded from Her aura with a flash of violet sparks, as if He'd struck a wall. Rivadus lay on the ground writhing, and then the Rune on His face burst into flame. He screamed.

Fire writhed about Veylistra. It curled about her body like a lovers' caress and her power fought to quell it, to dampen it. She was losing. Veylistra began to scream.

'Mistress.' Thorn's voice bore a world of agony and pain. He started to take a step through the Veil, which began to buck and crack.

'No' shrieked Veylistra and flames spewed from her mouth.

The immortals watched in impotent anger and rage as Veylistra raced towards Thorns' outstretched hand.

They could see the violet flame of Her own power burning bright within Her, but with each step towards Thorn it dimmed. The flame from the Rune on Her face was so bright now that they could barely look at it. Flame coiled about Her flesh and its fangs consumed Her. Light from the Veil pierced Her immortal flesh and speared it, breaking through, until She seemed almost translucent.

Veylistra shrieked in an agony beyond anything that mortal or immortal had ever endured and was no longer aware that she was doing so. And yet She still fought to hold onto the spark of Her power that remained. Her body was pierced now with holes of light and flame. All that She understood was Her lovers' hand, where it reached out imploringly from the universe beyond.

And then the fire of her power went out, the remaining violet flame was consumed by the fire that ravaged her.

Veylistra lunged.

Thorns hand was held out imploringly. He stepped forward slightly and firm fingers closed about her wrist and pulled her through the Veil.

The empty desolate cold of the void washed over Veylistra and the fires died.

Betrayed immortals shrieked in fury on the steps of the gods.

Cinder laughed.

****

Storms raged across a violet sky; thick blue clouds boiled like water. Comets arched in balls of molten flame to fall with terrible force into the earth, which moaned and bucked in pain. Violet lightning illuminated a horrifying landscape, torn and broken, where mountains rose like ragged teeth. It was a scene from the darkest nightmare.

Thorn stood naked and impassive on the shattered plain, as it groaned and bucked beneath his feet. Lightning flashed about him. The air was thick with hot ash settling onto his alabaster skin and sandy hair, an odd contrast to his eyes, which were totally black. The palm of his left hand glittered a sparkling blue.

The black eyes were riveted on the female figure before him. Her features were startlingly beautiful, though in a distant and untouchable way. Silvered armour adorned her body and gossamer silks rode the winds about her. Where a Rune had once scared her cheek, it was now pure and untouched. The only mark of her trial was the flames that licked across her armour and spat from her mouth when she spoke.

Veylistras' voice was everywhere; across the world and within his mind. The mind that once had been Thorn was tossed before it, like a leaf on the wind.

'You have done well, my servant, my lover. I am pleased.'

Thorn's mind registered the words, and though a primitive jolt of pleasure surged through him at the praise, his consciousness could not comprehend the immensity of the force behind it. What power would be Hers when She cast open the doors to the Hall of Fallen gods? It was almost incomprehensible. His mind began to recoil, seeking to protect itself. But the immensity of Veylistras' mind held him now, with no more difficulty than a man would hold an errant spider.

Thorn was also becoming vaguely aware of what he had begun to regard as his own 'power', responding to Her voice as She addressed him. Sparks began to crackle from his blue hand, stabbing randomly into his body; searing needles of fire. Thorn threw back his head in ecstasy, smiling.

Veylistra laughed, and it was like a howling gale. The earth bucked and comets responded, leaping across the violet sky.

'I see that you begin to recognise your ability now, Thorn, and that is good. But there is more…..so much more. What you are now is but a shadow of what you could become! You carry the seed beloved; let it take root in me. I can provide the sustenance you need. Become my herald and the powers of the avatar will be yours to wield. We can cast open the door to the Hall of Fallen gods together. Rune will be ours for the taking and the gods will flee before us.'

The power within Thorn rejoiced at the prospect; it coursed through him like lightning, crackling across his very skin. In his mind images of war and death danced and capered. Those who had once mocked him he crushed under foot; others he took more pleasure in slaying, enjoying watching them die terribly. How he'd make them pay for their folly! Armies marched at his back and Rune fell before his mistress' might. The divine orders crumbled.

Thorn barked a laugh, a dark and unholy sound. Deep within him, a solitary part of him fluttered alone in the encroaching darkness, screaming a warning, a tiny candle held against the enfolding dark. It flickered for a moment before its desperate light flickered and died.

Somewhere a ripple of concern flickered across Thorn's consciousness. That quiet, almost unheard voice shouted: this terror, this rage and primeval anger, it was not him. This dreadful malevolence was not the man that he'd become. He could see Alazla's kind face swimming in and out of his thoughts, and his mother's image too flashed past, but he could not seem to hear their words. He could not focus on them and the strength of the voice tore them from him.

Thorn lifted his eyes and gazed straight at Veylistra. As he did so, desire flooded him and he felt his very soul laid bare, vulnerable and weak as a newborn pup. 'I accept.'

Veylistra threw Her arms skywards in triumph. Volcanoes erupted anew. Lightning struck the ground all around Thorn, with such force that earth and rocks were cast hundreds of spans into the air. 'Grow,' She said.

A void opened up somewhere within Thorn, a void so vast that his immortal soul was swallowed and into its place rushed utter power, a torrent so vast that his mind screamed as his sanity was almost washed away. Bones exploded within his flesh and his skin ruptured. Agony and ecstasy became his world. He was only vaguely aware of his blood spattering upon the earth about him.

Power pulsed into Thorn from the void within, and with each beat of that black heart his being began to swell. Bones knitted anew, muscles twisted ropelike and vast, his skin became black as night. And just as he thought that the agony had passed and he began to look up, he was forced to his knees by a wrench across his upper spine that threatened to tear him in half. Ebony wings then burst from his back in a shower of blood, bone and sinew. A dark sword twice the size of a man appeared in his hands.

The avatar that was once Thorn looked up into the eyes of his mistress, and knew that he was magnificent. Bowing his head in obeisance, wings sweeping out behind him, he laid his sword at Her feet.

Veylistra smiled. 'Welcome, my child. Arise, Terran-Assail.'

- CHAPTER 20 -

Slave

After months in the slave mines, the novelty of looking at whole seams of gold had long worn off for Alazla. The yellowed beauty was now lustreless, and all he really saw in the gloomy darkness was yet another wall of unyielding rock.

Peering down the mine tunnel, he looked past the supporting timbers and other reluctant miners for his friends, but could not see them. The overseer behind Alazla grumbled and hefted his whip slightly, apparently even less enthusiastic to use it than Alazla was to feel it across his back. With a sigh Alazla lifted his pick again and started chipping away at the uncompromising rock face.

As was often the case during these endless hours, his thoughts drifted to home, which seemed dreamlike from the gloom of the mines. He wondered how his mother was, and fervently hoped that the divine order of Oldoth continued to keep its promise to support her. He remembered her face as clearly as the day she'd tearfully bade him farewell at the Dispensary. Perhaps she'd not even recognise him now though; gone was the puppy fat of his youth, replaced by a leanness that he'd never known before. A blond beard now covered his jaw, shaving not being the most practical habit in the slave mines.

Alazla wasn't one to bear grudges, being the philosophical type. But he also knew when he'd been well and truly stitched up, and that was his opinion of what had happened to him with the 'triple' murder. Certainly, he'd not been entirely innocent regarding Lorm, but he didn't deserve this dreadful fate and that allowed him to hold to his dream of one day being pardoned. Cantillion had relished the punishment he'd delivered to Alazla, pure venom dripping from his words. And if what Pell had said to Alazla in his cell before the trial was conducted was true, then it was Lorm's merchant father who had lined Cantillion's very deep pockets. Alazla had also grimly pledged to himself that one day he would 'pick up' the matter again with Lorm's father.

The sound of the gong being struck in the distance, signalling day's end, brought him out of his recollections and he realised that he'd filled both panniers on a rather overburdened donkey, which was looking at him quite mournfully. He ruffled the donkey's ears, which did little to appease it, and placed his pick in one of the racks. Then he joined the scores of weary, shuffling prisoners, making the long and dismal walk back to the surface.

Waiting for the lift, he spotted one of his friends, Kuoy, and walked over to him. Kuoy's dark skin and the colourful tattoos over much of his body marked him as one of just a few native Ylithians in the slave mines. Many rural Ylithians did not adhere to the recognised pantheon of nine gods and instead worshipped natural spirits of earth and nature. These spirits were represented in many of Kuoy's tattoos. Despite the fact that Korth and Ylith had not always got on especially well in the past, Alazla counted Kuoy as one of his few true friends in the mines. Kuoy nodded as Alazla approached, and both dropped into a weary, but companionable, silence as they waited.

The lift system was operated by the only Gek in the mines, fierce, flat faced creatures with jutting canines, only some ten hand-spans tall (and thus far shorter than Alazla) with an equally wide girth.

Alazla mused, as he passed, that the Gek's brutish appearance didn't reflect a lack of intellect. A highly intelligent race, they weren't prolific breeders, for which mankind was profoundly grateful. Alazla recalled the first time he'd seen one in a jacket, and had nearly split his sides laughing.

A grinning Alazla and Kuoy walked out of the lift and past more heaving, grunting Gek. Their 'home', a holding compound, was located out of the mines, so that the prisoners could have fresh air and a change of scenery when they rested. The slave mines of Crab Island were mainly about maximising gold production, gold that was extremely important to the economy of Korth. This requirement meant treating the prisoners at least moderately well.

The compound was essentially a stockade consisting of two wooden fences. The inner fence contained the prisoner compound and within the outer fence was the guards' barracks. At any one time the compound accommodated up to three hundred 'guests' (as the prisoners flippantly referred to themselves). The grizzled guards lounged against the timber fences, in their hardened leather armour, keeping a careful eye on the prisoners as they filed into the compound.

Thorn and Kuoy dropped onto their regular pallets located under one of the many simple shelters in the inner yard. (There were no buildings with walls, since this prevented the guards watching the prisoners completely.) They were soon joined by their friend Jacinth, who with her slender body and mane of red hair attracted a lot of attention from the other men. Alazla had initially got into several brawls trying to defend Jacinth's honour, as he saw it. Laughing, Jacinth had told him on each occasion that she was more than capable of fighting her own battles, and subsequently proved it by breaking the bones of a too-ardent admirer.

Jacinth flounced down next to them, grinning through a dirt-smeared face. 'So what news boys?' she said. 'No, no, let me guess. You've had a day of gold, rocks and back-breaking lifting. Amazing, me too! That's one of the things I love here, the sheer variety of the bloody work!'

Alazla and Kuoy both laughed.

Alazla had asked Jacinth on a couple of occasions 'what she was in for', this naturally being one of the main topics of conversation, and she'd always declined to discuss it. In many ways she was something of an enigma, in that she never discussed her family or her home, but she could fight like a cornered badger and got on well with Alazla, so that was enough for him.

Kuoy, though, was much more open about his life and had swiftly shared that he had been caught smuggling certain rare weeds and plants across Korth's borders. These weeds and plants had intoxicating and desirable properties that he had many customers willing to pay very handsomely for. It was just bad luck that it had snowed in the Blue Cinder Mountains and his trail had been found by chance and then followed by a Korth border patrol. Subsequently, Kuoy had been given five cycles' slave labour by none other than Loremaster Cantillion himself. Over the most recent two cycles of this, Kuoy had spent much of his time trying to persuade an always-laughing Alazla to go into business with him when they got out. He knew that with Alazla's knowledge and contacts in Korth they could become very rich men. To date, at least, Alazla had always declined.

'Our delicious evening meal arrives,' said Kuoy in his richly accented tongue. 'What I need is a few of my spices and I could soon liven this up!'

'Ha! And no doubt have us drugged and happily asleep for days afterwards,' responded Jacinth.

Kuoy grinned mischievously. 'Of course, a little sprinkling of Adja in our guards' food and I could have them bringing us banquets, ladies and gentlemen, as you like for your pleasure, and more importantly, the gate keys!'

'Adja? Not heard that one before,' harrumphed Alazla. 'I'm guessing it's rare and found only in Ylith, though: right? Not got any on you right now, sort of thing?'

Kuoy laughed. 'You're learning, my friend. We'll make a spice trader of you yet!'

'Excellent idea. Then I can get arrested again and sent back here by a gleeful Cantillion. This time, though, I'm sure it wouldn't be just for a mere thirty cycles,' said Alazla.

'Ah, whatever happened to that happy young man I first met two cycles ago?' asked Kuoy.

Alazla smiled, though did not reply as they retrieved their water and food tins to allow the circulating cooks to fill them up. The food was never great, but the cooks did not scrimp on portions and you could usually have more if you wished.

When they'd finished their meals, with Alazla still hopefully wiping round his food tin with a piece of bread, Jacinth said, 'I've heard more of those rumours again, you two.'

Both looked up.

'You know, the ones about war brewing and all. I've been buttering up Jerome some more,' she said, referring to one of the guard sergeants.

Alazla just smiled, knowing how Jacinth could get most red-blooded men eating out of the palm of her hand.

'Well, Jerome reckons that this tiff between the divine order of Sha and Arcanum has become bloody. Says some of those mage spires have been torn down by the Warlord of Athel-Loria.'

Alazla and Kuoy shared a look of surprise at this. If true, it meant a radical step in what until now had mainly been a war of words between the two orders, although nobody seemed quite sure how the dispute had actually started. Athel-Loria was the greatest military empire on Rune, where the order of Sha traditionally had the greatest presence. The order also took a significant role in the day-to-day governance of the empire. This suggested that the order of Sha had somehow persuaded the emperor to step up the game against Arcanum, the order of magi and beloved of Nim, god of magic.

'What about the other divine orders?' asked Alazla, surprised they'd not intervened to halt the escalation.

'Search me,' replied Jacinth, shrugging.

'You three!' a voice interrupted their politicking.

Looking up, Alazla saw a guard peering into their ramshackle shelter.

'You're all panning tomorrow. Report at first light to Jerome.'

They nodded in response, all sharing a secret smile. Most prisoners looked forward to panning for gold, since it got them out of the mines and into the hills for up to a week at a time. Although the panning itself could be boring, anything was better than hammering relentlessly at gold seams in the lightless depths of Crab Island.

'Nice, that's good news, if there's any such thing in this ruddy place,' said Jacinth. 'I'm turning in, then: we'll be walking a long ways tomorrow.'

With that she took to her blankets and was asleep within moments.

Kuoy and Alazla remained talking for a while before they too did the same.

They had already awoken when the cooks arrived at first light with breakfast. The three of them wolfed it down, eager to get out of the compound. Jerome and two guards waited for them in the outer yard, wearing their typical open-faced steel helms and boiled leather armour. Two more prisoners stood with them: Ibok and Nilm, surly types from the southerly realm of Bordan. Ibok sported a nasty scar across his nose and jaw from a wound that had also taken off much of his upper lip. He'd apparently won this trophy mugging the wrong person in Korth, which then landed him in the Crab Island slave mines. Nilm was small and wiry and had a vicious reputation.

As far as guards went, Alazla thought that Jerome was pretty much all right. It had emerged in conversations during previous panning expeditions that Jerome was also a native of Korth and had grown up in the Stone District, like Alazla, and this had enabled them to strike up conversations. It became clear to Alazla that Jerome actually missed Korth just as much as he did.

Jacinth always flirted outrageously with Jerome, and today was no exception. She flipped her blazing red hair over her shoulder and casually slipped her arm through Jerome's. Smiling, she said, 'Morning, Sergeant Jerome. Hope my favourite guard sergeant will be panning with us?'

Jerome, with a frank appraisal of Jacinth's form, firmly but not too quickly disengaged himself and, patting her on the bottom, said, 'Wouldn't miss you leaning over those stream beds for anything, Jacinth.'

Everyone laughed, although Alazla's was somewhat forced.

Alazla knew that occasional flirtation was part of Jacinth's way of handling some of the nastier and more important characters in the mines. It was hard here at the best of times, but he didn't have to like seeing her do it. Jacinth caught the slightly sad smile on Alazla's face and she gave him a brief, quizzical, look.

'Right, gear's all ready,' said Jerome, pointing to a number of large packs, 'so let's move out.'

Shouldering their gear, they set off. Since the quantity of gold found panning was far smaller than that mining, the panning parties did not usually take pack animals with them, which were in great demand in the mines.

Alazla knew that panning could take them to almost any location on Crab Island, since the whole place was riddled with gold seams, so he hung back and let one of the guards take the lead. Having been on the island for five cycles now, he'd only been on two previous panning expeditions and all within the last few months, since Jacinth had been shipped in. Alazla surmised that Jerome, who usually led these parties, was pulling a few strings for his favourite girl. Alazla certainly wasn't complaining, though: it was good to get out of the mines. He could see from Kuoy's light expression that he too was pleased to get out. Mining was particularly hard on Kuoy, since he'd never lived in enclosed spaces, spending most of his life living in the wild jungles of Ylith.

They spent most of that morning walking, stopping for just the occasional rest. Much of Crab Island was wooded but it was also heavily populated with wildlife, so there were plenty of trails to follow. Alazla could see from regular glimpses of the sea that they were following the coast and heading towards a peninsula on the east side of the island.

By noon they'd reached some wooded hills overlooking a small bay, which was partially circled on the farthest side by cliffs from a peninsula that jutted out into a grey and wind-tossed sea. The guards followed a track that they were obviously familiar with out of the woods and down into the bay.

'Right,' said Jerome, gesturing for the prisoners to come closer. Making sure he'd got their attention, he said, 'I've got leg-irons and manacles here, but you'll work a lot easier without them. So, unless you try anything stupid, I'll keep them off. You try running for the woods,' he said, pointing to the guards with crossbows, 'you'll get shot, simple as that. Korth won't mind one less slave. Am I understood?'

They all nodded, being used to this little speech, although they all had no doubt that Jerome meant what he said.

'Okay then,' said Jerome, 'let's get those tents up and then find some gold.'

Alazla and the others prisoners unslung their packs. The hulking Ibok was carrying the prisoners' tent and Alazla the guards, which they unpacked and assembled on sparse grassland just behind the beach, but far enough away from the trees that the prisoners could not easily sneak out into the cover of the woods.

When the plain dun tents were up they picked up their panning equipment and walked a short distance to the base of the hills. Here a number of streams left their underground hiding places to burble down to the sea. The guards allotted each slave a section of stream where they began to use their pans to sift through the gravel in the streambed, looking for gold.

The two guards with crossbows took up elevated positions on rocks, where they could keep a close eye on the prisoners. Sergeant

Jerome, seeing that all appeared in order, went off to the guards' tent, no doubt to enjoy the privileges of rank.

Panning was boring work: there was only so much interest that you could get from sifting through wet gravel. So when Alazla had panned a little gold from the rich streambed, he let his gaze wander across the island. He noticed that Kuoy, hunkered down beside his stream, was doing much the same and was looking at the woods with a slightly wistful expression. He caught Alazla's gaze and shrugged as if to say 'If only'.

Peering at the peninsula at the farthest side of the bay, Alazla could see that there appeared to be a small building of some kind located there, although he could not quite see what. He'd not been aware that Crab Island had any inhabitants at all, other than slaves, and so studied with interest the distant building. As his eyes lingered on the structure it seemed to him as if it began to slip away from him slightly. Frowning, he turned his attention back to the panning.

Eventually night fell and the guards collected the prisoners' gold and then conducted the ritual body-search for any gold the prisoners might have 'forgotten' to include. At this time, of course, Jerome reappeared and conducted a grinning Jacinth's body-search, personally. Alazla too could not help but smile quietly in respect for Jacinth, noticing as he often did the blood-red stone tied by a leather cord round her neck. He'd often wondered why the stone hadn't been taken from her, as all personal possessions were, but Jacinth had never seen fit to mention it and so he'd never raised the subject.

The prisoners were then shackled with leg-irons, preventing anything but a very loud and slow escape attempt during the night. Amidst much clanking, shuffling and muttered curses the prisoners and their guards gathered around the campfire and began to cook up their provisions. Fireside conversation was somewhat muted, since the guards and prisoners had little to say in each other's company and the five prisoners shortly took to their tent for as much sleep as they could grab.

Tucked into his bedroll, Kuoy spoke in his soft burr. 'Those woods sure look tempting. If we could get there, I could make sure they never found us, you know.'

'Nice thought,' replied Jacinth sarcastically. 'After all, you've only got to get these leg-irons off, dodge the crossbow bolts, fend for yourself with no equipment in a wood and then swim at least forty leagues to the mainland and you'll be free as a bird Kuoy!'

'All right! It was just a thought,' replied Kuoy in a slightly hurt tone.

Nilm, in his slightly nasal voice, interrupted the conversation. 'If you're bored with those two, Jacinth, you can always jump into my blankets! Mind you, we'll probably keep everyone up all night!' he brayed.

Ibok laughed coarsely.

Alazla felt his blood boil. Nilm and Ibok were scum at the best of times, but to have them lech Jacinth in front of her friends was too much. He sat up in his bedroll and started to say something that he knew would start a very nasty fight.

Jacinth, seeing the look on Alazla's face, reached out, laid a placating hand on his arm and, looking at the weaselly Nilm, said, 'I've seen you washing, Nilm, and believe me, I'd be surprised if you could keep any girl awake with that, for even five minutes.'

Everyone laughed at that, except Nilm, who, throwing Jacinth a vicious look, rolled into his blanket.

Hours later, a muffled clank awoke Alazla.

Opening sleep-fogged eyes, he realised that it was deep into the night. The campfire outside had burned down to its embers, judging from the muted glow outside the tent, and he could hear the gentle snore of the guard.

Nilm and Ibok were standing and talking in soft whispers. Their leg-irons were detached and heaped on a bed blanket. Ibok was pointing firmly at Jacinth, but Nilm was shaking his head, his long greasy hair swaying as he did so.

Alazla's jaw clenched in anger as he watched them carefully from beneath hooded eyes, all thoughts of sleep suddenly vanished. There was another moment's hesitation and then, apparently reaching agreement, they lifted the back canvas wall of the tent and slipped soundlessly out into the night.

Damn, thought Alazla, now we're in trouble. He slipped out of his blankets and moved over to Kuoy, placing his hand gently over his mouth to prevent him crying out, and then shook him awake. Kuoy opened his eyes, clearly surprised, but didn't make a sound. Alazla turned to wake Jacinth, but found her already standing behind him.

Their eyes swept the scene lit by a surreal sooty orange glow from the dying fire. Nilm and Ibok's empty bedrolls and the unlocked manacles were plain to see. Glancing at his friends, Kuoy moved over to the empty bedroll and removed a small needle-like object from the lock of one manacle, which he held up to the dim firelight to inspect.

Crouching close to his friends, Alazla could see the alarm in their eyes.

Whispering, Alazla said, 'Damn it, they've escaped.'

'State the obvious, why don't you!,' replied Jacinth, her face pale in the slight light, her voice dripping anger.

Alazla scowled at her. 'All right, but you know this will mean they'll organise a search party and cart us straight back off to the mines. We'll be back hacking at the rock face by tomorrow afternoon latest!'

Alazla could just make out that his friends were both nodding in agreement.

'And that's if they don't think we conspired to help them to escape,' whispered Kuoy.

Silence ensued.

Awkward moments passed.

It was Jacinth who broke the silence. 'Damn. They'll call in the divine order of Faed for sure and that'll mean they'll know that Kuoy's, at the very least, touched those manacles and lock-pick, if he didn't also help them to escape, and that implicates us all. At the very least we'll be sentenced to become gloomers,' she said, referring to those who were sent to the slave mines for life. 'But we could even be executed.'

Alazla cursed their luck, knowing that Jacinth was right. How could they be so damned unlucky, blast Ibok and Nilm! He could see panic racing across the faces of his friends as they all considered the options. Alazla knew with a certainty that he could not spend the rest of his life in the mines.

Reaching a decision, Alazla said, 'I'm going to run. We can go together if you want, but I'll not force you to come with me, although I don't really see that we've got much of a choice. I'm not going to spend the rest of my life as a gloomer.'

Laying her hand gently on Alazla's, Jacinth said, 'I'm with you.'

Moments passed as Kuoy stared at the open manacles upon the bed. He sighed. 'Fine. If you're going to survive out here, you'll need me too.'

Alazla smiled at his friend gratefully, knowing Kuoy was right.

Jacinth plucked the pick out of Kuoy's trembling hands and, peering in the slight light, put it into the lock of Alazla's manacles. She manoeuvred the pick for a moment, then there was a slight click and the manacles opened.

'Nice,' whispered Alazla, amazed.

Jacinth took a mocking crouched bow and then opened her own and Kuoy's manacles in the same way.

They slipped out the back of the tent and into the night. The guards snored on, oblivious.

- CHAPTER 21 -

The Broken Stone

For the first hour they simply ran, seeking to put as much distance between themselves and the guards as possible. They were lucky that it was a moonlit night. Trees whipped past as they raced through undergrowth; branches snagged clothing and scratched skin, but they didn't notice. They hurdled logs and streams with equal speed, hardly even stopping as they glanced back over their shoulders for signs of pursuit.

Alazla heard a muffled shriek, followed by a curse, from Jacinth and she called out for them to stop. Halting and looking back, Alazla could see that she had tumbled into a small stream, from which, muttering and cursing, she was now dragging herself, soaking wet. He couldn't help but smile at the sour look on her face, red hair curling into wet ringlets about her face, as she plopped down on the stream bank. A puffing Kuoy arrived behind him.

'Uhg. By Faed's black tits that water was cold. We need to talk,' Jacinth shivered, scraping back dripping hair from her face. 'We can't just keep charging headlong through these bloody woods at night without some form of plan or direction. And may the god of luck crap on Ibok and Nilm for causing this,' she added with venom. 'As I see it, if we're not already, we're shortly going to be hunted by mine guards who'll shoot to kill without question. We're trapped on an island just a few leagues wide, with no food, no weapons, and more importantly no means of getting off it.'

Alazla was fighting to keep the smile off his face and not doing a very good job, as he cheerfully replied, 'I'd say that you've pretty much covered it.' He wasn't sure why he wasn't panicking or feeling at least some degree of fear. He guessed that five cycles in a slave mine did a lot to harden a person to life's cruelties, but more than that he actually felt exhilarated.

Kuoy interjected quietly, dropping down on the stream bank beside Jacinth. 'Don't know if you noticed, though, Nilm and Ibok's trail split from ours a ways back. That means the guards are going to have to divide to follow us and I'm guessing that there are not enough of them to do that. I'd say that two of them will likely follow one trail while a third goes back to the compound for reinforcements, and that's a day's travel.'

Alazla and Jacinth both looked at their friend, surprised at the astuteness of his observation.

Alazla nodded. 'Well, let's hope that the guards follow Nilm and Ibok. Crossbow bolts in the back are what they truly deserve.'

'So now what?' asked Jacinth. 'Anyone got any ideas?'

'Well,' replied Alazla, 'when we were panning yesterday, I think I saw a house on that peninsula at the other side of the bay. We could go there and see if we can find some supplies.' (He certainly didn't like the idea of stealing from people, but for them this was genuinely a matter of life or death.) 'Looked like that peninsula would have some good views too. We could see if there are any other folk around here, and if there are, it's possible they've got a boat.'

Jacinth nodded. 'Well, I for one can't think of anything better and we certainly can't stay on this island: that's a ruddy death sentence for sure. Kuoy, got any other ideas?'

Kuoy shook his head.

'Right, let's go then,' she said.

It didn't take long to reach the peninsula, since by chance they had been travelling in its general direction. The wood thinned out as it reached the peninsula and the three escapees crouched down near its edge and cautiously scanned the area ahead, their breath steaming in the night air. It appeared quite bare in the darkness, covered largely just in scrub and grass. Moonlight illuminated a small stone house, its shuttered windows dark. Between the house and the edge of the peninsula was the occasional windswept tree, bent over and hunched like an old man. Beyond the trees was a single standing stone, its surface dark in the silver half-light. There was no sign of any life.

Alazla whispered, 'Doesn't look like there's anyone here, in fact it really seems abandoned. We'd better get back into the woods.'

Kuoy nodded his agreement and they turned to leave.

Jacinth, however, was still staring at the cottage. 'No,' she said.

Alazla and Kuoy stopped. Now that Alazla was facing away from the peninsula he was actually not quite sure why he was walking away. Whether the cottage was abandoned or not, they still might be able to salvage something from it. After all, they had little else to go on.

The dunk in the stream had washed much of the grime off Jacinth, and Alazla could not help but be struck by her beauty again, artfully highlighted now by the soft hues of the moonlight. She was staring, frowning, straight at the cottage as if she could bore a hole in it. Alazla noted that her teeth were gritted.

'Something's not right here,' she said sharply. 'I can smell enchantment.'

Alazla's hair stood up at the back of his neck at her words. No one said a word.

'Enchantment or not, though,' Jacinth continued, 'we're still in the crap. We need any equipment we can get our hands on.'

Alazla baulked slightly. 'If you think it's enchanted, though, Jacinth, shouldn't we just leave it alone?' The more he thought about it, the more this place filled him with a deep unease. 'We'll find someplace else to get what we need.' But even as he said it he knew that it wasn't true.

Jacinth was staring at him hard. Her reply was an angry hiss. 'What?! If you know where we can get the stuff need to save our bloody lives then I suggest you say so now, cause I'd love to hear it, Alazla.'

Alazla held her stare for a moment and glanced at Kuoy, who shook his head and then dropped his gaze.

'Fine, that's sorted then,' snapped Jacinth.

'All right,' replied Alazla, looking up, 'but one of us should keep lookout: they can whistle if they see any signs of trouble.' Jacinth nodded. 'Good idea.'

'I'll keep lookout if you like,' said Kuoy, Alazla thought just a bit too quickly.

Kuoy remained hidden in the brush and steeling himself, Alazla reluctantly began to creep forward with Jacinth. Moving as best they could between scrub and tree for concealment, they approached the cottage. Alazla's sense of unease began to increase as they crept closer. He found it easier to concentrate on the trees and ground rather than look directly at the cottage, which seemed to slide from his vision like oil.

As the cottage got closer, pins and needles began to crawl over his skin, and his sight seemed strangely blurred at the edges. He risked a glance at Jacinth as they crouched behind a wizened tree and noticed the bulge of her tightened jaw muscles and a slight sheen of sweat on her brow, although she seemed to stare straight at the cottage in a way that he couldn't. Looking back over his shoulder he could just make out the dark form of Kuoy watching them from the wooded eaves.

Struggling to ignore his irrational fear, Alazla continued to move towards the cottage, now solely guided by instinct. When it occasionally came into his immediate vision, bands of fear tightened about his chest. The only way he could move forward was to crawl towards it on hands and knees, with his face almost touching the grass. Finally his seeking hands touched cold stone and just as suddenly the feelings vanished. His blurred vision swam back into focus.

Taking in a gasping breath, he saw that the cottage before him was actually utterly derelict. The walls and roof had collapsed inwards, as if shaken by some massive force. Hunching behind the irregular remnants of the rear wall, they both gasped for breath, the air felt cool and calm. An odd dull reddish light was casting the walls, the grass and their skin into a sinister scarlet hue. A deep, reverberating drone thrummed from somewhere beyond the wall.

Alazla swore very quietly, and then for good measure beseeched a blessing from Oldoth. Clearly this was not what they'd been looking for. They'd stumbled into some form of unholy enchantment and now that cottage was clearly totally derelict, their hope for even basic supplies was clearly lost. Alazla grabbed Jacinth's arm and pointed that they should go back to the woods. Jacinth smiled, her teeth stained a carnivorous red in the light, and then slipped over the fallen wall into the cottage. Alazla cursed again for the second time in as many minutes and followed her.

They crawled through the derelict interior of the house, concealing themselves behind the cracked remains of walls and wooden posts. Shadows hugged the corners, despite the red hue that passed for light. The house had obviously been very simple, for it apparently had only two internal rooms. The front wall was largely tumbled down, but they found enough to hunker behind.

Looking past the wall took their breath away. The peninsula stretched away before them to the bluff. Where once a few hardy trees had stood, now only scarred stumps remained. There was a single standing stone at the very end of the peninsula which was now shattered, ripped down the centre like so much paper, its two halves bent outwards, curling in agony. The tearing had ripped apart the single rune of Oldoth that had once been carved upon the stone's surface. Within the centre of the shattered standing stone rotated a well of swirling darkness fed by veins of red light, its heart appearing almost to be the iris of some baleful eye, giving off a low hum that rippled through the ground.

Alazla stared, transfixed with both horror and fascination, at the rotating well within the stricken stone. He felt at once revolted by it, yet also drawn to it, unable to tear himself away, as a moth is drawn to a flame. It seemed then as he stared that its surface became somewhat less dark, and that if he looked harder perhaps he could even see something beyond. And then he realised something was looking back at him, something vast. He panicked, hands clawing up clods of grass, desperate to look away, but he could not. His mind was being drawn into its vast swirling depths.

Then there was a sudden yank and his gaze was physically pulled away from the heart of the stone. Alazla found himself being dragged unceremoniously back into the lee of the cottage wall by Jacinth, who dropped pale and shivering beside him.

'By all that's holy,' said Alazla, gasping for breath, convulsive shivers running through him.

Then he noticed a look of pale rage on Jacinth's face. Her face was contorted as if she struggled to control her emotions; her fists were clenched tight. Taken aback, Alazla slowly reached out and placed his hands over her fists. Her very body appeared to tremble with her rage. Horror or fear he would have expected, but this? He waited a moment then, just with his hands upon her fists, looking into her face.

'Jacinth,' he said, ignoring his own trembling, 'we need to go, we can't stay here… Jacinth.'

She looked up then, as if seeing him for the first time, and briefly nodded her assent.

Alazla, holding Jacinth's hand, stood into a crouching position. Then, keeping as low as they could, they stumbled numb and dazed back towards the woods.

****

The horse warriors had stood little chance. For all their much-vaunted battle prowess, all seven had fallen swiftly beneath her fangs. Oh, they'd been brave, as they always were, spotting her when she let them, letting them think they had the element of surprise. But it was they who'd been shocked, for despite her vast age Hercuba was still fast, perhaps faster than she ever had been, and she enjoyed playing. Their toy spears had simply bounced harmlessly from her lustrous fur, when she allowed them to strike her. For it would take greater weapons than that to harm such as her. They had even circled her at one time, and then she had taken great delight in tearing them one by one shrieking from their saddles and dismembering them before their fellows, as their battle-trained horses reared and whinnied in terror.

The last warrior had of course tried to flee and she'd let him; for she enjoyed knowing how her name had become a growing tale of terror and despair within the horse tribes.

This was a personal dance for Hercuba and her little horse warriors from Hamad. Ah, yes, they mostly avoided these hills now unless it was on some foolish quest to slay her and make a name for themselves. Consequently, they now mostly kept their herds and nomadic camps far from these hills, far from Hercuba and her children. What they did not realise was that this did not disturb Hercuba at all. She was not here for the horse warriors of Hamad, not even the delicious joy of menacing them. The horse warriors and their kind were just an unexpected bonus, there in hard times to keep her family fat.

No, Hercuba was here for the Forest of Shades. Hercuba's hills lay just south of that lush and verdant forest. Cursedly its powers were so great that she could not enter it, but often of course lovely fairy creatures would stray close to the edge of their enchanted forest, perhaps even to play in the hills or the lush Hamadian grasslands, and then she would have them. Chomping and grinding on their fine bones, she found the taste of their blood so very sweet. That was why Hercuba loved it here so. She stopped chewing for a moment on the carcass of a horse warrior, deliberating whether or not to set off for the boundaries of the forest. Her maws began to salivate at the prospect, steaming saliva dribbling onto the grass, burning it black.

And then she heard a whisper, so faint that at first that she ignored it and continued with her grisly meal.

'Hearken unto me.' There it was again, but stronger now. Hercuba looked up this time intrigued, her ears pricking.

She growled then in her hissing spitting language, 'Do not disturb my meal, creature. Begone.'

The response was a blast of wind so strong across the hills that the grass flattened and trees bent.

'Well, you've got stronger, I see,' Hercuba said conversationally. 'What is it you want then?'

The voice chuckled, a sultry feminine timbre. 'I'm glad to see that you still know when to growl and when to mew, my little Hercuba. I've a task for you, my darling, and you need to leave immediately.'

'Is that so, Veylistra?' Hercuba growled. 'I'm all ears.'

The voice laughed, an unpleasant sound. 'Somehow I thought you might be.'

- CHAPTER 22 -

Flight

Hercuba circled Crab Island in the soft dawn light, delighting in the play of the errant sea wind beneath her huge leathery wings. It tugged at the massive black mane in which she took so much pride, making it stream behind her like some unholy black banner. Hercuba roared in delight at the freedom, sending gulls shrieking from the cliffs beneath her.

Her six eyes analysed in minute detail the landscape below, the lush forest and small hills and cliffs against which the restless surf strove. There too sat the shattered stone of the poor godling Oldoth and some form of human settlement inland, judging from the smoke that arose. Interested, Hercuba banked and dropped downward for a closer look, but still stayed high enough to ensure it was unlikely she would be noticed.

Within the forest and hills the humans had despoiled a large area, now covered with wooden buildings, including a compound and what appeared to be a couple of watchtowers. The adjacent hill was pitted with black holes where the humans had apparently burrowed, perhaps looking for something or trying to build themselves new dens. In fact Hercuba supposed that if tunnelled deeply enough, the dens might actually be quite cosy; perhaps these humans weren't quite so stupid after all. She would remember this place, perhaps for a beloved cub or two.

The human settlement was well populated too, so it seemed likely that the manling she sought could dwell here. This was a good place to start her search. Folding her wings, Hercuba dived towards the mining town. The wind howled as she descended and she roared in glee, baring her massive fangs.

As the complex rushed up at her and the inevitable screams of the paltry humans began, she noticed that scores of them were neatly paddocked within a large wooden compound. Hercuba did not know what this portended but appreciated the convenience of it. She would feed well today.

****

Alazla awoke. For a moment he had thought that he'd heard a distant animal roar, but all about him seemed tranquil and his attention was quickly drawn to the delicious smell of cooking – fish, if he was not mistaken.

Sitting up from his impromptu bed of fern leaves, Alazla smiled. With dawn the worry of pursuit and spinning wells of darkness had receded. Kuoy looked up from a small firepit, his tanned face crinkling in a smile. 'Good morning, Alazla,' he said in his rich Ylithian accent. 'Feel better for your beauty sleep?'

Throwing off the ferns, which he actually had no recollection of picking, and rubbing his eyes, Alazla mooched over to the firepit and dropped down onto the grass beside Kuoy. Glancing briefly at Kuoy, Alazla peered into the firepit and saw within the fierce glowing embers small packages wrapped in leaves. 'I take it that's breakfast,' Alazla said, cheering up. 'I've got absolutely no idea where you got that but it's a blessing and that's all I really care about,' he added, and clapped his friend on the back.

'Where's Jacinth?' Alazla enquired, looking about.

'Gone down to the stream for a wash,' Kuoy replied, grinning. He hoisted one of the leafy packages out of the fire with a pair of scorched twigs and placed it in front of Alazla.

Barely able to wait, Alazla was so hungry that he burned his fingers several times getting the leaf wraps off his breakfast. He scoffed down great chunks of a delicious white fish, barely chewing. By the time Jacinth returned from the stream, Alazla was lying back content, staring forlornly at the empty leaf wrappers.

Damp from head to toe, her red hair hanging in ringlets, Jacinth had obviously washed her clothes too, since they appeared an almost different colour from yesterday and free from much of the dust from the mines.

'Oh,' she said, smiling as she walked over, 'See you've stirred at last. Thought we were going to have to leave you for the guards to discover, snoring blissfully.' Alazla smiled, running a hand ruefully through his shaggy blond hair, just pleased that his friend did not seem unduly affected by last night's strange experience.

'Fish is ready,' said Kuoy.

'Great, Kuoy, thanks,' said Jacinth as she sat beside the firepit and began to dig out her breakfast.

Alazla could not help but notice the way in which the damp clothing clung to her lithe and fit form. Looking up, he caught Kuoy grinning at him cheerfully, his dark eyes sparkling in mirth. Alazla had the good grace to blush.

Jacinth appeared not to have noticed the brief exchange as she tucked into her fish breakfast with almost as much gusto as Alazla had. Around mouthfuls she said, 'Don't know about you two, but despite what we saw last night, I recon our priority's still got to be getting off this bloody Island.'

Alazla surmised from this that she'd told Kuoy about what the two of them had seen.

Surprised, Alazla replied, 'How can you say that, Jacinth? What we saw last night changes everything! Didn't you see that....thing?! It looked like some god-cursed eye, or I don't know what, staring straight out from what had once been a sacred bloody stone of Oldoth.'

Alazla realised that he was raising his voice, but the emotion of the previous night had begun to come out. 'We need to put concern for ourselves aside here. This is not just about us any more. Captain Ixus at the mines needs to be told about the stone. I'd expect that he'll then send for help from the mainland. It, it might even help to get me pardoned, or my case reviewed at least, but if not….fine, I'll live with that.'

Taking a deep breath, he plunged on. 'I understand if you don't want to do that, so if you don't want to come back to the mine complex I'll go alone.' Swallowing slightly, Alazla looked within himself and knew that he meant everything he'd said. Finishing, he said, 'I'll just tell them that I lost you or something. They don't have to know where you've gone.'

The three ex-slaves all looked at each other for a few moments after Alazla's outburst.

Unusually, it was Kuoy who eventually broke the silence with his soft voice. 'I know you mean well, Alazla, but do you really think that they'll believe you? You'll just be a slave who tried to escape and failed. I shouldn't think you'll even get to see Captain Ixus and explain your unlikely tale. They'll just be happy to have caught a runaway slave and will march you straight down the mine, where you'll then sleep, live and work for the rest of your sorry life, if you're lucky. You probably won't even get to see the compound again, let alone daylight. Yours sense of honour is deluding you my friend.'

Staring at Kuoy and trying to find some fault in his argument, Alazla knew in his gut that his friend was right. Thinking deeply, with just the crackle of the fire to break the silence, he then eventually nodded reluctantly in agreement.

Jacinth said gently, 'So having persuaded our idiotic but noble friend here not to turn himself in….we can actually get back to the subject of what to do about what we've seen, and more importantly, getting off this confounded rock.'

Alazla knew it was meant partly in jest, but found himself slightly needled nonetheless.

'Well,' said Kuoy, getting up and pacing across the small clearing 'I think we should stick with just the one thing, getting to the mainland. When we get there, we can cut across the Blue Cinder mountains. I know a few hidden trails,' (at this he smiled indulgently), 'and make for Ylith. Once we're in the jungles of my homeland we will never be caught, that I can guarantee.'

'But what about that thing in the sacred stone?' said Alazla again, also getting up. 'We've got to tell someone about it. Someone will need to do something, it was,' he searched for the right words, 'horrible… it was just wrong.'

'All I'm hearing is someone, someone, someone,' Kuoy now shouted. 'What do you want three runaway slaves to do about it?! Even if you find someone prepared to talk to you, they will never believe you!'

Jacinth, looking up from her seat by the fire at the two men, said mildly, 'He's right, Alazla. What we saw is beyond us: we just need to get to bloody safety. There are other folk better equipped and better placed to deal with that than us. We need to look after ourselves now.'

Alazla, now angry, kicked a stone in frustration. Seeking at least some support, he looked from one face to the other and found none. 'So you'd have us hide in the stinking jungles of Ylith for the rest of our lives,' Alazla shouted at them both.

'Bugger it, both of you!,' snapped Jacinth, 'keep your voices down. The danger here is far from past.'

Then, looking at them, Alazla knew the answer. 'I know someone in power and I believe that he'll listen to us.' He didn't mention that he wondered whether this same person could also help to recind his sentence.

Kuoy began to come back with a taut remark but Jacinth held up her hand. 'No, let us at least hear him out, Kuoy. We owe each other that.'

Clenching his teeth, Kuoy nodded curtly.

Alazla hurried on, eager not to lose the moment. 'His name in Balthazar, he's a member of the divine order of Oldoth and Head of the Korthian House. He's helped me before and I know that we can trust him. If we get his support, he'll know what to do.'

Kuoy laughed and threw up his arms. 'You have got to be joking. You want us to go to the House of Oldoth in Korth, the capital city of the same realm that tried us and then sentenced us to slave labour?' He looked to Jacinth for support but quieted when he saw her pensive.

Jacinth said simply, 'Do you *know* that you can trust him, Alazla?'

Heart thumping, Alazla took a moment before he replied. 'Yes, I do. In fact, I owe him my life.'

Without pause, Jacinth said, 'Fine, then, I'll help you.'

'And I will not,' said Kuoy, raising his voice again. 'If you want to throw away your new-found freedom and walk into the dragon's den, then that is up to you, but you will do it without Kuoy.'

Regretfully Alazla nodded. 'All right, Kuoy, we'll work together to try and find a boat to get us off the island. At the very least the slave guards must have boats hidden somewhere; perhaps we can find those. When we land, though, we'll go our own way.' He looked sadly at his long-time friend, who only nodded his head in agreement, his face adamant.

Kuoy had cooked up plenty of fish, which, knowing they'd all be starved again later, they crammed into their pockets. They all reached agreement on first investigating the island's east coast in the hope that they might find at least a small settlement, from where they could steal a boat. This would also take them away from the direction in which the mines lay and also the place where they had been panning for gold the previous day. It was from that place they all believed the guards would inevitably start their search.

Kuoy offered to lead the way, and since his woodcraft seemed infinitely better than either of theirs, Alazla and Jacinth readily agreed. Setting off, Kuoy moved through the woods with hardly a murmur, scarcely moving branch or leaf. The others behind made their way as best they could.

Several times that morning they stopped briefly when Kuoy spotted something of interest to him. Alazla was amazed at how prolific the woods were with their bounty. Making a bag from the smock he wore, revealing an undershirt so filthy that it drew sarcastic comments about being downwind of him from Jacinth, Kuoy steadily began to fill his makeshift haversack. Alazla had no idea what many of the things were, but what he did recognise at one point was mushrooms and his mouth began to water in anticipation of their evening meal.

The woods did not have a particularly dense canopy overhead and so it was easy to tell the time of day as the morning chased away. Initially Alazla even enjoyed the walking across sun-dappled underbrush and mossy logs. Soon, however, the novelty began to wear off, as Kuoy kept up a relentless pace. Unfortunately the ground underfoot wasn't sparse: bracken, ferns and scrub were thick, and both Alazla and Jacinth were getting cut to bits keeping up with Kuoy. Both took turns at asking him if he was sure he was going in the right direction, or following the quickest route. Kuoy stopped answering, them in the end.

By Alazla's estimation it was gone midday by the time they reached the eastern coast. The wood stopped just a few spans before the edge of a low cliff, under which the sea crashed against the rocks, sending streaming fingers of spray clutching at the clifftops.

Jacinth dropped to the ground at the cliff edge, hanging her legs over it, raising her face to allow the sea spray to cool her. Kuoy grinned from the grass where he lay sprawled on his back. 'I think we've made good time. Unfortunately, also I think you two cut a trail that any reasonable tracker could follow with their eyes shut, but since we're talking about slave guards, well, we *might* be all right.'

'We'd better hope so,' replied Alazla.

Gazing out to sea, Alazla recalled his home. Korth's harbour was magnificent: its crystal walls would sparkle in the setting sun, the sea ablaze in turquoise and red, as merchant galleys from a dozen peaceful nations rubbed restlessly against the wooden docks. He dared to hope, briefly, that he may even see it again, something he had been sure he could never expect.

They did not linger long, but before setting off again they wolfed down the remainder of the fish and drank their fill from a nearby stream that ran gurgling happily off the edge of the cliff to join its big salty brother below. Then making sure that they could not see any signs of habitation along the coast within sight, they struck out, following the cliff line southward.

Kuoy took the precaution of keeping them within the tree line, even though the going would have been much easier in the short grass that typically grew from the tree line to the cliff edge. No one had to ask why this was.

As the afternoon wore on and the sun trod its track across a cloud-scudded sky, Alazla began to develop a slight sense of unease. Occasionally he found himself glancing back over his shoulder, and even once up at the sky. Puzzling, he could find no tangible reason why he should be getting edgy. I'm worried about pursuit by the guards, no doubt, he reasoned, although with the pace they were making he thought it unlikely that they would be found quickly. On somewhere as remote as Crab Island and with Kuoy's wood lore, he was beginning to think that they could evade capture for many days and even weeks perhaps.

Despite the fact that Kuoy was setting a rapid pace through the outer wood, Alazla found himself wishing that he would move more quickly and was almost dogging his friend's footsteps. Finally, Kuoy glanced back irritably and Alazla dropped back.

Jacinth looked at Alazla questioningly. He shrugged. 'Sorry, just getting a bit edgy.'

The light had almost fled when Kuoy stopped them. Even Alazla was grateful for the halt; blisters were now beginning to plague both of his feet.

'We should not go much farther today,' Kuoy said. 'Without the light the way will be treacherous.' The others nodded. 'I will seek us some more food, although I found some along the way as well. I'm afraid there will be no meat tonight.'

Alazla huffed sadly and Jacinth laughed.

As Kuoy moved off into the woods, Jacinth said, 'Go on, Alazla, find us some dry wood and kindling and I'll dig us a fire pit.'

Feeling rather like the errand boy, Alazla scowled slightly and, rubbing his flaxen beard, set off to seek dry wood. Having at least a little experience of gathering such, he knew where best to look, and it did not take him long to gather enough for a small fire. He also took the opportunity to gather armloads of ferns and pine branches for their bedding that night. Returning with his final armload, he saw Jacinth had located a stone that she was now using as a shovel to carve out a fairly deep firepit, some thirty spans or so within the eaves of the wood. He knew the pit should work fairly well to keep the flame and smoke from their fire to a minimum, in addition to the concealing embrace offered by the leafy canopy above.

While Jacinth was still excavating, Alazla took the opportunity to further explore their campsite. Leaving the woods, he walked to the edge of the cliff and looked out along the coastline. In the failing light there was little that he could see, although he did notice a small cove immediately south from their present location. He reflected that had they walked a little farther they could perhaps have made it there and tried to spear fish for their supper. Nevertheless he was grateful for being alive and free right now. A little hunger was a small price to pay.

As he reflected on this, a hand touching his arm made him jump. Turning, he saw Jacinth standing beside him. In the setting sun, she seemed even more beautiful than normal. Her curly red hair seemed ablaze with life, her skin was a soft white and her large brown eyes liquid. He realised with a start that he had reached out with his hand and was gently touching her cheek. Jacinth had not moved, but only smiled gently at him.

Softly she said, 'Would you like to tell me what's wrong, Alazla? You've been jumpy as a ruddy bullfrog all afternoon.'

Alazla dropped his hand and was silent for a moment, turning to stare back out to sea. His feelings churned inside him like the waves crashing against the cliffs below.

When he said nothing, Jacinth continued, 'You're worried. Is it about returning to Korth or even the prospect that you could even see your mother?'

All of these things were on Alazla's mind, certainly, and he wondered at how well Jacinth seemed to understand him. He was acutely aware of her warm presence beside him and her hand now resting lightly on his arm. Alazla wrestled with how to explain what he could describe only as a feeling and almost failed. The silence grew between them. Jacinth took her hand from his arm and began to walk away.

'Jacinth,' Alazla said. She stopped and looked back at him, waiting. 'I don't know how to explain it, it's just a feeling. I know that the guards are certainly a long way from us yet, but I feel… I feel… well, like we're being hunted.' There, he'd said it.

Jacinth smiled sadly. 'You worry too much, Alazla. That time will come, but not yet.' She began to walk back to the camp.

Alazla did not join his friends until much later, and Kuoy did not enquire. He ate the simple meal of cold roasted nuts, berries and mushrooms and then tucked himself into his fern bed. Watching the sun set into the rolling sea, Alazla slowly gave in to the gentle call of sleep.

- CHAPTER 23 -

Revelry

It was late into the night when Alazla awoke in a sweat, his breath coming in shallow gasps. His entire body was damp. The fire had long died and moonlight had turned the trees to precious silver. His companions were just immobile forms rolled deep into their leafy beds. The surf was only a distant hiss.

Alazla collected himself and willed his breathing to slow. As it did so his thumping heart also grew quieter and he realised then that he could hear faint music. Wondering if he was hearing things, he paused, listening again, trying to filter out the noise of the sea. There it was again: it sounded like some form of song.

Quietly rising, Alazla followed the sounds. He stalked to the edge of the woods, doing his best to keep quiet by imitating Kuoy's movements and doing at least a fair job. Seeing nothing beyond the wood line, he crept towards the cliff edge. As he approached he dropped to his knees, so as not to create a silhouette in the moonlight, and crawled forward. Hardly daring to breathe, he looked over the cliff edge and saw nothing save the restless surf.

Alazla swung his gaze south towards the cove and stopped in amazement. There were two ships anchored within the sheltering bay, their decks ablaze with lights. He could see little about them but cared not at all, that was enough for him. Keeping low, he raced back to the camp and quietly roused his two companions.

Jacinth and Kuoy pushed aside their fern bedding, waiting for Alazla to speak, knowing that he would not have woken them halfway through the night without good reason.

Alazla, grinning in his excitement, whispered, 'There are two ships, here now, in the cove just to the south!'

Jacinth and Kuoy looked stunned.

'Were they there earlier?' asked Kuoy quietly. 'Did we miss them?'

Alazla shook his head. 'Definitely not. I checked before we ate our meal and there was nothing there. They must have arrived within the last few hours.'

Jacinth seemed about to ask a question. Laughing slightly, Alazla held up his hand, to forestall her. 'I only had a brief look but we need to check this out, and quickly. It's possible they may leave with the dawn light.'

Jacinth and Kuoy both readily nodded agreement.

Kuoy took his customary lead a good way in front of his friends, moving quietly as a ghost. Beside Jacinth, Alazla watched his footing carefully, trying hard not to make any noise. Within a few minutes they had reached the nearest edge of the cove and Kuoy secured a position at the top of the bluff behind some scrub from which they could peer down with little chance of being seen.

The cove itself was small, with low grey cliffs running out to either side. Small tongues of rock poked impudently from the sea around their base. The sea was much calmer here within the shelter, Alazla noticed, than where they had made evening's camp. Rising gently on the low swell of the waves, two small boats rode at anchor, surprisingly close to shore. Alazla realised this must mean they had fairly shallow draughts. Their sails were furled and the rails and rigging were merrily hung about with lanterns of various colours, so as to give the craft a slightly carnival appearance. Their decks sported garish canvas canopies. Each boat was perhaps fifty hand-spans in length, with a small cabin at the aft end.

A couple of small rowing boats, no doubt landing vessels from the craft anchored farther out, had been dragged up the shingle beach. Their occupants presently appeared to be having a party. Fires burned merrily on the shingle beach, sending flicking fingers of flame crawling up the cliffs, illuminating laughing, dancing figures about the fires, clad in silks and satins of blue, red, purple and gold. Ladies swirled long skirts as they danced arm in arm with the singing men in tunic and hose, one also playing a violin. Occasionally one of the revellers would stop, gasping for breath and smiling, reach for one of the numerous bottles of wine propped up amongst the shingle.

From their seclusion the three escapees looked on, amazed. Ultimately it was Jacinth who broke the silence. 'You know, I've not been to a wicked party in ages. How about we go and join them?'

'Tempting,' replied Alazla, laughing softly, 'very tempting, but unfortunately I left my best silk shirt at home.'

Kuoy remained silent, still studying the scene.

'I've seen that type of boat before,' Kuoy said at last. 'They're coast-huggers, not true sea-goers, pleasure cruisers from Apolletta, most likely. That rowdy lot on the beach are likely nobles.'

Looking at Kuoy, Jacinth replied, 'What?! Surely everyone knows this is a prison island! Why on Rune would they want to come to this dump?'

Kuoy just shrugged but Alazla interjected, 'Crab Island is the nearest island to mainland Korth. I'd guess from what Kuoy has just said that it's about the farthest they can get to in those small boats. Bit of an adventure, maybe… and after all, no Crab Island slave guard is going to arrest a noble's son or daughter,' he added as an afterthought.

'I'd say,' said Kuoy quietly, his brow furrowed in thought. 'That lot are fairly well gone. If we're quiet we could probably sneak around them by keeping to the lee of the cliff. We could reach one of those landing boats, row out and then be away on one of those pleasure boats without them even seeing us.'

Jacinth was nodding in agreement, but with a concerned tone in his voice Alazla asked, 'But how are they going to get off the island if we take their boat?'

Kuoy looked at Alazla strangely for a moment and replied, 'Well, they'll still have one boat left. Their return journey may be a bit cramped, but I'm sure they can make it back to the mainland.'

Mollified, Alazla nodded.

Jacinth interjected, 'I hate to be the bearer of bad news boys, but has anyone noticed that we're at the top of a cliff and they're on a beach below us?'

Kuoy nodded. 'Obviously a good point. I'll take a quick look around and see if I can find us a way down.' With that he slipped soundlessly out from their scrubby hide.

Watching the revellers, Alazla thought that they looked increasingly drunk. The dancing was becoming more like staggering and the screeches from the violin strings showed that the violinist was also finding it more difficult to keep a tune, not that his friends seemed to have noticed. Alazla was reminded of the Decoram Festivities in Korth and of parting company with Thorn at the nobles' party. Perhaps if they'd stayed together Thorn would never have spent the night in that cursed crystal wood and none of this would ever have happened. But as his mother would say, you can't pick up spilled milk. He knew she was right, though that did not stop him regretting.

Kuoy was not gone long. On his return, his smile was white in the moonlight. 'Old stream bed runs down the other side. It makes an almost perfect track down to the beach. We should be able to pass easily… as long as someone keeps quiet,' he added with a meaningful glance at Alazla. Grinning slightly in chagrin, Alazla acknowledged the gentle caution.

Kuoy led them around the curve of the cliff top, being careful to keep them out of line of sight from the beach. On the farthest side Kuoy crouched down, his long black hair falling over his tanned face, and pointed with tattooed hands to a narrow trail downward, where once a stream must have chattered down the cliff towards the sea. From this side, Alazla could now see that the cliff was actually not especially steep, and during the daylight they could probably have negotiated it straight down by helping each other and taking their time. Right now, though, this old stream bed was a blessing.

Kuoy led again, followed by Jacinth and Alazla. Kuoy practically crouched as he moved surely downwards. Alazla tried to mimic his friend's movements. Often Kuoy would stop and feel his way where the stream bed lost the moonlight, in the shadow beneath the lee of the cliff. He would then halt, helping Jacinth and Alazla, especially down the regular steep drops. Alazla grew even more impressed at his friend's adeptness.

Kuoy and Jacinth crouched, waiting for Alazla as he stepped off the old stream bed and onto the shingle beach. He placed his feet carefully so as to make as little noise as possible. They all paused then, watching the revellers carefully.

Their caution was rewarded as a laughing young woman with long blonde hair broke away from one of the fires, running towards them, pursued by a grinning although not very coordinated young man in an embroidered blue velvet tunic. None of them moved as the running couple got closer to them. Fortunately the young lady did not appear overly frantic to escape and, slowing her pace, allowed the handsome young noble to catch her, upon which he grappled her to the shingle, meeting her in an ardent embrace. Their soft sighs and murmurs carried easily to the frozen group.

The whites of Kuoy's eyes were visible as he pointed towards the cliff just a few spans from them, and mimicked walking beneath it, to the shoreline and from there to the nearest landing boat. They walked deep within the shadow of the cliff towards the sea, trying to ignore the increasing sounds of ardour behind them. Alazla was sure he heard a muffled giggle from Jacinth.

The lapping of the waves was like the sound of freedom to Alazla and he found himself breathing heavily in excitement as they got closer to the boats. This really was it, he thought: freedom was almost a reality. They could see the nearest landing boat now. It was pulled none too securely up the beach, with the waves lapping at it, rocking it gently. Alazla realised that had they not been taking it, the mischievous sea would likely have pilfered it anyway.

Alazla stepped into the shallow surf and took the prow of the gently rocking vessel. He and Kuoy slowly began to move the boat into the water. As the prow lifted on a wave, Jacinth nimbly hopped over the side and set the oars into their locks. Kuoy too then hopped in and Alazla, now up to his waist in seawater, gave the boat a final gentle shove before grabbing the side, Kuoy helping to haul him in.

Jacinth began to stroke the oars easily into the water, pulling the small boat swiftly away from the shore.

It was then that they heard the screams. At first they took no notice, thinking it just more carousing. As the screams came again, though, they all recognised them as cries of fear. The music had stopped. Looking back, they could see figures struggling by the campfire.

Peering towards the beach, Alazla felt his stomach clench in anger as he recognised their fellow escapees, the filthy Nilm and the brutal, hulking Ibok. Nilm held a screaming young noblewoman clutched against him and was backing towards the beached landing boat nearest the nobles. His fist was wound tight into her long dark hair and he held something pressed against her throat. A laughing Ibok waved a massive branch as an improvised club menacingly in front of him.

Several of the young noblemen had drawn daggers, but dared not approach. One of their number lay on the ground before Ibok, the side of his head staved in, dark blood seeping onto the impassive shingle.

'Row faster,' hissed Kuoy. 'Give me one of the oars.'

Jacinth shifted quickly over, allowing Kuoy onto the small rowing bench beside her.

'What are you doing?' said Alazla in alarm. 'We can't just leave them with those murderers. Turn the boat around now, we have to help them.'

Kuoy did not smile when he said, 'We don't have time for this, Alazla. This may well be our only chance to escape.' Alazla looked hopelessly at Kuoy, recognising the uncompromising set of his face. Looking back at the shoreline, he saw that Nilm had almost dragged the young noblewoman to the other landing boat as her friends looked on helplessly.

'Fine, then go without me,' Alazla said.

'Alazla, no!' shouted Jacinth as Alazla dived into the sea.

The water was so cold it struck him like a blow, ripping the breath out of him. Alazla gave no more thought to his friends in the boat behind him as he clawed his way gasping to the surface and struck out for the shore. Although the sea was fairly calm, the waves rolled him around like a cork. His days swimming in Korth's harbour stood him in good stead, though. His rage was an almost palpable thing and it propelled him forward.

Despite the intense cold, Alazla slowed as he reached the shoreline and, moving his legs down, he sought the seabed. He stood then for a moment, the waters lapping just beneath his eyes, allowing himself to move with the motion of the sea. Letting the restless sea calm his mind, he settled on a simple plan of action. He knew that Nilm and Ibok would have the disadvantage, coming directly out of the firelight and into the night. With luck they might not even see him coming.

Alazla pondered as the waves lapped over his face. He had little doubt as to the fate of the young noble maiden should she be taken captive by his fellow escapees, and his fists clenched at his sides. Nevertheless he knew that without weapons he could never beat Ibok in a fight. He allowed himself a feral smile: Nilm, however, was another matter. Slowly, and keeping only his eyes visible, Alazla waded through the sea to where the second landing boat was beached.

Nilm had dragged the girl into the boat now. Alazla could see that she could be no more than his own age, perhaps some twenty five cycles. Her dark eyes were round with fear. Her purple satin gown had been torn at the bosom, exposing part of her white flesh, which a leering Nilm caressed with a filthy hand. With the other hand he pressed a sharpened piece of wood against her neck, drawing a slight trickle of blood.

Ibok was perhaps twenty spans from the landing boat, where the surf whispered on, uninterested. Alazla could see the jagged scar across Ibok's face, his part-torn lip and the ripple of his muscles through his ragged, filthy shirt. Four noblemen clutched daggers some few spans before him but stayed wisely beyond the reach of his makeshift club. Alazla had to admire their bravery, since they had already lost one of their number to the lumbering Ibok. Noblewomen were clustered behind the men, crying and weeping.

Alazla was so close to Nilm in the landing boat that he fancied he could smell the slave's putridity. The surf was so shallow that he had to lie down now, sinking his hands into the gravel to stop being moved around by the restless play of the sea.

'Come on, you bloody idiot,' Nilm shouted at Ibok, his voice unnaturally loud. 'You can play another time: there's other pleasures awaiting us now,' he brayed, kissing the cowering girl on the cheek for good measure.

Ibok grinned at the nobles, swinging his club. 'Can't I play with them, Nilm, just for a few more minutes?'

The nobles shifted at this. Hands used to holding wine glasses whitened on dagger hilts, yet they did not flee.

'Just get in the damn boat, you fool,' returned Nilm.

Hands scrabbling in the shallow surf for purchase, Alazla touched a large rock and his fingers closed around it, the surface smooth and cold. Seconds later he saw his moment. Alazla reared up behind the landing boat like some sea-bound cobra uncoiling from the watery depths, his face mottled with rage, hair spitting seawater like poison.

The noblewoman screamed and Nilm half-turned as Alazla struck him with the rock and the full force of his rage. Nilm caught the blow on the side of his face. He had barely time to shriek in agony as bone shattered and blood spewed from his mouth, spattering across the boat and his hostage. Nilm crashed forward to land half over the side of the boat, his face a fraction above the impervious sea, twitching and dripping red into blue.

Alazla lurched through the rolling surf and, steadying himself on the boat stern, grabbed the stunned noblewoman under the arms and hoisted her unprotesting from the boat. Staggering, he half-carried, half-dragged the sobbing girl up the shifting shingle and, falling to his knees, lowered her to the beach.

Two noblewomen had run around the men standing off against Ibok and were now standing just a few spans from Alazla. One was slightly plump and wearing a rather overbright lime-green dress, the other very plain-looking but in an exquisite gold satin gown, her intricate hairstyle fallen in disarray. Their eyes were wide in fear and faces tear-streaked. They hovered just beyond his reach, seemingly uncertain as to his intentions; Alazla realised that he must look an absolute sight. Climbing back to his feet, he gestured for them to approach the girl as he turned towards Ibok.

Ibok was trying to look at his fallen comrade and ascertain the impact of this new change of events, while keeping his club between him and the four dagger-wielding nobles. Alazla held no illusions and knew that at any moment Ibok was capable of charging straight through them, scattering them like leaves on the wind.

Ibok watched Alazla approach warily and Alazla finally saw recognition dawn in those piggy, bloodshot eyes. He understood then that Nilm and Ibok had not even known that the other escapees were there, in the very same bay. Seeing now that Ibok was soaking wet, he realised that they must have swum round the bay to get at the nobles. Both groups of fugitives had been within spans of each other and not even known it.

'You,' said Ibok, snarling, 'stay away. This ain't got nothin' to do with you, blondie.'

Alazla stopped, the gore-spattered rock still clutched in his fist. 'You could have just taken one of the boats and left these people alone, Ibok,' he said simply, rage still coiled in his muscles, and he tensed himself for the inevitable strike. But Ibok looked bewildered, as if at a loss as to what to say or do. Alazla considered: if the nobles backed him they could probably take Ibok down, but if not and he tackled him alone, it would be over all too soon. That decided, he settled for a bluff.

'You're outnumbered, Ibok. Take that piece of bleeding scum you call a friend out of the boat and head back into the island.' He took a deep breath. 'It's that or face all of us.'

Ibok frowned at Alazla and then looked at the dagger blades held almost convincingly in front of him. Moments seemed to become hours. Alazla tensed his muscles and prepared himself to spring at Ibok. He would likely only get in one good blow.

'All right, then,' Ibok finally said, and wagged his club at Alazla. 'But you watch out, blondie, I'll find you and pay you back for this!'

Alazla smiled grimly. 'You've got to get off the island first.' Then he mentally added Ibok to his list of enemies, a list that seemed to be growing almost as fast as his list of friends was shrinking.

Ibok lurched off towards the landing boat and picked up his accomplice's recumbent form. The whole side of Nilm's face appeared to have been staved in. Alazla could not tell whether he was breathing, and frankly didn't care. Nilm jouncing over his shoulder, the massive form of Ibok began to recede up the beach.

Alazla watched them go with a wash of relief before he realised that his peril might not yet be over. He cast his gaze over the assembled nobles and found that they were making no aggressive moves towards him, in fact quite the contrary. Some of the women were gently holding and soothing the sobbing lady that Nilm had held captive. A blanket had materialised and was now draped round her shoulders, covering her exposed modesty. A couple of the men had run back up the beach to the campfires and were now kneeling by the body of their fallen friend.

As Alazla quietly observed the proceedings, uncertain how to proceed, he was saved more rumination by the lady in the gold dress he had seen earlier. She detached herself from her friends and positioned herself in front of him. Alazla calmly watched her; the rage of the earlier battle had left him feeling hollow inside. Although stained and dishevelled, the lady held her head high and then shocked him as she made a small but perfectly formed curtsy. 'My thanks, noble sir: you have saved my sister from a truly deplorable fate.' Her voice carried a rich Korthian accent. She then appeared to be waiting for Alazla to reply.

'No problem,' replied Alazla, he thought somewhat lamely.

'Alas,' she continued, 'poor Roderick: he always was too brave.' Tears welling, she dabbed at her eyes gently with a flowery kerchief and looked sorrowfully up the beach towards the fire and the kneeling noblemen.

'Oh, but how rude of me sir: I should introduce myself. I am Lady Carine of the Altrune House of Apolletta, and my sister, the lady you saved,' she smiled, 'is Lady Caroline Altrune. Your name, sir: pray tell us, what is it?'

Alazla hesitated for a moment, considering their predicament as runaway slaves, and swiftly brought to mind several pseudo-names. Then he thought, well, the cat is certainly out of the proverbial bag now, and in fact halfway down the street, so there's no sense proffering more falsehoods than are really required. With a deep breath he said, 'Alazla, ma'am, Alazla El-Vanium.'

'I see,' she said. 'I do not know of you, but El-Vanium is a very old Korthian name, is it not?' and looked at him quizzically.

Alazla shrugged.

'I do not know how to thank you, Alazla. We owe you a debt truly beyond paying. However, first things first. It seems that we need to *give* you one of our boats,' and smiling, she gestured towards the sea.

Alazla turned to where Lady Carine pointed and saw the landing boat bobbing out to sea with Jacinth and Kuoy at the oars, apparently waiting for him. Jacinth waved.

Alazla smiled and turned to go. Doing so, he was stopped by a polite cough behind him and turned back to see Lady Carine extending her hand. Smiling, he stooped to kiss it lightly and then with a wave to his friends ran into the surf, striking out for the waiting boat.

He did not hear a smiling Lady Carine whisper, 'I think we shall meet again, fair Alazla El-Vanium.'

- CHAPTER 24 -

Unholy Rite

'I am vexed.' The voice rolled about the clearing, it was immense.

The immortal Cinder, wrung his gauntleted hands nervously. 'I am sorry Terran-Assail. We are trying to find the young men now. The bone-caster is....efficient.'

The avatar Terran-Assail, once known as Thorn, turned from where he studied the bone-caster working, to regard Cinder. The avatar towered to more than three times the height of the immortal. His massive ebony physique could barely be discerned in the darkness. Had he not been able to see him though, Cinder would have been able to feel him; the pressure of Terran-Assails' power, made the very air groan.

'Our success in this war depends on surprise Cinder. You understand this.' The threat in the rolling voice was implicit.

Cinder, scion of a god, and who had walked Rune for thousands of cycles, ran a nervous tongue over yellowed fangs and replied. 'I know Lord. Be assured that we will find out where they are going.'

'Our mistress is not as forgiving as I am, Cinder.' Ebony feathered wings creaked and stretched for a moment, veiling the stars.

The coals of Cinders' burning eyes flicked in fear. His voice dropped into an almost conspiratorial whisper. 'But why does She delay? We should open the Hall of Fallen gods now!'

'The time is not yet propitious. We must wait.'

Flame burst about Cinders fist as he clenched it in frustration. He did not see the smile that twisted the avatars'face.

'Propitious?!' Cinder spat. 'This war is irrelevant, compared to our greater goal!'

'There are realms and figures with the power to resist us Cinder. We must divide and destroy them.'

The bone-caster stared into the flames, and tried very hard not to listen to Cinder sweating; he had work to do and distractions, even ones as amusing as watching Cinder crawl, could prove fatal. With a wave of his hand the flickering images of Agastalen and Heath brightened in the flames and he capered in mad glee, the chains about his ankles rattling and clinking.

'I see them. I see them,' chortled the bone-caster.

Conversation between Avatar and immortal stopped, and their eyes turned to the bone-caster, where he danced about the firepit. His naked red-painted body was sinister in the firelight, his eye pits dark and soulless. Encircling his head and his eye sockets were tattooed circles of chains.

The sight of his manhood jiggling wildly another time might have been an amusing sight, but not now. Pandim, aide-de-camp to Baron Mytle, was staked out, spreadeagled beside the firepit. Gone was his finery now: his naked body was slashed with expert cuts, yet none so deep that he bled to death. Pandim's eyes rolled with fear and he whimpered pitifully around a wad of filthy cloth.

The bone-caster gestured curtly to two burly armoured guards, who held between them a soldier from the Barony of Wren. The soldier slumped in shattered chain armour that hung from him in strips; blood matted his hair and beard. The guards threw the battered soldier to his knees before the bone-caster.

He lifted the soldier's head, the chin cupped almost tenderly in his blood-red hand, and smiled, revealing teeth sharpened to points. The soldier opened his eyes briefly and laughed, his teeth caked with blood. 'You'll meet the gods for this, you unholy bastard.'

The bone-caster giggled, 'I'm counting on it,' and drove his twin-pointed dagger into the soldier's heart.

As the soldier lay upon the earth, gasping and clutching weakly at the dagger driven into his heart, the guards lifted him up and threw him casually into the huge fire pit. The flames roared unnaturally high and the bone-caster raised his red arms, shuddering in ecstasy.

'Human souls,' the bone-caster commented casually, and skipped closer to a whimpering Pandim with a rattle of chains: 'nothing like them!'

Pandim moaned in fear around his gag, his eyes rolling wildly. 'Your wily master may have escaped but you were not so lucky, were you?'

The bone-caster recalled with a brief sigh of pleasure the staged retreat by Baron Mytle's battered force. Cinders's pursuing forces had been lured into a pre-prepared trap and huge logs had been rolled down upon them from above, crushing more than a hundred of his best horse. The wily baron's forces had then made good their escape, leaving Cinder to rage and rant. He recalled with delight the fire pit he had built then and the dying soldiers that he had cast into that pit. Of course Cinders' troops now shunned the bone-caster, unless they were under a direct command from Cinder to help him, a command from which they often would not return.

The bone-caster revelled in the soldiers' fear. His power receptacle veritably groaned now. He lovingly caressed the finger bone strung about his neck. Of course, a time would come though when he would not need such trinkets. Terran-Assail would reward his most faithful servants lavishly, and the bone-caster was most faithful indeed. He lusted for a time when Cinder would answer to *him*.

With a skip, the bone-caster plucked the filthy rag from Pandim's mouth.

'Please, please don't hurt me. I beg you,' screamed Pandim. 'I'll tell you what you want to know. I beseech you. In the name of all the gods, I'll tell you. Please just don't hurt me. Just don't hurt me.'

'Oh, the gods is it?' replied the bone-caster, leering. 'Well, I'm sorry to say that that's not going to make much difference.' He thought he heard the Avatar chuckle at that.

He sliced the skin of Pandim's white belly, expertly cutting through the skin and fatty tissue to the muscle beneath.

Pandim squealed and cried, soiling himself. Gasping, Pandim whimpered, 'The two men have been sent to Shael to alert Queen Iodarii. They bear the baron's own blade as proof!'

'I see,' the bone-caster replied, his face now so close to Pandim's that Pandim could smell his stinking breath. 'In that case there's good news and bad news.'

Pandim, bearing pain unlike any he'd ever felt, nevertheless managed to nod in hope. 'The good news is that I'm feeling quite full right now. The bad news is that I also enjoy my work.'

With that he drove his dagger into Pandim's heart. With a final squeal the aide-de-camp jerked and then lay still.

The bone-caster arose, leaving the dagger quivering in Pandim's cooling heart. He was pleased. This was good work and and the deep rumble of pleasure from behind him asserted that Terran-Assail was also pleased.

Thinking of the glory that would be heaped on him by the winged one, he tore the finger bone from his neck and crumbled it in his hand. Red light blossomed from his hand, casting his face into a hellish glow. Power suffused him and he struggled to contain it. Even as he revelled in the ecstasy his body quivered with effort, his muscles spasmed and sweat sprang from his pores, running through his body paint in rivulets.

A moment later he opened his palm and a globe of fire blossomed, occasionally pulsing as if something struggled within it. He threw the globe towards the deceased Pandim, where on touching his chest it vanished in a bloom of red fire that suffused the entire corpse. The fire pit dulled and then roared skyward.

An awful scream borne upon the wind ripped across the encamped army and Pandim sat up.

His shoulders slumped wearily but infused with glee, the bone-caster cast about, to find his friend crouched down by the warmth of the belching fire pit. As he knelt, the bloated red spider scuttled over to him. The bone-caster picked up the shadow spider, cradling it in his palm, stroking its red fur gently. Its yellow eyes regarded him as its legs quivered in pleasure and a deep purr arose from its tiny body. 'I think it is time you wove us a gate, my friend.'

Regarding the returned Pandim, he said, 'And then we'll send those young men a gift from Terran-Assail.'

The shadow spider waved its mandibles and chittered.

****

Bella the grey mare proved to be a passive and affable travelling companion. She showed no signs of missing her previous master and at the end of a day's travel would tolerate Agastalen and Heath's clumsy attempts to tend her with only a rare nip. They took turns riding Bella and found that they tired much less quickly than when travelling solely afoot, and managed to increase the amount of ground they were covering each day quite considerably.

Agastalen and Heath had agreed that delivering Baron Mytle's message to Shael wouldn't cause them much inconvenience, since it was their next destination anyway, and they also agreed that the beleaguered baronies could certainly use the help. So, they decided that when they managed to make it to Shael, they'd do their best to deliver what they sadly believed were likely to have been amongst the last words spoken by the brave, if somewhat effete, Baron Mytle.

Their journey to the south coast of the baronies, from where they intended to follow the coast east, nonetheless took them some two weeks, passing across rolling hills and through wide vales. Occasionally they would come across a farmstead or small community which they usually approached to buy food, when they were not met with icy stares or doors shut in their faces. They were able to supplement their limited diet with the dwindling supplies from Firs Deep and a knowledge of foraging, limited to nuts and berries. The weather was reasonably tolerant of their travels and they only had to shelter from poor conditions on two occasions, the latter of which, though, caught them square upon the side of a hill with no visible shelter. They spent the miserable night hunched beneath an equally miserable-looking elm.

Approaching the coast, they found themselves shadowing a southerly proceeding tree line, marking the boundary of a large wood. The distant tree line followed them south for two days before they set eyes upon the coast. After what had seemed endless leagues of grassland and woods, the sight of the sea put a smile on both their faces and poor Bella was forced to gallop the last stretch encumbered by both an exuberant Heath and Agastalen.

Their fare that night was limited to a ration of salted pork and some shrivelled apples, but neither of them minded. Bella cropped grass contentedly and had not nipped Agastalen once as he had rubbed her down with the remnants of an old shirt designated for the purpose.

'Hadn't realised shrunken apples could taste so good,' said Heath, who'd wasted not even the apple core.

Agastalen had to nod his head in agreement. 'I'd have turned up my nose for sure if they'd tried to serve these up in the spire,' he agreed.

Agastalen looked, as he had many times, at the dagger Baron Mytle had given to them, as proof to Queen Iodarii as to the truth of their message. The elabrorate enamelled crest that surmounted the hilt seemed somewhat out of place in this remote part of the world.

'Do you think the Queen will agree to see us?' he asked Heath.

Rolling himself into his cape for the night, Heath murmured, 'If she doesn't I'd say it's certainly going to be her loss! It's not going to take Cinder long to chew up the rest of the Peldane baronies, and he doesn't seem to me like the sort of guy that respects borders very much. But personally I'm not going to beat myself up about it. As soon as we're on that ship from Shael, we're as good as back in Arcanum and that's enough for me.'

Although not sharing his friend's slightly casual disregard, Agastalen knew that Heath was fundamentally right, but for him it was not enough, so many things had happened. 'But can it ever be the same, Heath? The magi used to be at least accepted and sometimes even loved in almost every corner of Rune. Even if they find a solution to the crisis, are we now going to be despised? Will there be places we can longer ever go, where we are outcast?'

'Not much of a loss, that,' replied Heath from his bedroll. 'They'll be the poorer without our skills. There's a magi counsellor attached to almost every monarch on Rune. You don't think they'll all just come home, do you?! Come on.'

Agastalen sighed as he recalled his family, and the pride in his mother and fathers faces when he'd been accepted to Arcanum. He'd been young, but it was one of his most precious and lasting memories. 'Maybe you're right, but everyone at home knows that I've become an apprentice. What if I can never go back?'

Heath's snores said what he thought, though it was a long time before sleep claimed Agastalen, as old memories of his family played through his mind's eye.

Next day it became clear that the coast road was not especially well travelled and was in places little more than a track. It seemed that the barony traffic to Shael did not favour this particular route.

The woodland that they had traced to the coast for part of their journey stayed with them now, and they appeared to be skirting its southern boundary. The wood rarely strayed close to the track itself, though, remaining at a distance perhaps of a stone's throw. It became progressively darker and thicker as the eastward-proceeding leagues rolled under Bella's hooves.

During the afternoon it was Agastalen's turn to ride upon Bella and he found himself often glancing towards the wood. It was so thick now as to be almost impenetrable to the eye. The trees on the wood, or *forest*, boundary, he now corrected himself, were tall and old, their craggy boughs wrapped in ivy. The more he thought about it, the stranger he also found it that the woods stayed a regular distance from the track. He could not shake the feeling that somehow the forest returned his stare.

Agastalen glanced down at Heath, curious as to whether his friend had noticed anything. Heath's jovial face was slightly pensive and he caught Agastalen's eye. 'You feel it too, do you?' asked Agastalen in a deliberately open-ended fashion, hoping to draw his friend's thoughts.

'Don't quite know what it is,' returned Heath, glancing at the forest. 'It's almost like we're being followed or watched by something, something that won't come out.'

Agastalen nodded in agreement. 'Maybe, if we tried not to look,' Agastalen suggested hopefully.

Heath laughed, scratching at the black stubble on his chin. 'Anything's worth a try,' he said.

The feeling did not go away though, and that evening they made camp as far from the forest's edge as possible, in the lee of rocks that overlooked a small damp beach that smelt strongly of overripe seaweed. They talked of small things and did their very best to ignore the forest. Agastalen found himself unable to shake the feeling that it wanted them to look at it.

In the end their attempts at conversation petered out and Heath took to examining the red stone brooch that Agastalen had recovered from the museum in the spire, presently being use as a clasp for his cloak.

'I'm glad you like my brooch,' said Agastalen, hoping to needle his friend briefly.

Sadly Heath did not rise to the bait and replied, 'You can have it back if you want it: the stone's cracked.'

Agastalen's face showed surprise and he leaned forward to see where his friend was pointing. Indeed there was a crack deep within the ruby, which spiralled out like a web throughout most of the stone. It was likely only the stone's metal setting that was holding it together.

'That must have taken some force. Never seen anything quite like it,' said Agastalen, sitting back.

'You can have my bronze feather if you like,' said Heath, grinning. 'We'll get you a fine hat in Shael and you can stick it in it. You'll look quite the gentleman!'

Agastalen laughed. 'Good night, Heath,' he said as he rolled into his bedroll.

'Good night,' Heath managed, his voice already sleepy.

The red-haired spider scuttled out of the rocky shadows. The two men were apparently already asleep. As it chittered, the spider's mandibles started to weave back and forth. Lines began to appear between its mandibles, web–like, and as it wove they grew, finally becoming a pulsing black hole in the darkness of night.

Bella's scream woke them. The mare was bucking and whinnying in terror, her eyes rolling and wide.

Agastalen and Heath lurched to their feet, scattering their bedrolls, blinking the fog of sleep from their eyes as they cast about, searching for the source of her distress.

Heath ran towards Bella, calling out her name. The mare was rearing in terror, pulling at the rope that tied her to a sapling. As he raced towards her, though, the sapling bowed and the rope pulled over the top of it. Bella galloped off into the darkness, leaving Heath spitting curses.

Agastalen's shout of alarm alerted Heath, who turned to see a naked figure running at him from the darkness. At first Heath was surprised as he realised that it was Pandim who ran at him. For some reason, he briefly wondered if the aide-de-camp had come after them, seeking his beloved mare Bella, and even whether his nakedness was some form of statement. And then he noticed the fluidity with which Pandim moved; his muscles rippled with a strength that the slightly overweight aide had never possessed in life, and his stride had the pace and fluidity of a hunting cat as he powered out of the darkness. The look of surprise on Heath's face turned to one of horror.

Pandim struck Heath before he had even drawn the breath to cry out. Heath was slammed to the earth and then Pandim was on him like some maddened beast. Blows struck Heath about the face and he desperately delved within himself, seeking his well, but the blows came too hard and fast. His vision was blurring and he knew that he was losing consciousness.

Agastalen watched dumbstruck as the naked aide-de-camp tore from the darkness and struck his friend with an impossible speed. Heavy blows rained down on Heath, even as Agastalen sought to gather his thoughts.

Not knowing what else to do, Agastalen desperately reached into himself and his well blossomed open at his touch. Had he not been concentrating on his friend's dire need he would have been amazed at the speed with which he did it. His single binding responded to his touch and golden energy coursed into him. Not understanding exactly how, Agastalen let instinct guide him and he collected the energy into a concentrated ball within him. He released the form with a slightly clumsy gesture. His aim was almost straight as the fist-sized ball of golden energy arched from his hand, crackling and fizzing into the night air.

Agastalen gasped at the empty void within himself as the energy left him, the unconscious part of his mind noting, though, that he'd not used his own life force to create the form.

The ball of energy struck the creature Pandim a glancing blow to the back of the head. There was a hiss of flesh as it struck, and it dissipated in a golden flash that briefly illuminated Heath's bloodied and gasping face beneath. Where it had struck Pandim, the hair had been burned away to reveal scalp and blackened tissue beneath.

Pandim leapt off Heath and raced towards Agastalen, loping on all fours.

Agastalen desperately struggled to draw more energy through his binding. Energy throbbed into him, although it seemed far more sluggish than it had before. Agastalen deliberately created a simple form this time, one taught to all apprentices.

Pandim leapt at Agastalen, his teeth bared. Agastalen released the form and the simple weave created to lift mundane objects struck it, deflecting the creature away from him. The creature Pandim ricocheted off the form with all of the pace that it had created and struck the rock directly behind Agastalen with a crack of bone.

Agastalen did not wait to see what had happened then, but ran towards Heath, who was swaying groggily on his feet. Grabbing Heath, knowing it was their only chance, he half-pulled and half-dragged Heath towards the dark looming forest. Earlier today the forest had seemed too close, and now, as their breathing laboured, it seemed as if they'd never reach it. Heath's legs kept giving way beneath him and Agastalen knew that at best he had one more form left in him. The creature was far beyond their ability to stop.

Risking a glance back, Agastalen could see that the creature Pandim already pursued them. Yet its strides were no longer fluid.

Now it moved with a staggering gait, as if its legs had been damaged. Its pace, nonetheless, was at least equal to theirs and their short lead was being slowly eaten away. Agastalen whispered a prayer to Nim as he increasingly carried Heath's weight.

They made it into the forest with the creature perhaps just fifty spans behind them. Beneath the canopy of tall trees and with only moonlight to guide them, they could barely see. Agastalen could faintly discern the dark outline of tree trunks. Branches slapped at his face and briars snagged his clothing. His heart hammered and his lungs clawed for air as he laboured to bear the weight of his friend. Even though he had Heath's weight on his good shoulder, his injury from the arrow had barely healed and it burned with pain, stretching newly healed skin.

Save for the crash and snap of their own passage, the forest remained quiet until the sound of the creature Pandim entered the forest behind them.

Heath muttered incoherently as they ran, but Agastalen had no breath to ask what his friend was trying to say. Heath worked his legs, staggering as best he could to help Agastalen, but often he would simply collapse, a burden, close to pulling his friend down with him.

Something struck Agastalen in the face. Pain blossomed in his forehead and he was thrown from his feet. He landed in the damp earth, gasping. Heath collapsed beside him. He raised a hand to his head and it came away wet. He was barely able to make out a thick branch at head height in the thick gloom above him.

Heath was trying to get to his feet and failing. The noise of Pandim crashing through the brush brought Agastalen back to his feet with a lurch and he dragged Heath up.

As they stumbled, the sounds of pursuit were now even closer. Had Agastalen had the breath left he would have said a prayer to Nim, but his heaving chest allowed him no opportunity. The metallic taste of his own blood ran into his mouth. Blood pumped in his veins with a force that caused his head to throb.

Desperate to grasp any chance before the creature descended on them, Agastalen reached within himself to find his well and quickly brushed it with his mind; even now his discipline did not fail him. Yet his strength did. As he poured all his effort into their flight his well opened briefly, but he could not sustain it and as quickly it closed again, like a door snapping shut on the light of day.

They could no longer catch their breath fast enough and their pace was beginning to slow. Agastalen's mind raced, desperately seeking a solution, determined not to give up. It was clear from the crashing and snapping behind them that Pandim was just seconds behind them and their own noise made them an easy target to follow.

Knowing that there was just one option left to them, Agastalen decided to hide. He dived into a thicket of what he found to be brambles, pulling Heath with him. He ignored the thorns tearing at his exposed skin as he wormed deeper into the thicket. Then suddenly his feet were scrambling to find purchase as the bramble thicket abruptly ended.

With not even the breath left to cry out, his arms windmilling, seeking balance and finding none, he fell. For a moment Agastalen simply fell head over heels, the air rushing past him, and then he began to strike damp walls, careering off them as he rushed downward. Mud and stones scattered and his hands grasped fragile roots to have them snap in his hands as he tumbled. He drew a breath, only to have it slammed from him a moment later, as with a force that made his vision swim he struck the ground belly first.

Agastalen groggily raised his head, spitting leaves and dirt from his mouth, and then Heath landed on him, driving the air from his abused lungs in a whoosh and his face back into the dirt. Agastalen lay in the dirt for a moment, taking respite in simply drawing even shallow breath. He realised then that Heath had not moved from where he'd landed on his back. Rolling over, Heath slid off him with a dull moan.

Agastalen had no way to tell where they were; it was pitch-black and the air was thick with moisture. Even the dim outline of the trees had gone. Righting himself, he strained his hearing, but he could hear no signs of their pursuer. He didn't dare hope that they had thrown Pandim off. They'd certainly fallen a long way though, their fall apparently having been broken by a thick bed of old mouldering leaves and branches. Luck may yet be with them, provided Heath was all right.

He knew that his eyes should have fully adjusted by now, but could still see nothing. The air smelt still and musty, as if it were little disturbed. He had no way to check on Heath or their surroundings without light, so he decided to wait in silence, hoping that dawn would shed light on their predicament.

- CHAPTER 25 -

Tomb

Slithering rocks and mud tumbled down from above, their broken echo the footsteps of doom.

Lurching awake, Agastalen realised that he must have dropped off to sleep. He held his breath and listened. There it was, unmistakable: something approached, climbing down from above.

His entire body ached with fatigue and his head throbbed from where he had struck the branch. Muffling a sob of anger, he groped out in the darkness and located Heath and frantically shook his friend.

'Wh, what?' gasped Heath.

Agastalen's sigh of relief was audible and he whispered, 'I think that thing's found us again, we need to move on… and quickly.'

Heath cursed softly. 'But what is that thing, Agastalen? It's not Pandim, it's something else, but what? The way it moves. It's, it's, like some form of hunter.'

'Search me. Not heard of anything like it before. The strength, though, it's as if there's something else inside it. There's no way we can beat it,' said Agastalen.

There was a pause amidst the darkness.

'So what now?' said Heath. They could both still hear the sounds of movement from above.

Agastalen's voice was soft as he replied. 'We keep running and pray to Nim that we can lose it.'

Agastalen extended his arms, groping blindly as he moved, trying to ignore the sounds of skittering mud above them. His hands touched a wall of damp earth. 'Here,' he whispered, 'I've found a wall.'

Groping for a moment, Heath finally wrapped a hand in the back of Agastalen's cloak, the other set against the wall, and they started walking, trying to stay as quiet as possible.

The dark was relentless. They had no way to tell if it was still night or whether where they had landed was simply perpetually in the darkness. From the stale smell of the air Agastalen worried that it might be the latter. He fervently hoped that the creature Pandim was as encumbered by the darkness as they were. He worried for his friend, given the blows to the head that he'd taken, but there was nothing he could do about it now. The silence and the darkness might be their only ally.

They both heard the thud as something landed in the earth behind them. Pandim, it seemed, had just finished scaling down the drop.

Agastalen speeded up, one hand groping out blindly in front of him, the other touching the damp wall. Fear and anger coursed through him. He bitterly reflected that a mage like Winfod or Lei-Weya would likely have swiftly sent such a creature screaming back to whatever hell had spawned it. He vowed that one day he would hold that power and woe would befall the cursed Cinder when their paths crossed then.

Casting aside such thoughts as irrelevant for now and drawing his mind back to their fraught task at hand, he thought that if he was not mistaken they had been following a slight downward gradient. He blinked, thinking for a moment that his eyes were deceiving him, but the excited tug on his cloak and hiss from Heath told him that they were not. Dull, even in the darkness, there was the faintest of illuminations ahead, so slight that it could almost be overlooked.

They picked up their pace, faintly encouraged. Agastalen reasoned that they would have to bolt as soon as they made it into daylight, but without him having to carry Heath now, they had a real chance of out-distancing the injured creature.

The slope caught them unawares, and their legs went from under them. Stones skittered as they hurtled down it feet first. Limbs flailed as they tried to slow their descent, having some slight effect.

Suspended in mid-air for a moment, they came to a crashing halt in a tangle of limbs and bodies. Unfortunately not all of them were their own. Heath gasped, jumping up from the pile of cracked and dried bones they'd landed in, his breath steaming in clouds in the cold.

The light was dull now, a faded and even musty yellow glow, partially illuminating a long and narrow earthen chamber through which mist curled and whispered. Into the earthen walls were carved hollows in which rested the bones of the dead, their slumbering ranks marching on far beyond the dim illumination. None of the deceased, though, were human: horns jutted from foreheads, tusks from elongated maws, and giant snouts were filled with wicked teeth. Some clutched bizarre and ancient weapons in death, even though their grip on life had faded.

Agastalen stood up, detaching himself from a yellowed jawbone set with tusks. His fingers were already beginning to grow numb from the cold. Heath looked frantically about, his red brooch flashing slightly in the half-light. His face was thick with dark bruises, his lips swollen and one eye almost shut.

Agastalen quipped, 'You've certainly looked prettier.'

Heath didn't smile, a look of horror stretching across his face. Agastalen followed his friend's gaze and he took an involuntary step back.

The mist curled and boiled with a life of its own, rolling towards them. The light dimmed to almost nothing. Mist was the creature's cloak. Terrible clawed hands raised a blackened blade and unholy yellow eyes held them from beneath an ancient iron helm. The breath of deepest winter raced before it.

Frost crept across Agastalen's skin. Fear like he'd never felt clutched his heart, but his body seemed frozen and unable to obey his silent, shrieked commands. All thoughts of his slender mage power fled from his besieged mind. He was paralysed, his consciousness a prisoner to fear. His heart fluttered in his breast like a trapped bird.

The mist coiled about their frosted feet, rising up their legs like a serpent ready to strike.

Agastalen regarded its hate-filled yellow eyes, and as the terrible blade rose above him, he feared that he could hear a whisper of lust from it. His heart pattered feebly and he knew that even should the blade not strike him, he was dying. His head drooped, unable to hold its terrible gaze.

A slight fresh light bloomed into the darkness of the chamber and with it came the scent of a summer's morning. The mist stirred and curled, recoiling from the light.

'You shall cease,' a female voice rang out.

Its hate-filled gaze passed from Agastalen and Heath towards the welling summer's light. Its voice was like the grind of snapping ice. 'Our hunger burns; these mortals are as nothing.'

The female voice returned. 'They have been marked. You may not have them. Feed instead upon that which pursues them. It is infused which much power.'

The unholy creature Pandim landed then with a clatter amidst the bones.

Yellow eyes swung from the mist to regard it.

The beat of Agastalen's faltering heart slowed, and darkness closed upon him.

****

Agastalen awoke beneath a canopy of broad-leafed trees.

Sunlight streamed down in sparkling golden fingers to caress the river bank in dappled, warming light. Flowers nodded gently to the attention of bees and opened their blooms to the suns touch. The clear river rushed by, singing its gurgling greeting to any who would listen.

Bewildered, Agastalen sat up and shed a blanket of thick green moss. Alarmingly, the moss then proceeded to crawl away, having apparently assumed that he'd finished with it.

Heath slumbered quietly beside him. The bruises on his face had faded to a dull yellow.

Agastalen touched his forehead, recalling his collision with the branch, and found that barely a scab remained. The remaining wound in his shoulder too had vanished, replaced with a fresh pink scar.

He stood up and stretched, and suddenly blushed when he realised that he wore only his smalls. There was a titter of feminine laughter. He looked frantically about and started pulling on the clothes he spotted on the grass. Apparently they had been washed and mended and now smelt of a spring morning.

Heath stirred and sat up, blinking sleep from his eyes. His expression must have mirrored that of Agastalen's just a moment before.

Agastalen just shrugged to his friend's enquiring look. 'My last recollection is the same as yours.' He shuddered briefly at the memory and continued, 'If that recollection is correct, though, I believe that the singularly unpleasant Pandim was just about to become that mist creature's next snack.'

Heath nodded and, arising, began to dress, and said, 'And I remember him as being such a pleasant young man. Baron Mytle would be mortified at his behaviour!'

Agastalen laughed and, sitting down, said, 'And what do you make of this, then? We appear to have an unexpected benefactor.'

'Ouch,' said a voice under Agastalen, who jumped up in alarm. He had sat down on what he assumed was a rock. Apparently the rock had different ideas, though, since it had now sprouted a face, arms and small legs, standing to about the height of Agastalen's knee.

It waved a knobbly hand at him and said, 'You've got real bony buttocks: you'd best be careful where you put them. We're not all as nice as me, you know; some of us bite!' Having said its piece, the grey rock-like thing waddled off, huffing to itself.

Agastalen and Heath looked at each other and burst out laughing. They laughed then until tears rolled down their faces, and the darkness of the recent few weeks lifted from their shoulders. It felt better than any healing tonic.

Wiping the tears from his face, Heath chuckled. 'Well, seeing as we've lost all our supplies, I'm all for finding some food. Let's see what we can find. I sure hope the berries don't talk back, though!' Miming eating a berry begging for its life, he had Agastalen in stitches again.

Fortunately the berries and other fruits did not talk back, and it was not long before they returned with their arms loaded. The forest had provided for them in abundance and seemed totally unlike the sinister and dark place they'd recently raced through in fear for their lives. In fact wildlife abounded; birds sang in the trees and nature seemed in perfect harmony.

With the forest fruits reduced to nothing more than a pile of pips, they sat back, licking their fingers.

Birds sang in the trees and, soaking up the warmth from a patch of sunlight, Heath asked, 'Any ideas on what had been done to Pandim,

Agastalen? He looked quite dead to me, but I've not seen or heard of any kind of magic that can do that!'

Agastalen looked at his friend stretched out and soaking up the warmth, for a moment feeling a chill as he recalled the fluid grace and power with which Pandim had moved. 'Me neither,' he agreed. 'But, although we're well schooled in mage law, our knowledge of *divine* magic is much more limited. It's possible that whatever created it was of divine origin. We know few priests, though, let alone one who'd want to send something like that against us. I also can't believe that any of the divine orders would condone magic like that.'

Heath nodded his head in agreement, dark locks waving, and said, 'Then that leaves the why. The only thing I can think of is the message the baron gave us.'

Agastalen nodded, impressed as always with his friend's perceptions. He had considered something similar himself, but now that he'd heard it from Heath too he was certain, and said so.

They lay there then, enjoying the comfort of the forest's tranquillity and each other's presence. After a harrowing few weeks, it seemed like a soothing balm.

It was Heath who eventually broke the silence. 'One thing I know for sure, though … is that we stink! I'm off for a dip. Then perhaps we can talk about who saved our skins from the mist….thing?'

Agastalen agreed and Heath raced down towards the river, peeling off clothes as he went. He leapt into the broad river with a whoop of glee, followed by a splash that threw water onto the bank.

Agastalen settled back, amused by his friend's antics. They'd both had their fair share of fun at the Spire of Arcanum, but Heath's antics had just as often got him caught. Had it not been for his enormous natural talent (and a very tolerant arcane mistress), he would likely have been tossed out, to return in shame to his family.

Heath's happy splashing suddenly turned to a shout of alarm. Agastalen surged to his feet, all manner of possibilities racing through his mind as he sprinted down towards the river bank. Heath's shouts continued as Agastalen closed, but now he could also hear laughing female voices.

He arrived at the bank to find Heath treading water in the centre of the river, surrounded by laughing women. There were perhaps ten of them and all quite beautiful, their long hair a fan in the water about them. Their faces were wild in glee as they laughed and shouted in a rapid, jabbering tongue that Agastalen did not recognise. They pulled and tugged at Heath, who splashed and swam, trying his best to avoid them. When he managed to evade one, another set of reaching hands would successfully dunk him or tweak his ear.

Noticing Agastalen, Heath shouted, 'Help me, help,' just before he went under again with another burble. He surfaced with a splutter and shouted, 'They're trying to drown me. Help!' The women laughed and, seeing Agastalen, gestured, calling out in their strange language. Although he could not understand the words, he quickly defined their intent; that he jump in too.

They all were utterly enchanting, Agastalen realised, and without exception. Their faces were youthful and striking in their beauty, their skin a soft blue, their long hair ranging wildly in colour from green to purple to orange and even the purest gold. Their sparkling eyes and smiles were bright and full of life. Agastalen stepped cautiously back from the river bank, shaking his head. There were disappointed murmurs from the water.

Even as he walked back up the meadow, shaking his head at Heath's apparent good fortune, he heard his friend's shouts of outrage turn to those of joy. It would not be long before Heath was getting his own back on the cheeky water creatures.

The antics in the water continued on well into the afternoon. Agastalen knew his friend well enough to realise that when enchanted with something he could be quite tireless, so he dozed and waited for Heath to return. Agastalen looked down on one occasion to see Heath seated on the grassy river bank, surrounded by six of the beautiful creatures. Their hair ran in watery cascades down their shoulders and he could see that they wore only the briefest of clothing, made of river reeds. They jabbered at him in their rapid tongue, but occasionally Agastalen could hear a word spoken by them in the common Runic tongue. Apparently they were very quick learners.

Eventually growing bored of waiting, Agastalen decided to explore the vicinity. There were a lot of questions which they needed answers to, so perhaps he could find a few while Heath was 'distracted."

His walk through the forest was tranquil. As the sound of Heath and the women's laughter faded behind, he became grateful for the peace. The forest was bright and welcoming and the terrifying encounter with Pandim seemed far away now. Tall broad-leafed trees stretched towering limbs to the sun, and beneath their shady hands grew pools of nodding bluebells, ferns, violets and other things for which he had no name. A family of red squirrels chattered at him as he wandered under their home in the bough of an ancient elm, and birds sang in the trees for the delight of it.

Agastalen reached out and plucked some yellow feril berries from a small mature bush. He munched on the lopsided fruit thoughtfully, half-keeping an eye out for the small rock-thing that had sprouted legs earlier. If he could find it, it might be able to answer a few of his questions, he considered. An ingenious youngster from the family of squirrels that had chattered to him earlier obligingly scampered along behind him, picking up the feril pips as he dropped them.

He had wandered late into the afternoon before he realised that he should think about getting back. He'd not told Heath that he was going anywhere, not that Heath would have noticed his absence, he strongly suspected. During his stroll he'd taken note of a few landmarks, including a lightning-blasted tree and a silver willow trailing lazy branches into a brook, so was fairly sure that he could find his way back with a good degree of accuracy.

Turning about to return along the animal trail he'd been following, he noticed that at the top of a small adjacent rise the forest appeared to open out, perhaps being the forest edge or even into a glade, he considered. Intrigued, Agastalen decided to take a quick look; a bearing on their surroundings might certainly help them.

The slope was slightly steeper than he'd thought, and after a long afternoon of walking he paused for a moment at the top of the rise to catch his breath. The hill top opened into a glade, ringed by ranks of towering oak trees of almost uniform height. Their branches stretched out across much of the glade roof, as if seeking to enclose it from the prying eyes of the sun, moon and stars. Yet nevertheless the late afternoon sun encroached and fell upon a circle of stones at the heart of the glade. Eight weathered grey stones, twice the height of a man, encircled a horizontal bier. The glade about the stone circle was carpeted in a sea of miniature yellow flowers, their heads like roses; Agastalen had never seen anything like them before. There was a sense of stillness about the glade; the rustle and chatter of the forest behind him was absent here.

Agastalen felt no fear and only a sense of wonder. Without hesitation he stepped into the glade and walked towards the circle of stones, taking care as he trod not to crush the yellow flowers, although he was not quite sure why.

As he approached the stones, the stillness became more profound. They ringed the bier like eight craggy, ancient sentinels. Their faces once had born carvings and sigils that nature's hand had now all but erased. The bier in the centre of the standing stones was carved from a different rock, though, its hue a faint red. Agastalen suspected that he could see markings chasing across its surface.

As he halted before the circle the oak trees rattled their branches, stirred by an errant wind. Agastalen traced his fingers across the surface of the adjacent standing stone. Its surface was gnarled and pitted, flaking slightly under his touch. A diagonal crack ran across part of its breadth, dividing a faint image that teased at Agastalen's mind. He traced its surface gently with his fingers, making out the serpentine body and wings. 'Dragon,' he whispered quietly. He recalled only scant legends of the allegedly mythical creatures. The other runes and glyphs were largely too faded for him to interpret, but he fancied that he could see the figures of other fantastical beasts, some with horns and wings and running on many legs, not just two.

The hair stood up on the back of his neck as he suddenly recalled the creature's bones that they had seen in the forest tomb. They bore an uncanny resemblance to some of the outlines on the stone. Stepping back sharply, he realised his palms had become clammy. Bits of flaking rock clung to them, and he wiped them against his shirt.

Perhaps the bier itself would yield more wholesome answers, he considered. As Agastalen started to walk past the stone and into the circle a voice called out, 'That would be a foolish step to take, mortal!'

Agastalen jumped out of his skin and with a curse span to see an odd creature propped casually against the stone he had just been inspecting. Standing perhaps to Agastalen's shoulder, the grinning creature appeared almost human save for two small horns protruding from its forehead and the fact that its lower torso appeared to be that of a goat. Wiry hair, the same brown as that of its legs, covered its more human upper body sparsely and also gave it what looked to be an immaculately trimmed short beard.

Raising a set of wooden pipes to its lips, it blew a brief trill and skipped a few feet away and executed a graceful bow. 'I am known as Deyus and you may also call me…. Deyus.'

Agastalen's jaw hung open.

'Are you perhaps not gifted with the power of speech creature?' said Deyus, and cocked his head to one side.

Mustering himself, Agastalen managed, 'But, but, you're….half-goat.'

Deyus's brown eyes widened. 'It saddens me that such must pass for manners in your domain, ungainly one. I am a faun and Fae at that!'

With a look that Agastalen realised must pass for disgust, Deyus turned and with an insolent trill upon his pipes skipped away.

'Wait,' called Agastalen. 'I'm sorry. It's, it's just that umm, I've never seen anything quite like you before.'

Deyus turned at that and with a wicked gleam in his eye smiled, revealing sharp teeth. 'And likely thou wilt never again, fragile and fleeting creature, but your apology is accepted nonetheless, for I am nothing if not gracious.' And executing another brief bow, he then seemed to wait.

Belatedly realising that Deyus was waiting for him to introduce himself, Agastalen said, 'Oh, um, sorry. I'm Agastalen, an apprentice mage, sorry, I mean um, recently demi-mage of Arcanum.'

Intuition telling him that Deyus posed no discernable threat and knowing that they needed information, Agastalen decided that it would be in his best interests to try and win over Deyus, so he also introduced Heath, even though he wasn't present.

Deyus smirked knowingly as Agastalen mentioned Heath. 'Ah, the mortal who cavorts with the Sylphs. He should beware, for his heart could become captured!' he laughed, and capered on the spot.

Concerned that the seemingly fickle Deyus could vanish as just quickly as he'd arrived, Agastalen decided to ignore the faun's reference to Heath, for the moment, and press for more urgent information. 'Deyus, we stumbled into this forest while we were being chased by some form of dead creature and then fell into a tomb of some kind. We'd have died there, either slain by the tomb's guardian or by the thing that chased us, but we were saved, by something here. Later we woke up in the river meadow.'

Cutting to the heart of the matter, Agastalen said, 'Was it you that saved us, Deyus? If it was you, why? Are we still in the barony woods?'

Deyus laughed then, which was more of a bray than anything else. Agastalen waited patiently until Deyus had finished and huffed,

'Mortals, so full of questions. Rushing at things as if you have so little time, which perhaps you do not at that!' He brayed and hooted again, finally saying, 'The answers you seek, though, are no and yes, to the first and last questions.'

Agastalen waited, not quite certain what the faun meant, and paused, endeavouring to work it through.

Deyus finally scowled and continued, 'No, it was not me that saved you, but it was one of my kind, and yes, you are still within the barony woods, as you call them, but that is not their true name, although that name you could not pronounce. To you this is the Forest of the Fae and we are the Fae. I am of that same race. As to the why, well that is equally simple. The stone that your mortal companion bore in the form of a brooch was once carried by one of us: it is a Fae Stone. That is why you were saved.'

Deyus then apparently grew bored of their conversation and started to skip his way through the yellow flowers. A jaunty melody from his pipes followed him into the woods.

Intuition told Agastalen that there was little point in pursuing the faun, so he was left alone to ponder beside the brooding stones.

- Chapter 26 -

The Fae

Agastalen returned to the river meadow that night with a marginally better understanding of their situation than he'd had earlier that day. The gaps in his knowledge frustrated him, though, and he looked forward to reasoning it through with Heath.

Heath was already at what Agastalen thought of as their camp, although he had apparently and unsurprisingly not missed his friend.

Lounging on the grass, Heath surprised Agastalen in demonstrating that he too had garnered some brief information concerning the Fae from the flighty Sylphs, largely confirming what Agastalen already knew.

'You should be careful, you know,' said Agastalen, his tone serious. 'We know almost nothing about these Fae. Those Sylphs, beautiful as they are, could well carry magic or charms that we don't understand.'

Heath picked idly at the grass and replied, 'But they're so beautiful, the way they laugh, the way they move, with such grace. They make the girls in Loria seem so, well, boring.'

As he leaned towards Agastalen, Heath's face split into a wicked smile. 'I see no harm in enjoying myself a little. You should join us tomorrow, you know. I'm sure Elya could find you a friend.'

Agastalen took note of his friend's reference to this one sylph by name and, ignoring the offer, tried again. 'There's a lot here we don't understand, Heath. I'm just saying, maybe, we should be careful.'

Heath sat up, a spark of anger in his green eyes, 'To the hells with being careful. We've been chased, harried and shot at ever since we left Loria. I say we should relax and enjoy ourselves while we're offered the chance.'

Agastalen did not press the issue further, knowing that doing so would just make Heath more entrenched in his viewpoint.

Agastalen awoke the next morning to the sound of liquid laughter. He sat up, rubbing the sleep from his eyes, and saw Heath being tumbled from his bedroll by a lithe, blue-skinned Sylph, that he assumed was Elya. Her hair was liquid silver, with full, even pouting lips, and eyes like dark pools. She was without doubt utterly captivating.

'Come on, Heath,' she giggled. 'You mortals are so sluggish in the morning. We must swim. I have many things to show you.'

Agastalen was shocked that the Sylph was apparently fully fluent in the Runic language after just one day.

Elya pointed with a laugh to Agastalen, who was trying to keep his mossy blanket from walking away again at an inopportune moment and said, 'Would your grumpy friend like to swim with us? My friends would love to play with him.' She pointed to where several beautiful Sylphs huddled down at the water's edge, pointing at them and giggling.

Heath looked at Agastalen, a cheeky smile on his face. 'Well?'

It took a great deal of willpower for Agastalen to croak out, 'Errr, no thank you. Uumm, I think I'm going to explore the forest some more. Yes, that's it, explore.' It sounded lame, even to him.

Heath shrugged, 'Your loss, friend,' and raced off hand in hand with Elya.

There were disappointed sighs from the river's edge when Agastalen did not make to join them.

Watching the stunning Elya and her fellow Sylphs, Agastalen was in fact not remotely sure about his decision and wondered whether he would come to regret it, and in fact, whether he did already. He watched his friend swim off with the Sylphs, but he noticed that a couple remained loitering hopefully by the river bank. Knowing that his willpower would shortly fail him completely, Agastalen pulled on his clothes and decided to return to the stone circle, hoping to catch Deyus again.

He strode purposefully away from the river meadow, trying to put as much distance between himself and the captivating water creatures as possible.

Reaching the shady glade more quickly than the previous day, Agastalen was pleased to find Deyus sitting beside a standing stone, playing softly on his wooden pipes. The melody was haunting, and walking across the glade he did not interrupt, but settled down beside the faun to listen.

As the faun piped, Agastalen fancied that he could see lush forests, stars wheeling overhead and Fae creatures at play; as many racing across the sky as scampered among the trees. He let out a soft sigh of regret when Deyus finished, the melody haunting the glade for moments after the pipes had grown silent.

Agastalen did not wish to break the silence, treasuring the tranquillity and fleeting imaginings.

It was Deyus who spoke first and his voice was slightly sad. 'You will not know this, Agastalen, but Fae mate for life. Even now your friend makes love to Elya in a secluded pool, the water is warmed by the sun and her beauty is radiant. Your friend is utterly captivated and from this moment she is his. But when Heath leaves here, Elya will never love another. Heath, too, whether he realises why or not, will never be able to take the love of another Fae.'

If Deyus expected a reply from Agastalen he did not get one, since he found himself utterly at a loss.

'When Heath departs this place, Agastalen, Elya will spend the rest of her days remembering the warm touch of her mortal love, even when his bones are but dust upon the wind and no one remembers his name.'

Stunned, Agastalen had no words with which to reply. He just looked into Deyus's large dark eyes and saw no mockery or even anger, but only sorrow. He also knew, undeniably, that Deyus spoke the truth. In his mind's eye suddenly he could see their pleasure, the sparkle of the clear pool in the woodland glade and the soft moans of their intimacy, on the wind.

When Agastalen eventually spoke, his voice seemed harsh in his own ears. 'But why? Why take a mortal mate then?'

Deyus hung his head, looking at the earth, and whispered, 'Because, Agastalen, we are dying. The Fae are dying.'

He looked up into Agastalen's eyes and shrugged, perhaps to himself, and said, 'There seems little harm in your knowing the truth. The history is ancient and means little to the world now. There are none left to care, save us. Even the gods have turned their eyes from us.'

The faun placed his wooden pipes on the ground before him and shifted his bovine legs so that they were folded beneath him. 'The Fae are old, Agastalen, and once as countless as the stars. We were not always confined to such as this, you know.' His hairy arm swept out to encompass the beautiful forest. 'Before the order existed that you now know as the world of Rune and universe beyond, Ione´ and gorGoroth the female and male dragon gods slept. The Fae were conceived of their dreams and we flew the heavens. We laughed, we danced and we loved with wild abandon. The Fae were as numerous at the stars. The dragon gods cared little for us and so, when they awoke and wove the universe about them, we roamed and danced across the wild and new worlds as we saw fit.'

The Faun paused then, fiddling idly with his pipes, as if for a moment thinking. 'But when the war in heaven came we had to make a choice, a choice that would later come to rule our fate. Though some of us remained neutral, many of the Fae lords and their hosts sided with the male dragon god gorGoroth. They went against your younger gods and humankind. Within this stone circle rest remains of one such Fae lord. Had you entered that circle, you would have been consumed by the powers that bind his slumbering spirit.'

Agastalen glanced in horror at the passive stone circle, edging slightly farther away.

Deyus clenched his lightly furred first and said, almost spitting out the words, 'And when gorGoroth fell, so did the judgement of your gods fall upon the Fae. Many of us were trapped on your world and here we were condemned to remain for eternity, even those who took no part in the conflict. Your gods called it compassion not to kill us, and congratulated themselves on their judgement.'

Deyus's voice grew quieter, falling almost to a whisper. 'And we may not pass beyond the boundaries of these lands. These beautiful forests are our tomb, our prison, our doom. Here we will die and fade, until even the memory of our race is lost.

He met Agastalen's eyes then. 'The final curse from your compassionate pantheon smote us barren. We may never bear children. As each age passes, so more of our kind simply fade.'

Agastalen's mind reeled at the scale of what he was being told. He'd been aware of the mythical existence of dragon gods, since that was taught at Arcanum, but that they'd preceded the human gods and had created the universe was an utter revelation. This was something that could turn religion upside down on Rune. Humanity, it seemed, was far from supreme. And that the Fae could live, essentially unknown, to the other races on Rune was nothing short of stunning.

'I think I understand what you're saying to me, Deyus, though the implications… are vast. But how does this relate to Heath?' asked Agastalen.

Deyus nodded and somewhat reluctantly said, 'Simply this: the Sylph Elya in mating with Heath will seek to bear his child. Because Heath is a mortal man and so also beloved of your younger gods, such a mating is not bound by the magics that strike us barren and it is possible that Elya will conceive. If she does, then the child will carry both Fae and mortal blood. That child will then be able to pass beyond the bounds of this and any other Fae land, unlike us. In this way the Fae or at least a part our race will continue, even when we have faded into memory. There are some few across Rune who are the children of such encounters, although their true ancestry may perhaps be unknown to them.'

A riot of emotions and thoughts tumbled within Agastalen. He didn't know whether to be overawed at the telling of such a vast and unknown history, to be saddened for the tragic fate of the Fae, humbled by Elya's sacrifice or perhaps even angered at the way that his friend was being manipulated and used.

Deyus waited patiently. In the end Agastalen settled for anger. He rose to his feet, his face red and towering over the diminutive Fae, and raged, 'You should have told me! You are as much a part of this manipulation as Elya is. Heath must be warned!'

The faun was apparently unmoved and watched Agastalen calmly from his seat on the grass. 'Seek not to judge me, Agastalen. You know little of this. I told you such only out of respect for the strength that you demonstrated in resisting the Sylph charms that surely would have overwhelmed most mortals.'

He chuckled at the look of shock of Agastalen's face. 'Oh yes. Be assured that had you been female, Agastalen, you would have been greeted by the male sylphs whose charms are equally as…. overwhelming as those of the females!'

Agastalen shook his head, his face still mottled with anger, and raising his voice, said, 'Whatever your platitudes, I'm leaving to warn Heath. Do not try to stop me.'

The smile on the faun's mischievous face vanished as he replied, 'It is too late, Agastalen, their love-making is complete. You cannot unmake what has been done. Elya may conceive now and she may not. As for stopping you, be assured that I could. However, you are not my enemy and you should remember that I am not yours.'

Struggle as he might with the faun's logic, Agastalen knew that it could not be disputed. Deyus had been honest with him. Once they reached the borders, he and Heath needn't ever come back to this enchanted forest. What was done was done and unless Agastalen told him, Heath might never know that Elya had mated with him for life and hoped to bear their child.

Agastalen's shoulders dropped, his anger draining away, leaving him feel empty and spent. He nodded reluctantly in agreement.

'Come,' said Deyus, jumping up. 'There is something that I would show you.'

The faun companionably took Agastalen's hand in his own, and with his other hand holding his wooden pipes he began to pipe a merry tune. The haunting notes from the pipes lifted Agastalen's spirits and he found worry melting away, becoming a distant thing. He noticed then that with his journey to the glade and conversation with the faun, the day had fled and it was already late afternoon.

Holding Deyus's hand, the faun laughed and skipped beside him. They left the glade and the slumbering anger of the Fae lord far behind, with only the fading melody of wooden pipes.

Unexpectedly Agastalen realised that he now danced beside Deyus. He moved and swung with an ease and grace that normally escaped him. The woods began to race by, the haunting melody of the pipes always preceding them. Agastalen fancied that at times he could hear the birds singing their hearts out in accompaniment as they leaped. Occasionally he noticed faint figures racing beside them as they danced, fleet as leaves on the wind. Often the figures were small and faun-like with horns, others were wrapped in cloaks of leaves or flitted looming and winged beside them.

Agastalen laughed with an abandon that he'd not felt since they had left the Spire in Loria. It left him feeling giddy. Where anger and resentment had coiled inside him, now instead there was joy. They danced so fast now that his feet hardly touched the ground. Deyus piped with abandon and, capering madly, would often spin with one of the figures that ran beside them.

Eventually, and to Agastalen's regret, the music slowed, its pace becoming gentle and soothing. Agastalen found himself slowing, his cloak settling about him again.

They stood on a grassy promontory that jutted out into the sea. White horses crashed against the base of the rock and fans of salty spray showered the air, coating the sparse fir trees that clutched even the edge of the promontory, as if attempting to declare that this land would one day belong to the sea. The sun set to the west, its dying fires settling into the sea with ripples of hazy orange and red. Agastalen thought for a moment that the promontory bore a carpet of golden leaves and then gasped as the area of his attention stirred, with the shift of great feathered wings.

Without a thought Agastalen started forward and didn't notice the slight look of surprise as the faun lowered his pipes. The creature was beautiful, its gold furred flanks shimmered in the setting sunlight, as they rose and fell in the peacefulness of sleep. Its white and brown feathered wings were furled across its back, the giant beaked head resting upon enormous feline paws.

It appeared unaware of Agastalen. Now that he was closer he noticed that the creature's once beautiful beak was chipped and cracked, the golden flanks were mottled with grey and the feathers were faded and dull, in places missing altogether.

'Griffin,' said Deyus, beside Agastalen now. 'Once one of the most beautiful creatures of all the Fae, she is the last of her kind now. This is the farthest southerly boundary of our realm here and we can go no farther. She watches the farthest skies here, knowing that she can never fly into them again.'

Agastalen looked to Deyus, who placed an affectionate hand on the old griffin with an unfathomable look.

'She fades,' whispered Deyus.

'You must leave, you know,' said the faun, looking sadly to Agastalen. 'The longer you stay, the more difficult it will be for you to go. We can take you to our farthest boundary, close to Shael, at dawn.'

Agastalen nodded and didn't ask how Deyus knew of their destination.

He slept that night in the river meadow and dreamed of a dying griffin, its golden skin fading to silver and then to dust, as a crimson sun arched across the sky and fell like a bloody comet into a boiling sea.

Heath did not return that night and it was not until noon the next day when an impatient Agastalen saw his friend appear smiling from the woods hand in hand with Elya. The sylph walked with a sway beside Heath, her arm about his waist.

Heath waved and called out a greeting.

Agastalen noticed as he approached that Heath's chest was bare and he wore a skirt of woven river reeds and his hair was braided with grass. There was no sign of the other female Sylphs.

'Where have you been?' asked Agastalen, somewhat more harshly than he'd intended.

A scowl crawled across Heath's face and he replied, 'I've been enjoying myself, and if you weren't busy being so stuck up, you would have been too!'

Elya whispered something in Heath's ear and giggled.

'Come on, why not join us?' said Heath placatingly, and smiled. 'I just came by to see if you were here. Elya says there's an amazing waterfall high up in the hills, and we're going to dive off it.'

Agastalen's face must have shown his lack of interest and even annoyance, since Elya stepped forward and placed a delicate hand on his cheek and said in a voice that shimmered like the water, 'Dear Agastalen, let go of your concerns, they are those of the world. Stay with us for a while. Come and swim with us today. The tumbling rivers in the hills are wonderful to behold and I will have friends there, should you wish.'

Agastalen felt himself go weak inside at her touch. Her beauty was without question, her face sculpted by the finest artist; her eyes were the liquid depths of pools.

Heath started momentarily, seeing the look of desire that rippled across Agastalen's face, but Elya stepped back and placed her hand on Heath's arm and the smile returned to his face.

Agastalen wanted to go with them with all his being. Everything that was male about him was as taught as a drum skin; he throbbed with it. He knew that it would only take the slightest murmur of agreement and shortly he too would be fulfilling his most erotic dreams with a creature from his fantasies. Yet within him echoed the faun's warning. If he gave in, he knew that they would likely never leave. To many this would not be such a terrible prospect, to live your life in the arms of such a beautiful creature and perhaps even to see your own children grow. But even if they put aside their holy vows to Arcanum, they had also made a promise to Baron Mytle, a promise on which thousands of lives could depend. Whether his desire wished it or not, Agastalen knew that he had to keep that promise.

'No.' Agastalen almost gasped the word but he managed to say it.

Elya raised her eyebrows in surprise and looked at Heath, disappointment and surprise evident on her face.

Heath shrugged and turned to walk away, calling, 'Your loss, my friend. We'll see you later.'

Knowing that he had to strike now or likely for ever lose his friend, Agastalen ran after Heath and pulled him around. 'No, you don't understand. We need to leave today.'

'What are you talking about?' returned Heath with acidity. 'We've only been here just over two days. We deserve a rest.'

Elya rested her head on his shoulders, her long hair falling across his bare chest. Heath began to look very distracted.

Not knowing what else to do, Agastalen placed himself squarely in front of Heath and put a hand on his friend's shoulder. 'Heath, we have people that are depending on us delivering that message to Shael. We made the baron a promise. Thousands of lives could be at stake. We cannot wait for another day. Cinder is butchering innocents in the baronies even as we speak. We are rested and healed, Heath, we need to go.'

Concern etched Heath's face and he nodded slightly. 'You're right as always, Agastalen.' Taking a breath, he said, 'You carry the message. I'll stay here with Elya.'

Elya's smile was radiant and she let out a cry of glee, smothering Heath's face in kisses.

Taking a breath, Agastalen plunged on. 'We gave that commitment together, Heath, and unless they release you, you're also bound to Arcanum by vow. You can't just toss that aside.'

Agastalen then noticed the diminutive form of the faun Deyus, standing behind Heath and Elya. His face appeared sad and worn.

Heath drew a breath to speak, his eyes fixed and hard.

Deyus cut in then, 'Your friend is right, Heath, you must go. Your place is not here, at least not at the moment: your race….your world, needs you.'

Elya spun to regard the faun, who looked utterly miserable, her eyes flashing, and spat a string of words at him in a language that neither Heath nor Agastalen recognised.

Deyus regarded her solemnly but did not reply.

It seemed as if Heath reached a decision then and a new look, one touched with resolve, filled his face and he turned to Elya. He placed his hands to either side of her face and drew her into his embrace. When they parted, Elya's eyes were filled with tears and wide with astonishment.

Agastalen did not miss the gesture when her hand reached down to touch her stomach. His heart went out to the Sylph then and he wept inside for her, understanding the extent of her grief, knowing that she could never love another and that Heath clearly did not know.

'They are right,' Heath said, oblivious to his friend's tumbling emotions. 'I did make a promise and I am also bound to Arcanum, though the gods know that right now I wish that I weren't. I *promise* I'll return to you though, my love.'

Elya gasped and barely nodded, tears streaking her face. She whispered something then to Heath that only he could hear, and raising his hand, placed it on her breast above her heart.

The faun then began to pipe. The haunting notes filled the air and Agastalen barely had time to raise his hand in farewell to his diminutive friend before the forest spun and blurred.

- CHAPTER 27 -

The Grey City

Agastalen and Heath awoke from their enchanted sleep atop a bluff.

The day was cold and grey; a piercing wind sliced through their clothing and tugged at the grass. The dark and foreboding border of the Fae Forest marched like an omnipresent sentinel, just a few spans behind them.

They rested uncomfortably with their backs against the outside of a small ring of standing stones. Recalling his conversation with the faun about such stones, Agastalen muttered a curse and rolled away from them.

Trying to wipe the fog of enchanted sleep from his eyes, Agastalen stood up and looked over the bluff, just twenty spans from them, where it plunged down a dizzying depth until finally reaching a vast natural harbour that churned with a turquoise sea. A grey city clung to the cliff at the farthest edge of the bay, like some huge stone spider.

A wet nose in his ear made him turn. Bella, their mare, had apparently made their enchanted journey with them and was now trying to rifle his pockets, looking for goodies. Agastalen rubbed Bella's nose, delighted to see her. He'd not liked to think of her alone in the wild. Bella's packs were intact and a glance showed him that Deyus had even provisioned them with food and a little gold coin, even if the coins did look a little green and old. He whispered thanks to his fickle friend.

Heath rose, yawning, and scrubbed at his hair. His eyes had a slightly haunted look. He walked to the bluff edge and peered over incautiously. 'Cheery place,' he muttered. 'I'm hoping that's Limfrost, capital of Shael?'

Agastalen nodded slightly. 'How are you feeling?' he asked cautiously.

'Like I just awoke from a deep magical sleep, cast on me by some capricious faun,' Heath snapped.

Agastalen ignored the fact that Heath had obviously not answered the question. 'Look, I'm sorry about what happened and that you had to leave Elya. I know… it must be hard.'

Heath caught Agastalen's gaze and replied grimly, 'No, I don't think you'll ever know how hard it is.'

Wrestling with what the faun had told him, Agastalen was not sure what to say. He hung in a moment of indecision. To tell Heath the truth about Elya and the dying Fae, and how she could never love another, could well break his heart or maybe even send him dashing back to the woods of the Fae. But if he kept the faun's secret, then he knew that Heath could forever regard him as the one that had torn Elya from him.

Trying for the middle ground, Agastalen failed to find it. 'Look, there were things going on there that you really didn't understand.' Even as he said it, he knew how cryptic it sounded.

'And you did, I suppose, oh Arch-Mage Agastalen. Please, spare me the superiority.'

'That's not what I meant,' Agastalen said.

'Then tell me what you meant.'

Agastalen paused and took a deep breath. He was rushing towards the truth but could still not bring himself to say it. He needed Heath and they were both bound by vow to Arcanum, not forgetting their duty to the baron and humanity.

'I was trying to protect you,' he said.

The heat in Heath's face began at his neck and started to rise towards his face. Agastalen saw the warning signs of his friend's impending fury and cast about for something to keep the peace.

'Protect me?' said Heath. 'From what? From the love of a mythical creature more beautiful and caring than anyone or anything that you or I could ever hope to meet?'

Stepping close so that his face was barely a span from Agastalen's, he said, 'The only person you were trying to protect was yourself. You just didn't wany to make this journey alone... friend.'

'I'm sorry,' Agastalen managed as Heath started to turn away.

'Sorry?' Heath replied. 'Have you ever been in love, Agastalen? No? Well, neither had I.'

In an astonishing change of tone that left Agastalen mystified, Heath shouldered his pack and, setting off, said, 'Come on, we've got a message for a queen.'

Agastalen scuttled to catch up, guilt hanging thick on him like a cloak.

They left the circle of standing stones to continue its impassive regard of the equally impassive and distant grey city.

The road into Limfrost harbour was not difficult to locate, since it teamed with traffic, there apparently being just a single route down to the grey city. An impressive causeway had been carved into the cliff face with sufficient width to easily accommodate four carts abreast.

It took at least a half-hour to negotiate the causeway down into the harbour, since it burgeoned with traffic. Agastalen recognised regional dress from Athel-Loria, Shael and Immiriel amongst those that he did not. It also swiftly became clear that they were expected to make way for carts, pack animals, merchant caravans, occasional nobles atop pawing destriers, and in general anyone slightly bigger than themselves. They frequently found themselves pressed up against the cliff wall in an attempt not to get crushed.

Huge stone gatehouses spanned the width of the causeway at regular intervals. Guards in grey cloaks diligently watched the throng from atop tower battlements.

By agreement, they halted at the next gatehouse and Agastalen, avoiding a rotund merchant with a train of braying mules, approached one of the guards, who stood at attention, a spear in one hand and a round shield featuring a grey fortress and ship device on the other. The guard watched him approach impassively through a visored helm.

Agastalen halted in front of the guard and politely said, 'We have information that we need to get to Queen Iodarii. Could you tell us how we can get to see her, please?'

A moment passed as Agastalen stood under the guard's scrutiny and then the guard shrugged, 'Best way would probably just be for you to attend the open court, sir. Anyone can attend and present a petition to the Queen then. Queen Iodarii receives open court once a week, sir. Next open court is two days from now, at the palace.'

When nothing else was forthcoming from the guard he nodded briefly in thanks and rejoined Heath.

'That seems easy enough, then,' said Agastalen cautiously, trying hard not to precipitate another argument and giving Bella a bit of purple Fae fruit from the saddlebags, which the mare seemed to enjoy immensely. The prospect of delivering the message had obviously lifted his spirits somewhat. 'I'd suggest that we find lodgings, with stables for Bella of course, and in the time between now and this open court thing see if we can find ourselves a ship to Arcanum.'

Heath's tone was neutral, for which Agastalen was profoundly grateful. 'That's fine with me. We'll have to be frugal with the lodgings, though. Two berths to Arcanum could be pricey. It's possible we may have to work some of our passage as well.'

Agastalen's returned expression was sour, as he realised that Heath could well be right.

Lower Limfrost was a bleak city, built around the harbour. Its uniform grey granite buildings seemed to huddle together for warmth and had the stout appearance of having been built to weather storms. Agastalen considered that Cinder would have a hard time trying to take the place, if it ever came to that, he added to himself. And the people of Limfrost themselves seemed little bothered with finery too, their stout grey cloaks marking them out from the more garishly coloured folk from Immiriel or those from Athel-Loria who often wore animal furs.

The first couple of inns clearly denoted themselves as being too rich for the pair's meagre purse and with reluctance they passed them by. The Cheerful Octopus, however, which sported a faded metal sign of the said sea creature with a mug of ale in each tentacle, in what was clearly a slightly poorer part of the city, looked much more promising, if less cosy.

After some haggling with the landlord, and including a stable for Bella, it turned out to be so cheap that they surmised they could afford to stay for over two weeks without exhausting their funds. After a quiet discussion, they wisely decided to tip the landlord a little extra to ensure that Bella was well cared for, fearing that she might otherwise 'vanish' from her stall one night.

They ate a watery stew at a slightly lopsided table in the Cheerful Octopus bar. The oil lamps burned with cheap oil and the light was yellow and dull. A half-dozen poorly clad customers nursed their beers, perhaps hoping that they would last the whole night.

Heath's gaze was far away as his wooden spoon made circles in his stew. Agastalen's attempts to draw him into a semblance of conversation had failed and so he decided instead to talk to the landlord, in the hope that he might be able to give them some guidance as to where they could find a ship to Arcanum.

The landlord was a cheery sort, a burly fellow, obviously an ex-sailor from his rolling gait. He kept a cudgel hung in plain sight upon the wall behind him. Although poor, he kept a clean inn, and Agastalen thought that once you got to know him, he probably wasn't a bad sort. He watched Agastalen approach and rubbed a meaty hand over his bald pate, probably hoping that he was going to order some more beer. Sitting at a bar stool, Agastalen decided to do so, knowing that Heath would drink it even if he was off his food.

While the landlord drew the ale Agastalen said, 'We're looking for passage on a ship bound for the Free Province of Arcanum. Could you point us in the direction of an honest sea captain who could help us?' He had deliberately avoided reference to Arcanum city itself, concerned that it might draw too many enquiries. The province of Arcanum itself had many small villages and towns to which they could easily be travelling.

The landlord frowned and plonked two tankards of foaming ale on the bar as Agastalen slid over a small coin. 'Well nows, sir. Bit of a problem there. You not eard? Athel-Loria's declared war on Arcanum!'

Agastalen gaped, only managing to shake his head.

Even Heath looked up from his stew.

The Landlord leaned on the bar, obviously warming to his subject. 'That's right. Tore down all dem mage spires cross the whole empire. Dat not being enough either, Warlord's vowed to exterminate order of Arcanum to a man. Divine order of the war god Sha all got together and marched, with all the legions of Athel-Loria too. Dey've got half a million troops camped on border of Immiriel! Dey're waitin for free passage cross Immiriel to Arcanum. Don't sees how the Queen can say no meself. Can't stop Athel-Lorians with an army like that at dere back.'

Agastalen thought that was probably a bit of an understatement, as he struggled to make sense of what he'd heard. In all the history of Rune nobody had ever declared war on the magi. Wars between the divine orders themselves had certainly happened in ancient history but Arcanum had always managed to remain neutral. And if what the landlord said was true, this was more than a war: it was a vow of extermination, by the greatest military empire in the world. He knew with utter certainty now that if they'd not fled Loria, they'd certainly have lost their lives.

His mind racing, Agastalen also realised that he had been right to keep their connection to Arcanum secret. Although Shael was apparently not involved in the war, the influence of the mighty Athel-Lorian empire directly on its border could prove substantial. Their very lives could now be threatened in these northerly countries, if it became known that they were sworn to Arcanum.

Heath was now beside Agastalen at the bar, apparently having been stirred from his dark contemplations by the news. Heath took a sip from the fresh beer. Agastalen, though, could see the shock that he was trying to hide.

Wiping his lips and trying to sound casual, Heath said, 'But why does this stop us taking ship to Arcanum?'

The landlord frowned and said, 'Dose bloody Athel-Lorians sailed half their fleet round and dey're blockading whole Immirien peninsula.'

Agastalen knew that the peninsula concerned was where the small free state of Arcanum sat.

'Day're letting nothin in nor out. Few ships tried to run it first, course, but dey was sunk to a man.' The landlord cursed and spat on the floor. 'Hit trade hard, damn em. Stopped all shipping east, just like dat.'

The landlord seemed keen to continue the conversation, but not wanting to draw too much attention to their interest in the subject, Agastalen thanked him as he and Heath returned to their table.

'Nim's shiny balls,' cursed Heath quietly, sitting down. 'What do the Athel-Lorians think they're playing at? There's not been a war on this scale for hundreds of cycles. Even with their military might, they don't really believe they can win against Arcanum, do they?'

Agastalen did not look at Heath as he replied, 'With the order of the war god allied to them, they really could, Heath. Arcanum could be utterly destroyed.'

Heath sat aghast, but as the feeling of dread coiled in his stomach he knew that Agastalen was right. The war god's order was unparalleled in its strength on the battlefield, and if it were allied to the greatest military force upon Rune he understood that the threat to Arcanum was dire indeed. Heath's throat constricted for a moment as a fleeting image of his mistress Lei-Weya, cut down before the empire's hordes, assailed him.

Putting a hand on his friend's arm, Agastalen said, 'We can still get to Arcanum, Heath.'

Heath looked up, surprised. 'But how? It's blockaded.'

Agastalen rubbed his jaw stubble thoughtfully and replied, 'The cut of Shael is to the north-east of here. We can make for there and then head south towards Arcanum. The only problem, though, is that time could be against us. We'll need to get there before the legions of Athel-Loria start their march south through Immiriel. If we find ourselves behind their lines we'll never make it.' He didn't add that should they be caught by the Athel-Lorians and exposed as magi, their lives would certainly be forfeit.

Heath nodded, his face resolutely set, and said, 'In that case we need to get this message delivered sharpish and get out of here, as if Nim himself were shipping us.'

Agastalen laughed, trying to keep his voice down, pleased at his friend's new resolution and determination, and said, 'I'd say that's about the size of it.'

****

Unfortunately, the queue was enormous.

It seemed that the entire population of Limfrost had decided to petition their beloved Queen today. The queue of huffing merchants, parents with screaming children, finely clad landowners and people from all walks of life, trailed from beyond the great double doors of the grand palace, through the cobbled courtyard and far into the boulevard beyond. Grey-cloaked guards discreetly kept order and without comment occasionally escorted a queue-jumping opportunist to the very back of the line.

Being keen to deliver their message and get out of Limfrost quickly, Agastalen and Heath had set out from the Cheerful Octopus as soon as a reluctant sun cast its first dreary dawn rays across the grey city. They'd made good time through the lower city and harbour, to the upper city citadel walls, where its imposing battlements were paced by the Grey Guard.

Their hearts had dropped, though, when arriving at the rearing grey palace at first light; they'd joined a queue of jostling folk that already stretched almost out of the courtyard. It was now noon and Heath had gone to find them some lunch.

Agastalen craned his neck again, hoping that they were a few spans farther forward, noticing that they were perhaps almost halfway across the courtyard. With a sigh, he returned to studying the distant temple of Aevarnia, goddess of love, perched amidst Upper Limfrost. The eye was naturally drawn to the soft white of the pillared mother temple of Aevarnia: it seemed a dove amongst dirty grey pigeons.

Heath returned with their food: hot parcels of fish, seasoned with pungent juice from Yich fruit, which grew on craggy silver trees hanging precariously on the cliffs about Limfrost. Agastalen thought as he munched that picking such fruit must be a pretty precarious task. Heath grouched around mouthfuls about the slow progress of the queue.

By late afternoon they'd not yet reached the palace door and it was clear that they were not going to make it that day. The courtyard began to cool as such meagre warmth that the sun offered began to cool and finally failed altogether as it slipped behind a dark bank of clouds. Agastalen started to approach a guard, intending to ask how long they had before the Queen retired for the day, and was answered pre-emptively as several dozen penitents were ushered out of the palace and the great black doors shut behind them with a boom. Grey Guards promptly took up station in front of the doors.

Agastalen and Heath spat out simultaneous curses. There was a low collective groan from the crowd and the scores of disappointed folk turned to make their way from the huge courtyard. Grey guards began to call out in low voices as they ushered citizens through the gate.

Agastalen and Heath didn't move. 'What now?' said Heath, his green eyes worried. 'If we wait another week until the next audience, that damned Athel-Lorian army could be marching through Immiriel, even if they're not already,' he finished.

Agastalen nodded agreement. 'I'm also not sure that the baronies can spare a week either, with Cinders army running amok, and there's nothing to stop them.'

Looking worriedly about he spotted what appeared to be a guard officer, judging from the white plumes rising from his helm. 'Let's talk to him,' he said, pointing.

'Right,' agreed Heath.

The plumed officer watched them approach without comment, his hand resting easily on the hilt of a short sword. His helm was open-faced and his look was one of weary resignation. Before they could speak, the officer said, 'Don't ask, the answer is no. You'll just have to get here earlier next week.'

'You don't understand,' said Agastalen, 'we have an urgent message for the Queen from Baron Mytle in the Peldane baronies.'

The officer shook his head and said, 'You're right, I don't understand, and for that matter I don't want to. Move along, please.'

Heath stepped in, his voice slightly frantic. 'Please, the message really is urgent. There are lives at stake!' The officer gestured to two of his grey-cloaked guards and they moved towards the two young magi.

In desperation Agastalen drew the baron's dagger from his belt, intending to show it to the officer as proof. The officer, misinterpreting his intentions, took an alarmed step back and drew his short sword in one fluid movement. Shouts of alarm went up from the guards and they raced towards their officer.

'No, no, you don't understand,' shouted Agastalen, desperately waving the dagger around. 'This is from Baron Mytle: it bears his crest, its, its proof of what we say!'

Rough hands grabbed Agastalen from behind and wrenched his arms behind his back. The baron's dagger fell to the cobbles with a metallic ring. A cry of alarm went up from Heath as he too was grappled.

'Cease, and bring me that dagger,' snapped a lady with a martial voice, striding towards them. A grey silk cloak snapped out behind her and her sculpted metal breastplate caught the failing sunlight. Those guards not holding the two young mages saluted and the officer stooped to retrieve the dagger. He handed it to the lady, hilt first.

Agastalen judged the lady to be a high-ranking officer from her attire, although she could not be more than his own age. She inspected the dagger crest with hard blue eyes, which then examined the two of them, seeming to take in every detail.

'Release them,' she snapped.

The guards stepped back immediately.

'Now leave us and close the courtyard gate.'

The officer saluted and ran to attend his mistress's duty.

The female officer handed the dagger back to Agastalen, who took it cautiously, as if half expecting it to bite.

'My apologies,' said the officer. 'We're used to dealing with loud and stubborn petitioners who don't wish to leave. Occasionally even tempers as well modulated as those of the grey guard grow thin. My name is Commander Jalda, commanding officer of the palace grey guard. I'm familiar with the family crest of the Mytle barony and know the baron himself well enough to recognise that as his personal dagger. If you genuinely have a message from the baron you may give it to me and I will ensure that her majesty receives your message…. in full.'

Her voice hardened further and she added, 'But if you're just thieves who have stolen a dagger from a respectable man, then you can expect a hard and cold justice here.'

Agastalen knew that they had little choice but to trust Jalda. Their chances of reaching Queen Iodarii today were now effectively zero. A senior officer, though, he hoped would see their pledge to the baron fulfilled. Agastalen looked to Heath, seeking his friend's assent. Commander Jalda did not miss the significance of the look that passed between the two friends and waited patiently.

Heath nodded his reply to Agastalen's unspoken query.

As the grey guard set watch on the palace walls, Agastalen explained then to Commander Jalda of their encounter with the Peldane barony forces and the terrible outcome of the barons' battle against the immortal Cinder and the forces of Taed. Jalda asked few questions, listening attentively as the compound fell into shadow. Agastalen did not explain why they were travelling in the first place, and neither did the commander ask.

When he'd finished, Jalda's face was grim, her cold blue eyes flashed in anger. 'Under the baron's personal crest I see the truth in your words. Sadly it also confirms much that we had suspected, brave sirs. I thank you on behalf of Queen Iodarii, and I assure you that she will hear your message this very day. Your word to the baron is fulfilled and you must also consider us in your debt. Should at any time you require assistance or favour, you may call upon this office. Farewell.'

With that Jalda turned sharply, and with a billow of her fine cape departed.

A slightly bemused Agastalen and Heath were escorted to the palace gates.

- CHAPTER 28 -

Dove

The sails cracked and snapped in the morning air.

The pleasure craft from Apolletta leaped merrily through the frothing waves, bunting and brightly coloured lanterns making it appear as if it had just escaped a carnival flotilla. Standing at the helm, hands firmly grasping the wheel, Alazla smiled in real mirth for the first time in cycles. Blond hair streaming back, he laughed aloud as despite her shallow draft the small ship, which they had come to discover was named Dove, turned willingly and with only gentle guidance. Feeling the tremors in the wheel and watching the taughtness of the sails and rigging, he urged her on to greater pace. Dove responded by canting over, cutting a swathe though the waves. Silk cushions and bottles rolled across the deck, precariously close to falling into the racing surf.

Jacinth and Kuoy at the prow were hanging onto the brass rail as if their lives depended on it. Jacinth, her hair streaming in the wind, comfortably shifted her body with the rock and swell of the ship. Kuoy appeared to be having a less easy time and was clutching stiffly at the rail. Reluctantly Alazla eased off the pace of the ship, realizing that Kuoy had very little nautical experience and even less tolerance for chop. Dove righted herself easily, with the jangle of lanterns and bottles.

342

Jacinth turned and with a consoling pat on a slumped Kuoy's shoulder walked along the deck towards Alazla, her hips rolling easily with the motion of the ship. 'Ahoy there, captain,' she laughed as she approached, pushing back a tumble of wavy red hair from her face. 'I see you've never sailed before, then,' she said.

'Oh, just one or twice,' said Alazla, smiling, revelling in the eager pull of the little ship. 'Mum saved up and bought me a leaky old tub for my birthday once. I thought she was the most beautiful thing I'd ever seen,' he said, remembering her fondly. 'She let in more water than she kept out! Patched her up though, mended the sails sanded and painted her up. Called her Qizoth. Thorn and I used to race her round Korth harbour. We'd take it in turns to buzz the merchant vessels coming in.'

He shook his head, his guts twisting at the happy memories of his closest childhood friend, and with his voice husky with emotion continued, 'Harbour master locked Thorn up for it once. I was sailing, and got too close to an Immiriel Galley. It almost took out a Korthian warship trying to avoid us. Thorn said it was him, though. Cost his parents a week's takings at the inn to get him out. He had to work it off scrubbing floors!'

Jacinth laughed gently as Alazla recalled the fond memory.

Even though cycles had passed, Alazla knew that he had still not accepted Thorn's loss. Although his friend had been taken during the battle at the House of Oldoth, he had not seen him slain or even injured. A part of him still held out hope that, somewhere, Thorn remained alive.

His thoughts must have shown in his eyes, since Jacinth, ever perceptive, said, 'There's always hope, Alazla. Of all the people there when Thorn was taken, for some reason they took Thorn and only Thorn. Not even a beloved son or daughter of Oldoth but Thorn, the lowly son of an innkeeper. I'll be Nim's own imp if there's not a reason for that! There's a chance, even if small, that your friend still lives.'

Alazla looked at Jacinth and smiled in thanks, grateful for her support. It helped him to believe that he was not clutching at moonbeams, holding out just a fool's hope.

Kuoy emerged from below decks later that morning with armloads of brightly coloured clothing and other assorted bric-a-brac. After he'd made several attempts to outfit Alazla in quite garish noble finery, Alazla was at last able to settle for a white cotton shirt, black pantaloons and blue cape, with a small but serviceable dagger. Kuoy was similarly attired, although such cosmopolitan clothing looked somewhat out of place on his feral, tattooed body.

Jacinth emerged from the cabin grinning and seemed not at all surprised at the looks of grinning admiration from Alazla and Kuoy. She had washed her hair and tied it back at the nape of her neck. A tight black velvet doublet displayed an ample cleavage. Her green velvet skirt was slit up the side for ease of movement and displayed flashes of creamy leg. Jacinth curtsied to a wolf-whistle from Kuoy.

They ate well that evening, as the Dove raced on an unerring south-westerly course, scudding within a league of the Korthian coast. The nobles had been well provisioned and the escaped slaves all fell on the food with the gusto of those who aren't sure where their next good meal is likely to come from.

As Kuoy and Jacinth discussed the best place to put ashore, Alazla nibbled on some fruit and contemplated the distant coast. Occasionally he could see the twinkle of lights from small communities, their families no doubt now retreating inside for the warmth of fire and companionship. His feelings as they approached Korth were mixed: he knew that they did so as escapees, yet his heart surged at the hope that he might see Liandra, his mother, again, although pragmatically he also understood that this was one of the first places that any authorities seeking them would look.

Alazla now came to understand that his fight with Lorm, ultimately resulting in the death of the bully, had forever changed Korth for him. No longer was it his childhood home, a place of fun, learning and the reassuring comfort of his mother's hearth. There was a legacy of anger there for him now, of injustice. The innocence of his youth had been brutally shattered and what should have been happy memories of the place where he had grown up were left jaded and tarred. And yet he had nowhere to direct this anger. Certainly a grievous injustice had been dealt him by Loremaster Cantillion in sentencing him to the slave mines. It was not his blow that had slain Lorm, although he'd certainly premeditated the attack on him. Despite his anger Alazla understood that Cantillion himself was not wholly to blame. Not wholly, anyway, he thought. Perhaps if he could somehow get himself pardoned, he could go back, at least in part, to the way things were. Perhaps.

Hearing beloved son Balthazar's name mentioned, Alazla turned his attention to the conversation between Kuoy and Jacinth, who was heartily tucking into a well-stocked plate of smoked meats and fruit.

'I will not be dissuaded, this Balthazar is nothing to me and certainly neither is Korth, who condemned us to those cursed mines,' Kuoy was saying, his weathered face set firm in resolution. 'When you and Alazla put ashore close to Korth, I will take this vessel and make for Blue Bay, from where I can put into Ya-Guth, in the land of the horse people. Korth has no dominion there and I should be able to make my way overland to Ylith, although the way will be long.'

'But you can't sail, you jackass,' laughed Jacinth, her dark eyes sparkling.

'I will do well enough,' retorted Kuoy. 'I have been watching Alazla and do not believe that it is so very difficult. I will do well enough.'

Jacinth locked eyes with Alazla, who had as yet said nothing. They both knew full well that Kuoy sailing this ship, small though it was, would certainly be a sight to see.

'The issue for us, though,' said Alazla, interjecting, to Jacinth, 'is how are we going to get to Balthazar, to tell him about that' – he struggled for words – 'swirling light, the well, in the stone.' He tried to ignore the feeling of dread that came back to him when he thought of that moment. Continuing, he said, 'We can't sail into Korth's harbour. The papers of all boats coming in and leaving are checked.'

Jacinth said, 'Alazla, it's unlikely that the Korth authorities yet know there's been an escape, after all we're fortunate that we escaped the island quickly and our guards would've had to get back to alert the compound before anything else could be done. As long as we don't take too much time getting to Korth city after we're ashore, we should be able to get in before the authorities are alerted and our descriptions circulated. Once we're in, even if they look for us there, we can just go to ground.'

'There goes my good reputation yet again,' muttered Alazla. 'Not only condemned to the slave mines and then the talk of the city at that, but my face is now likely to be plastered on every wall as an escapee!'

Jacinth laughed and replied, cupping his chin, 'But what a handsome face it is too! You could become one of those handsome rogues that all the ladies of court sigh and pine over.'

Alazla shook his head, unable to remain morose in the face of such levity. 'Very well,' he said, 'by my guess we should be within sight of Korth sometime late the day after tomorrow. When we're within a half-day, we'll tack closer to the coast and look for a suitable place to get ashore. This boat's got a fairly shallow draught, so we shouldn't have to swim too far.'

They were all replete, and with little else to discuss they settled back into the cushions to rest. Alazla lashed the wheel and took a bearing as the stars came out from under their cloak of daylight to shine happily in the encroaching ebony above them. Then he joined his friends and proceeded to lecture an attentive Kuoy as to how to pilot a small ship.

Sometime later, with Kuoy and Jacinth drifting off to sleep in a sea of silk pillows, Alazla continued to wrestle with his feelings about his impending return to Korth.

It was then that the wind died. The ship began to slowly coast to a stop until she sat bobbing in the play of the waves. Alazla climbed to his feet and stepped out from under the gaudy deck canvas. His boots echoed dully on the planking, the only other sound the gentle slap of waves against the hull. It was possible that they were caught in a lull, Alazla considered, looking out from the deck rail: such things certainly were not unheard of. With a chill, though, he realised that the sails did not stir at all, not with even the slightest murmur or sigh of canvas; they hung utterly limp from the spar. The hair slowly stood up on the back of his neck.

Close to the spar the still air suddenly seemed to thicken, become misty, swirling slowly. Alazla took an involuntary step back until his hand touched the cold metal starboard rail.

The air became thick with moisture, beading on his skin and the deck, until the mist had become a cloud above him, now thick and coiling. Slowly the cloud coalesced into a coiling and misty shape, vaguely human in outline. Yet the likeness stopped there, for it was at least twice the size of a man. From its head rose a wispy crest; its face was slightly pointed and set with silver eyes the colour of the moon, its maw filled with rows of wicked-looking fangs. Sweeping airy wings arose from its back, high into the air above the boat.

Alazla tensed himself, ready to shout to his still slumbering companions.

And then the creature bowed with whispering grace, ephemeral wings stretching behind it. Its hissing voice stirred the sails upon the spar. 'III briiing youuu greeeetiiings Hakooon… frooom beeeloveeed sooon Balthazaaar.'

Alazla's mind raced furiously as he tried to suppress the fear that threatened to overwhelm him. Sweat beaded upon his brow despite the chill. His muscles coiled and quivered with adrenalin barely held in check. Think, he forced himself, think! Had the creature wanted to attack, surely it could easily have taken him unawares. It had used Balthazar's name; somehow it knew or apparently knew *of* the beloved son whom they sought, even now. There was a remote possibility that this could somehow work to their advantage.

Seeing his hesitation, the airy creature extended its arms towards Alazla in what he assumed was meant to be a placating gesture but which made him attempt to recoil another step, bumping into the rail behind him again, allowing him to proceed no farther without taking a watery dive.

'Theeee beloveeed sooon saiiid yooou wouuuld hesitaaate,' hissed the airy creature, 'soo I muuust say thiiiis. Youuur moootheeer iiis weeell aaaand heee haaas keeept hiiis pleeedge.'

Alazla recalled immediately the promise that Balthazar had made to him after he had been condemned to slave labour on Crab Island: that he would ensure Liandra, his mother, would be cared for by the House of Oldoth. Only Alazla and Balthazar knew of this pledge.

Its towering form ebbing and curling, the creature waited patiently while Alazla considered.

Certainly Alazla understood that as a beloved son of Oldoth, god of sun and storm, Balthazar could well have power over airy creatures like this. Having decided to trust, a slight cold touch upon his arm made him turn his head. Jacinth and Kuoy stood silently beside him. Transfixed, he had not heard their approach. The airy creature made no overt acknowledgement of their presence and appeared to keep its silvered eyes fixed solely upon Alazla. Kuoy and Jacinth's faces were ashen and beaded with moisture.

Barely moving his lips, Kuoy whispered, 'We can all make it over the side if we go at once. On my mark.'

Alazla shook his head, in the negative.

Disbelief widened Kuoy's eyes.

'The creature was sent by Balthazar,' said Alazla, deliberately speaking aloud despite Kuoy's previous whisper. The creature bowed low at Alazla's acknowledgement, sweeping its arms wide.

The air then seemed to lighten, and once more Alazla realised that they could see the sky, although he had not noticed in his initial panic that it had vanished. A fresh sea breeze rushed across their faces and the sails caught the air with a dull boom. The pleasure craft lurched gently into motion once more. The airy creature remained by the sails, its presence now an ebbing and ghostly translucent outline in the daylight.

Summoning his courage, Alazla regarded the creature as Dove raced merrily ahead again, as if glad of the reprieve. Jacinth had assumed a position at the ship's wheel, her face a mask of controlled calm. Alazla's mind was ablaze with questions, the least of which being how Balthazar was even aware that they were here, but instead Alazla simply said, 'What does Balthazar want with me, spirit?'

'III wiiill beeaaaar youuu tooo hiiim nooow. Preepaaare yourseeelf.' Surprised, Alazla took a step back and held out his hand as the spirit's huge cloudy hand reached out for him.

Beside him, Kuoy was visibly shaking.

'Wait,' Alazla shouted, with more than a little panic in his voice. 'Just, just hold on. Where is it we're going?'

The spirit cocked its head to one side and hissed with a rush of cold breath, 'Not weee, youuu tooo, Balthazaaaaar.'

'Okay,' said Alazla, trying desperately to rationalise. 'Balthazar sent you to bring me to him, is that right?'

The spirit affirmed this with a slight nod.

'Fine,' he said with satisfaction, 'I'll go, but you'll have to take Jacinth as well.' He knew that given their earlier conversation and his present state, Kuoy would certainly not agree to come. Kuoy could stay on the ship and change the present course for Blue Bay. He glanced then at Jacinth, who returned a thin-lipped but firm nod of affirmation.

'Nooo,' hissed the spirit. Alazla began to draw breath when it continued, 'I haaave nooot theee pooower tooo beaaaar twooo beiiiings oof fleeesh. Youuu muuust cooome alooone.'

'I won't go alone,' said Alazla, firmly crossing his arms on his chest, although he certainly did not feel as brave as he pretended. 'It's both of us or nothing.' Despite his brave affirmation, he was quite sure there was nothing he could do should this spirit decide just to scoop him up and race away across the sea.

Minutes passed as the spirit waited, perhaps for Alazla to say more, or perhaps it was just thinking in whatever remote manner air spirits thought. Then its form seemed to coalesce into something more solid and momentarily they were able to define more of its face, covered in lush azure feathers and silvered eyes with cat-like pupils. The head snaked forward without the body moving and hissed in Alazla's face, 'Agreeed. I shaaall conveeey thiiis craaaft wiiith aaall speeeed, whereiiin Balthazaaaar waaaits.'

Without another word the little ship leapt forward as a strong wind suddenly bellied the sails with a tight crack of canvas and groan from the mast. Jacinth squealed in alarm and Alazla raced to the wheel to help her as the ship canted alarmingly.

- CHAPTER 29 -

Ancient Huntress

Hercuba lazily rolled in the air currents, revelling in the race of the wind through her lustrous black fur. She dived and arched through clouds, unaware that the sheer force of her massive leathery wings would often tear apart their pillowy softness.

Hercuba had been watching the small ship that harboured her modest prey all morning. Despite her prowess, she always liked to check for surprises before engaging an enemy, even one as weak as this, and thus had kept a cautious watch for a while. Easily picking out the tiny figures upon the deck, several leagues below it seemed that these creatures were just what their scent on the island had suggested, mere mortals and nothing more. And if Hercuba thought that the ship raced across the waves with an unnatural haste, she did not appear overly concerned. Human practicalities and minor magics meant little to her.

Hercuba did truly wish that the immortal Veylistra had set her a more worthy prey, though. She would have to discuss it with her next time. The hunt had certainly been interesting, she decided, and definitely appetising, but mortals were poor opponents at best and had an awful tendency to cry before being eaten. Alas for the true mortal heroes, she thought; where were they when you needed a truly worthy morsel?

Reflecting sadly on the state of the world these days, Hercuba folded her wings and with a lazy roll dived down towards the boat.

The first warning they had of the attack was when a shadow fell over them.

Alazla looked up just in time to a see an enormous winged creature plunge downward and strike Dove's mast with a blow like a detonation. The small ship canted madly and Alazla was catapulted with his friends across decks. He struck the starboard rail with a crack that forced the breath from his lungs. Tumbling over Alazla, Jacinth struck the railing head first, lying motionless where she fell. Kuoy appeared little better off than Alazla, gasping and clawing air back into his lungs.

Timbers groaned and shrieked, deck planking buckled and rigging snapped like string as the winged terror rose back into the air, tearing out the entire mast with the shriek of tortured timber.

Stunned and gasping, Alazla knew that they faced a creature from fable and legend and it was a terrible thing. Three heads writhed and roared upon a body of ebony fur, spitting steaming saliva from jaws that roared impossibly wide. The central head was that of a black lion, its mane cascading down onto the muscled torso of the beast. The second head was that of a terrible crested serpent, its scales rippling with sinuous movement, and finally the third was that of a goat, with baleful scarlet horns. Her body must have been fully forty spans long and the bat-like wings beating in the air to support it were at least twice that. The creature was bigger than the ship!

The chimera's mighty wings beat and it rose into the air with a rush as its roar shook Alazla's bones.

The lion head tore rapaciously into the clutched mast as if it were a carcass. The mast was rent like kindling, raining down onto the sea, the ship and its terrified occupants. Then folding its leathery wings slightly it dropped, landing with a boom on the cabin at the aft end of the small ship. The cabin simply collapsed under the massive weight of the chimera and the aft end sank into the sea, causing the prow to rear crazily, dripping foam. The chimera roared, an almost deafening sound, its terrible heads writhing and snapping, the wings beating slightly lest the entire boat simply sink beneath its massive weight.

As the wounded ship reared up, Alazla canted along the deck towards the bellowing chimera. Eyes wide with fear, he grabbed at Jacinth, whose hair was thick with matted blood, as she rolled past him. His free hand flailed frantically for something to grab but found only air. His feet scrambled desperately in denial as he skidded and rolled down the deck while holding on to Jacinth, eyes fixed in horror upon the snapping maws of the ebony beast, drool dribbling steaming onto the deck planking. If he had been able to double-check his glance, he would have been sure that the creature was grinning. Suddenly his shoulder wrenched painfully as his free hand coiled about the frayed end of a piece of rigging, and he swung to a stop perhaps fifteen spans from the snapping heads.

Kuoy was not so lucky. With a scream he tumbled past Alazla, his feet scrambling and hands clawing at the deck planking in a desperate attempt to stop his plunge. His dark eyes met Alazla's briefly in a silent plea for help. The chimera watched eagerly as the tattooed tumbling form of Kuoy rolled helplessly down the elevated deck. It raised an elegant furred paw and wicked curved talons extended slowly from it.

The paw plunged with deadly speed and Kuoy screamed in agony as it pierced him clean though the gut. He lay nailed to the deck, gurgling, upon the end of an elegant curved claw. With a slight wrench the chimera unhooked its paw from the planking and blood blossomed from Kuoy's mouth. Kuoy rose, impaled like some grisly delicacy upon the end of the claw, until he was level with its lion head. The goat and snake heads hissed and spat with glee.

The chimera looked at Kuoy quizzically for a moment, as if he were some child's curiosity, a dreadful intelligence burning in its eyes. Kuoy's legs kicked of their own volition, unable any longer to obey his commands. Stretching its maw impossibly wide, the chimera then casually bit off Kuoy's head. Blood sprayed onto its ebony fur and rained down onto the deck and into the sea. The chimera casually chewed Kuoy's head with an awful crunching and then cast his corpse into the sea, where it bobbed in an ebbing red tide.

A sob of horror escaped Alazla and then the three heads of the chimera fastened their hungry gaze on him. Fighting to hold on to both Jacinth and the rigging, he felt utterely helpless. He cast desperately about, seeking some way to extricate himself, but the tiny, wounded ship, appeared reluctant to reveal any such secrets, if indeed it held them.

The chimera almost playfully raised a giant paw and struck the deck of the ship. The vessel boomed with the impact and sank farther into the sea. Alazla gripped desperately at the rope as he swung wildly side to side, his shoulder flaming in agony. Tears of frustration and sorrow ran down his face: there was nothing he could do as the creature played with him in some macabre game of cat and mouse. Then again the chimera struck the deck and the heads hissed gleefully, tongues lolling out to lick at giant maws. Alazla's grip slipped, chasing down the rope and burning his hand. He knew that he could not hold on much longer.

Suddenly there seemed to be a slight pause in the wind. Had Hercuba looked then, she would have seen the waves curling and being sucked skyward some distance from the ship as something raced towards them with immense speed. Then, with a boom that almost spun the beleaguered pleasure craft fully around, the wind spirit struck the chimera. Hercuba was launched clean from the boat with such a force that she was sent tumbling and spinning into the air, and only a desperate snapping and clawing of her bat-like wings prevented her from tumbling into the sea. Alazla almost screamed in relief and dared for a moment to feel hope, as he desperately held on to Jacinth.

Alazla could make out the almost insubstantial outline of the wind spirit crouched protectively over the ship, its airy wings arched forward ready for battle. Hercuba roared in rage as she righted herself, her wing tips scudding the tops of the waves.

Despite the immensity of the blow, Alazla could not see that the chimera carried any injury from the strike. Its heads weaving and snapping in wrath, wings beating as she hovered above the sea, it spoke to the wind spirit in a deep and sinister language unrecognisable to Alazla, that thickly rolled and boomed across the waves. The only response from the wind spirit that Alazla could determine was perhaps an increase in the wind across the waves.

Then, her hissing voice reverting to the mortal tongue, she said 'You are no match for me, creature of Oldoth. I am old even to those of your kind. For this moment, though, I am content, and for that you should be thankful. Be assured that I will yet taste that mortal creature's flesh.'

Laughing, Hercuba rose into the air with a beat of her wings and flew slowly away.

- CHAPTER 30 -

Beloved Son Balthazar

The remains of the once pretty pleasure craft Dove had been dragged up onto the beach. She was now barely more than a tattered wooden corpse. Lacking both mast and cabin, Dove looked as if some giant creature had sat upon her, which of course, it had. Certainly its previous owners would not now recognise her. However, Alazla reflected, the wind spirit had managed to push it to shore without it sinking, and though quite dead, Dove even now provided them with wood for their fire. Oddly, he felt somehow grateful to the brave little ship.

Jacinth sat staring without seeing into the campfire flames beside him. The red stone about her neck winked softly, reflecting the flickering firelight. Her head wound had been cleaned and bandaged, and beside concussion and several days of headaches, she seemed to be as well as could be expected, in the circumstances. Alazla had told her about Kuoy, and after her sobbing had finished she was able to accept his loss with the stoicism of one who has spent cycles in a slave mine and seen many companions lost.

The wind spirit had left them, presumably to return to Balthazar, and another airy messenger had subsequently arrived and instructed them to make for the Seagull Inn, located in a small town called Ulm, two days' walk south-west, towards Korth. There Balthazar had said that he would meet them. Alazla had received this news from the messenger with slight disappointment, realising this meant that he would not be going home, to Korth, at least not for the moment.

Alazla had decided that despite any threat to them, he was not prepared to travel at risk to Jacinth, in her wounded condition. So, they'd made camp under a waterproof canvas for three days now, concealed by brush and shrub in a small ravine off the beach, onto which Dove's carcass had been dragged. They were certainly not short of food either. Whilst many of the foodstuffs had received a good salty soaking, the ship had been well stocked and many had been packed in waterproof wrapping and remained more than edible for those as unfussy about their food as an escaped slave.

Understanding Jacinth's sorrow over Kuoy – the gods knew he felt the same – Alazla knew that they nevertheless still had to survive themselves. They certainly could not remain in the gulley indefinitely: the small ship, even though it had served to provision and clothe them, now also acted as a marker to their location. If Jacinth was well enough, they needed to move on. Deciding to broach the subject, he said, 'How are you feeling?'

Hunched beneath the canvas and without looking up, Jacinth replied with slight acidity, 'Like a dragon sat on me.'

'Okay,' said Alazla patiently, 'but do you feel well enough to travel yet? If we can, we really need to be moving on. Every day we stay here now increases our risk of discovery.'

Looking up then, a flash of anger in her eyes, Jacinth said, 'Alazla, if you're so worried for your own precious bloody neck then just go on without me. It's you that's so damn well committed to getting information to the country that condemned us all to slave labour anyway. Personally, I'm not sure that we owe them anything. Kuoy was probably right to think simply about escaping.' She added the last with a slight catch in her voice.

Alazla felt for her grief: the bitterness of that grief throbbed in him too. But they had to make a decision. Reaching out and touching her arm, he said, 'Look, in wanting to leave Kuoy was doing what he thought was right, by him. The difference is that we're doing what we think is right by others and not just ourselves. It's important that someone in authority knows what we've seen and it may even help to clear us, get our sentences revoked, you know, maybe go back to a normal life. But, if not, then at least we've done our part.'

Jacinth yanked her arm away from Alazla, her face red with fury. 'Don't you speak ill of Kuoy, you ignoble idiot. And do you think the Korth authorities will give a damn about your pious bloody gesture and pardon you?! They'll just take your stupid information and then order both you and me straight to the gallows, where we'll swing until we rot, as an example to all escaped slaves.'

With that Jacinth stormed across to her bedroll and rolled herself into her blankets, her back to Alazla.

Watching Jacinth as she sobbed quietly to herself, Alazla knew that even though she'd spoken in anger, she was probably right. Once he'd told Balthazar about the situation on Crab Island, there'd likely be little that even one as positively inclined as Balthazar had once been could do to help, or indeed would want to do for them. But that did not stop him yearning to return home. As an escaped slave, the gallows would almost certainly await him. Whilst Alazla could make that decision for himself, he knew that he could not for Jacinth. She accompanied him due to a misplaced sense of loyalty. Jacinth was free now, and unless she accompanied him, could likely live out the rest of her days in peace in the wide and varied lands beyond the borders of the kingdom of Korth.

Alazla slipped out of the hidden gulley alone, just before dawn. Jacinth slept quietly and oblivious in her blankets, having eventually cried herself to sleep. Alazla had left the best of the supplies behind for her and knew that they would support her for several weeks if she was frugal. There had also been some coin on the boat, which he also left, bar a few coppers.

By Alazla's estimation Ulm was perhaps a two-day brisk walk to the south-west. He'd never visited Ulm before but was aware of the small town's location and knew that his old friend Pell certainly had relatives there.

Alazla crested the rise leading down into Ulm on the afternoon of the second day. The town was nestled in the protective arms of its own fertile vale, which in turn opened out directly onto the sea. Chimney smoke waved happily in the gentle sea breeze and a small river, on which Alazla could see at least one mill, circumvented the town, running down into the sea.

Alazla had already decided that he would enter the town under cover of darkness, to reduce the risk of anyone recognising him. This would also mean that the Seagull Inn, in which he was to meet Balthazar, would likely be busy with its evening trade, again meaning that he would bear less scrutiny. Accordingly, he settled down beside a farmer's hedge and tucked in to his provisions to while away the time. He had no regrets about leaving Jacinth on a rational level and knew that he could well have saved her life by doing so. He also knew, however, that he was going to miss her company a great deal. They'd got on famously ever since she'd tucked him under her wing on his first arriving in the mines and helped him to survive, which many slaves failed at. There had been a sense of relief in him when Jacinth had agreed to accompany him, and now that relief was replaced by an assurance of having done the right thing, but that did not stop him from nevertheless feeling empty. In many ways Jacinth was the last friend he had left. His old childhood friends such as Penny, Ash and even Thorn were now as remote to him as Korth itself. They existed in a life that he was no longer part of, but still yearned to return to. Jacinth was a part of his new life, and he harboured the hope that she could share a life in Korth with him one day.

The fading light interrupted Alazla's pondering and with a slight sigh of regret he started down the track to Ulm. As he passed the hay bales piled in the fields and livestock lowing with the approaching night, he knew full well that this stroll down into the vale of Ulm could well be his last. Balthazar, if he even came himself, and the authorities could shortly put a swift end to his brief stint of freedom.

The Seagull Inn was simple to locate as it was on the shorefront overlooking Ulm's small harbour, beyond which the sun was setting in a dramatic orange splash. Several fishing vessels were moored for the evening, no doubt to be out again on the dawn tide.

An inviting yellow glow spilled out from the inn's bottled-glass windows, and a faded and peeling painted sign of a gull above the door swung in the light breeze. Alazla took a deep breath and stepped inside, to a tumult of noise and laughter.

The inn, being one of only two in the town, was burgeoning with boisterous patrons. Alazla briefly wondered whether it was a holiday of some form, it was so full. After the isolation of Crab Island, the press of human bodies shocked Alazla as he made his way into the shouting and laughing throng.

Alazla had always been well built, but with his time on Crab Island he had lost the puppy fat of youth and now his frame was hard and well muscled. If nothing else the overseers had always ensured that they were well fed, since a weak slave achieved little. Alazla pushed his way easily through the crowd, able to see over all but a few heads. If at times he pushed a little too hard without meaning to, those who would have said something swallowed their comments when they saw his swarthy bulk.

He had forgotten what it was like to be this close to scores of other folk. Alazla could hardly hear himself think amongst the haze of talk, smoke and drink. It was stiflingly hot and he couldn't turn without bumping into someone, drawing an acid glance for slopping their ale. There was not even a table to be had. How could he keep pushing back and forth through this throng looking for Balthazar, who could be almost anywhere?

Alazla's breath began to come a little shorter and the bar took on a slightly blurred and hazy cast. Was it the smoke, he thought? He couldn't tell. He needed to get out. These people were squeezing the breath out of him.

Alazla turned with a gasp and lurched towards the door, the room blurring on all sides. A rotund man in a plain wool cloak cursed as Alazla barged into him, spilling his ale across his chest.

'Here now,' shouted the man, 'what's your game?!'

Another voice cut in then, feminine and familiar. 'Sorry sir. My brother's not used to crowds. Please take this copper and buy yourself another ale.'

Grumbling but mollified, the man took the coin with a bitter glance at Alazla.

A firm hand on Alazla's arm guided him away from the overly moist gentleman towards the bar. The figure cast back a hood to reveal a tumble of red hair and Jacinth's grinning face. Poking him in the chest with a finger for emphasis, she said, 'You've got a good heart, Alazla, but you're also a prat at times. You're going to need at least one of your friends to get you out of ruddy trouble.'

Jacinth signalled briefly to the barkeeper for ales as relief flooded through Alazla. He scooped her up in a hug that almost crushed the breath out of her.

'Bloody heck. Easy now,' she huffed, 'I've only just got over a knock on the head, remember?!'

Alazla put her down with a little reluctance, and pushing back an errant lock of hair from her face, said, 'I'm just glad you're here. I didn't like the thought of doing this without you.'

Jacinth flushed and took a swig from her mug of ale, eventually replying, 'Yes, well, idiot, just don't try to make my decisions for me. I'm old enough to make my own, thank you.'

Smiling, Alazla nodded, and taking a sip from his ale, said as a thought crossed his mind, 'How did you get here before me, though? I came by a pretty direct route.'

Wiping the froth of ale from her mouth, Jacinth replied, 'You're not as fast as you think, you great ox. Passed you this morning and you didn't even realise. Good job I knew where you were headed, though.'

Alazla had to agree with the sentiment as he looked about the tavern, using his height to best advantage. 'Can't see Balthazar yet,' he said.

Jacinth nodded. 'Can't be much help there; given that I've never met him.'

A tap on Alazla's arm turned him towards the innkeeper, a wiry gentleman with a craggy face and shock of grey hair. 'Your friend's in the back,' he said with a jerk of his head towards a door at the far side of the inn, 'through there and first on the right.'

Alazla did not wait to enquire how the innkeeper knew who they were and simply nodded his thanks. Not forgetting to pick up their ales, they headed to the indicated door, endeavouring not to repeat Alazla's earlier performance.

Beyond the door a corridor was illuminated by oil lamps upon small trestle tables. Several doors gave access to what Alazla assumed were private dining rooms. Placing his hand on the closest door handle, Alazla met Jacinth's eyes, knowing that once they entered the room, their future fates were likely sealed. Her lips set firm, she gave him a slight nod and they entered.

The room was shadowed and had about it a peaceful feel. The walls were panelled with oak, and thick velvet curtains were drawn across the bay window into which was set a dining table and six stylised high-back chairs. Three leather armchairs sat before the blazing hearth; only one was occupied. Balthazar, beloved son of Oldoth, sat reading a book and looked up as they entered. His long lustrous blond hair was tied back from a stern and tanned face and unusually, he was modestly clad in a simple sky blue robe, tied with a leather belt. His one concession to flamboyance appeared to be a thick golden chain, largely hidden by the neck of the robe.

Balthazar smiled slightly as they entered. Alazla thought it almost looked like relief. Certainly this was not at all what he had expected; Balthazar appeared to be alone without either other city officials or even guards. He was not sure what this suggested but he sat in the offered armchair and waited for his old acquaintance to speak.

Balthazar regarded the two of them steadily from his chair. The only noise was the crackle of the fire in the hearth as minutes passed. Once Alazla would have been unnerved by those eyes without pupils, that seemed to roil with clouds. Instead, now, he felt somewhat calmed by Balthazar's steady gaze; he could find no menace there. Even now, and not having said a word, he found himself trusting the son of Oldoth.

Unexpectedly Balthazar then said softly, in his deep voice, 'I have kept my pledge, Alazla. Your mother is well, although she misses you greatly.'

'I knew you would,' said Alazla, nonetheless with some obvious relief in his voice. He felt something of a slight weight lift from his heart. 'Does my mum know about my… present situation?'

'She does not, and neither is she likely to. It would not be… safe,' said Balthazar, his face grim.

Then, looking at Jacinth, he said gently, 'And who is this, then? I knew, of course, that Alazla had a companion, but forgive me, for I do not know your name.'

Jacinth introduced herself and noticed then Balthazar's gaze lingering upon the ruby pendant about her neck, his eyebrows raised slightly in surprise.

'Ah yes. I recognise the name now, a fellow escapee no less. That is a fine pendant for a slave,' he said.

Alazla had never commented to Jacinth on the stone or asked how she had managed to keep it concealed from the slave guards. He had decided that if she ever wanted to talk of it, then she would raise the subject herself.

Jacinth hastily tucked the pendant into her doublet under Balthazar's scrutiny and made no reply to his enquiry.

Balthazar smiled slightly and turned his attention back to Alazla. His face then lost all semblance of a smile and the room seemed to darken. 'That you have come here of your own volition speaks well for you, Alazla, and also for you, Jacinth. But I am not a Loremaster and so I will not seek to judge you.'

Alazla's heart lifted on hearing this.

'As you are by now perhaps realising yourselves, there is much more at stake here than the sentence of a few escaped slaves, and I believe that is why you have come, is it not?'

Alazla nodded.

'But you must tell me *all* that has happened to you since you escaped the mines, fully and without omission. After that, well, we shall have to decide what to do with you.'

Alazla knew that he had to trust Balthazar fully, and so with a quick glance at Jacinth, who gave him a reassuring smile, he commenced their harrowing tale from the enforced escape after Ibok and Nilm broke loose during the gold panning, to their sight of the appalling well of darkness within the holy stone of Oldoth. Here Balthazar held them, the clouds within his irises swimming with intent as he probed for every detail, from what they'd seen to even the terror they had felt. He held them, particularly, when Alazla mentioned that he felt as if something had been looking back at them. Balthazar's impassive expression revealed little, though.

Jacinth too, added additional detail that Alazla overlooked or perhaps had even blocked from his mind. They explained their desperate trek across the island and their decision to inform the authorities as to what they had seen, the cavorting Apollettan nobles and ultimately the attack by the chimera, leading to Kuoy's terrible death.

When the tale was fully told and Balthazar had exhausted all of his questions, the night was nearly done. The oil lamps were guttering and the light of dawn was beginning to creep through the gaps in the velvet curtains. Even the embers from the fire were long dead. Silence draped the room like a shroud. Balthazar's face looked worried and drawn.

Eventually Balthazar spoke again. 'Your escape after sight of that terrible thing you describe as a "well" upon Oldoth's own holy ground may well have been a blessing from our beloved god himself. I do not believe it was happenstance that you laid eyes upon such a thing and indeed that you had the rare strength to approach it and bring this news to me,' he said, with a smile for both of them. 'As for the chimera, well, this speaks of great and dark power abroad in the world.' His fingers steepled in front of his face, he then said softly and almost unheard, 'But which power, and is it connected to the war that now unfolds in the north, I wonder?'

He rubbed his eyes then, and glanced at the sunlight peeking through the curtains. Getting up from his chair, he stretched and walked across to the bay, where he drew back the curtains upon a beautiful dawn sky. He cast open the windows, letting fresh air flood in. For just a fleeting moment Balthazar's outline glowed with a golden light. 'The sun is always so comforting, don't you think?' he said as he gazed out.

Turning back to them then, he looked grim as he said, 'This matter is beyond me and must be brought to the attention of both the Head of my order and the ancient Guardians of Korth. They will know what to do. Fear not, though,' and held up a placating hand at the alarmed look on Alazla and Jacinth's faces. 'You need not come. I will go alone and will discuss with them what is to be done – and also done with you' he added.

Pacing vigorously back down the room, he pulled a pouch from his belt and cast it upon the table. 'There is money in there and more than you will need. Take rooms here at the inn and keep a low profile. Alazla, you should keep your beard, it hides your face well. Jacinth, you will need to dye your hair, it is too recognisable by far.'

Jacinth raised a protective hand to her radiant red locks.

'Be assured that I will return or send instruction for you.' With that Balthazar whispered a few words, and for a moment power seemed thick in the room and then he simply vanished. The curtains blew wide and the windows rattled in their frames. A sudden wind raced from the room and across the Vale of Ulm.

- CHAPTER 31 -
The Guardians of Korth

'Really, Balthazar, you must show more decorum,' huffed Endoril, First Councillor of Korth, his wizened old head rattling elaborate gold and emerald earrings.

A palsied hand pointed at the fuming beloved son of Oldoth. 'You storm in here, and by quite unconventional means I might add, giving a number of our most illustrious dignitaries a terrible fright, and then simply demand an immediate audience with the Guardians!'

'My dear beloved son,' Endoril sighed, looking quite swamped for a moment by his enormous white and gold robes of office, 'you must understand that I am doing all I can, but even I cannot just change a state visit by the Prince of Zerad-Dun and trade depositions from the senior Bordish ambassador.'

Balthazar continued to stalk across the small antechamber that had been his home for more than five days now. His official blue robes swished as he walked, echoing his agitation. 'Endoril, this delay is simply not acceptable. Grave matters are afoot here and they simply cannot wait. If I must barge into their confounded illustrious presences then be assured that I will!'

Endoril drew himself up, momentarily patting his grey hair, and then, folding his hands in front of him, said, 'Beloved son, be assured

366

that even one such as yourself could not penetrate the inner sanctums of this palace should we not wish it.'

Balthazar began to return comment, his eyes stormy, but Endoril forestalled him, continuing, 'It would certainly speed matters up greatly, though, if you did not require a private audience. Surely these matters could be said before the court, could they not?'

Balthazar noted that Endoril was far too discreet to enquire what the matters might be. 'No, and no again, Endoril,' he said, trying desperately not to become irate with the First Councillor, who he knew was honestly doing his best in this unexpected situation. An audience with the Guardians, even if granted, was often arranged a cycle in advance. 'This is for the Guardians' ears alone, Endoril, and none other.'

Endoril nodded gently. 'Very well, beloved son, please send for any refreshments that you may require. Are you sure that I cannot accommodate you in a suite here at the palace, to ease your waiting?'

Balthazar shook his head briefly, having turned down this offer several times before.

'I will keep you informed,' said Endoril, and with a graceful bow as if to an equal, that Balthazar knew must strain his ancient joints, swept from the chamber.

The summons, when it came, caught Balthazar napping in his chair. From the dim blue glow of the room's crystal walls, Balthazar surmised that it must be well into the night.

Trying to pat his rumpled robes into something resembling respectability, Balthazar followed the messenger, who led him unerringly down a labyrinth of enormous vaulted passages until they reached huge arched double doors, where, with a bow, he departed.

As Balthazar approached, the huge double doors swung silently open, allowing him entrance to the great hall of the palace. The hall's length clad in a shimmering soft blue radiance raced away before him, almost impossibly long. Vaulted walls met with whispered grace perhaps two hundred spans above his head. Buttresses cunningly crafted into representations of the nine gods, avatars and many creatures of legend writhed up the walls, from where they stared down in impassive and eternal watch.

As he walked down the length of the great hall, alone now, Balthazar's steps sent chasing echoes before him. Save for the Diamond Fist guards, still as statues at the hall's edges, he could have been the only living creature. The place, Balthazar realised, had about it the still and ancient feel of a temple. Although well it should, perhaps: legend held that the Guardians were immortal and had governed the kingdom of Korth since it was founded five-and-a-half thousand cycles past. Balthazar could not vouch for the truth of this, but he knew that during the many cycles that he'd been admitted to the Guardians' presence for, he'd never seen them age.

Balthazar knew that he was approaching his destination when he spotted the two great statues that flanked the apex of the hall. Two mighty dragons, one black and one silver, towered upward, maws agape, their ridged spines supporting the arched gables above, from where they balefully stared down on anyone who dared to approach the Guardians' thrones. Balthazar had often thought it unusual that the nine younger gods had only minor representation within the hall.

The Guardians, Illurien and Alliandra, sat silently upon two intricately carved diamond thrones, each surmounted with the gem crest of Korth. They appeared almost statuesque, their forms painfully thin, skin without imperfection and alabaster-white. Although to the glance they did not seem old, their hair was silver-white and bound back by circlets of gold. Their only movement as they watched Balthazar approach was that of their hooded violet eyes, tracking his approach.

Balthazar's footsteps seemed painfully loud to his ears.

Reaching the foot of the dais, Balthazar bowed low, as deep as he would to his own master, Aolandar. Rising, he was forced to crane his neck slightly, the dais upon which the thrones sat being some thirty spans in height.

'Hail Balthazar, beloved son of Oldoth. The Guardians greet you. You are welcome here.' The First Councillor's formal announcement made Balthazar jump: he had not realised that there were others here, hidden in the shadows at the foot of the dais.

First Councillor Endoril stepped forward in a rustle of white and gold finery, allowing Balthazar to see him better. Endoril gestured briefly to the other side of the dais, where now that he was paying greater attention, Balthazar could make out two other figures. A frowning Sorbek nodded briefly in recognition. The proud most beloved son of Lorethian, god of justice, appeared partially dressed for war in a silver breastplate bearing the open-hand sigil of Lorethian, with a sweeping skirt of chain mail links. Beside Sorbek stood a figure whom Balthazar did not recognise. The young man, perhaps no more than twenty cycles of age, had close cropped dark hair and a welcoming smile that was slightly lopsided. Clearly he was a mage, from the dark blue robes that he wore, bearing the golden bands that spiralled up from the hem, denoting his bindings. Balthazar judged that he must have displayed great talent to have reached the magi ranks at such a tender age.

'I believe that you know most beloved son Sorbek,' said Endoril, 'but unless I am mistaken, you are not familiar with Vodan, Mage of the Korth Spire of Arcanum. Mage Vodan is present as arcane advisor, since the most esteemed Arch-Mage Feroul is attending the present 'crisis' in Arcanum.'

The young mage Vodan bowed slightly to Balthazar in the way of greeting.

Not wanting to seem rude, but acutely aware of the impassive regard of the Guardians, he whispered to Endoril, 'I requested a *private* audience.'

Endoril smiled somewhat indulgently. 'This is about as private as it gets here, Balthazar; just one religious and one arcane advisor, plus myself of course. You should regard yourself as privileged.'

Endoril then formally said, his voice echoing loud 'Please state your petition, beloved son of Oldoth.'

Having had considerable time to consider his approach, while waiting, Balthazar had already decided to forgo the usual formalities. Taking a brief breath, and setting his eyes firmly on the serene faces of the two Guardians, Balthazar began to simply but sombrely tell the tale of a well of darkness within a sacred stone of Oldoth and the escape and pursuit of three slaves from Crab Island, by a creature from fable.

His account of the tale was succinct, without embellishment, and for that all the more chilling. As he wove the terrible story the great hall carried his voice about, sending stirring echoes to chase his own words. Yet during the account there was one detail that Balthazar deliberately omitted: that of the slaves' names.

During his recount he was not interrupted, and when he concluded, minutes passed before his last words echoed slowly into silence. The expressions on the Guardians' faces barely changed during his account, as from time to time they tilted a head slightly, in an odd and almost birdlike manner.

Minutes seemed to pass as the Guardians' hooded violet gaze rested on him. Tired now, and beginning to feel like he wanted to shake someone, Balthazar nonetheless bore the scrutiny stoically, knowing that these seemingly frail and even enigmatic figures were likely one of the most potent and goodly forces to walk the face of Rune.

With a sinuous grace Illurien stood from his throne and Balthazar realised that whilst extraordinarily thin, the Guardian must be perhaps sixteen spans tall, well over the height of even the tallest man that he knew of. And yet, as Illurien descended the steps, white boots not making a sound as he trod, Balthazar knew that here was an opponent that he would not like to cross. Whilst he appeared thin, almost to the point of fragility, it seemed as if the very steps seemed to bow slightly with his weight. There was about him, somehow, a sense of enormity.

Balthazar dropped his gaze, collecting his thoughts for a moment, until raising his head again he looked up into the smiling face of Illurien. He placed his hand upon Balthazar's shoulder and Balthazar almost gasped at the weight that threatened to drive him to his knees. Looking in amazement at the Guardian, he could see that Illurien exerted no pressure and even seemed oblivious.

Illurien's voice was light when he spoke, carrying an undercurrent of some hidden potency. 'We must be grateful to beloved son Balthazar for this news, and to those who carried it to him.'

Balthazar was sure there had been a slight twinkle of laughter in those violet eyes then.

Illurien continued, 'And thus, we must talk of things now which to some are unknown and with which some,' he looked then to Sorbek, 'will disagree. But whether or not we here like it, this does not change something, if it is fact.'

At the inherent acceptance of his words given by Illurien's reply Balthazar felt a weight lift from his heart. Concern as to the apparent credibility of his tale had gravely concerned him. Personally he knew Alazla well enough to believe him fully, but the tale of an escaped slave, whether recounted by a beloved son or not, could also just as easily have been dismissed here. A glance at a scowling brother Sorbek suggested to Balthazar that at least he remained far from convinced.

Illurien then lifted the hem of his intricately woven gown and sat himself upon a lower step of the dais, in a surprisingly informal pose. 'Forgive me if I appear to ramble here,' he said, 'but I believe the dark tale that beloved son Balthazar has brought to our attention is part of a wide and complex issue.'

'Your pantheon of gods is known as the younger gods for a good reason, Balthazar. They were born well after the universe itself was created by the dragon gods, gorGoroth the male and Ione' the female.'

This, Balthazar already knew, though he noted that the conservative Sorbek was scowling so hard that his bushy black eyebrows almost hid his eyes. Had times been better, he would have smiled.

'Humanity, I'm afraid, was created by the power of the dragon gods. As with many of the dragon gods' servants, they were born to serve a specific task.'

Balthazar was staggered. He had never actually conceived that humanity could have been created by the dragon gods. Although since the younger gods had not existed then he could see that it made sense.

'Ridiculous!' exploded Sorbek, his forked beard jutting out in outrage.

As Illurien regarded him with narrowed eyes, Sorbek took a breath. 'Forgive me, Guardian. I merely meant that such is conjecture on your part. The order of Lorethian believes that humanity was created from the dreams of the sleeping younger gods. They later awoke to the cries of the suffering of the children born from those dreams.'

'As you wish,' said Illurien easily. And with a smile that reminded Balthazar of a crocodile, he continued, 'So what would you say if I told you humanity was also created to provide the dragons with food – you were in fact nothing more than fodder, bred and managed in herds. Dragons fed and grazed on humanity much the same as you now do with fields of wheat or the livestock that you farm.'

The giant draconic statues behind the Guardians' thrones seemed to loom large with menace with the Guardians' words.

It was the first time that Balthazar had actually seen Sorbek speechless. All colour had drained from his normally ruddy face.

For himself, Balthazar was not sure whether he actually believed Illurien. He wondered whether he was seeing a slightly more capricious side to the Guardian here that he had never before seen.

'Forgive me,' Illurien continued as Sorbek continued to regard him in stunned disbelief.

Balthazar interjected, surmising then for himself, '*This* is the misery, then, that awoke the younger gods. We had always believed that the misery concerned was just that of... *slavery.*'

'My mate Illurien is taking a little too much time to come to the point.'

Gazes moved to Alliandra, who was now walking down the dais steps. She too was tall and swayed gently with an otherworldly grace. Raising long delicate hands for emphasis, the Guardian said, 'That most of your gods fell in the battle you do not contest. Can we agree on this?'

She smiled then, with such warmth that Balthazar found himself returning it. He and Sorbek then both nodded.

'Have you ever considered where your gods may lie? Their remains, if you will?' asked Alliandra.

Balthazar was somewhat thrown by the change of direction, yet again. For himself he could not see where this was going, but at a nod from Sorbek spoke for them both. Rearranging his sky-blue robes in an attempt to gather both his thoughts and his somewhat battered dignity, he replied, 'There were no remains to speak of. The ninety-one gods and their avatars were consumed in the heavenly battles.'

Illurien, with a smile for Alliandra, continued. 'I see. I'm afraid yet again that is incorrect. The remains of the fallen ninety-one younger gods and their heralds were eventually gathered by the few surviving younger gods and laid to rest in a tomb beyond the bounds of mortal realms. That place is known as the Hall of Fallen gods.'

For himself Balthazar was at quite a loss. He wanted to disbelieve the Guardians, but their words had an appalling sense of truth, or at the very least partial truth about them.

Sorbek, clearly somewhat numb now, but obviously dreading as much as Balthazar where this was going, rumbled, 'The divine orders have no knowledge of this hall of which you speak.'

Illurien shook his head, silver hair swaying. 'You must find it in you to accept that there are some things in the universe that perhaps the younger gods have chosen not to tell their disciples, most beloved son.'

'Whilst I am following all of this,' said Vordan, stepping into the conversation and for some reason grinning as if the mage found the whole thing exciting, 'I perceive little connection within your references to that of which beloved son Balthazar has informed us.'

Illurien's smile vanished. 'And therein, dear Vordan, lies the nub. Within the stone upon the island the young slave saw the Bridge of Mourn.'

Balthazar recalled the name as being that of the fallen god of the dead, but certainly did not recall any connecting reference to a bridge.

Illurien's gaze was piercing when he said, 'I'm afraid that the Bridge of Mourn leads to The Hall of Fallen gods.'

His mouth as dry as old parchment and fervently wishing he had a seat to hand, Balthazar croaked, 'By Oldoths' holy name! We must close it then!'

'That,' rang out Alliandra, 'would require the power of all nine of your gods' highest representatives, Balthazar. And it seems that two of your orders are presently at war. Somehow, I do not think that they are likely to co-operate.'

'Who did this?' managed Sorbek.

Balthazar glanced at him gratefully, not sure that he had any words left.

'If we but knew,' Alliandra replied, her voice rolling about the hall in anger, 'then we would have undone them by now. It seems not only must we discover the face of our enemy, but we must also swiftly find another way to close the bridge.'

'Equally,' Illurien replied, taking the hand of his mate, 'we must understand the why! Why it is that some force has opened the way to the tomb of your fallen gods?'

Balthazar's mind whirled and tumbled with the implications.

- CHAPTER 32 -

Freedom

Alazla and Jacinth laughed on the veranda.

The evening cooled and the birds sang lazily in the trees. The wine, a red from one of the Peldane baronies, was excellent and they were slightly tipsy.

The two escaped slaves had quickly decided that since they would not be running away this time, they should also not be shy about spending Balthazar's generous purse. So, with the reckless abandon known only by those who've seen truly desperate times, without hesitation they took the finest apartment that the Seagull Inn had to offer. Alazla had been grateful that it had two beds, thereby avoiding any awkward conversations.

Alazla and Jacinth with great commitment had also embarked on sampling the finest wines, foods and clothes that the small town of Ulm could provide. Neither of them had noticed, or perhaps even cared, that their spending had led to them being referred to as the 'young nobles from out of town'. Certainly, given the true nature of their status, they would have laughed at the bitter irony of the label.

Jacinth had followed Balthazar's advice and dyed her recognisable red locks a jet black; they were now piled artfully atop her head with silver pins. To Alazla's eyes she looked more lovely than ever in a new close-fitting white cotton dress. Her dark brown eyes were bright and her smile wide as she laughed at another one of his jokes.

Alazla was less comfortable with his beard, now that he actually had a choice whether to wear it, and so had settled for shaving it off, wearing a hat to cover his shaggy golden hair when out and about 'shopping in town'. He had yet to stop the 'rubbing his face phase' with the beard gone. He would have blushed had he realised that while laughing, Jacinth admired the way his clean-shaven appearance showed off his strong jawline and how the cut of his new shirt showed the breadth of his muscled shoulders to best effect.

The ruby ever present at Jacinth's neck caught Alazla's eye and he resolved at last to ask about it. 'You've worn that ruby necklace since the day I first met you in the slave mines. I was always surprised that the guards never took it from you or commented at the least.'

The smile left Jacinth's face and she looked at Alazla thoughtfully. As always, she saw no malice within him and knew that his question, which had sat within him unasked for months, was purely derived from a genuine interest. Her reply caught Alazla by surprise. 'It was a gift… but you, you git!' she emphasised the last word, 'should not even be able to see it!'

Alazla was not sure how to react to that; it was certainly not the response that he had expected. 'What do you mean by that?' he asked carefully.

Jacinth reached for the wine bottle and topped up her own glass and then Alazla's. 'By that I mean that it is hidden by bloody enchantments, Alazla. What power do you have that lets you see it? That, is more the question than why the guards didn't!'

Alazla sat somewhat flummoxed as to how Jacinth had managed to turn the table on his question and gentle enquiry, and he now found himself slightly defensive. Not having an answer, he just shrugged and said, 'Can I see it?'

Jacinth seemed to freeze at his question; her wide eyes displayed shock. When she set her wineglass down, her hands were trembling.

Alazla, surprised by her reaction, started to stutter out an apology.

Jacinth held up her hand and stopped him. She carefully unclasped the ruby pendant and handed it to him.

Alazla reached out and took it from her, noting that the chain shook as her fingers trembled.

He held the stone up to the light of the veranda's oil lamp. The ruby spun and flickered on its golden chain. The depths of the stone burned as if with an inner fire. Its surface was flawless and for a moment Alazla was mesmerised by its beauty. He reached out to stop it spinning and realised that there was a soft heat about it.

Not quite knowing why, Alazla stood and walked to Jacinth, the fiery stone hanging on its chain from his hand. Her eyes seemed unnaturally wide and bright, and in an odd way she appeared more frail and vulnerable than he had ever seen her. Alazla knelt down before Jacinth's chair and gently fastened the stone about her neck again.

Her lips parted wide and she seemed about to say something when Alazla forestalled her by placing a finger upon her lips. He reached forward and gently kissed her on the cheek.

Jacinth's eyes never left his.

A discreet cough from the other side of the veranda disturbed them. Balthazar in dirty blue robes, so crumpled that he looked like he'd slept in them, appeared slightly embarrassed. 'I apologise. I appear to have arrived at a most inopportune moment.'

Alazla stood up, flushing, and Jacinth giggled in her chair.

'Not at all,' said Alazla, hoping fervently that the dim lighting upon the veranda hid the fire in his cheeks.

Balthazar continued, walking towards them, cutting straight to the heart of the matter at hand. 'I have successfully met with the Guardians in Korth and returned here in great haste. The situation is most dire, and the implications are... um, startling. There is, I'm afraid, good news and bad.'

Alazla and Jacinth exchanged a concerned glance.

Not even bothering with a chair, Balthazar started to pace the veranda, his stomp lending a steady rhythm to his words. 'I will be frank with you. In doing so, though, I will tell you things that may challenge your religious beliefs, but you must keep an open mind.'

Alazla and Jacinth shared a look of surprise. Jacinth shrugged.

'That which you saw within the stone on Crab Island is a doorway, to a place called the Bridge of Mourn. Take my word for it when I say that this in its own right will mean nothing to you.' He rubbed a hand wearily through his tangled golden hair.

Alazla was struck by how tired Balthazar looked.

'I will not seek to hide the truth from you and so I will tell you what I know. Amongst other places, this bridge leads to the Hall of Fallen gods. I know that will mean nothing to you, but in short, it is the tomb where the fallen ninety-one younger gods lie.'

'Great,' said Jacinth crisply and with the faintest hint of a smile. 'Anything else, while you're at it?!'

Balthazar returned her slight grin. 'A little more. You will ask why such a gate has been opened, and to that, and also as to the whom, as yet, we have no answer. Equally worrying is that we presently have no way to close the gate to the Bridge of Mourn. Normally, with the combined resources of the all nine divine orders we could achieve this, but as you know there is now a war being waged by the order of Sha and the empire of Athel-Loria against Arcanum and so such a thing just cannot be conceived.'

'Is that the good news or bad?' asked Alazla quietly.

Balthazar smiled wearily. 'Fortunately that, Alazla, is the bad. The good is that we received a missive from a noble, one Lady Carine Altrune, validating part of your tale, including how you saved her life and that of her friends.' He turned his face to hide his momentary smile and added 'It seems that she was quite taken with you.'

Alazla did not notice Jacinths' eyes boring into him. It seemed that Balthazar did though since he hurried on. 'Yes, well, Lady Carine is in herself very influencial and with her account and mine, the guardians felt that they were obliged to offer you a full pardon, for all....alleged crimes.'

Balthazars smile literally illuminated the veranda. 'It's unconditional Alazla, you're free, and Jacinth too.'

Alazla hung his head, unable for a moment to speak. He felt Jacinths' arm slip about his shoulders. Somehow he dared not believe it. With everything they'd been through, it seemed surreal. Justice had at last been done, or perhaps he corrected himself, injustice had been undone.

'You've done it' whispered Jacinth, her voice thick. 'You've bloody done it! You're free. *We're* free!'

Tears stood unashamed in Alazlas eyes 'I, I can go home.'

Balthazar's smile was radiant.

********** Here ends Book 1 of Heaven's War **********

Read more about the world of Rune and Alazla's adventures in book 2 of Heaven's War.

GLOSSARY

Cast of characters

Aegon	Most beloved son of Ondalla
Agastalen	Apprentice Mage and native of Immirriel
Alazla El-Vanium	Son of Liandra and friend to Thorn
Alicia	Beloved Daughter of Oldoth & friend to Thorn
Alliandra	Female Guardian of Korth
Anemon	Primus & Arch Mage of Nim
Aolandar	Most beloved son of Oldoth
Ash	Friend to Alazla
Balthazar	Beloved Son of Oldoth
Cantillion - Loremaster	Chief Loremaster in Korth city
Caroline - Lady	Lady Caroline - youngest daughter of the House of Altrune of Apoletta
Catherine	Mother to Thorn
Cerine - Lady	Lady Cerine - eldest daughter of the House of Altrune of Apoletta Korth
Dantifus	Beloved Son of Oldoth
Dak	Farmer in the Peldane Baronies
Deyus	Fae Lord, bound by the younger gods to the Fae realm
Dynnari	Most beloved Daughter of Aevarnia

Elya	Sylph and Fae lover of Heath.
Endoril	First Councilor of Korth
Heath	Apprentice mage and friend of Agastalen
Hercuba	Chimaera and heathen spirit
Ibok	Crab island escapee
Illurien	Male guardian of Korth
Il Terrannon	Warlord of Athel Loria.
Imdalla	Most beloved daughter of Elishar
Iodarii - Queen	Queen of Shael
Jacinth	Ex slave and friend to Alazla
Janda	Commander of the Grey Guard in Limfrost
Janine	Head cook at Thorn's parents inn
Jord	Most beloved son of Tyche
Jouran	Father to Thorn
Kuoy	Native of Ylith and escaped slave, slain by Hercuba
Lei-Weya	Female mage and tutor to Heath
Liandra	Stepmother to Alazla
Lisa	Serving girl at Thorn's parents inn
Lyarra	Companion & dancer to most beloved son Jord
Master Fafner	Teacher in ancient lore
Mistress Mimb	Diminutive teacher in military studies
Mytle - Baron	Baron of Mytle and brilliant strategist
Nilm	Crab island escapee
Oquanor	Beloved Son of Oldoth based in Korth House
Pandim	Aide-de-camp to Baron Mytle
Pell	Friend to Alazla
Ranticus	Thorn's parents horse

Reon	Beloved Daughter of Oldoth, based in the Korth House
Sorbek	Most beloved son of Lorethian
Terran-Assail	Once Thorn, now Avatar to the immortal, Veylistra
Thorn	Son of Catherine & Jord, friend to Alazla, becoming the Avatar Terran-Assail
Trib - brother	Beloved Son of Oldoth
Valeya	Most beloved daughter of Sha
Vodan	Mage at the Korth Spire and deputy court advisor
Winfod	Mage tutor to Agastalen.
Wren - Baron	Baron of Wren. Slain in the battle of Peldane

The gods
Dragon gods

ione'	Dragon mother and co-creator of the universe. Goddess of the universe
gorGoroth	Dragon father and co-creator of the universe. Fallen and cast out during the first war in heaven

Surviving younger gods

Aevarnia	goddess of love and music
Eli-shar	goddess of life and healing
Faed	god of shadow & stealth
Lorethian	god of justice
Oldoth	god of sun and storms
Ondala	goddess of nature

Nim	god of magic
Tyche	god of luck and chance
Sha	goddess of war

Immortals
The Council of
Seven Thrones

Veylistra	Aspect the scarred moon. Daughter of Nim and Slayer of the Avatar
Kythera	Queen of Dreams. Daugher of Tyche
Cinder	Son of Oldoth and wielder of Kalak Dane
Rivadus-Hex	Aspect bad luck. Son of Tyche.
Mahomet	Aspect books/knowledge. Son of Nim
Lodbrog	Aspect secrets. Son of the Fallen god, Mourn
Grimm	Aspect the assassins blade. Son of Sha

Lightning Source UK Ltd.
Milton Keynes UK
15 December 2010

164439UK00002B/73/P